MW00534979

THE ACADEMY

PREVIOUS BOOKS BY DAVID POYER

Tales of the Modern Navy (The Dan Lenson Novels)

Arctic Sea
The Weapon
Violent Peace
Korea Strait
Overthrow
The Threat
Deep War
The Command
Hunter Killer
Black Storm
Onslaught
China Sea
Tipping Point
Tomahawk
The Cruiser
The Passage
The Towers
The Circle
The Crisis
The Gulf
The Med

Tiller Galloway

Down to a Sunless Sea
Bahamas Blue
Louisiana Blue
Hatteras Blue

The Civil War at Sea

That Anvil of Our Souls
A Country of Our Own
Fire on the Waters

Hemlock County

Thunder on the Mountain
Winter in the Heart
As the Wolf Loves Winter
The Dead of Winter

Other Books

Writing in the Age of AI
F-35 (with Tom Burbage, et al.)
Heroes of Annapolis
On War and Politics (with Arnold Punaro)
The Whiteness of the Whale
Happier Than This Day and Time
Ghosting
The Only Thing to Fear
Stepfather Bank
The Return of Philo T. McGiffin
Star Seed
The Shiloh Project
White Continent

THE ACADEMY

A DAN LENSON NOVEL

David Poyer

ST. MARTIN'S
PRESS
NEW YORK

This is a work of fiction. All of the characters, organizations, and events portrayed in this novel are either products of the author's imagination or are used fictitiously.

First published in the United States by St. Martin's Press, an imprint of St. Martin's Publishing Group

www.stmartins.com

Library of Congress Cataloging-in-Publication Data

Names: Poyer, David, author.
Title: The Academy / David Poyer.
Description: First edition. | New York : St. Martin's Press, 2023. | Series: A Dan Lenson novel ; 22
Identifiers: LCCN 2023031028 | ISBN 9781250273086 (hardcover) | ISBN 9781250273093 (ebook)
Subjects: LCSH: Lenson, Dan (Fictitious character)—Fiction. | United States. Navy—Officers—Fiction. | United States Naval Academy—Fiction. | LCGFT: Novels.
Classification: LCC PS3566.O978 A63 2023 | DDC 813/.54—dc23/eng/20230707
LC record available at https://lccn.loc.gov/2023031028

First Edition: 2023

10 9 8 7 6 5 4 3 2 1

To those who will step into our places
in the shield-wall

I will not bring shame upon my sacred arms, nor desert my comrade, but guard and defend our altars and our homes. I will not betray my country, but leave it greater and better than I inherited it. I will obey those appointed over me and submit to the laws. If anyone disobeys or attacks the constitution I will defend it, alone or with others. I will honor the holy things. Let the Gods witness: Agraulus, Enyalius, Ares, Zeus, Thallo, Auxo, and Hegemone.

—*Oath of the Athenian Cadets, circa fifth century* BCE

I

THE YARD

1

Annapolis, Maryland

Early, before dawn. A morning like so many others, yet different. Streamers of fog eddied above the sluggish dimpled platinum of the river. A closely mowed expanse of grass stretched like a tightly fitted green sheet between a wooded hill, only barely visible through the mist, and a concrete seawall.

The runner was still lean, though his hair was graying. No longer speedy, but still persevering, he rounded the far end of the field and headed back. He could only see a few yards ahead. The layers of early fog twisted above the grass, like spirits uncertain of their proper tenancy.

A sail drifted noiselessly past, propelled by the faintest breath of air. A haze-gray Yard Patrol craft lay motionless, welded to the river surface.

Under Daniel V. Lenson's running shoes the soft soil, still wet from heavy rain the night before, squished treacherously. He stumbled, nearly turning an ankle. But recovered, and plowed on.

Not many other runners were out this early. Just a few much younger figures in USNA athletic gear.

* * *

July, after a conflict that wrecked two continents. The nuclear exchange had cost both China and the United States cities and cropland. Both still struggled with disease, famine, and revolt.

The Allies had declared victory. But neither side had truly won.

Rear Admiral, Upper Half, Dan Lenson ambled to a halt at the wooden footbridge arching over College Creek. He bent, panting, hands on knees, recalling bitterly how effortlessly he'd sprinted across these same fields as a teen.

Maybe he was pushing too hard. He was still exhausted from five years at sea. Captaining a cruiser at the war's outbreak, he'd rocketed in rank as America rebuilt its fleet, smashed a submarine blockade, and island-hopped back across the Pacific. Still battling radiation exposure, too, from a cross-country hunt for his daughter. Thank God, she'd surfaced again. Nearly starved, but alive.

"You okay, sir?"

A thin-faced blonde, incredibly young. She seemed to float, defying gravity, as she jogged in place. "Y'okay?" she said again, a mountain twang to her voice.

"Fine . . . just trying to catch my breath."

She glanced over a shoulder. "Should I call somebody?"

"No. Thanks. Just . . . needed a break." He straightened, fists to his back, trying to get a full breath past the scar tissue in his throat.

She looked him up and down. Taking in, no doubt, the nonreg running gear, the black leggings and nonreg tee. "Do you, um, work here, sir?"

He couldn't help chuckling. "Yeah, starting today. Actually, I used to run this circuit. Around the Wall. When I was a mid."

Her eyes widened. "You're the new Supe."

When he nodded she glanced around. "At least we got one of our own this time."

Dan frowned. "Excuse me?"

"Um . . . nothing, sir." She edged away. "I just meant, um, welcome aboard, sir."

He nodded again, still puzzled, but she'd already turned away, accelerated, climbing the arched footbridge with a grace and unstudied power that left him feeling twice as tired.

Forcing reluctant legs into motion once again, he jogged up onto the same scuffed weatherworn planks he'd sprinted so lightly over before . . . when he was young.

* * *

The grounds of the United States Naval Academy were divided into Upper and Lower. The cemetery and some of the playing fields lay to the north, across College Creek from the original footprint of old Fort Severn. They constituted the "Upper Yard."

As he clattered off the footbridge, leaving the river fog behind, the Lower Yard came into view. To his left loomed the granite-and-glass bulwark of Nimitz Library. Beyond it rose Hopper Hall, computer science and cybersecurity. To his right, the massive gray slab of Alumni Hall.

Cutting a right, he jogged past the Vietnam Memorial to Decatur Road. He took a knee to catch his breath again beside Worden Field, the Academy's drill ground. He remembered hot sweating days in ranks, laced into the pigeon-breasted coatee and leggings as his knees buckled and the sweat ran down his face and the suspended rifle gathered the weight of the planet. Across the field stood Captain's Row, decorous brick homes built early in the previous century. Senior staff lived there.

The captains and commanders who'd work for him, starting today.

Beyond them rose a gray brick wall. And past that, Historic Annapolis, capital of Maryland, a city tiger-fiercely protective of its traditions, history, and its tourist-dependent economy.

Hoisting himself again, he forced reluctant joints back into motion. Past the beaux arts mansarded granite of the main academic buildings. To his right, the Museum, with such obscure attractions as an admiral with four eyes and Chester Nimitz's saddle.

Stribling Walk. He circled the level, meticulously groomed red brick paths that wound between monuments to fallen midshipmen and stone and bronze figureheads from long-gone ships. Past colorful beds of lilies and tulips and green-patina'd cannon. Past the massive, copper-domed Chapel. Below it, in a hushed crypt, lay a rebel Scotsman, American captain, and Russian admiral: John Paul Jones.

Ahead loomed the sprawling octopus of Bancroft Hall. Mother Bancroft's eight wings and five stories of French Revival granite had housed the Brigade of Midshipmen since Teddy Roosevelt's time. In the early morning light it seemed to levitate, ephemeral, illusory, like some castle of dream.

He'd come of age here. Passed from frightened plebe to blasé firstie, from youth to adult. He couldn't help glancing up to check the window of his old room. And then, to another window, where . . . yeah, that memory still hurt.

He trotted past the green-painted flanks of captured torpedoes and down through an underpass. Near the eighth wing he angled right again, past the armory, recalling tea dances, racks of rifles, furtive kisses in a coat-filled nook. Athletic buildings, then the verdant expanse of more playing fields, flat as the tarnished gleam of the Chesapeake Bay beyond.

Fatigue dragged at his bones. He slowed to a walk, looking longingly at the tumbled boulders of the seawall. Back then he'd taken them at a sprint, vaulting from block to block, exulting in his body's quickness, its sure invulnerability.

He frowned. The waves lapped only a few feet below the rocks. Had they lowered the seawall, since he'd been here?

Jogging again, though, he was getting winded. Toward the white-painted foremast of USS *Maine*, salvaged from Havana Harbor and reerected here. Past a memorial to the submarines and men lost in World War Two. Then north again, past the hulls and masts of the boat basin.

The Yard was wrapped, embraced, surrounded by salt water and the intangible arms of tradition. The river. The bay. The sea. It was beginning to stir now, as cars filled the parking lots, streetlights winked off, as the whole great machine and institution woke to the day.

The day when he would take its helm.

* * *

Not that a new superintendent simply showed up and took charge. He wore the hats of a base commander, a university president, and the boss of a major university athletic department. Dan had requested the billet as his twilight tour. The courtesy was granted now and then to senior officers ending their careers. The possibility had hung fire for months. Then, suddenly, in an all-too-familiar routine, he was behind schedule and had to hustle to catch up.

He'd paid his first official calls while being vetted by congressional staff. He'd phoned two previous supes to ask what their biggest challenges had been and how they'd met them. The nomination itself had happened in the dead of night, the last item of business before the Senate adjourned. He suspected his wife had greased the shipways. Once approved, he'd paid more calls: the CNO, for steering guidance; the chairman, Senate Armed Services; the commandant of the Marine Corps; the secretary of the Navy.

Then on to Annapolis, and the transient quarters above the Officer's Club. Over the previous week the outgoing supe, Admiral Arminius Cree, had briefed him in. Showed him through the massive official residence where he'd live and entertain. Then, over three days, introduced Dan to the major players. What he called the "cost center heads": the commandant of midshipmen, the academic dean, the athletic director, along with Financial and Legal, the command master chief, and the second-tier department heads.

Unfortunately, Cree had warned, USNA was on a collision course with several icebergs. Dan would have to deal with falling application numbers. Pressure to reduce expenditures. And reports of sexual assault, harassment, and intimidation were at a new high. "Seems like, the more open we are to accusations, the more we get," Cree had sighed. "Young men and young women . . ."

He hadn't finished the sentence, but Dan got the idea.

As a war hero, and holder of the Medal of Honor, he'd be expected to rebuild the Academy's image.

* * *

Back at the Q. A quick shower, and the first of several changes of uniform he'd go through today.

But there was another formality before he could take charge.

* * *

He stood in the parqueted quiet of Memorial Hall, looking up at the flag.

DON'T GIVE UP THE SHIP, it read, crudely stitched on a blue background. The selfsame banner Commodore Oliver Hazard Perry had flown on Lake Erie, when he'd defeated the Royal Navy and drawn a line between empires.

Below it lay a bronze tablet with hundreds of names. They'd died in flaming gun turrets, in sinking, flooding ships and submarines, in the sky, in muddy trenches and steaming jungles. The Honor Roll immortalized those graduates who'd given everything in the line of duty.

He wished Blair could be here, or his mom. But his mother had passed, and as the first female secretary of defense, his wife had her hands full at the Pentagon. He'd invited a few classmates, though most were retired now.

A cameraman was setting up. Looking into a speckled antique mirror, Dan checked the hooks of his choker whites. Tucked his cap under one arm. Acceptable . . . but he had to try not to look tired.

"Attention on deck," someone called, and even the civilians straightened.

A captain stepped to the lectern. "Welcome to the promotion ceremony for Rear Admiral Daniel V. Lenson. For reappointment to the rank of vice admiral and assignment as the superintendent, United States

Naval Academy. His most recent billet assignment was with the staff of the chief of naval operations in Washington, DC. He'll be sworn in by Vice Admiral Shaynelle Hlavna, chief of naval operations."

Hlavna came striding in trailed by four staffers. She centered herself beneath the flag and nodded. "Stand at ease."

Dan had asked for a streamlined ceremony, without official honors or the national anthem. Hlavna went briskly through a welcome, and regrets that Dan's spouse and daughter could not attend, then paused.

"The Academy occupies a special place in the Navy's heart. Not all our officers, or even our best, graduate from this institution. But it preserves our traditions of heroism and duty. It produces leaders dedicated to a career of naval service, with the potential to someday assume the highest responsibilities of command, citizenship, and government.

"Daniel V. Lenson assumed those responsibilities, in missions behind enemy lines, commanding warships and task forces, and planning and directing significant operations both in peacetime and in war. He holds a variety of decorations in addition to the Medal of Honor. They include the Navy Cross, Silver Star, the Legion of Merit, Defense Superior Service, several Armed Forces and Navy Expeditionary Medals, the Purple Heart, the POW Medal, and various service medals and unit commendations. He also holds significant foreign awards, including the Israeli Medal of Courage, the Korean Order of Military Merit, and the French Legion of Honor.

"One noteworthy absence is the lack of commendation and achievement awards other officers typically receive. But then, true warriors often neither receive nor require those routine attaboys.

"For true warriors are sometimes called to step over the line. And now and then, Dan Lenson has been so bold as to do so.

"Such actions usually end military careers. And for good reason; regulations and orders are lessons learned from centuries of experience. But now and then, individual initiative, that pride of the naval service, proves wiser than the regulations. The mature officer owes the country more. We expect him, or her, to know when to choose a different path.

"But Dan's not just a hero. In the deepest sense, he's a servant. He cares, not just for his own people, but for all those affected by his decisions and operations.

"For all these reasons, I believe he's the right person, at the right time, to lead the Academy into the future."

She looked his way. "Front and center."

He had his head down, abashed by the praise. He'd never felt he had much choice in those decisions. They'd always simply seemed the right thing to do.

Though, to be honest, often it had been a close call. . . .

The chief of staff stepped up. "Attention to orders. 'Headquarters, Department of the Navy. The president of the United States has reposed special trust and confidence in the patriotism, valor, fidelity, and abilities of Daniel Valentine Lenson. In view of these qualities and his demonstrated potential for increased responsibilities, and in accordance with the authority vested in the chief of naval operations, he is hereby authorized to assume the title and wear the uniform of vice admiral, United States Navy.'"

Hlavna nodded to an aide, who handed her a small box. Reaching up rather awkwardly—Dan bowed to help out—she replaced his epaulettes with the solid gold, silver anchor, and three silver stars of a vice admiral of the line.

She stepped back to applause from the audience. It echoed eerily from the high ceiling, from the paintings of long-ago battles.

Hlavna said, "Please raise your right hand."

He repeated the oath; that he would support and defend the Constitution of the United States against all enemies, foreign and domestic; that he would bear true faith and allegiance to the same; that he took the obligation freely, and would well and faithfully discharge his duties.

Then it was his turn to speak.

He stepped to the lectern, and paused. He had no lofty sentiments to deliver. No prepared remarks. "CNO, thank you for coming today," he began. "It's an unexpected pleasure. Members of the staff, honored guests, ladies and gentlemen. We all have a number of other duties today, so I'll be brief. But I do want to say just two things.

"First, how humbling this moment is. I hope I can live up to this trust.

"Second, that no one achieves high rank on his or her abilities alone. A couple of people I want to recognize are here with us today." He nodded at them. "Master Chief Donnie Wenck and Commander Amarpeet Singhe. I'm glad they've been able to accompany me here. But far more are absent; on duty, retired, more than a few on eternal patrol. Without them, I wouldn't be alive, much less be standing here.

"But with the help and advice of everyone here, I'll give it everything I have."

* * *

He shook hands and accepted congratulations. He was chatting with the head of the alumni association when the CNO's aide cleared his throat beside him. "Sir? Admiral Hlavna has to get back. A word before she leaves?"

Dan joined her at the great bronze doors. She crossed her arms. "Dan, again, congratulations. I think this is the right fit."

"Thanks."

"Please maintain contact. Your official chain runs through the N7 but you need to keep me and the SecNav in the loop."

"Will do, ma'am. Weekly updates."

"Good. New issue: Remember Linwood Naylor?"

"The historian. On my staff for the invasion of Hainan."

"His book will be a movie soon. It makes you look like a cross between Patton and Halsey. We're getting calls, invites to talk shows. Interested?"

"Um, we discussed this before, ma'am. I'd rather not."

"How about going to LA for the premiere? The studio's invited you. CHINFO will set up travel."

He wavered for a moment; Blair would love it. "Uh, well, I'm really sorry. But thanks."

He watched as she descended the marble steps, crossed the black-and-white-tesserated floor of the Rotunda, as she passed through a second, larger set of bronze doors. The sunlight outlined her. Then she was gone.

* * *

He sat down to lunch with Cree and his wife, a petite Black woman with mousy hair, in the rose garden behind the Supe's House. The scent of jasmine hit him suddenly, and he remembered, out of nowhere, how sweet it had smelled outside the mess hall that first evening of Plebe Summer. He had to blink and winch his attention back to what Mrs. Cree was saying.

"I'm so sorry your spouse couldn't attend, Dan. But she's so *very* important, you probably won't see much of her here. At all."

Dan smiled, ill at ease. He'd never mastered small talk. And this woman seemed to have some kind of axe to grind about Blair. Politics? Or just resentful that Dan's wife was secretary of defense, while as far as he'd seen, Eleanor Cree confined her interests to the Red Cross and the Annapolis Junior League.

"We've had such a marvelous time here. Arminius manages to get in eighteen holes nearly every weekend. Do you play, Admiral?"

"Uh, not so much. I sail, though. Thinking about breaking my boat off the hard, sailing it up here from Norfolk."

"What sort of craft, Dan?" Cree put in.

"A thirty-two-foot sloop. Just big enough to go offshore."

"The Labor Day regatta's in September. The Shields Trophy, Hammond Cup, the Offshore Championship—"

"Sounds great," Dan said, "but I'll probably be running pretty hard, trying to take over from you."

"Oh, this billet's a piece of cake." Cree leaned back so far the garden chair creaked. "Almost on autopilot. Ellie and I, I have to say, I couldn't do it without her.

"See, ninety percent of this job is social. We entertained twenty thousand people last year. Second only to the White House. The alumni dinners, the Army-Navy gala, class reunions, visiting congressmen—we're the only service academy so close to DC." Cree waved away a questing hornet. "To be honest, Dan, the supe has very little direct control over what actually happens around here. The commandant runs the Brigade. I leave the other details to Burkie and the Dean. By the time issues reach our level, the answer's either obvious, or there's nothing we can do anyway."

Dan nodded, but wondered where this philosophy had come from. In his experience, the easy decisions got made far below flag officer level. Only the toughest problems rose to where a general or admiral had to get involved. In fact, Cree's casual demurral made him suspect there might be some sores that so far had not seen the light of day.

He glanced at his watch. "Shouldn't we be getting—?"

"Relax, Dan." Cree chuckled. "They can't very well start without us. Can they?"

* * *

The change of command was in what he remembered as Tecumseh Court, though it had a different name now, a yellow brick expanse in front of Bancroft. Only a hundred yards distant, so when Cree got up at last Dan rose too, and their aides fell in behind them, and together they strolled unhurriedly out and down what he remembered as Buchanan Road, though it, too, had been renamed. Ancient oaks towered to his left. A faint, exquisitely welcome breeze breathed off the river, cooling the sweat on his brow.

Commands echoed ahead. Shouted cadences reverberated on the heating air. The summer Brigade, over a thousand new plebes and their upperclass trainers, were forming up. Mrs. Cree chattered nonstop as they walked. The outgoing supe himself was silent, apparently sunk in thought.

They stood in the shadow of the second wing as the companies wheeled into position. The plebes were in white works. Dan remembered their aroma, a pang of memory whenever he ripped open the plastic on new clothes. Dixie-cup sailor hats with blue bands. White jumpers, shiny black shoes, sailor-style neckerchiefs tied in square knots. Their marching was pretty ragged. Well, hell, they'd been civilians a month ago.

He remembered the shock and awe of those first hours. Your personal identity was ground off along with your hair and clothes. The blur of inoculations, gear issue, rifle issue, paperwork. The peremptory shouts of the cadre, intimidating, incredibly buff young studs in impeccable trop whites.

"They've only been here for three weeks," Mrs. Cree said, beside him.

He forced a smile. "I was just thinking that. Remembering what it was like."

"Arminius says the memories get sharper, the older he gets."

High youthful voices rose in the sunlight. Swords flashed. The summer stripers reported to the summer commander, who at last turned to the commandant, executed a graceful, if rather too flamboyant sword salute, and snapped his sword tip to the bricks. "Brigade present and accounted for," he shouted.

Colonel Leslie Danelle Stocker, USMC, a short woman in Marine greens, returned the salute, then placed everyone at parade rest. Taking the mic, she reminded the mids of Cree's record, his stewardship, and wished him and Eleanor fair winds and following seas.

Cree took the lectern. He, too, was brief: honor, inclusivity, duty, pride. Then he introduced Dan, and outlined his combat career, awards, and decorations.

Dan stood with hands locked behind him, feeling two thousand eyes searching him. He knew what they were wondering. What kind of leader would he be? What changes would he demand? Or maybe they were just zoned out. He remembered nothing of what his own supe had said, years before. Back then, even your company officer was a remote presence. What mattered was what your firstie thought, how your classmates ranked you, and whether you'd make it through the semester. Or not.

"Present arms," Stocker barked. The cadres' swords lifted, then dropped; they executed precise about-faces and shouted in fifteen voices, "Present . . . *arms.*"

A thousand right arms lofted wood and steel, a thousand left hands slapped the stocks in a rippling applause that echoed between the enclosing walls. A thousand right hands snapped the rifles vertical, floating their stacking swivels in front of a thousand noses.

Dan faced Cree in the cloudless flooding sunlight, in the bright wind off the Chesapeake, so like the day he'd stood here himself for the first time, and saluted. "I relieve you, sir."

Cree returned the salute, then extended a hand. "I stand relieved."

The band blared out. Dan trailed Cree and the rest of the official party out onto Stribling Walk again. Behind them the ranks shouldered arms, swung into columns, and stepped out for the next event in a packed day of drill and exercise and indoctrination.

Dan smelled jasmine again, cut grass, the briny wind off the Bay. The massive and warlike figurehead of USS *Delaware* scowled down at them. The grim chieftain was no longer called Tecumseh, but he'd always think of it by the old name.

Cree, a few steps ahead, was patting his wife's arm, his step sprightlier than it had been minutes before. The former supe glanced back, and their gazes locked.

It's your problem now, his wink seemed to say.

The wind shifted then, and from the massed marching ranks more scents reached him, smells that lit again recondite and long-slumbering neurons. Cotton and soap and sweat, gun oil, hot bricks, the stink of exertion and stress, too-hasty showers and the grim eye-gritty weariness of never enough sleep.

And for just that moment, the years between fell away. . . .

2

Forty Years Earlier

The afternoon was sweltering, but the idiots he was trying to coach shouldn't be doing *this* bad. Throwing a time-out signal to the ref, Dan angrily waved them in from the field.

The players trotted up, sweating through gray USNA tees, sticks bobbing randomly. They looked beaten already. The chubbier mids were wobbling on their feet, pale, close to collapse. Yeah, it was hot, but you couldn't call a game for heat. He huddled them around the water-beaded aluminum cooler and handed out Styrofoam cups. "Hydrate," he snapped, eyeing the other team across Dewey Field. Beyond them, out on the Severn, a yawl was tacking upriver. Very slowly, in the nearly airless, sun-scorched day.

Battalion lacrosse, the run-up to the Brigade championship. He wiped sweat off his forehead, scowling at the other team and evaluating his options. Which were few.

He wasn't playing, himself. Coach Knauer had cut Dan from the varsity, so Lieutenant Oleksa had volunteered him to coach the battalion team.

The clock ran fast in lacrosse, with four ten-minute quarters. He'd pressed hard from the get-go, and they'd made two goals, but second batt had four big firsties on defense and after that they'd battered in vain. There was no shot clock, so you could control the ball as long as you wanted. So for the second quarter his guys had passed, danced, run it, and held the lead. But when the other side got the ball again they'd scored three times, then run out the clock in turn.

With sixty seconds left the score was tied. But there were no "ties" in lacrosse. If the score was even, the game went into sudden-death overtime. And it didn't look like his guys had much left.

"Take another cup, and pour it on your head," he snapped. "Now listen up. Control that damn ball! If you get the shot, take it, but go right back to defense. I know some of you segundoes and firsties figure it's on you to win. But this is a team effort. So let's work as a team." He eyed each in turn. A husky midfielder, but short legged, always a little too slow. Two tubby third class. A second class, fast, but with a laid-back attitude.

And Midshipman Fourth Class Mario Patterson. A plebe, but he did have one trick, a roll dodge Dan had seen him practice. He'd swap sides on the stick, setting his opponent up, faking him out. Then whip his body around a hundred and eighty degrees and blow past.

But Patterson didn't seem to have his mind in the game. He kept missing opportunities. Reacting, but a step behind the play.

Dan decided to try something different. "Sam, grab a mom stick," he told his face-off guy. To the others, "If you can get the ball, and Patterson's in the clear, hike it to him.—Patterson, make sure you keep your fuckin' stick up as you roll. And stash that ball deep in your pocket."

They nodded and he jerked his thumb at the field. "Beat Army!" they yelled, though it wasn't Army they were playing, and trotted back onto the crisp singed grass.

Dan braced hands on hips, watching them line up.

Last year he'd played on the national championship team at Michie Stadium. Navy had won seventeen national championships, nine the past ten years. Made six postseason NCAA tournament appearances. Coach Knauer was worshiped like a god. But that first day of this season, he'd brought in last year's team and this year's picks. Read out the list and paused, his lean, hard face expressionless. "That's it, folks. Those whose names I didn't read, thanks for your effort."

"Thanks for our *effort*?" one of Dan's teammates had muttered. "We won the fucking national championship, and he's cutting his top five?"

But you didn't question the coach, any more than the crew of USS *Boise* would've second-guessed Mike Moran when he said to pick out the biggest and commence firing. Dan, and the others who hadn't made the cut, had filed out, masking their shock and disappointment. Even now, weeks later, no one had an explanation.

Now the ump was out on the field, readjusting two players' positions. Dan paced the sidelines, sloshing a cup of cold water over his own T-shirt. He eyed a fireplug. Last year, as a second class, he'd managed to smash into it during a passing drill. Despite the pain, and possible internal bleeding, he'd checked himself out of sick bay after two days and gone back to practice.

Then the next year I get cut, he thought, kicking angrily at the wilting turf.

"Down," the ump yelled. The face-off men dropped to their battle stances, glaring at each other. "Set."

The whistle blew. Baily got the ball clamped and pumped it out ten yards to McFetridge, in front of him. McFetridge passed to Snell, who ran left, faked his guard, and passed to Patterson, ten yards closer to the goal.

Dan tensed. The plebe was in motion! Big steps. A wide stance. The Second Batt lineman loomed. Patterson swapped sides on his stick, bent, faked, and spun left. He blew past the lineman, swapped sides on the stick, and went to shoot.

A scuffed sphere left his stick and looped through the air. "Crap," Dan muttered, not believing what he was seeing.

The trailing player recovered the ground ball after one bounce and quick-sticked it to midfield.

The attack men converged. A clear shot. Dan's goalie bent, intent. Dan prayed it would go to his strong side—the guy was weak to his left—but it homed torpedo-straight into the five slot, between the goalie's legs.

The umpuffed his whistle, cheeks red, holding up his stopwatch. And that was it. The game, and the battalion's shot at the championship.

* * *

Patterson was trotting past, looking spaced out, when Dan beckoned him in. The plebe bopped over. Halted and came to attention. Pipe-thin arms trembled. Sweat gleamed on knife-blade shins. "Yes, sir?" He took on the usual plebe frightened-deer expression. "Sorry, sir. Guess I blew it out there, huh?"

"Know what you did wrong?"

"Not exactly, sir." He dipped his head, as if expecting the worst.

Dan looked away. "I *told* you to keep that stick up. Keep it semi-vertical when you came out of your roll. The ball came out the back as you went to do your overhand."

"Yes, sir."

"Which your fuckin' coach just told you exactly one minute before! Were you giving it all you had out there, mister?"

"No excuse, sir." There were only five acceptable responses as a plebe: "yes, sir," "no, sir," "no excuse, sir," "aye, aye, sir," and "I'll find out, sir."

Dan sighed. “I wasn’t *pinging* on you, ploob. Just *asking.* Were you giving it all you had?”

Dropped gaze. “Maybe not, sir.”

“Yeah, that was obvious. Why not?”

The plebe hesitated, glancing across the field. Dan looked that way, shading his eyes against the sun, but saw nothing. God, it was hot. The knockabouts drifted motionless on the Severn, mainsails drooping limp as used condoms. Heat boiled off the tumbled rocks of the seawall.

“Permission to speak freely, sir?”

Dan sighed again. “Make it a short squirt.”

“I haven’t had much . . . chance to sleep lately. Sir.”

Dan rolled his eyes. “What, they’ve got you under two mattresses? In your laundry bag? No, you wouldn’t fit . . . so what’s the issue, you can’t keep your mind in the game?”

A prominent Adam’s apple bobbed. The kid glanced across the field again. This time Dan caught a hefty upperclass frowning from the sidelines, arms crossed. Bob “Easy” Davis. A fellow firstie, though not from Dan’s company.

The kid was scared shitless. Still, it was standard for plebe year. During their first summer, it was one upperclass to fifteen freshmen. Now, with the Brigade back from cruise, Pensacola, jump training, it was four to one. “Five pair of sweat gear. Sir.”

Yeah, the heavy gray sweatpants and hoodies, in the unair-conditioned rooms, would make for an uneasy sleep. Still . . . “We’ve all been through it, Mister Patterson. If we could do it, so can you. I expected more effort out there.”

A tremor of the lips; was that a tear? “You’re *cutting* me, sir? Sir, please . . . this is the only thing I’m really good at.”

“But you’re not that good at it,” Dan said. Then immediately wished he hadn’t. But upperclassmen didn’t apologize to plebes. “Aw, hell. I’ll give you one more chance.”

Patterson compressed his lips on what was probably a thank-you. Another forbidden phrase. Dan jerked a thumb. “Now shove off the fuck out of here.”

He gave it a beat, then strolled toward the sideline. Davis watched him come, arms still crossed. Squinting into the sun.

“Hey, Bob, got a minute?”

Davis lifted his chin. “It’s about Snowflake, right?”

Snowflake? “If that’s Patterson, yeah. What’s his story?”

Davis opened his eyes wide. "Where do I start? He's great Army material."

"He says he's not getting any sleep. We're supposed to give 'em six hours a night."

Davis's chin lifted farther. "What fucking business is it of yours?"

"He's on my team. He could play better if you didn't have him sleeping in five pair of sweat gear."

Davis shook his head wearily. "Is that what he told you?"

As a company honor rep, Dan went on internal alert. If Patterson was lying, it was an honor violation. A hearing, possibly separation. "It's not true?"

His classmate shrugged. "What if it is? You saw him out there. Can't field. Can't throw. Can't do chow call or remember his rates. I give him 'til the end of the semester. If he doesn't put in his letter first."

Dan nodded. Every company had its shit magnet. There had to be someone at the bottom of the grease list. And once your classmates graded you low, and the company officer wrote you off, there wasn't much chance of a comeback. He was stepping away when something made him turn back. "Bob?"

"What?"

"Can you spare me a come-around?"

"With him?" Davis looked surprised. "He's not in your company."

"I know, but how about it? Maybe tomorrow. If you can do without him for half an hour."

"Shit, you can have that dork for a roommate." Davis started a smirk, but quit halfway. He shrugged again. "I'll give him the word."

* * *

Dan hadn't had that great of a plebe year himself. He'd done well in high school. Lettered in two sports. But at Annapolis, he was surrounded by standouts. Valedictorians. Former enlisted, combat Marines. Salty petty officers. Golden Gloves boxers. Eagle Scouts. Football captains. Geniuses who held patents. Often, guys (and a few girls) who were several of the above at the same time.

The torments had been refined over decades. Shoving out, dead horses, the green bench, leaning rest. Carrier landings and crab races. Sweating a penny to the bulkhead, along with salamanders, hello-darlings, hanging around, and greyhound and bunny races. A plebe's brain became a catalogue of trivia. His body, an engine for converting food into push-ups. Dan had gained notoriety from being able to eat while clamped on (attaching himself to the table without the use of a chair, with elbows and knees). Once, his firstie had asked for his least-favorite foods. For a month, all Dan had eaten was coffee ice cream and brussels sprouts.

Nine months of hell, but once you climbed Herndon, you could almost be grateful. At least you knew that, short of being captured by the North Koreans, you'd just survived the worst year of your life.

A lot of his classmates hadn't, though. Bilged for grades, for conduct, for failing physical readiness. Or they'd just quit; given their upperclass a final finger, walked into the company office, and vanished. As the commandant had warned them, that day they'd been sworn in. "Look at the man on your left," he'd said. "Then the one on the right. Out of the three of you, only two are going to graduate."

Dan had resolved then he'd be one of the survivors. It wasn't heroism, or even ambition. Just that he had nothing to go back to. Not back to Bumfuck, Pennsylvania, that was for sure.

Now, to his surprise, he was a striper. Part of the Brigade leadership. Not, he felt sure, from any inherent talent. More likely just that he was tall, looked good in uniform, and could flourish a sword for the tourists.

His mind recurred to a fresh worry. Fourth-year calculus. From an A in high school math to Ds at USNA.

Facing, once again, being expelled. Within months of graduating.

He grabbed a stick off the bench and flipped up a ball from the ground. Cradling it, he gazed out once more over the field. Heat shimmered above the grass. The sails drooped. The clouds hovered, frozen in place like painted scrims. As if time itself had halted, becalmed, withheld. As if nothing would ever change forever, ever, ever.

He tossed the ball and caught it. As if that single motion restarted the universe, a breeze from the Bay heeled the boats. The zephyr swept toward him, ruffling the Severn into glittering ripples of light, flattening the grass. Until at last it cooled his chest and arms, bringing with it the sweet-salty scent of the sea.

Cradling the ball, he jogged back toward Bancroft.

* * *

Evening meal. Under the laminated beams of the largest dining facility in the world, hundreds of tables resounded with the clatter of plates, the clash of trays as the Filipino servers slammed them back into metal carts. The incessant bawling from a thousand plebe throats, reciting "The Laws of the Navy," the names of the football first-team lineup, the movies out in town. The hot air was thick with food smells. Tonight's menu was lobster tails, broccoli, fried potatoes, with ice cream as dessert, frozen into huge stainless-steel bowls from the USNA Dairy.

He squinted down the table at one of the youngsters, an overweight sophomore, who was intent on scraping the last lobster tail onto his plate, which already held four. "Mister Sheldon."

"Sir?"

"Can you leave a little protein for our fourth-class animals? And you might want to go easy on the ice cream. Given your last score on the Mile Run."

"Yessir." Looking resentful, the youngster scraped the smallest tail back onto the tray. The stares of the four plebes at the table—rigidly braced up, chins in, backs straight—tracked the wizened morsel hungrily.

"Morton, if you please, the lighthouse," Wilseley, the other first class at the table, said. Each condiment or item on the table had its pet name: the cow, the lighthouse, the redeye, the twins. The lone Army cadet at the table, an exchange student named Donderbeck, often looked confused.

Suddenly a chorus of shouts erupted two tables down. "Wild man! Wild man!"

Heads whipped around. "Fuck, he's headed this way," Wilseley said, grabbing the edge of the table. "Plebes! Barrier strategy!"

The shouts grew deafening. A dark head bobbed above the uniforms. Dan and Wilseley's plebes bolted to their feet, then froze, uncertain how to deploy.

A stork-like figure jerked free of the scrum, a blue-and-gold half-gallon carton in an extended hand. Before Dan could react, Patterson upended it over his head, drenching him in icy milk. "Wild man!" the plebe screamed, face distorted.

Dan combed milk from his eyes. It ran down his shoulder boards. His trop whites, ruined. "Fuck," he muttered.

Plebes didn't initiate a wild man. Like a wire-guided torpedo, someone had dispatched Patterson on his course of destruction. Most likely Davis, for Dan sticking his oar in at the game. The plebe looked stricken. "Sorry, sir," he muttered.

"Get the fuck out of here, Patterson," Dan snapped.

* * *

Study hour. The period after evening meal when the assiduous midshipman hit the books. Dan and his roommate, Ted Scherow, a stubby guy from some Podunk town in the Midwest, opened the windows, turned on the red lights on their desk lamps, and lit cigars.

Scherow was the most colorless guy in the company. As a third class, he'd reported two minutes late to watch squad inspection. Had strolled to his place in ranks directly in front of the officer of the watch, as LCDR. Leighty was bawling everyone out for slackness, yet *Leighty had never noticed him.* Oddly, or maybe because of his unnoticeability, his roommate yearned to be onstage. He tried out for every Masqueraders production, but usually only got bit parts or walk-ons.

Dan couldn't get his mind on partial integrals. He tried again to make sense of the equations. Nada.

Scherow crunched an empty Fresca can and lofted it to a clanging two points in the shitcan. "Doin' any good over there?"

"Not much."

"Feel like a Benny's run?"

Dan fought his better instincts and lost. He slammed the calc book closed. "Grab Donkey and we'll go."

"Donkey" was DuKay, a plebe from a three-man room next to Dan and Ted's. Donkey, Bozo, and Muff were their go-to plebes for Coke runs, window-closing details, and any other shitty little jobs the firsties could dream up. With habitual submissive expressions, stubbled heads, and rumpled, sweated-through uniforms, they could only with difficulty be distinguished from their equally cowed classmates.

The gates were closed on weekday nights, and the ten-foot wall was surveilled by the superannuated watchmen the mids derided for some generations-forgotten reason as Jimmy Legs. A section behind the Chapel was usually unguarded, but crossing the central Yard was risky; it was open ground, and illuminated.

Fortunately another route existed, word-of-mouthed from class to class.

In black trou, black pullovers, black watch caps, and black dress gloves, Dan, Ted, and their classmate Corwin Haley, followed by DuKay, met at a grated door deep in the basement of the first wing. They carried flashlights, and Dan had a chunk of wooden batten tucked into a pocket. The grate was padlocked, but some obsessive mid in the deep past had tried combination after combination until he lucked out.

It unlocked with a snap. DuKay supplied a drop of 3 in One to keep it working—no one wanted it to be replaced—and the grate groaned open. Beyond lay darkness, smelling of old steam, moldy damp, and rat turds.

The tunnels dated from when God was a pup. They ran from a boiler plant at the far end of the Yard, supplying heat to the academic buildings and ultimately Bancroft.

Dan nodded to the plebe, whose long face looked ghoullike in the near dark. "Go ahead," he muttered.

A clang as the grated door went home. A double ratcheting click echoed as DuKay hasped the heavy lock behind them, on the far side of the grate and out of reach from within.

When Ted snapped on his flash, it illuminated a long, low-ceilinged passageway that echoed with the slow drip of water into dank puddles. Scurrying claws scratched as something unseen fled, squeaking. Scherow advanced, carefully placing his steps. A hundred yards in, the tunnels branched. They took the left-hand passage, toward the Chapel.

Two hundred paces more, and they halted at a rusty set of steel rungs. This time Haley took the lead. Bracing his back, he levered a manhole cover upward. Steel scraped and rang.

"Coast is clear," he muttered.

Dan pulled the shim from his pocket and wedged it up under the cover's lip, keeping it from setting flush. They dodged to the shadow of a tree and froze, listening.

The Yard lay dark, silent, save for the drone of an aircraft far above. The querying hoot of a roving owl.

Scherow stepped out, reaching the wall in quick strides. A leap, a swing of his legs, and he was over.

Haley went next. He hung for a moment, unable to quite get a leg over. Dan scooted across and gave him a boost. Atop the wall, his classmate extended a hand. Then Dan, too, was over, dropping to the silent brick pavements of Hanover Street. Lights glowed from ancient windows, houses that dated from when the British flag had flown over Maryland.

"She'll be right around the corner," Scherow muttered.

True to his word, a darkened Pinto with two girls in it idled on King George. Scherow and Zusana exchanged a peck, then the other girl got out so the mids could cram themselves into the back. Dan crouched, bent under the sloping headliner. Zusana declutched, the little motor tapocketa'd, and they rumbled off down the cobbled street. Two blocks on, she pulled the knob for the headlights.

"I brought Kendrick," she said. "From my dorm. Kendrick, this is Ted, Corwin, and—uh—"

"Dan."

"And Dan."

"Do you guys really have to sneak out?" Half turned to them, the new girl's profile was attractive. Chin a little pointed, but a nice nose.

The car turned toward the fish market and the city dock, then uphill. The tires flubbered on bricks. Past darkened storefronts, boarded-up shops, abandoned buildings.

"Affirmative," Corwin said. In the flashes of light from passing cars, his bony, rawboned face looked like the mask of Death in a medieval engraving. Redheaded, awkward, he'd shocked the company by bringing a violin back from Christmas leave and playing it with an artistry that had won him grudging credit with Brenton and Lormer, their then-firsties. A truly sadistic pair; who would have thought they'd be music lovers? Lormer had a set of weight-loss electrodes he liked to put on plebes, then make them shove out—sitting on thin air, essentially—while being shocked every fifteen seconds. And Brenton had fried Dan for not polishing his belt buckle. The *back* of his belt buckle.

"So what happens if they catch you?"

"Oh, demerits, some walking tours," Ted muttered.

Kendrick laughed. "A walking tour sounds nice."

"Not with an M1 over your shoulder, squaring the corners," Dan said, but the sharp-chinned girl seemed to have locked onto Corwin. Well, he had a girlfriend already. Who knew where it was going with Mignon, but the perfumed letters on linen stationery kept coming. . . . He sat back, catching the loom of the oaks on State Circle, the scents of honeysuckle and Confederate jasmine on the wind. The little car, vibrating as it hit speed, arched up and over the bridge to the far shore of the night-bound river.

Craning back over his shoulder, he glimpsed the Chapel dome, the sick-yellow lights along the seawall. Someday he'd look back for the last time. Graduated. Done. Finished forever with the fucking place.

One thing was for certain fucking sure. Once he got out, he'd never be coming back.

* * *

Benny's lay a full seventy yards outside the seven-mile limit. It had been carefully surveyed by a Brigade navigational team, with the results on file in case some overzealous company officer crashed the party. The bar was attached to a bowling alley, which came in handy with girls; it sounded harmless, going bowling. But the tavern was the main attraction.

They settled at a table and ordered pitchers and pizza. Kendrick sat with Corwin, Zusana with Ted. Dan took his first sip and grimaced. He hated the sick yeasty taste, but the way it made him feel made up for it. Warm. Relaxed. Accepted.

When he tuned back in, Zusana was asking Ted what kind of car he was getting. Firsties could own cars, on paper, but couldn't take delivery until spring semester.

"Porsche. The two-point-four liter, with the Targa top."

Zusana snuggled prettily. "That's the convertible, right? Oh my God. What color?"

"Red."

"But I told you I liked green!" Her hand slid under the table; Ted's face reddened. "You said I could pick out the color!"

"Okay, okay . . . green. But remember, I can't park it in the Yard until after Christmas leave. You'll have to keep it at your place."

She leaned closer, hand busy under the table. "As long as I get to drive it."

"What're you getting, Dan?" Kendrick asked, without taking her attention off Corwin.

He cleared his throat. "Uh, well, I was talking to a guy out in town with a used MG. He's offering me a good deal."

"That's awful small, isn't it?" But before he had a chance to answer she was tugging Corwin to his feet. "Do you *really* play the violin? Zusana said so. Let's go outside a minute, it's so smoky in here. Or wait, where's the restroom?"

"Wait up, I'll go with you," Zusana said.

The cigarette haze was getting to Dan too. His eyes burned. An occasional Wolf Brothers during study hour, fine. But he couldn't imagine smoking all day long.

When he reached for the pitcher it was empty. He signaled the waitress for another. Checked his wallet; low, but enough.

A while later two of Dan's teammates—*former* teammates, he thought sourly—joined them from the bar. Harry Orczek, "The Orc," was a goalie, the toughest position to play, and Karl Glase, a defenseman. Both had won Black Ns—the dreaded Class A punishments of one hundred demerits each—on the same night. Partying hearty on an alum's boat in the town harbor, the Orc had fallen overboard. Glase had dived in to save him. Unfortunately, the next boat over had belonged to a retired general. When they were fished out, sopping wet and reeling drunk, the Marine had called the Main Office to come get them.

Dan tilted his chair back. "I'm surprised to see you guys. Aren't you still on restriction?"

"Officially." The Orc burped and rubbed a hand over a nearly bare scalp. "What're they gonna do? I got an offer from the Lakers."

The fresh pitcher arrived. Glase and Orczek threw dollar bills on the table and topped off everyone's mugs. They talked about the last game, against Air Force, then about the coach. "I hear he's gonna get fired," Harry said. "After letting you guys go? Nobody understands why he did that. Did you do something we don't know about?"

"If we did, I don't know about it either," Dan said.

"Where's Mignon, Dan? She not make it?"

"Oh, this was kind of a ad hoc thing. It's hard for her to get away except weekends."

Glase nodded. "Uh-huh. Hey, either'a you thinking about service selection? I had a great time at Pensacola. Five years obligated, then I'll pull down the big bucks with TWA. How 'bout you?"

"Either subs or surface ships," Dan said. "I barely got out of that upside-down spin. If I have to go someplace, I'll let somebody else fly me there."

"Yeah, when you get to be an admiral," Zusana snorted.

The girls had come back from their head call. Kendrick giggled. Dan examined her closely. Was she really an airhead? Or was she on something?

"If any of you idiots make admiral, the Navy's really screwed," Zusana observed, cuffing Ted playfully. Scherow started to refill her glass, but she slapped his hand away. "No, I gotta drive. And we should get going. Don't you guys have to get up at . . . what do you call it, zero dark thirty?" She stood, smoothing her skirt. The mids threw quarters on the table for tips and followed her out.

* * *

They crouched in the shadow of the wall. Boosted to the top, Dan peered around for ambushers. At last he beckoned.

The shim was still there under the iron cover. They pried it up and groped with their feet for the ladder down. Ted found his light where he'd staged it. Sliding the heavy disc back into place, they trotted back down the tunnel.

They halted beneath the central court, where the Brigade would be falling in in a few hours for morning formation. "Grab my ankles," Dan muttered.

This access was a few yards inside T-Court, beneath where Tecumseh bent his scowl toward the bricks. Dan noodged the cover up a couple inches and aimed the light carefully from beneath it up at the company windows. Long flash, short flash, long.

He grinned, still slightly lit. Remembering the trick question fired at them as plebes. How many bricks did it take to complete T-Court?

The answer, of course: one.

They waited. Muff should reply with the countersign: short, long, short. Then DuKay would hustle down to unlock the gate and let them back in.

But no answer came. Dan blinked the signal again, shading the side glow with a cupped hand.

Nothing.

"Shit," he muttered. The beer high was evaporating. If they couldn't get that gate unlocked, either they stayed here until dawn, and racked up a Class A, or risked a dash in the open beneath the windows of the Main Office, under the full illumination from the Yard lights and the moon.

"What's goin' on?" A hiss from below; Haley, sounding anxious too.

"They're not answerin'," Dan muttered.

"Fuck. Fuck," Scherow whispered.

Dan glimpsed motion from the corner of one eye. A small figure, striding along purposefully. For a moment he thought it was a Jimmy Legs. Then a flash of dull green trouser hem brought the horror home.

It was Black Bart. The Black Ranger.

Someone had filched Major Truxtun T. Bartranger's prized Mameluke saber, ground off most of it in the machine shop, and replaced it in its scabbard. So that drawing it at Color Parade, the major had saluted a three-star admiral with a two-inch stub. In revenge, he'd sworn a vow to fry a mid for each and every article in the reg book. Unfortunately Bartranger, too, had done night crawls as a firstie, and tended to stick his nose into the most obscure places at the most inopportune times.

Dan eased the lid down so slowly it seemed to be healing. He updated the others in a whisper, then hunched, waiting, as footsteps carried through the brick, the soil, down to reverberate in the sealed narrow space. Bartranger wore steel heel guards, which made it easier to track him. But it also lent his steps the ominous metallic click of approaching doom. Like actors in a World War Two submarine movie, the three mids crouched in the depths, waiting helplessly for the enemy destroyer's depth charges.

Tap. Tap. Tap. A pause.

A distinct *click*, directly on the manhole cover, as if testing it for play. They flinched, exchanging looks.

The steps moved on. Faded.

Dan hissed out a breath. Checked the luminous hands of his watch. Gave it five minutes more, then slowly, slowly lifted the cover again and periscoped the horizon.

A shielded light flashed from a window. Short. Long. Short.

He checked again—still clear—and flashed the countersign. Then eased the cover down as the others retreated toward the gate.

His last glimpse was of Tecumseh, still scowling forbiddingly out over the empty pavement.

3

The air was still cool this morning. Mist haunted the oaks. In the distance the cadenced chants of double-timing plebes awakened memories. Early morning come-arounds, chow call . . . the day started early here.

Larson Hall, the Academy's Administration building, crouched in the shadow of the Chapel. It dated from the same era, a two-story French Revival design of white brick and green-stained copper. Dan let himself through tall oak double doors into a spacious lobby lined with maritime art. Most were original oils, donated over the years. The first floor held PR and other staff. He climbed marble stairs, handrailed with ornate, turn-of-the-century cast iron, to the second floor, his office and that of his deputy.

"Good morning, Admiral. I hear the change of command went smoothly." A middle-aged woman in a tweed suit dress that looked like a hand-me-down from Agatha Christie, sensible shoes, and tortoiseshell glasses rose from her computer station.

"Thanks, Valerie." The flag secretary, Valerie Marsh, had served four previous superintendents. Unlike the other service academies—West Point, Colorado Springs, and New London—Annapolis had been staffed by a mix of civilian and military personnel from its earliest years. The uniformed members turned over at intervals; he'd have to depend on the civilians for institutional memory.

"You asked for sit-downs with the major cost center supervisors. I set you up with everyone, including the dean, throughout the day. You also have lunch with the governor at Government House, twelve-thirty. That's on State Circle, in town. Will you want a car?"

"Thanks, I'll walk." He flipped through the schedule she handed him as two larger-than-life-size men in whites let themselves in. Shaven-headed, saturnine Kareem Abimbola was the Academy's command master chief, the senior enlisted. Cree said he had to be prodded to speak up, but always gave good advice. "Captain Jack" Burke-Bowden, Dan's chief of staff–slash–deputy superintendent, was a decorated submariner. As a Navy quarterback, he'd held the NCAA rushing record for three years.

The tall sun-filled windows of Dan's office looked out over Stribling Walk and the Upper Yard, with a glimpse of the silver Severn between the trees. His curved ruby-lacquered desk was set with brown leather chairs in front. To the right stood the usual sofa and coffee table setup, also in government-issue brown leather. The floor was pale wood, with a russet Persian carpet. Two long bookshelves were empty except for bound copies of *Proceedings*, *Shipmate*, and the *Naval War College Review*. The walls were bare; Dan hadn't yet unpacked his I-Love-Mes—his three-star flag, the plaques and inscribed photos from his previous commands.

A rather pudgy, anxious-looking lieutenant stood as they came in. Vince LeCato was Dan's flag aide, a do-everything dogsbody who also served as an extra set of ears when necessary. Next door was a conference room, with blue leather-covered chairs, a long polished table, another truly magnificent figured carpet, and black-and-white photos of former superintendents with various presidents, cardinals, kings, and other heads of state on the walls. Dan wavered for a moment between office and conference room, and settled on the former.

"Jack, Master Chief. Grab a seat." He waved at the couch. "Lieutenant, could you bring the whiteboard in?—Coffee, guys?"

"We're good," Burke-Bowden said. "All moved in, sir? Over at the House?"

"Admiral and Mrs. Cree will be leaving this afternoon. I'll move in tonight." He nodded to Abimbola, asked again about coffee. The chief shook his head silently.

When they were settled in, Dan opened. "I'm still getting the lay of the land, but I'm going to want this office to be more proactive than I sense it's been in the recent past. For one thing, I've asked Commander Amy Singhe to investigate and report back to me on three specific areas. First, how we can put an end to sexual assault and harassment. For good. Second, to deep-dive our administrative overhead, and see if there's fat there we can cut without hurting our academic ranking. And third, review our suicide prevention programs and make sure we're doing what we ought to.

"Okay, over to you. Additional thoughts?"

Burke-Bowden smiled as if he'd just been complimented. Which he hadn't been. "Absolutely, Admiral. Give us our orders and we'll move out."

Dan turned to Abimbola. "Master Chief, I've been reading your posts. You seem to have ruffled some feathers online."

Abimbola remained impassive. "I say what I think, Admiral. If people don't like that, they can come to me, and we'll have it out in person."

Dan looked at him again, noting a resemblance to his old rabbi, Barry Niles. Yeah, he ought to give his former boss a call, see how his recovery was going. "You take on what you call the Eighth Battalion. What exactly is that?"

The Brigade, of course, had only six battalions. The "Seventh Battalion" was a nickname for an informal self-help network among minority midshipmen.

The master chief said, "Sir, we have an issue in certain circles. Both staff and mids. It's not entirely a white male problem, but that's the core of it. They're not top dogs anymore, and they don't like it."

Dan nodded. "Hate speech on the wall of the head in 5-3."

"A noose on a mid's bunk in Fourth Company. And posts on social media that don't make any of us look good."

He remembered the blond mid while he was out running: *Well, at least we got one of our own this time.* Did she mean . . . yeah, probably. Since Stocker was Black and Cree had been at least part Native American. He cleared his throat. "Let's talk more about that later. Maybe with the commandant, and our equal opportunity person in the room. But I agree, we need to address it."

He took a breath. "Actually, as I see it, we have several simultaneous challenges. If we can get ahead of them, we'll stay in a good space. But any one of them can take us down."

They watched wary-eyed as he went to the whiteboard. "The most public, I guess, is this." He wrote *Recruiting Scandal.*

Burke-Bowden shrugged. "Sir, due respect, that's a bump in the road. You'll see when you talk to Coach Virjay. We're above seventy percent wins in all our Division One sports. Just between us, you don't get that without some serious recruiting."

Dan considered his response. With thirty-three divisional sports programs, the athletic department ran almost independently of the rest of the institution. Football income and alumni donations funded most of it, and any interference risked a mob of Old Grads waving pitchforks and demanding heads. "Have we privileged getting the best athletes over clean recruiting?"

"Like every other school in the country, Admiral." The captain spread his hands. "I can get Virjay in here now, if you want to get down in the weeds. I know he's got another million-plus penciled in for his next season."

"He wants a *plus* in the budget?"

"Only if we want to keep winning, Admiral." Burke-Bowden looked smug, as if he'd delivered the final harpoon.

"Yeah, let's discuss that. But later." Dan turned to the board again. Wrote *Admissions.* "Our applications are down twenty percent over the last two years. I know, Big Navy's got the same problem. But we have to make ourselves look attractive to a new generation. We need to move fast to have an effect next year. Public affairs, our Blue and Gold officers, the head of admissions—"

"I'll take the lead on that, sir. Convene a working group. Get some solid recommendations for action—"

"By the end of next week," Dan said. He wrote *Flooding.* "I talked to Jerry Bonar at public works. We're flooding for ten days a year and it's getting worse."

"We raised the seawall," Burke-Bowden said. "We were going to carry that around the Yard, but money dried up."

"Yeah, I saw that yesterday on my run. But that doesn't stop flooding. Bonar wants a half-billion-dollar drainage project. We need to think a century out."

The deputy said, "We have a sea level rise advisory council—"

"Advisory councils aren't action," Dan snapped. "I want concrete plans, with hard numbers." He regarded the board again, wanting to mash that button harder, but this wasn't the time.

He wrote *Professors' Revolt.* The civilian academic staff wanted curriculum changes the officer staff opposed. Both his staffers were silent. "No comments? No advice?"

"You need to deal with the dean on that one," Burke-Bowden said. "Admiral."

Congress and Budget, he wrote next.

The master chief stirred. "Speak your mind," Dan told him.

"Admiral, you got the inside track on that, right? Your wife being the SecDef and all. And the vice president was your direct CO, during the war."

"Secretary Titus will have an input, sure. But her mandate's to reduce costs. That could pit her priorities against ours."

"Is that a conflict of interest?" the deputy said. "With your wife, I mean?"

Dan didn't answer, because he didn't know. Just hoped it wouldn't be an issue. He looked at the board again, the list, suppressing a sigh. As far as he could tell, Cree had let every major issue slide. Left his subordinates to manage the place day-to-day, with only an occasional meeting or committee report instead of a strategic plan.

Unaddressed, problems didn't go away. They festered, until suddenly the patient presented with toxic shock.

Burke-Bowden stirred. "Sir, on the social front, don't forget, you have Plebe Parents Weekend coming up. It's tradition for the supe to host a reception. Then, the quarterly meeting of the Board of Visitors."

"I know. I'll have to make a report, and recommendations. And speak to the alums at homecoming. And get ready for the ten-year Middle States accreditation visit." He glanced at his watch. "I've got the dean next, then a meet with the governor for lunch. Master Chief, I'll want you and HR in later regarding what we talked about." He gave them both a curt nod. "We've got to stop kicking the can down the road, and take action. I'll depend on you to make that happen. Understood?"

They agreed, of course. Murmured their aye-ayes. But their faces were unreadable as they stood to leave.

* * *

The academic dean was officed in Nimitz Library. Dan headed that way—he wanted to walk whenever possible, both to show the flag and get the exercise—past a Flagg-built academic complex. He remembered it as Maury Hall, but it had been renamed for arguably the Academy's most famous graduate, President Jimmy Carter. And recalled the stinks of hydrogen sulfide, equations on screeching chalkboards, the droning tedium of recitations. . . .

Dr. Grantham Mynbury had been a professor of economics at Northwestern, chief academic officer at U of Nebraska, and associate vice chancellor and dean of graduate studies at Notre Dame. At USNA for ten years, he would likely outlast Dan, since the civilian leadership had no expiration dates.

Mynbury's office was bigger than his own, and newer too. The provost-slash-dean was a lean graying wisp in a houndstooth jacket and what Dan assumed was a university tie. He met Dan at the door, bushy eyebrows raised. "You didn't need to come here, Admiral! I'd have been happy to meet you in Larson."

"Thought I'd check out your digs," Dan said. "Doctor."

Mynbury patted his shoulder. Condescendingly, or just being friendly? "Grant, please. Shall we show you some of our newer facilities? Brag off a bit?"

He nodded, and the dean led the way to a new building next door, all granite facing and dark glass. "Hopper Hall, as you probably know, is named after Admiral Grace Hopper, a pioneer in computer programming. Legend has it she discovered the first computer bug . . . literally; a moth, caught in a relay of the Mark II at Harvard."

Mynbury strolled the bays, pointing out a robotics laboratory, a gamma ray lab for 3D printing, CAD systems, classrooms with racks of servers. The old wires courses Dan remembered had evolved into cybersecurity, IT, and autonomous weapons. On the fourth deck they peered into a Pentagon-level sensitive compartmented information facility. "This is the only top secret SCIF outside Washington. We hold State videoconferences and National Security Agency exercises here. Our mids screen for NSA and ONI fellowships."

"We're teaching them how to hack?" Dan's turn to raise his eyebrows.

"Absolutely. Our cyberwarfare team routinely infiltrates other universities' systems. And they try to penetrate ours, of course." Mynbury smirked. "I flatter myself we're leading the pack. Not least, because of several really brilliant mids. They keep our faculty on their toes."

An elevator down, and Mynbury led him along a subterranean passageway. Key-carding a locked door, he waved at a subcritical reactor. Several mids were busy around the array of stainless-clad rods that held the enriched uranium. A counter clicked languidly from a bulkhead. A first class explained they were running a capstone project on nondestructive testing of submarine pressure hulls, using a neutron generator and artificial intelligence to inspect weld seams.

Dan smiled benignly, pretending he understood her explanation of hybrid parallel particle transport algorithms and monoenergetic beams. They seemed smarter than the mids he remembered. Especially when the dean mentioned the accelerated master's program in nuclear engineering.

Back at the provost's office, Dan accepted coffee. They chatted for a few minutes about what he'd just seen. At length the prof leaned back. "We're also preparing accessions for the Space Force, in astrophysics, and we do surveys for near-Earth asteroid detection with two half-meter telescopes. But . . . enough patting our own backs. You probably wanted to discuss our current in-house, um, differences of opinion."

Dan set the cup down. “I’ve heard about the New Reformers. Or the ‘Rowdy Twins,’ as I understand they’re called.”

The bickering had made the national news. Cree had fired two professors, but they’d been reinstated by a federal court and returned to their classrooms. They’d published journal articles and online blogs attacking the whole idea of “military education.” In the latest twist, they’d sued to remove the Mexican Monument as a celebration of imperialism and racism.

“Really, Admiral, you needn’t bother with them,” Grantham said. “We have internal procedures. The faculty senate will deal with the issue. Nor do you, ahem, need to send outside observers to examine our administrative overhead.”

“If you mean Amy Singhe, I expect you to cooperate with her,” Dan said. “And as far as the academic senate dealing with the Twins, they haven’t for the last two years. How about if I met with this couple? I understand they’re a husband-and-wife team.”

Grantham sucked air through his teeth. “A personal meeting? Oh, I’d advise against that. I don’t think that would be productive. At all.”

“Why not? If I may ask.”

“Both the individuals concerned, and I have to say, the rest of the teaching staff, would see that as . . . intimidation. No matter how pure your intentions, the optics . . . it would not be helpful.”

“Well, I won’t insist. But can you tell me more specifically, what do they want? How big’s their following? Give me some sense of what we’re dealing with.”

Mynbury tented his fingers. “Well. Yes, they’re controversial. What do they want? To some extent, the same things we all do. To serve the client, that is, the students, more effectively.”

Dan wasn’t sure the mids were the “clients” here. Maybe in a civilian setting, like the universities Mynbury had come up through. But wasn’t the government, the Navy and Marine Corps, the Academy’s actual customer? He held his objection as the provost went on. “They urge us to move into new ways of teaching, new areas of scholarship. Gender studies. Critical race studies. Updated history texts. They see us as a fossilized, authoritarian, sexist, racist institution in need of radical change.”

“Renaming monuments? Revising history?” Dan was trying not to show anger. “I understand renaming the buildings named for Confederates. But I read they want to restrict uniforms to parades.”

Mynbury smiled. “That may be simply testing the envelope, as the saying goes. I have to agree that some aspects of our institution are outdated. I suspect you may too, Admiral."

"Well . . . sure. So, you're sympathetic?"

Elevated eyebrows. "I didn't say that. We just don't operate by the chain of command. We evolve by consensus. And I want to make one more point, sir."

"Go ahead." Dan was trying to keep an open mind, but it wasn't easy.

"Congress is reevaluating the whole military education system. Transforming the Academy into a more modern institution might build support from progressive elements. To forestall action that may not be in our best interests. I also have to say, it might help increase the number of our applicants. Make us look more welcoming to those who would otherwise not consider a military career."

Dan nodded. Both reasonable points. Among a lot of others. He glanced at his watch; a quarter 'til. "I have to leave. But I did want to mention two things I hoped to put more emphasis on. Academic-wise."

"Certainly, sir." Mynbury adjusted a stack of papers on his desk. "A course change, as they say around here?"

"We need more emphasis on data analytics. Not just cybersecurity—I see we're doing well there—but winnowing actionable intel out of the data."

"That's part of what goes on in the internship programs. But, yes, I could talk to Dr. Schultz. See if there's a way to make our studies more relevant to the needs of the Fleet. Is that what you . . . ?" He spread his hands, an apparently habitual gesture.

Dan nodded. "Great. Also, outside of engineering, we need to reemphasize foreign area studies. I fought side by side with Indonesians, Vietnamese, Taiwanese, Koreans. We need specialties, majors, and more languages. Less deep math, unless it's going to be useful in their majors."

The dean nodded. "And?"

"One final question. Brianna Court."

Court, a second-class mid, had hit a stump on an ATV on summer leave, severed her spinal cord, and been left without use of her legs. Returned to Bancroft to await discharge, she'd filed suit to stay on, with a promise to apply for Cyber Command on graduation.

Mynbury looked grave. "Her retention, or not, isn't really an academic decision. But if you asked me, I'd recommend you approve her application."

"It'd set a precedent," Dan said. "One we might not like. First off, she might not be the best candidate for Cyber. Individual preference, great, but would she be taking a slot from someone better qualified? And, think about accessions. We'll have kids in wheelchairs applying for entrance, then suing under the Disabilities Act."

Mynbury spread his hands again. "You could address that on a case-by-case basis."

"More lawyers, more bad publicity. Aside from the real question: whether it's smart to graduate officers who can't fulfill basic physical tasks, during an attack or other emergency." Dan checked his watch once more, then rose. "I'll need to think about that. Thanks for your time, Doctor. Until later?"

"You're welcome anytime, Admiral." Mynbury rose gracefully and held the door.

When Dan glanced back at the end of the hallway, the dean was still regarding him, looking thoughtful.

* * *

Ms. Marsh reminded him again about Parents Weekend. "Someone needs to look over the plans for the reception, Admiral."

He nodded, checking himself in the mirror, grabbing his hat, on his way out. "Uh, can we just redo whatever we did last year?"

"Certainly, but the contracts have to be re-advertised and rebid. Federal law. Unless you want it catered by the Mess. Or use your personal account."

She regarded him so expectantly he felt ashamed to mutter, "Personal account?"

"You have a small budget to use as you wish. Mainly from alumni donations. Superintendent Cree let his wife draw on it for redecoration and social expenses." His secretary looked away. "Who *will* handle your social events, Admiral? I take it your wife will be . . . busy elsewhere."

Yeah, Cree had warned him how much entertaining a supe did. "Uh, let me think about that."

"Certainly, Admiral. I'm just saying, we can't wait too long. Or it will be GSA potato chips and generic ginger ale in paper cups. That may not convey the impression you want."

Actually he had no problem with soft drinks and chips, but yeah, the parents probably expected something more elegant. He sighed, and called to his aide.

* * *

He hiked out Gate 3, returning a hurried salute from a startled-looking marine. He avoided Bilger's Gate—the northern exit, traditionally used only by those leaving in disgrace—and headed up Maryland Avenue. LeCato fell in behind him on the narrow sidewalk. Dan looked up at the colonial brick homes, and déjà vu struck dizzyingly. Or not déjà vu, exactly, since he'd walked these streets before. Many times. As a mid.

The old seaside town had been sad and dirty then. It had gentrified since, and the tobacconists and used bookstores had been replaced by upscale florists, fancy coffeehouses, antique shops, yacht brokerages, art galleries.

The grade steepened. Stepping around a gap where the bricks were being replaced, he remembered how slick they'd been covered with ice in the winter. How the wind had howled down the street, stinging his face with drift. Not as bad as Alaska, though. Where he'd almost died a year ago.

The white-and-gray, almost Slavic-looking tower of the State House rose ahead. Like many of the homes, it dated from before the Revolution. Congress had met there during the negotiation of the Treaty of Paris. Washington had resigned his commission there, setting a noble precedent for the new nation. Annapolis had been the nation's capital until operations moved to Philadelphia, and later, to a new city on the Potomac.

Government House was a stately nineteenth-century brick mansion, surrounded by elaborate gardens. Dan stopped to scope out a gap in the trees off what had been Bladen Street when he was a mid. Now it was a pedestrian mall. LeCato gave him a questioning glance, but said nothing.

* * *

Touching base with the governor was a mandatory courtesy. Walter Thornton was bluff, balding, and reputedly corrupt, which seemed to be par for Maryland. Dan stayed on his guard, but nothing untoward was broached over the lobster salad.

The mayor of Annapolis had also been invited. Mrs. St. Audrey Larkin was a pleasant, slightly fussy redhead in a floral Hermes scarf that Dan thought Blair would have liked. Larkin knew his wife's family, of course. The Tituses and Blairs dated far back in the state's history. "Along with the Larkins, of course," Mrs. Larkin said brightly, patting Dan's knee in a way that might have been perceived as intimate in a different setting. "My husband's ancestor was one of the first colonial governors."

"How interesting," Dan murmured. He sipped tea to mask a yawn. Really, if the job was going to be like this, lunches and talks and receptions, Valerie was right. He needed help. But that wasn't in the budget, of course.

"I understand you have a daughter who's a doctor," Larkin pursued.

"Um, not exactly. I mean, she holds a doctorate, but it's in biochemistry. Infectious disease."

"How fascinating."

He straightened; was she making fun of him? The mayor smiled so sweetly he couldn't tell.

"And where is she now, Admiral?"

"She was headed for Switzerland, but that's on hold." He sipped again, and suddenly had an idea. Nan was between jobs . . . and he needed help.

The governor grunted, hoisting himself to his feet. "If you'll excuse me. Great ta lay eyes on you, Admiral. Good luck over there. If I find you in my garden some night, we'll talk some more."

Larkin frowned after Thornton as he left. "His *garden*? What was that about?"

"I have no idea," Dan lied.

* * *

The afternoon wasn't going to be as pleasant, if you could call his meetings with the dean, governor, and mayor pleasant.

"Mr. Gupta's in your office," Valerie said as he hung his cap. Its sweatband was soaked. The mirror showed stains under his arms. He needed to buy . . . he turned to LeCato. "Mid Store? Here's my card. I need two, no, make it three more summer white shirts. Chest forty. And a pack of tees."

His flag aide hesitated, and Dan corrected himself. "Sorry, I didn't mean—that would be a personal errand, wouldn't it? Sorry."

"I can relay that ask to your enlisted aide, sir. But, um, you shouldn't ask them to get the T-shirts. They aren't uniform items. Officially."

Dan nodded. "Thanks for the save, Lieutenant."

"No problem, Admiral."

"Be right there," Dan called to the outer office. He ducked into the head and shrugged into a jacket. The A/C was on, thank God.

The athletic director jumped to his feet. Gupta looked sweaty too, probably having walked over from his own office. They shook hands, a custom COVID and then the Central Blossom epidemics had almost killed, but that was returning. "Thanks for coming in, Virjay. We have some issues to discuss."

"Yes, sir, Admiral. I brought you the printouts for our budget request. Also your pass for the Golf Club."

Dan laid the pass aside. Why did everyone assume he was eager to play golf? Meet the new boss, same as the old boss? He studied the printout. "Captain Jack says you want a plus up. A million."

"One point three five million, Admiral. Just to keep up with inflation."

"We have to find places to cut, Virjay. The city's bumping up our sewage fees at the same time DoD wants a budget trim." He forced an expression of reluctance. "I'm thinking, five percent. Not to your department overall, just to intercollegiate. I want to beef up PE for the Brigade. See if there's anything we can steal in West Point's new holistic fitness program. And MacDonough Hall, the workout rooms, they're unsatisfactory. Rust, mold, exposed rebar, broken heaters. The combat training pool's leaking twenty-two hundred gallons of water a day. Those're the facilities that serve the ninety percent of mids who aren't varsity. That strike you as fair?"

Gupta studied the floor. "Fair? Maybe not, but . . . you lettered in lacrosse, Admiral. And in cross-country. You know how hard these kids work. How vital sports are to our recruiting. Which is in trouble, from what I understand."

"It's not an easy call, I know. But I need you in my corner on this."

The director looked away. "I'm not sure I can promise that, Admiral. I'm not sure you understand yet how important alumni support is. Without that, we'd have to shut down a lot of our programs."

Okay, there it was. Gupta felt strong enough, with the backing of the alums and probably the Board of Visitors, to dig in. Well, at least the guy was up front about it. Far worse to have him feigning buy-in, then stabbing Dan in the back.

Still . . . "Well, that's the way my budget's going in," Dan said. "Football's valuable. It's a unifier. And, yeah, it builds leaders. But it's gotten so it's wagging the dog around here. I think there are ways to spend the money that'll benefit everybody in the Brigade, and give the Fleet a better product.

"I suggest midlevel coaches. Offer early retirement to the ones without a good win record. Give the junior guys and gals more responsibility. I'm sure you know the drill."

Gupta frowned, but nodded. He didn't offer to shake hands as he left.

* * *

The last interview of the day, and the one he'd been looking forward to least. The commandant of midshipmen, the *'dant* in Academy shorthand, ruled Bancroft and its often-unruly four thousand uniformed students. Subordinate to the superintendent, but with a power inverse-squarely greater in its influence on the mids. When the students trekked across the Yard to the academic buildings, they were Mynbury's. When the athletes were in gym gear on the playing fields, they were Gupta's. The rest of the time, their blue-clad butts belonged to Colonel Leslie Danelle Stocker, United States Marine Corps.

Stocker had offered to come to Dan's office, but again, he'd wanted to meet in her native habitat. After pinning his ribbons on a fresh shirt, taking a tuck, and checking his gig line, he and LeCato walked the heat-shimmering bricks down Stribling and across the yellow brick courtyard. The mids did double takes as he passed, saluting with pathetic eagerness. As they climbed the granite steps into the hushed lofty space of the Rotunda Dan remembered watch squad inspections here, and the night one of the plebes, with the same name as a legendary prankster, had thrown flour on the immaculate ranks from an upper balcony.

Stocker waited in the center of the brightly waxed tile passageway. Husky, instantly impressive, she stood with boots at shoulder width, immaculate in pressed greens, hair high and tight, hands locked behind her. One pace to her left stood a slim, graceful-looking midshipman with thin gold stripes on his, or maybe her, epaulettes. Dan recognized the mid who'd saluted so elegantly at the change of command.

Stocker came to attention. "Good afternoon, Admiral."

"Colonel. Carry on, please." Dan forced a casual tone. "Want to introduce your assistant?"

"Yes, sir. Sir, this is Midshipman Brigade Commander Kerry Evans."

The Brigade was run day-to-day via an internal command structure staffed by the senior mids. The brigade commander helped set the schedule of events and planned training. Evans's first name didn't give Dan any pronoun clues. "Good to meet you," he said.

"Honored to meet you, Admiral."

Stocker said, "Mister Evans came in during his summer leave, to help get ahead of the curve. And he is a direct descendant of Robley D. Evans."

Okay, Evans was a he/him. "Really? And proud of it, I would guess," Dan said.

"Fighting Bob" Evans, graduated in 1863, had been a buffalo hunter and Indian fighter before attending the Academy. He'd commanded his first ship at seventeen and was wounded four times at Fort Fisher before killing his tormentor. When surgeons tried to amputate his legs, he swore to murder whoever tried. He fought again at the Battle of Santiago, and dragged himself aboard the Great White Fleet on crutches. Evans had been gruff, cranky, boastful, and so profane *The New York Times* had chastised him for it.

"We can meet in my office, if you like, Admiral," Stocker said.

Ushered ahead, Dan reviewed what he knew about the 'dant. A fighter ace, with the POW Medal from Syria and the Navy Cross and Silver Star from combat over Taiwan and southern China. Cree had told him Stocker ran a tight ship in Bancroft. "Without a hard-ass over there, your job'd be a lot tougher," he'd said. "With her riding herd, there's no need for you to worry about the mids."

They settled in the office, which was much barer and more worn than either Dan's or Mynbury's. Stocker offered iced tea; Dan declined. "So, sir, how can we help you?" she said, folding her hands. Evans stood by the door, at ease.

"This is mainly just a get-acquainted visit, Colonel. But there are a couple issues I wanted to surface."

"Shoot, sir."

"I was talking to the provost about Brianna Court."

"The crippled girl."

"Uh . . . right. He's proposing we let her service-select for Cyber. Ask DoD to waive her physical."

"No," Stocker said. "She can't walk, she can't fight; too bad, but we can't use her. Waive the military obligation and let her go."

Dan looked to the mid, who stood silently, pale blue eyes registering neither support nor disagreement.

The 'dant added, "Sir, I know about your record, and the Medal of Honor. We're both warrior types. You have fights coming up with Washington. We have your back. There's no need for you to worry about things over here."

Dan sat back. "I respect that, Colonel. And I try not to micromanage.

But I don't believe in 'hands off.' I plan to be more involved than the previous supe. Let's see if we can work together."

They discussed it for some time. Stocker liked his plan to deemphasize varsity sports and beef up PE, while Dan wondered how she'd heard about that so damn fast. She added, "I would suggest, as part of that, sir, that we add mandatory hand-to-hand combat for the youngster class. Like our Marine martial arts course, only for everybody. Every cadet at West Point takes combatives. Why don't we? Build confidence. Correct the drift toward pure academics."

Evans cleared his throat. "There could be options, Colonel. Krav Maga. Jujitsu. Karate. Tae kwon do. Ninpo. Kickboxing."

"I like that," Dan said. "Send me a proposal . . . no . . . just start. Coordinate as necessary."

Stocker made a note. "I'd like a tear gas chamber too."

"Well, let's not get ahead of ourselves. That'd require capital funding. And we're gonna have to fight to keep what dollars we're getting now."

"Copy." She glanced at the window, where a company was practicing small-unit drill. "But in the last analysis, we're preparing these kids for battle. I didn't have an easy time here. A woman of color? They *ran* my ass. But, you know what? Without that I couldn't have survived captivity.

"We get great material, except they're so fucking out of shape, and they don't know how to think ahead or recover from a setback. Most of 'em, they've led easy, privileged lives. Their parents protected them. Made things easy. It's the same in their schools.

"We're here to produce leaders. *Combat* leaders. Everything else, DoD can hire on the open market. And eighty percent of *our* problems come from the lowest five percent. We fire them, the service is better off."

Dan nodded. He half felt that way himself. But only half. "I see your point. But if we'd bottom-blown all our marginal mids years ago, we'd have lost some of our most notable grads. Halsey, who used to drink beer on the roof and toss the bottles down into T-Court. Merian Cooper. Philo McGiffin. Oley Oldendorf. John McCain."

"That was a long time ago," Stocker said. "Sir. And the plebe regimen was tougher then. It case-hardened those old grads. It's why we used to win wars."

"You mean hazing."

"It had a purpose." Stocker narrowed her eyes. "Like I said, the tougher we make the process, the better product we put out."

Dan nodded, not much liking the way she described the mids. But they could argue that later. “New subject. I understand someone submitted an extracurricular activities application for a white pride group.”

Stocker shrugged. “Well, that’s not the actual name, sir. They call it the ‘Anglo-Saxon Culture Study Group.’” She glanced at the mid by the door. “Actually, Mr. Evans here submitted the application.”

“Really.” Dan twisted in his chair to study the firstie, who looked levelly back. “Your explanation, Mr. Evans?”

“Just to honor my people, sir. Like everyone else honors theirs.”

“Evans. That’s Welsh, isn’t it? Not Anglo-Saxon at all.”

“True, sir. But still British.”

“You know, you’ll be leading all kinds of people, in the Fleet,” Dan told him. “I’ve served with them. Fought beside them. Any idea whites, or Anglo-Saxons, as you call them, are superior in some way . . . it’s not just against Navy policy. It’s just plain mistaken.”

Evans inclined his head slightly, but didn’t argue. Just said, “I hear you, sir.”

“I’d like a word with the commandant.”

Evans looked to Stocker, who nodded. He snapped to attention, about-faced, and left. When the door closed, Dan said, “About this, uh, Anglo-Saxon bullshit.”

Stocker said, “Frankly, sir, I don’t think we need to go to general quarters over it. Yet, at least.”

“Really? What about these racist tweets Master Chief tells me about?”

“Admiral, I think it’s just teenaged idiots doing what teenaged idiots do, before they realize the consequences.”

Dan must have looked surprised, because she went on. “I had the kids in front of me who posted them. Believe me, they won’t be doing it again. And as far as a club goes, there’s an African American network. The Academy Women’s Network. Spectrum, our gay-straight alliance. Why not one for whites?”

He must have looked doubtful, because she added, “If anything, having them in one place lets me keep my microscope on them. If they go supremacist, we cancel their asses. Like I did with *The LOG*.”

The LOG had been a mid-edited humor magazine when he’d been here, irreverent but harmless. This was the first he’d heard about a ban. But a white pride club, greenlighted by a Black woman? He said, “But we’ve always banned fraternities. They hive off one group from the rest. Isn’t this the same thing?”

Stocker shrugged. "We force these kids together every day. A few hours a month with people they choose to be with won't hurt 'em. We have separate chapel services, right? Believe me, I'll keep a close eye on it. And if it does go in an unhealthy direction, I've got a plan."

Dan wavered, then decided to revisit it later. She was closer to the problem than he was, anyway. "Okay, to move on . . . I reviewed these numbers on sexual harassment. They seem to be rising year on year. Shouldn't they be falling? We've spent enough time on counseling, warning."

Stocker compressed her lips. "They're rising because we keep defining harassment downward. You compliment somebody's hair, now it's verbal assault. I'm sorry, I have no patience for that crap. Women who can't stand a little teasing won't be able to handle the Fleet, or the Corps, or a squadron ready room. If they can't deal, they're better off at a civilian school."

Dan nodded, struck with both her fervor and how out of step it sounded compared to official guidance. Cree's hands-off policy had let her go too far. Redirecting her—if Dan decided that was needed—wouldn't be easy. His other alternative, relieving her, might be harder still.

"Well, appreciate the sit-down," he said at last. "I'll see you at the weekly meeting, and we can pursue these issues further. Including *The LOG*—maybe we can stand some teasing too."

He glanced out the window as he stood to leave. At the marchers, out on the court. Their unlined faces; the slim, straight bodies; the energy in their steps as they wheeled and countermarched.

Had he ever looked that young?

It was hard to imagine.

* * *

Blair was due in for dinner, but at six, with him still in his office, she rang his cell. *"Dan? How's it going?"*

He disengaged his brain from the budget review, still wondering how he could whittle down the maintenance account for twenty-two diesel-powered Yard Patrol craft. "Uh . . . hi. Getting settled in. Moving into Buchanan House—I mean, the Supe's House—tonight. When will you—"

"I'm going to be held over here. Rocket attack on our embassy in Algeria. But for sure, this weekend. You have a helo pad there, right?"

He blinked. Called, "Valerie, do we have a helo pad?"

"Never mind . . . they say here you have one across the river, at the NSA." The Naval Support Activity was a sprawling complex of workshops, rifle ranges, athletic fields, a Navy Exchange, and housing for the junior staff. All part of Dan's empire, along with the Academy proper.

"Wouldn't that be use of a government vehicle for a personal visit?"

"I'm inspecting a DoD facility, all right? Don't worry, I'll run it past the beagles."

They chatted for a few more seconds before she had to go.

Valerie left too. Dan propped his head on his hands, alone in the office. Trying not to give way to depression. Yeah, he was tired. Maybe he should have taken that medical retirement. Traded his sloop in on something bigger, and pursued his old dream of sailing around the world.

His thoughts milled, buzzed, trying to reconcile everything he'd heard that day. But of course, they couldn't. Two radically different courses existed for the institution he led.

And there existed a darker possibility, worse even than choosing one side over the other. They could join hands, to frustrate and roadblock a superintendent who fell between the stools.

As the summer darkness fell, the lights in the upper windows of Larson Hall were still burning.

4

The Naval Academy Natatorium

Zero five hundred, long before dawn. The huge old pool echoed with yells and clanks and splashes under the cast-iron arches as if from some tunnel bored deep into rock. The eye-scorching tang of chlorine, and the stench of a hundred years of mold and lead paint and creeping rust.

Midshipman First Class Lenson was powering through the tenth lap of today's self-assigned fifteen. He'd worked his way up to a mile, alternating crawls, backstroke, and the relaxed, easygoing sidestroke the Academy taught as a way to stay afloat if you got blown overboard, or your ship went down.

He couldn't complain about not being well trained. Rehearsing a drop from a forty-foot deck edge. Swimming through fire. Improvising flotation from your trousers. Was he really going to have to do all that shit? He doubted it.

He hit the end of the pool, considered a flip turn, but decided not. If a mid touched the gutter during the Two Hour Swim, he didn't graduate. If he drowned, he didn't graduate. Scuttlebutt had it that sometimes the coaches would tip oil into the water and torch it, to make things more realistic. And how once someone whose dad was a fisherman had come back from spring leave with a huge dogfish. He'd snuck it into the pool, and the swimmers had bleated and scattered as an ominous gray fin wove among them.

Unfortunately, Dan hadn't grown up near a pool, and had nearly panicked in the water. At last, realizing he wasn't going to graduate otherwise, he'd started getting up at 0400 each morning, trekking to MacDonough, and forcing himself through lap after lap. Now he felt at home in the water. Maybe he'd sign up for SCUBA in the spring.

In the end, that was what the Academy taught you, along with how to fold your skivvies and squeegee yourself down after a shower and polish worn-out shoes to a gloss that would shame a Manhattan bootblack. A setback meant you gritted your teeth and worked twice as hard. And if *that* failed, *four* times as hard. Until whatever brick wall you were head-butting cracked and toppled.

He collided with another flailing, slippery body. Nearly choked, but came up, sputtering, and fought back into the rhythm of the crawl.

Still . . . two fucking hours of this? With eight hundred other bodies thrashing and flailing in the same turbid slime, climbing over one another, elbowing, kicking, fighting their own classmates as much as the water itself?

He'd have to reach down deep, to make it through that.

* * *

When he got back to his room three plebes stood braced up tight beside his door, chins rigged into their spines. Two he knew. It took him a moment to recognize the third, clad in blue-and-white gym gear. Apparently what Davis specified as a come-around uniform. The gawky kid, Patterson, looked as scared as he had the night before, when he'd wild-manned Dan at his table.

Dan pointed at his own fourth class. "You two, beat feet. Four minutes to put a better polish on those cap brims, then report to Mr. Enders.—Mister Patterson! Eyes in the boat!"

"Sir." Already beads of sweat dotted the kid's forehead. He was tall as Dan, but aside from that didn't look seventeen, the minimum age to be admitted.

Dan looked him over again. "Why's your T-shirt inside out?"

"Mister Davis says I don't rate wearing the Academy crest, sir."

"Well, fuck that. Put it on right, and assume the position."

Patterson stripped, reversed his shirt, and dropped to the push-up posture: back rigid, arms straight, legs at the proper angle, toes and palms the only points of contact with the deck.

The passageway filled suddenly with yells. A squad of plebes pelted past, naked except for socks, gym shoes, and marshmallows tucked into their jockstraps. "The last guy back gets to eat them all," a second class shouted after them.

"Dimmy, get those guys dressed," Dan yelled angrily. "There's women in the p-way." To Patterson, "What's for lunch, maggot?"

The plebe unloaded the menu, then the list of midshipman stripers as Dan changed into working uniform blue alpha: blue-black trousers and shirt; black tie; black belt; black socks and shoes. He centerlined his buckle in the mirror and set his cap square. Adjusted his collar devices. Primped his Spiffy, the thin, spring-loaded wire brace that anchored a mid's collar points. A properly bent Spiffy was a work of craft.

In the passageway a female plebe was screaming out the uniform for formation, the menu, the officers of the watch, at the top of her lungs. Down the hallway, up from the stairwells echoed other screams, other bellowings, a hellish incessant clamor building to a deafening yammerdammerung. She ended with, "Time, tide, and formation wait for *no man*! Ten minutes, *sir*," as Dan opened his calculus book.

After several minutes' helpless gazing at the same function, he strolled out into the p-way again. "Come aboard," he told Patterson. The plebe scrambled up. "Against the bulkhead, mister! Now, explain why you wild-manned me last night."

Perspiration was running down both sides of the kid's too-prominent nose. "Sir, I was ordered to."

"By whom?"

"Uh, permission not to bilge—permission not to bilge an upperclass, sir."

"Permission not granted. Was it Mister Davis?"

"Sir, I cannot—"

Dan moved up to stare him full in the face, practicing his most intransigent scowl. "*Bullshit!* An upperclassman asked you a question. You owe him an honest response. Not this sea-lawyering horseshit! *Who?*"

"Sir, it was Mister Davis, sir."

Dan shook his head sadly. The system put smart, determined kids under more stress than anyone could reasonably be expected to take. Then evaluated their ability to think, remember, and decide. The kind of performance that would be expected of them in shipboard fires, in battle, in infantry firefights, in bomb runs through heavy flak. Not just to build character, but to weed out weaklings who'd get their people killed.

Was this kid one? Was Easy Davis right, the Navy would be better off without him? Dan wished he could see behind those bulging orbs. X-ray inside that sweating forehead.

He sighed and glanced down the hall. Two frightened-looking girls were braced up near the ladderway. A male second class was shouting in their faces. Not touching them, but jabbing his finger at their chests. Women were new at Bancroft, and for most of the mids the jury was out as to whether they were really Navy material.

He turned back to his current problem. "Your own firstie, and you bilge him the first time somebody applies a little pressure. I hope you can stand up more than ten seconds when the Commies take you prisoner. Whattaya think, that a realistic expectation?"

"I'll find out, sir."

"I'd say it doesn't seem likely. What's the mission of the Naval Academy?"

"Sir, the mission of the US Naval Academy is to develop midshipmen morally, mentally, and physically and to imbue them with the highest ideals of duty, honor, and loyalty in order to graduate leaders who are dedicated to a career of naval service and have potential for future development in mind and character, to assume the highest responsibilities of command, citizenship, and government. Sir."

"What are the qualifications of a naval officer?"

"Sir, John Paul Jones—"

"Did he spoon you, Patterson?"

"Sir?"

"Are you his personal friend?"

"No, sir. Sir, *Commodore* John Paul Jones wrote, 'It is by no means enough that an officer of the Navy should be a capable mariner. He must be that, of course, but also a great deal more. He should be as well a gentleman of liberal education, refined manners, punctilious courtesy, and the nicest sense of personal honor. He should be the soul of tact, patience, justice, firmness, kindness, and charity. No meritorious act of a subordinate should escape his attention. . . .'"

When he ran out the quote, Dan said grudgingly, "Okay, not bad. . . . but do you think that describes you, Patterson?"

"No, sir."

"No? Why not?"

"I don't have any subordinates yet, sir."

The five-minute call went. A passing firstie grinned. "Got yourself a wiseass, eh, Dan? Hey, isn't that Easy Davis's negat?"

"He's coming around to me."

"I hear this kid's a little light in his loafers. A red mike. You should smash him in the fucking mouth, Dan."

A "red mike" was Academy slang for a woman hater. The other firstie said, "How many of our fucking classmates does it take to run one of these wusses out of here?"

"I guess we'll see," Dan said. "Are you a red mike, Patterson?"

"No, sir. I like girls."

"And a nonperformer? I guess we'll find out, right?"

"No, sir."

Again, a response he hadn't expected. "No?"

"Firm negative, sir." For the first time the kid looked less scared. He flexed his shoulders and looked past Dan to the far window. Then his gaze dropped, to the book in Dan's hand. "You havin' trouble with that, sir? Maybe I can help."

Dan blinked. Tutoring, from a plebe? He'd never live it down. "Uh, I don't think so. Enlighten me, how'd you get so famous, Patterson? As a shit magnet, I mean?"

For a moment, silence. Then, for the first time, his gaze sought Dan's. "Sir . . . Mister Lenson. I need help."

Dan grinned. "First smart thing you've said."

"I'm serious, sir." His voice low, confiding. Pitched so that in the clamor of the passageway, no one else could overhear. And the way he was looking at him . . . Dan backed away an inch. *Was* the kid what they were hinting at? It was grounds for discharge. If not federal prison time.

"Mr. Davis's trying to run me out. I haven't slept for days. I'm . . . afraid. I can't go home. There's nothing for me there. You're my coach, right? Isn't there anything you can do?"

Dan leaned back, arms crossed. That line about not being able to go home . . . for a second he almost identified.

But Patterson wasn't his responsibility. "That's between you and him, amigo. For now, why don't you drop and give me fifty. And while you're at it, the line corps of the Navy and their insignia."

"Sir! Sir, the line corps of the Navy is, the line corps of the Navy are, Medical Corps, gold spread oak leaf with one silver acorn surcharged in center; Dental Corps, gold spread oak leaf with two silver acorns attached to stem. Medical Service Corps . . ."

* * *

The air was heavy with the thiol stinks of butanoic acid, mercaptoethanol, formaldehyde. Not just the reeks of today's demonstration, but of generations of bored, anxious mids, seeped into the bulkheads and overheads and decks of the ancient musty basement. The chem lab stuck to your uniform long after class, making your roommates wrinkle their noses and the other mids in ranks edge away.

Dan titrated carefully, eager not to screw this one up. He wasn't doing well in theoretical either. Fortunately, organic was mostly memorization. But the blackboard work . . . sometimes he couldn't grasp how the reactions made one structure into the next one, much less the one after that.

Obviously he wasn't going to be a chemist. But if he was going to subs or surface ships, he might not need to know that much about carbon bonds. Anyway, it all came down to time management. Grinding away until you at least could fake knowing what you had to. Like the novel he was reading in Professor Gilliland's Literature of the Sea course. The character who had no idea how a frictionless bearing worked, but who'd memorized the description, regurgitated it verbatim, and passed his exam with flying colors.

The next period. Microeconomics. His eyelids drooped and his head slowly declined as a droning voice floated upward and buzzed against the ceiling. "The marginal product equals the change in the amount of product as we change the amount of labor employed. It is the slope of the curve delta TP dividing by delta L. Note the slope of the curve and the point at which it crosses the zero line and goes negative. . . ."

A pencil stabbed him in the back. A classmate, behind him. Dan snapped his head up and faked making a note as the prof gimlet-eyed him.

French. The prof was a distinguished French Navy captain, with the *de* in front of his last name. Scuttlebutt said he was descended from one of Louis the Sixteenth's mistresses. The class was reading Apollinaire's poetry; a surprise, since usually everything, even the liberal arts classes, was focused on the needs of the Navy. He wondered if the teacher was sticking to the lesson plan. Or if he even had one.

Sous le pont Mirabeau coule la Seine
Et nos amours
Faut-il qu'il m'en souvienne
La joie venait toujours après la peine
Vienne la nuit sonne l'heure
Les jours s'en vont je demeure

D'Estaintot's gaze fastened on Dan. "Want to give it a try, Mister Lenson?"

"Uh . . . yes, sir. Um . . . 'Under the Mirabeau Bridge flows the Seine. And our love; must I remember, joy always follows suffering; come the night,' uh . . ."

"The bell . . ."

Bell? "Uh, 'The hour strikes? And . . . in days to come, I will . . . endure'?"

"Well, *pas exactement*, but not bad." The prof nodded. "The next stanza . . . Mister Schrade, please."

Leaving Dan with a glow of approval. He wasn't going to write any poetry. But it was nice to have *one* class where he didn't feel like he was a cunt hair away from going down in flames.

* * *

The glow didn't last. Fourth period, before noon meal, his calculus prof said, "Mister Lenson? Could you stay for a moment?"

Dan hesitated by the door. It was a long haul back down the muddy torn-up construction site the mids called the Ho Chi Minh Trail. "Yes, ma'am."

Mrs. Colson held up the work Dan had just turned in. "I'm not sure you're grasping the essence of Sturm-Liouville theory. Though I've presented it in a very elementary way. Your thoughts?"

His thoughts? "Uh, well . . . I guess yeah, I get that it's uh, like a second-order linear—"

"A *real* second-order linear ordinary differential equation. Yes. And the solutions correspond to the eigenvalues and eigenfunctions of a Hermitian differential operator in an appropriate function space." Colson, one of the few female professors, flourished Dan's pop quiz bloody with red ink. "That you could memorize from the text. But in terms of solving the equation, you're not even close."

He tried to avoid looking down her blouse, but it wasn't easy. She was ancient, easily in her midthirties, but so well-endowed most of the male mids were lost in fantasy each time she stretched up to chalk an equation. To his horror, he was growing a hard-on. He muttered, "*Et nos amours, faut-il qu'il*—"

Her eyes widened. "*What?*"

"Uh, nothing. Sorry, ma'am. Yes, ma'am, I *am* a little fuzzy on exactly how to execute some of these operations—"

"It's evident in your work, believe me." She pushed the paper into his chest. He froze, a moth paralyzed by pheromones. His hard-on was nearing its asymptote. “My advice is: study, um . . . harder. If you need extra instruction, ask. Otherwise, you might want to consider other options than graduating from this institution.”

He lingered, hesitating. Extra instruction? From her? He dwelt on that fantasy a moment. Then muttered, “Yes, ma’am. Excuse me,” and sprinted for the door.

5

Dan stood on the deck of his sloop in the mooring basin, hosing down the topsides. She hadn't done well in storage. A smell of decomposition in the forward cabin had led him to a leaking hatch. The zincs were gone, signaling possible corrosion in the shaft and bronze through-hulls. On the plus side, the surveyor had okayed his standing rigging, and the sails were safe in their sealed bags.

After a haulout at Pretty Lake, new bottom paint, and a sole replacement, he'd wanted to run her up to Annapolis himself. But his schedule made that impossible. A hired captain had brought her in the day before. Now he was looking forward to day-sailing the upper Bay, maybe taking a cruise down the Eastern Shore.

And once he retired, the ocean would be open to him.

The weather had turned cool. The Brigade was back from its far-flung summer deployments: cruises, sub school, Pensacola, marine training. Apparently one of the travelers had brought bedbugs to the sixth wing. Mattresses were being replaced and insecticide sprayed. Stocker and the medical team assured him the infestation was contained. Dan had gotten through Parents Weekend, with help from his daughter.

"I might have to take off at short notice, if they need me in Basel," Nan had told him when he'd called. *"The Global Virome Project the CDC set me up for. But I can break my lease and come down, until they're ready for me."*

Dan had felt guilty. It felt like an imposition, and he couldn't pay her, except out of his own pocket. Which he was happy to do. But then again . . . she'd spent most of her growing-up years with his ex-wife, while he'd been at sea and then at war. It would be great to spend some actual time with her. "Sure, okay," he'd said at last. "It'll be great to have you here. If you really don't mind."

* * *

He was in his office at 0800, going over sewage treatment with the rep from town, when Mrs. Marsh poked her head in. "Sorry to interrupt, but the commandant's on the line." She smiled at the rep. "Maybe you could return tomorrow?"

Dan excused himself, intuiting from her tone it was bad news. Once alone he picked up. "Lenson."

"Stocker here, sir. Figured you'd better hear this from me first. Midshipman Evans was found dead, out on Farragut Field."

"What? Oh, no. The brigade commander?" That tall, graceful, self-assured young midshipman. A moment later he remembered: who'd also founded the Anglo-Saxon studies club.

"Yes, sir. A promising young officer."

Farragut Field was the stretch of level green fronting the open Bay. "What was he doing there? And what's Medical say?"

"One of the groundkeepers found him. In running gear. Bruises, but no definite cause of death so far. Maybe an aneurysm? It might take a formal postmortem."

The first death in the Brigade during his tour. Though in a student body of over four thousand, accidents and medical issues weren't unknown. During PT, athletics, even fit young human beings sometimes simply . . . gave out. He asked what the procedure was. Stocker said, *"We can request a consultation from the armed forces medical examiners. They'd send someone from Baltimore. But we need your chop for that."* Stocker didn't sound upset, but then again, she'd fought in Syria and Taiwan.

"Have you called the parents?"

"Not yet, sir. I'll do so now."

"No, that's my job. LAN me contact info, and a summary of his record."

"I'll write a statement for the PAO to release," Marsh said.

"Verbal, or signed?" Dan asked Stocker.

"Sir?"

"The request for coroner assistance. Verbal, or signed?"

"It'll be a digital signature, Admiral. I'll send it to Valerie ASAP." A pause, then Stocker added, in a lower tone, *"There are also several rifles missing."*

Dan tensed. Each mid was issued an Army-surplus M-14, kept in their rooms. They served for drill and parade better than modern weapons, which were less tolerant of abuse than walnut and steel. "Uh, those aren't fireable, correct?"

"No, sir. Barrel torch-cut, welded bolt face, no firing pin. But still—"

"Right, we have to account for them. ASAP. Should I come over?"

Stocker said that was up to him.

* * *

He phoned Evans's parents—a difficult conversation, but one he owed them—then hiked over to Bancroft. Dark clouds threatened, but rain didn't seem imminent. A steady flow of mids streamed past, and each one had to salute him. By the time he got to Bancroft his arm was sore.

Sick bay was how he remembered it. Sterile blue tile walls, waxed decks, the mingled astringencies of wintergreen and Betadine. The medical officer led him down a row of cubicles. A marine stood before one. He drew the curtain aside for Dan as Stocker came in, accompanied by a short, possibly pregnant blonde Dan recognized after a moment as the Academy's public affairs officer, Commander Madison Burnbright, USNR.

Evans lay nude save for blue-and-gold running shorts. He looked unchanged except for chin stubble. Eyes closed, he could have been asleep. On one pale arm, the blue tracing of some kind of runic tattoo. Tattoos were regulation now, as long as uniform sleeves covered them.

Dan nodded to the doctor. "What about this bruise on the side of his head?"

The doc, in green scrubs, crossed her arms. "Best guess, he was running the seawall. Missed his footing, went down, struck his temple. Fell into the water and drowned."

Dan nodded thoughtfully. Tragic, but he could see that happening.

"That's mainly based on where we found him." Stocker looked both grim and not that upset. As if she was used to it. Dan had seen corpses before too, but few so young and godlike. Usually they'd been ripped apart by high explosive or charred by flame.

"I heard aneurysm," he said.

"We really can't say just yet." The doctor bent. "One thing I noticed, here." She turned the boy's head to the left, revealing a small raised pink spot on the neck. Moved down to the torso and pointed to another.

"What are those?"

"I don't know. I doubt they're responsible for his death. But there are other possibilities. Than simply slipping and falling."

"Such as?"

"Well . . . usually, when someone this age dies, this fit, it's some form of congenital anomaly. Myocarditis. Hypertrophic cardiomyopathy. Also . . . drugs could be involved. Or even too many energy drinks, if there's an underlying condition. But I'd need permission to investigate."

She didn't mean parental permission. Mids were emancipated as soon as they took the oath. But he had a tough time believing the brigade commander had been into cocaine or meth. Finally he said, "I'll request assistance from the military, uh, investigators. Coroners. Have the specialists handle this. Any problem with that?"

"No, sir. We installed a chill locker during the pandemic."

"Good." Dan nodded to Stocker. "Do we have eyes on the seawall? See if we have camera coverage. Maybe that'll give us a better idea what happened. Also . . . we have a deputy brigade commander, right? To take over his responsibilities?"

"Yessir. Midshipman First Class Juliane Oshry. From New York. Supe's List, NCAA champion gymnast, a born leader since her Plebe Summer. She won't miss a beat stepping up."

Dan halted as a suspicion flared. "Wait a minute. Uh, what company was he in? Evans?"

"Eighth, Admiral," the doctor said.

"I was addressing the commandant, Doctor. Colonel, the missing . . . equipment. What company?"

Stocker murmured, gaze averted, "Eighth."

He frowned. "I'd have considered that significant, if you'd mentioned it, Colonel. Why didn't you?"

"I just found out before coming down here, sir."

"Get the company officer on deck. The company commander. The rest of the firsties in Eighth. Cross-reference them with the membership of this white studies group. Then I'll—"

Burnbright, the public affairs officer, put a hand on his arm, then removed it. "Admiral? If I can put in a word? I'd advise you not to talk to them. At least, not yet." She hesitated, as if gauging his anger, then went on. "There'll be media interest. Especially with the stolen weapons."

"Weapons?" said the doctor.

"We don't know they're stolen, yet," the commandant said. "My suspicion is they're still in Bancroft somewhere. Let me deal with this, Admiral. It's a 'dant responsibility."

"I agree," Burnbright said. "It's better to put distance between them and you. So you can be seen as objective. Whatever action you decide to take, when the situation clarifies."

Dan looked from one to the next, the doctor, the PAO, the colonel. "All right," he said at last. "Commence your search. I want a report by 1200. Tear this fucking place apart, Colonel."

"I plan to do exactly that, sir," Stocker said.

* * *

He headed back to Larson. He didn't feel comfortable leaving a mess in the hands of others, but Burnbright was probably right. Maintain distance. Let his subordinates work. The conventional guidance for flag officers and CEOs: Do only what *only* you can do.

If the death really *was* questionable. Athletes did die unexpectedly, from undiagnosed conditions, or even just from a blow to the chest in just the right place. He'd run those massive rocks himself. He could see it. Evans slips, falls, hits his head. Blacks out. Rolls into the Bay and drowns.

The fly in the ointment was those rifles, missing from the same company. And that Evans had been starting what might be seen as the rootstock of a white supremacist cell.

But if Stocker came up with the rifles fast, and if the death really was an accident, the problem could resolve itself. He might even be able to keep it out of the media.

Out in the Yard, the walks were thronged with mids hurrying to class. He ducked out the gate and circled around behind the Chapel, avoiding most of them, but still having to return salute after salute. Great, he had visibility, but his shoulder was really starting to hurt.

He shook his head, wondering at himself. Was he hoping for a cover-up? Funny how where you stood really did depend on where you sat. He glanced at his watch and hurried his steps. Today would be his first "Way Ahead" meeting. He'd asked the department heads to look at a 5 percent cut, just to be prepared for the next federal budget.

And also, to take a serious look at another question.

* * *

They were all there when he arrived. Burke-Bowden, Mynbury, Abimbola, Gupta, and the chief financial officer. Chairs against the wall held the second-tier folks: legal, strategy, information services. And Chief Wenck, whom he really hadn't seen much of since they both came aboard. He nodded as everyone stood, said, "Be seated, please," and took his chair at the head of the conference table. Valerie had set his tablet there; he opened it with a tap and cleared his throat. "The 'dant won't be joining us right away. Maybe later. So, two big issues today. Planning for cuts, number one. You submitted them to the deputy—"

"Sir, on that." Gupta raised his hand. "We haven't submitted, since a cut's not possible. I outlined why in my email."

"It wasn't a *suggestion*, Virjay. You and I discussed where to make reductions."

"Sir, firing line coaches is not a way to keep our win percentage up."

"Win percentage is important. But it isn't the only metric that counts, Virjay. Let's discuss that later, off-line." Dan said, making it plain with his tone that though he didn't want to dress him down publicly, Gupta's feet would be held to the fire. "Everyone else: the CFO, myself, and Captain Burke-Bowden will review your inputs and craft a plan. Again, not set in stone. But it's better to be ready if the axe falls.

"Next." He glanced at his tablet. They were all watching him. No doubt gauging his preferences, to adjust their own. Which wasn't really what he wanted. "Our approach to borderline students.

"Here are my thoughts. Clearly, plebes and third class who'll clearly never meet our standards should be separated. The Navy doesn't owe them anything. An early disenrollment's better for everyone.

"The senior marginals, anchormen, outliers—whatever you want to call them—they're a tougher call. Yeah, we could shitcan them. But looking over our history, a lot of our most famous grads were marginal performers while they were here, or didn't fit the mold in one way or another. It seems to me that often it's our 'misfits' who become stellar leaders later in life."

He paused, surveying the room. Blank faces. He forged on. "But you could also argue that's anecdotal evidence, those were the exceptions, and in different times. That a bad fit here will also be a nonperformer out in the Fleet, or in the Corps.

"We have two choices on the close calls. Either help and heal them, or separate them too. Treat 'em like broken parts, and save ourselves the trouble."

"The bottom five percent give us eighty percent of our problems," Burke-Bowden said.

Dan nodded. "The 'dant gave me the same readout, Jack."

Mynbury lifted a finger. "If I may."

"Professor," Dan said reluctantly, hoping the dean wasn't going to pontificate.

Mynbury tented his hands, gazing at the ceiling. "Today's students, Admiral, are quite unlike those we accessed in the past. They're much more technologically savvy. Plugged into social media. Smarter. And less motivated by what I might call old-fashioned patriotism. I'm not saying it's good, or bad, just that even for those who want a military career, we're being outcompeted. Why should they, um, *suffer through* Colonel Stocker's draconian regime, when they can receive as good an education, and a reserve scholarship, at a civilian college? Where they can live more freely, and date their classmates? That's important in the late teens, early twenties."

"We should allow them to date each other?" Dan said, interested. At least someone was thinking creatively, even if it would outrage the alums.

The dean shrugged and spread his hands. "That would be a Navy decision, Admiral. To be kicked upstairs, probably. I'm just pointing out a disincentive."

"So, in terms of separation versus help, you're saying . . . ?"

"We've already moved with the times. Minority, women, gay, trans. If we furnish a wider tent, and they meet academic standards, your 'separate or heal' dichotomy becomes moot."

Dan was almost glad Stocker wasn't there, though he was also getting anxious about her absence. Did it mean they couldn't find the missing rifles? He could guess how she'd react to Mynbury's cool dismissal of any standards, period. Other than grades, of course.

He sighed and looked along the table. "Who else agrees with the dean? That we basically keep anyone, I guess, who can maintain a two point five average?"

"And hasn't been convicted of a felony," the JAG officer put in.

"Two point oh," Mynbury corrected Dan. "It hasn't been two point five for a long time, Admiral."

A lieutenant commander in the outer row of chairs lifted a tentative hand. Receding chin, rimless glasses. Dan smiled inwardly; sometimes the best suggestions came from lower down in the chop chain. "You're info tech, right? Go ahead."

"Sir, there's another possibility, though I'm not sure everyone will like it."

"It's rare everyone likes anything. Let's hear it."

The officer hesitated, licking his lips. "Well, sir, it's based on technology developed during the war. Mainly by the Chinese, but I understand we worked on it too. In animals, mammals, there's like a go–no go circuit that allows them to overcome operant conditioning. The Chinese used focused ultrasound to ablate those areas of the brain. Bejing called it 'normalization.'"

Dan stared, astonished. "Are you suggesting we fry parts of our people's brains?"

"No, sir, no, I'm just suggesting we might look into something along those lines rather than separation. Once we invest a million dollars in a mid, isn't it worth investigating if we can make him, or her, more suitable for the job? More disciplined, a better fit all around? They'd probably be happier too. It doesn't impact reasoning ability—"

"No, just turns them into robots!" Dan was about to unload on him, but restrained himself. He'd asked for suggestions. He couldn't blast the first junior officer who made one. He compromised on, "Let's let somebody else try that first, okay? I, uh, do appreciate your input, though."

Burke-Bowden said, "Sir, all this about separation versus remediation isn't a new issue. Admiral Cree and I had this discussion many times. I copy your wanting another look, but maybe it needs further study? A smaller group, maybe headed by Strategic?"

Dan sat back in his chair. "Well . . . okay. But we're not going to sit on our hands. I need concrete suggestions. A draft policy. By our next meeting."

A moment of silence, then he went on. To the next issue on the agenda, and the next. As slowly, slowly, the bars of sunlight from the windows micrometered across the papers and screens.

* * *

He tried Stocker's phone when the meeting ended, but it went to voice mail. He debated going back to Bancroft, see what was shaking out, but resisted. Instead he drove over to the Upper Yard.

Halligan Hall was a rambling, terra-cotta-tile–roofed, much-rebuilt pile not far past the baseball field. Dan found the public works director in the basement, contemplating a tabletop model perhaps ten feet long by eight wide. He recognized the Chapel first, at the highest point, with the town inland of that. Below it lay the Lower Yard, the buildings, the athletic fields. Outboard of that, the river and bay. Missing were the library, the alumni auditorium, and the new cyber center.

Bonar, a lanky, ugly man with a jaw that could have cut glass, rose, dusting his hands. "Admiral."

"Jerry."

Bonar waved at the model like God at the freshly risen land. "They built this back in seventy-one, when we first started to think about subsidence. Used to run a hose in here and fill up the Bay, see what flooded first."

"Used to?"

"We do digital now. Faster, more flexible, easier to reconfigure."

He led the way upstairs, and rotated the big screen on his desk so Dan could see. This model included the newer buildings.

He went over what Dan already sort of knew, but in more detail. The Academy's history was generally divided into four eras. The first "naval cadets" had been billeted in old Fort Severn. But only a sixth of the land the current Academy occupied had existed in 1845. The first expansion, in the 1850s, had filled in the shoals that bounded the property and bulkheaded the new land with stone.

After the Army trashed the grounds during the Civil War, the sixth superintendent, David Dixon Porter, had bought the old Government House and four acres from the state, then ten more acres on College Creek from St. John's College. He also bought Strawberry Hill, now the Academy Cemetery. He built the New Cadets' Quarters, and physics, steam, seamanship, and instructor residences.

These had in their turn been obliterated in the massive reconstruction circa 1904–13. The "Flagg Academy" included Bancroft, MacDonough, Dahlgren, Mahan, the Officers' Club, the Chapel, and the hall that housed Dan's office.

Bonar darted arrows around the screen. "That was when we did the biggest landfills. The southeastern shoreline along Spa Creek got pushed out into the harbor. Filled areas circled Dewey Basin, where the sailing fleet is now. They built more playing fields to the west with sand and muck from the bottom of the Bay."

He called up a photo dated 1908. "MacDonough Hall was actually built as a shiphouse. That huge arched entry was so boats could sail inside. Unfortunately, at high tide their upper rigging got tangled in the steel roof supports. Ernie Flagg was not happy."

After Flagg, little had changed until 1941, when acreage to the south was bought from private owners who'd filled it for a lumberyard. To the north, another shoal was landfilled outboard of Hospital Point, and more "made land" pumped on the north side of the Severn. After World War Two, Dewey and Ingram Fields were filled and bulkheaded, and a new area of reclaimed spoil jutted two hundred yards farther into Spa Creek.

Bonar said, "That gave us room for two new wings to Bancroft and three new academic buildings. But during the final fills, in the nineteen sixties and seventies, poor-quality water-saturated clay started to migrate back into the river. We had to hang a bridging structure from the library's foundation out to pilings." He called up a more detailed plat. "That made room for Alumni Hall, the library, and the nuclear and cyber buildings. But we can't push out any farther into the river. And, environmentally, we can't dredge and fill anymore."

He turned from the screen. "To put this in perspective, Admiral, look at the other academies. We have about four hundred acres total. West Point has fifteen thousand. Colorado Springs has over eighteen thousand. We're pinched in by the Bay and the town. There's nowhere else to go."

The engineer went on. "Now, remember, all this made land was hydraulic fill. Pumped up from the bottom of the river. Soft clay, silt, shell, and muck."

"Yet we built on it," Dan said.

"Not exactly. Our major buildings—Rickover, Nimitz, Chauvenet, Michelson, Bancroft—were built on wooden pilings."

Dan was getting a sinking feeling, no pun intended. Remembering the rot on his boat. *"Wood?"*

"Oh, as long as it's below the water table, it'll last. Venice was built on pilings. But what they're driven into is not only soft, it's permeated. Dig down four feet, you hit water." Bonar sighed. "And all this soft, wet material's still consolidating. Settling. So far, almost eighteen inches since it was put in place.

"Add to that the general subsidence of the whole Chesapeake Bay area. That's about two millimeters a year. Then sea level rise. NOAA calls that at four millimeters annually.

"Put it all together, triple whammy, and this is what you get."

Bonar called up the model of the Lower Yard again. He keyboarded, and a year callout began scrolling. As the future unfolded the fields sank, the sea rose, the Bay crept in. Dan bit his lip as the lower floors of Michelson, Chauvenet, and Nimitz vanished beneath a blue tide. When Bonar stopped the clock at year 2100, fully half the Yard was underwater.

He said, "This is what things'll look like at least a hundred days a year, by then."

Dan bent closer. Stribling Walk, gone. Only the obelisk of the Midshipmen's Monument emerged. The classrooms, flooded. The athletic facilities, under several feet of water. He straightened. "I didn't realize it would be this bad, that soon."

"I presented to the Board of Visitors. Half of them called it a hoax. Admiral Cree had a plan, increase drainage, but then the war came—"

"Yeah, that derailed a lot of plans." Dan rubbed his chin, contemplating the screen. They would be flooded by De Nile. Ha ha. But not really funny. Annapolis was going the way of Atlantis. Apparently every supe had studied the issue, but done little more than raise the seawall a little. "Your big drainage project. Won't that help?"

"Temporarily, but not long term. Our storm drains dump into the river. When the Bay rises, it backs up through them. Basically, you can't stop water. If it's not coming over the seawall, or back through those drains, it'll percolate up through the ground."

Dan felt sick. "Okay, I'm convinced. What are our options?"

Bonar looked serious. "There aren't any easy ones. Tell you that up front."

Dan nodded. "Give me the choices, Jerry. And I'll try like hell to do whatever's needed, to rescue this place."

* * *

Back in his study at the Supe's House, he drooped like a wet rag in an armchair. Bonar's presentation had been depressing. Frightening.

The problem wasn't just the Academy's, of course. Every Navy installation on the coast would have to relocate, rebuild, or be abandoned. Humans had looked away from the problems they'd caused for too long. Now the bill was coming due.

Stocker had reported in. None of the missing rifles had been found. Tomorrow, Dan would have to call the CNO and the secretary of the Navy, then release the news to the media. Which he wasn't looking forward to.

A tap at the door. "Yeah," he called.

Nan stepped in, tucking a phone back into a pocket. "You okay up here, Dad?"

He forced a smile, submitting to a hug. His daughter was still thin, but she looked a lot better than she had after being kidnapped by Covenanter rebels. Nearly starved then, and with typhus from contaminated water. Now she was filling out. Her hair was growing back too. No longer a shining sable cascade, but brown stubble was better than the alternative.

He was lucky to still have her. He patted her hand. "What did you do today? Anything new from Switzerland?"

She dropped into a chair and slung a leg over its arm. "They're still waiting on a UN grant for my position."

He said tentatively, "But it still looks good?"

"I guess. But I've been calling around, looking at alternatives."

"Biochem?"

"Drugs. After LJL 4789 I seem to be a hot property. There's a launch in Baltimore that's setting up a lab."

LJL 4789 was the chain terminator antiviral, developed by the team of Lukajs, Jhingan, and Lenson, that had halted the spread of the Central Flower virus. He nodded. "Sounds promising. Heard from your mom?"

"Not lately. Birthdays and Christmas mostly. Remember, she has the younger kids . . . how was your day?"

"Ha. Don't ask."

"That bad? Sorry. What did you want to do for dinner? I could heat up something, if you want."

Dan roused himself. "Let's go to Cantler's."

She pulled a mock frown. "It's good, but . . . again?"

The restaurant was one of his favorites, a homely, ramshackle establishment whose vast screened porch overlooked a tidal creek. The real attraction, though, was flounder, clams, and other seafood that had slept the night before in Chesapeake Bay, as the saying went. He was trying to think of another choice when his phone went off. He looked at it. "It's Blair."

"I'll be downstairs. Say hi for me." She unslung her leg, stood, and sauntered out.

He picked up. "Hey."

"Hey."

"Pentagon fighting the bit?"

A tired chuckle. *"No surprise there. But that's not why I'm calling. Dr. Corris has been trying to get hold of you."*

Dan closed his eyes. Mukhtar Corris was the Swiss attorney Blair had found for him. He specialized in defense before the International Criminal Court. He remembered Corris's warning: *The Hague moves very deliberately. But once you are indicted, the trial date set, suddenly it will seem all too fast.*

The accusation dated from early in the war, when Dan had ordered his task force to stand clear of a torpedoed tanker. Rendering assistance, with the attacker still at large, would just have meant losing another ship.

Unfortunately, Berlin hadn't seen it that way. "Uh, he hasn't called here. Is there a new development?"

"Afraid so. They've issued the indictment. Your court date's next month."

He couldn't stop a shocked intake of breath. "Uh, the previous administration, their policy was that no US citizen would be extradited for war crimes. That's changed? Is that what you're telling me?"

"Not exactly. There are folks pushing for that, yes. But since the next person they'd go after would be our vice president, I doubt that's going to happen. But Corris needs to talk to you. Failing to appear doesn't mean the process won't go forward. You just get tried in absentia. He can defend you, but staying away won't help your case.

"Really, Dan, you need to talk to him, not me. You have his number, right?"

"I'll call first thing in the morning. Europe, he'll be out of the office now."

"Okay, but don't put it off. This is serious."

They talked for a few more minutes, before she had to sign off. *"Another late meeting,"* she said. *"Appropriations. Given the political reality, we're going to take significant cuts . . . anyway. I'll try to visit next week, okay? Take care of yourself. And best to Nan."*

He sat alone again in the darkened room, pondering his choices. Fight the charge? Go to Holland, defend his actions?

And run the risk of prison?

Or: Ignore it? Most likely, the administration would stonewall any extradition orders.

If he didn't respond, though, he'd be confined to the United States. If he went to a country that honored the warrant, he'd be detained and turned over to the court. Imprisoned, if found guilty in absentia.

He sat there still as darkness seeped in the windows. Until at last he grunted, got up, and went to join his daughter downstairs.

6

Saturday morning. Back in his room, after his self-assigned early swim, Dan couldn't resist the siren song of his rack. He asked Scherow to run the morning come-around, and crashed.

When the ten-minute call went, he woke groggy and sweating. It had to be ninety degrees. Through the open window pulsed the ominous drone of millions of cicadas. He lay disoriented for a moment, then bounded off his bunk, suddenly eager.

He was picking up his car today. And, not only that . . . Mignon was meeting him in DC, and she'd agreed to spend the night with him.

Saturday classes went by in a nodding blur. By noon meal most of the tables were nearly empty. The second class and first class had liberty after their last Saturday class.

Back in his room, he grinned as he changed into chinos and a short-sleeved madras shirt from Peerless. He wavered between gym shoes and his class shoes, and decided on the black leather.

* * *

The seller lived in Arnold, across the river. The MG was in the front yard when Dan's taxi pulled in. A luscious dark green. Freshly waxed, it gleamed in the sun. He stood admiring it, and the emerald lawn that sloped down to the river behind the big, obviously well-cared-for house. A sailboat lay moored at the end of a long pier.

He rang the doorbell and handed the owner, an old guy with a pointed beard, a check for his down payment. More than he'd figured on, but the seller was cool with getting the rest by the end of the month. Until then, he'd keep the title, and Dan would house the car there, in the guy's garage, until he rated parking in the Yard.

"Want the top on today?" the guy said, looking Dan up and down.

He checked the sky. "Is it gonna rain?"

"Doesn't look like it."

"Then I'll take it without. Sir."

"Sir? Heh heh. Well, enjoy her," the old guy said, handing him the keys. "The engine hesitates if you hit the gas too hard. But keep up with the maintenance and oil, and she'll get you around."

Dan climbed in. It felt strange and new. His first car. He patted the driver's-side door, fitted the key, and fired it up. Depressed the clutch, and ran through the gear changes in his head. He'd hardly ever driven before, except his uncle's station wagon. He'd scraped a telephone pole and had to mow lawns all summer to cover the repairs.

So, take it slow . . . he slammed it into first, let up on the clutch, and the car bucked to a stall. Grimacing, he tried again.

He rolled out of the driveway and up the hill. Braked at a stop sign and turned onto Ritchie Highway. Steering cautiously, he eased up to thirty. Thirty-five. The motor purred. The wind ruffled his hair. He flashed on the house again. The boat.

Maybe someday he could have a place like that. . . .

* * *

Beltway traffic sucked. Trucks kept cutting him off, bulling over into his lane. A thicker coat of wax, and the rig would have sideswiped him. His hands were shaking on the wheel by the time he got to Mignon's college. The old stone pillars braced the gate like two plebes at rigid attention.

"Dan, you're late. I was getting worried."

She had a sweet smile, and she seemed to care about him. Mignon M'Naughton was petite, blond, and cutely pretty in a light blue summer dress that looked like silk, a paisley scarf, and the sleeves of a knit sweater over her shoulders. She was majoring in education and planned to teach elementary school. They'd met at one of the Academy dances popularly known as Pig Pushes or Tea Fights. He liked her, but he wasn't sure it was going anywhere. So many mids got Dear John letters that *The LOG* ran them as a regular column. So far she'd allowed him deep kissing, a brief exploration of her breasts, and a hand dipped inside her panties in the parlor of the drag house on Randall Street.

She looked the car over. "So, this is it?"

"Like it?"

"It's cute, but . . . Dan, what did this cost? Can you afford it?" Frowning a little, she slid her overnight bag into the back seat. Tentatively, as if it might be repossessed along with the vehicle.

"No worries. I'll be getting an ensign's pay come June." He helped her in; she seemed to appreciate gentlemanly attentions like that.

* * *

They were nearly at the hotel when traffic slowed, clotted, and stopped dead. She sat patiently for a while, hands folded in her lap. Finally she smiled at him. "Do you still have my picture in your hat? The one of me at Virginia Beach?"

He grinned at her. She *did* look good in a swimsuit. "I'm the envy of every plebe in the company."

"Something's going on," she said, craning to look down the avenue. "Oh yeah! Some of the girls were going. It's the march, today."

"March?" He blinked, uncomprehending. "Uh, I get enough marching, thanks. What if we—"

"Just for a minute. Please?" She turned a sweet pleading look on him.

Okay, whatever . . . He spotted a space down a side street, locked their overnights in the trunk, and followed her down the avenue.

Toward a clamor of shouting. A pulse of cheers, like a pep rally, but with a menacing undertone. They edged between black-and-white pedestrian barriers. A pair of uniformed cops scowled at Dan when he nodded to them. Then looked Mignon over, with obvious appreciation.

When they came out on Pennsylvania Avenue Dan halted, astonished.

Hundreds—no, thousands—of demonstrators thronged the pavement, milling, circulating, but gradually flowing north. Most were young, though a few older folks hiked along with them. Some carried banners or placards. No one seemed to be keeping step. The boys were long-haired, in mustaches and frayed Levi's and sandals. The girls wore bell-bottoms and halters, or embroidered peasant dresses and headbands. He smelled burning leaves. They chanted, "Hell, no, we won't go," and "Ho Chi Minh is gonna win." He sucked air; felt his back stiffen. These were the people he'd be defending?

Mignon tugged his arm. "Let's march. For a little ways. Okay?"

"What? Uh, I don't know—" But he interrupted himself. "Sure. Okay." Despite his revulsion, he was curious too. They could tag along a few blocks, see what it was all about, then duck out and circle back to the car.

At least he was in civvies. He glanced back, noting the cross street, then grabbed her hand and joined the throng.

They hiked along, Dan feeling awkward, even sort of treasonous just being here. Mignon joined in the chant, "Stop the bombing, stop the war," but he just looked around, keeping his mouth shut. Who were these people? Communists? They looked like regular kids, his own age. Except for the older ones. Those must be the leaders.

A bearded guy stared at Dan's head. Yeah, the high and tight. "You military, buddy? Like, a vet?"

"Uh . . . sort of."

"What, they draft you? Sending you to Nam?"

"Uh, not yet. I mean, not exactly."

"Whatever, cool of you to come. Appreciate the support."

"I'm not really *supporting* this," he muttered under renewed yelling from up ahead.

"Hey, it's you guys that are getting killed over there."

"So, what, we just leave the Vietnamese to the Communists?"

The guy looked confused. Mignon pulled at Dan's arm. "Isn't this great? They're protesting all over the country today. Dow Chemical. The White House. The Pentagon. We're making history." She stopped herself, glancing up at him. "It's not, I mean, like, anti-military. If that's what you're thinking—"

"Whatever." He put a hand on her back. "Is this far enough? How about if we—"

The marchers around them slowed, bunching up. Someone was shouting up ahead. They were packed subway-close now. He smelled sweat, perfume, hot asphalt, grass. Puzzled murmurs shivered through the crowd. Then shrill cries lifted. Shouts of alarm.

A short, rapid popping. Then, screams.

"Shit!" Dan dragged her down to the pavement as something zipped past overhead. The screams grew louder. The crowd surged, falling back as the marchers in the lead recoiled, shouting, knocking an older woman to her knees. A siren scraped the sky.

A mist drifted over them, and his eyes started to sting. "Tear gas," he yelled, and the warning was taken up, repeated, back along the route.

The crowd tried to scatter, but cop cruisers and National Guard jeeps were pulling up, blocking the side streets. People started hammering on the doors of the buildings, but they were locked. Kids were smashing windows, then boosting each other into them to escape. A girl sobbed, working a glass shard out of a bloody palm.

The cops came in with clubs drawn and started cracking legs and arms, knocking people down. Vicious-looking dogs lunged on short leashes, barking and slavering, teeth bared. The mist thickened. It became a choking, throat-burning smoke. He pulled his shirt up over his mouth and nose, and helped Mignon wrap her scarf over her face. Half dragging her, he headed off the avenue. Realizing, belatedly, he'd stumbled into trouble.

Just then he tripped over an overweight man in a coat and tie and jacket. Dressed like a math teacher. He was slumped on the curb, coughing and choking. His ridden-up shirt exposed a pale hairy belly. He was gasping, cheeks cherry red, legs kicking feebly. A knot of students surrounded him, looking helpless.

Dan dropped to his knees, recalling buddy-care and field trauma training. Airway, breathing, circulation. Mignon knelt too, looking anxious as he rolled the guy onto his back. She pulled off her sweater, folded it, and stuck it under the man's neck.

"Asthma," the guy choked out, rolling a terrified gaze up at them.

"We gotta get him out of this gas," Dan told the students. "Give me a hand."

A bearded kid bent to help, then others. Dan got his arms under the upper body. "And . . . *heave*," he grunted. They hoisted, together, and staggered off with their burden down an alley.

Only to run into another line of District cops. They were collaring protesters, dragging them off to vans. One, in blue uniform and gas mask, spotted Dan and hustled over. "What are you doing?" he shouted through the mask diaphragm, above a renewed *pop-pop-pop* of more gas rounds, farther up the avenue. The wind was blowing it back down on them, channeled between the buildings. A German Shepherd, barely held in check by a tough-looking female cop, lunged snarling at Mignon, who screamed and backed away.

Dan yelled over the noise, "Officer, this guy's having some kind of seizure. Needs medical help."

The cop grabbed his collar. "Tough shit for him. You, you're under arrest."

"Arrest? For *what*?" Dan nearly threw the hand off, then lowered his arm. His career could end here and now. Arrested at an antiwar protest . . .

that had to be something like a Class A infraction squared, if not grounds for outright dismissal. "Sir, look. I'm military."

"Yeah? Makes you a fuckin' traitor."

"Sir, honestly, we didn't plan to be here. I was just taking my girl on a date. We just got . . . caught in the crowd."

"What's the trouble?" An older cop, obviously senior. His tone didn't convey sympathy.

"Says he's military, didn't mean to be here, was just scorin' points with his girlfriend."

"Accidental protester, huh?"

Dan said earnestly, "No, sir, I'm on weekend liberty. We were on our way to our hotel, and just . . . wondered what all the fuss was about." He was sweating now. The dog kept lunging at them. Mignon was sobbing. "And this guy here, he needs a doctor. His airway's closing up. He could die."

The cop eyed his haircut. "What're you, a marine?"

"Navy. Naval Academy."

"Annapolis, huh? Should'a known better than to get mixed up in this. Book 'em both."

"Take me, then, but let her go. Please." Dan took Mignon's hand.

The older cop shook his head wearily. "Oh, fuck it. Let these two lovebirds go. And call the EMT, get that guy some help. Jee-sus *Christ* in a basket.—I said, get *out* of here, you two!"

Dan pulled a limping Mignon, who said she'd turned her ankle, along to D Street. They fought their way over discarded placards and wind-tumbled trash in what he hoped was the direction of the car. Coughing, eyes and noses burning, tears streaming down their cheeks. Behind them the avenue was a welter of gas, smoke, shouts, and weeping. To his relief, he found the little green sportster parked where he'd left it. And his new key, thank God, was still secure in his trouser pocket.

* * *

The hotel was a faded redbrick pile that had hosted presidents and lobbyists in its nineteenth-century glory days. Since then it had decayed, to put it mildly. But Academy scuttlebutt had it that the desk didn't look too closely at unmarried guests. Which turned out to be true; the clerk signed them in without a question. Dan pushed cash across—more than they'd said when he'd called on the phone, but he was afraid to object—picked up his AWOL bag and Mignon's overnighter, and headed for the elevator.

They both went quiet, not looking at each other as the car ascended. She said in a low voice, "I've never done this before. Stayed in a hotel with someone, I mean."

"Um, me neither." He rubbed his stomach, fighting nausea. They'd had dinner at an Italian place north of the Capitol. Now pork cutlets and pasta churned in his gut. His eyes and throat still burned. Maybe his first-ever glass of wine and a big meal hadn't been a good idea.

He ventured an arm around her. She leaned into him, and they looked at themselves together in the flyspecked elevator mirror. "You smell really nice," he said. Even with her hair messed up and her eyes still red, she was cute. She smiled up at him. But her lips trembled.

When they got to the room, she disappeared into the bathroom. He went to the window. It was getting dark. The avenue was clear now, traffic flowing again, lights coming on. Should he get undressed? He let down the dusty shades and sat on the creaky bed.

She came out with her hair loose to her shoulders, in a knee-length nightdress he could almost see through. The curve of her breast, the shadow of nipple, made him catch his breath. She went to the window and pulled the curtain closed over the blinds he'd already dropped.

Alone at last, without the Drag Mom back in the kitchen, her ear tuned to anything going on in the parlor. They kissed. He cupped her breasts, then slipped two fingers lower. She lay back with eyes closed, as if pretending to be asleep.

When his fingers grew warm and wet, she shifted on the bed. Sighed. Her thighs parted. She murmured, "That feels so . . . Can we put the light out?"

He grew bolder in the dark. With her eyes closed, she did as he directed. He was close to coming, but he wanted more. From the way she kept shifting her hips, so did she.

He rolled atop her. But the moment she felt him hard against her belly, she stiffened. Tried to roll away. "Dan. No."

"What? I thought you wanted—"

"No. Not yet. Not until—you know."

At the push-up position above her, hands on hers, he realized he had her pinned. Now she wanted to back out? He felt a sudden surge of frustration. Lust. Anger. Positioned his hips again, preparing to drive home.

"Don't," she murmured. "Dan. Stop. *Please.*"

He swayed suspended on his forearms. She was sweet. Pretty. He liked her. But enough to get married? Besides, he'd be at sea for years. What good would it do either of them?

"I've got a condom," he tried. "It's safe."

"Oh, Dan. You thought I'd let you go all the way?"

He whispered angrily, "I don't get it. Why the fuck did you come, then?"

She turned her face away. Was she crying? Again? "You said, a weekend in DC. Museums. I didn't think you wanted to—do this."

"What? You knew I did. You *knew.*"

"Maybe. But I changed my mind. Can't we just—I can do what you liked before, make you come that way."

He hung poised for another second, then rolled away, cheeks burning. "Shit," he muttered. "Okay. Whatever."

Afterward he lay in the dark, the blinds up and the window open again, the night air carrying the distant many-stories-up hum of the streets, cooling them as they lay no longer speaking. A distant light moved across the sky. Not Venus. An aircraft of some sort. Its landing light waxed and waned, as if it was searching for something; for its home port, its goal, its landing place; and finally disappeared.

II

THE TRIAL

7

Norfolk Naval Base, Norfolk, Virginia

Standing on the tarmac with Blair, he waited impatiently for a call from his attorney. His wife had driven over from DC in the rain. It had fallen off and on since dawn as gray squalls blew in from seaward.

He patted her back, realizing just how much he'd missed her. Getting a smile in return. Yeah, absence *did* make the heart grow fonder.

But they were both so busy . . . she probably even more than he, trying to keep her head above water in Washington while the country struggled to recover. President Holton's offer of a cease-fire had ended the active rebellions. Yet the Covenanters still held out in the Midwest, and the Reconstituted Confederacy was a power in the South.

"They're pushing to defund the Department of Defense," she was explaining to the captain who escorted their group. "And it's hard to argue, considering how much needs to be rebuilt. Cities. Farmland. Industry. Eighty cents of every dollar we take in goes to war debt. Something's got to give . . . but we can't entirely gut the forces. There are still threats out there."

Dan checked the charge on his phone. He didn't want to miss this call.

Matters at Larson Hall were settling into the time-worn grooves of military administration. The investigation into Evans's death had wrapped. Dan had imagined someone giving the sprinting white-power leader a shove at an opportune time. The jagged rocks would finish the job. But there was no video coverage of the seawall, and the DoD autopsy had come up with little more than Sick Bay had. Bruises, a cracked tibia, water in the lungs. Dan had approved a slip and fall as the official finding.

He regretted the death, as he would have regretted anyone's under his command. The kid could have gone far, once he got rid of whatever misguided sense of superiority he'd carried.

And the missing rifles had turned up at last, hidden in the bottom of a laundry basket, ready to be smuggled out and presumably sold on the black market. One of the civilian cleaning crew had vanished the same day, an ex-con with a burglary record, making him the prime suspect in the theft.

The 'dant, Stocker, said the initial meeting of the Anglo-Saxon studies group had been yawningly unthreatening, devoted primarily to an argument over whether it had been Æthelstan of Kent or King Alfred of Wessex who'd founded the first English Navy. They'd elected a new president to replace Evans, Midshipman Galadriel Stewart.

So he seemed to've been granted breathing room on some of his concerns. The waiting passengers retreated under the terminal's awning as rain spattered anew. Party of six: himself and Blair, the SecDef looking 1940s in a khaki trench coat and low pumps and her hair up. A shaky, graying codger in blues so faded they must have been pulled out of the back of his closet. He'd introduced himself as the CO who'd put USS *Horn* into commission.

That seemed fitting: his old destroyer's first skipper, and her very last. And three enlisted plank owners. A separate group a few paces off would go in the second shuttle. Blair's protective detail—two CID agents—and the shipyard personnel who'd tended to the old can during her long quarantine at Portsmouth Naval Shipyard, across the Elizabeth River. *Horn* had moldered there pierside for fifteen years. She'd pegged the radioactivity meters, contaminated by alpha fallout hammered so deep into decks and bulkheads and cableways no high-pressure washer could flush it out.

But the readings had gradually fallen. And today his former command would perform her final duty.

He stood remembering the rain-soaked day he'd taken charge, over at Pier 8, not half a mile from where they stood now.

Remembered the disgraced and retiring skipper he'd relieved, and the cynical advice Carter Ross had offered.

"Ever heard about the three envelopes?" Ross had said, turning his coffee cup in gnarled fingers in the CO's in-port cabin. Dan had wondered why the guy was so nervous, as if in the waning minutes of his watch some disaster might still overtake him.

Dan had cleared his throat. "Envelopes?"

"Fellow comes on board to relieve, the outgoing CO gives him three envelopes. Says, when you get in trouble, open the first one. When you get in real trouble, open the second. And when you're ass-deep in gators and there's no way out, open the last one.

"So sure enough the fella screws up and he opens the first one. It says, 'Blame your predecessor.' So he does and it works. Later on he gets in real trouble. He opens the second envelope, it says, 'Reorganize.' So he does and gets out of the shit. But then at last he gets in such deep kimchee he can't see any way to avoid a court-martial. He opens the third envelope."

"So what's it say?"

"'Prepare three envelopes.'"

Horn had been a challenge, all right. Not just an engineering nightmare, but an experiment: the first warship to integrate females into wardroom and crew. Commonplace these days, but revolutionary then, with a lot of voices predicting he'd fail.

But it hadn't been the women who'd doomed her.

Blair looked up from her phone. "He hasn't called yet?"

The International Criminal Court at The Hague had discussed holding trials after the end of the war. Generalissimo Zhang. Marshal Chagatai. Admiral Lianfeng. General Pei. For aggressive war, crimes against humanity, and war crimes. They'd planned to indict senior officers from the Allied side as well, to show impartiality. It had taken years, but now, after many delays, his turn in the barrel might be here. He smiled tightly. "Uh . . . nothing yet. No."

"Like I said last night, he'll want character witnesses. If they decide to prosecute. And if you decide to go. Which is up to you . . . If you do, I can't accompany you. Administration policy: no interference in the judicial process."

He nodded. "Copy. But I'm wondering if—"

Heavy wingbeats interrupted him. The aircraft droned in from seaward. It roared over, circled the basin, then transitioned from level flight to VTOL mode. It hovered, lowered itself, hovered again, finally settled.

"Don't forget these." The captain passed out cranials with ear protection. Dan arranged Blair's, unsnagging a lock of her hair, then donned his own.

Bent low, they scampered across the tarmac toward the rear ramp. To the snarling thud of huge engines driving gigantic proprotors, they lifted into the overcast.

* * *

He peered out as they churned over Virginia Beach, giving Norfolk International a wide berth. Pink and white hotels reared from the sand to the sky. The twin lighthouses of Cape Henry dropped astern. The sky cleared as the land receded. Two-to-three-foot seas, he estimated, looking down, with predicted winds of ten to fifteen knots. Good sailing weather.

Except for a very few historically significant units, obsolete warships were worthless. The costs of disassembly, recycling, and safe disposal exceeded their scrap value. A SINKEX put decommissioned hulls to use one last time.

But first, the Inactive Ships Office scrubbed them down. They removed oils, fluorocarbons, polychlorinated biphenyls, mercury, and solid plastics. They pumped out fuel, lubricants, and hydraulic fluids, and steam cleaned tanks and piping. A tug towed the ship out to the exercise area. There, a party went through one last time, securing watertight doors and hatches and scuttles to reflect wartime compartmentation. After a final muster, they debarked, abandoning the forlorn vessel.

Then her executioners moved in.

* * *

Finally he glimpsed her, far ahead: a speck on the blue that grew quickly into the familiar shape of a Spruance-class destroyer. The bladelike bow. The towering, complex, nearly vertical superstructure, so unlike the smooth, slanted surfaces of newer ships, designed to shrug off enemy radars. That huge sail area had nearly blown him down on a Dutch frigate when a tug had dropped gears. . . . The V-22 lost altitude and made a circuit of the target, maintaining a half mile's distance.

She looked the same, Dan thought, yet not the same. Rust stains ran from her scuppers, as if she were weeping blood. Her paint was faded, ghostlike, less haze gray than off-white. Holes gaped in her upperworks, where equipment had been stripped out. There were transplants too; new antennas, different from those sheared off by the blast. An unfamiliar enclosure, on the helo deck.

"Does it look like it used to?" Beside him, Blair squeezed his hand.

He squeezed back, but didn't answer. Still staring out.

Horn had been his first real command. He remembered: Claudia Hotchkiss, his exec. Lin Porter and Kim McCall. Marty Marchetti, "Mister Machete," hadn't made it. Too close to the burst, and instantly vaporized.

And little Cobie Kasson, fireman, who'd given her life for her shipmates.

"I remember the day you left on her," Blair said.

He nodded, pulling his mind back. Glancing at his wife.

She projected inaccessible professionalism in public. But she had a passionate, even reckless side. She had a doctorate in operations research, a Juris Doctor degree from George Mason, and a stepfather who owned six thousand acres in Prince George's County, Maryland. He could see how some found her intimidating. Doubly so now, as secretary of defense.

They'd met in the Persian Gulf, in a sandstorm, when he'd been exec of *Turner Van Zandt* and she the defense aide for the late Senator Bankey Talmadge. Then again in Bahrain, where one passionate night had interlocked their lives like enzyme molecules.

It had never been a traditional marriage. They'd grabbed weekends and holidays together, flying from coast to coast, scheduling meetings around each other's commitments. Sometimes he honestly didn't understand how it worked. They were just both so damned busy.

But maybe once he was out of the Navy, and she retired too, they'd get to spend some good years together at last.

He squeezed her hand again. Shit! He was going soft. Mooning over an old ship. Which was after all just a hunk of rusty metal.

Except . . . no. A ship wasn't just steel and copper and paint. It was freighted with memories. Joys, and terrors, and regrets.

This one had been sentenced to a deep grave, far beyond the hundred-fathom line.

* * *

USS *Ffoulk* was a wartime Burke-class destroyer, named after a Marine hero of the Taiwan campaign. Dan and Blair airlocked in and were led to the wardroom for coffee and cookies. The skipper explained there'd be a holdup. One of the prep crew had fallen down a scuttle and injured his leg. Meanwhile, they were welcome to relax in the wardroom, or observe from the bridge.

Blair settled in with her tablet; Dan took the offer, and climbed to the pilothouse. A junior officer handed him a printout, and he ran his gaze down the exercise order.

It would begin with *Horn* under power at fifteen knots. A single turbine and screw had been returned to service for the exercise, remotely steered by a joystick-and-console on *Ffoulk.* The first attack would come from massed drones. Following that would be cruise missiles from a German destroyer, with dummy warheads to prolong the testing opportunity. The next assault would be something classified, still in prototyping. The op order also mentioned a countermeasure, though it didn't specify what. The final event was left open too.

He unsheathed binoculars from a holder. *Horn* leapt closer, sharpening as he focused. An ache ignited in the region of his heart. Dropping the RHIBs in the Gulf for boarding and search. Liberty in Bahrain, and the captain's mast he'd held afterward, when he'd caught the male crew circulating topless photos of their shipmates. Then Operation Adelaide, in the Red Sea.

Ffoulk's CO drifted over. "Understand you were her skipper when the bomb went off, Admiral," he essayed.

Dan lowered the glasses. "Uh-huh."

"A stolen nuke, in a dhow, is what I heard."

"Pretty much it, Captain," Dan said. "Fallout-enhanced with strontium-based animal feed. Would have poisoned a lot of innocent people, if it had gone off closer to land."

The skipper stood beside him for a few more seconds, probably yearning to know more, but finally was called down to Combat for STARTEX. He invited Dan to accompany him, but he said he'd stay topside, at least for a while.

Blair came up, and was ushered to the captain's chair. Her protective detail stood back by the chart room.

The exercise creaked into motion, the drone-swarm buzzing in from seaward like killer wasps. Launched from a sub, apparently. Small, dangerous-looking cruciforms skimmed the wave tops. As they jinked and dodged, even diving in and out of the sea now and then, *Horn* changed course to uncover her stern. Fighting on her own, like another ship he'd known long before: USS *Barrett*, in the Windward Passage.

So many ships. So many memories . . . *Reynolds Ryan*, *Bowen*, *Barrett*, *Van Zandt*, *Oliver C. Gaddis*, *Horn*, the two *Savo Islands*. And the missions: Iraq, the White House, the Tactical Analysis Group . . . then, crowning everything, commanding fleets in wartime.

He'd dreamed of such a career, as a mid. But resigned himself to the probability his fantasies could never come true.

Yet somehow, they had . . . just not in the ways Midshipman D. V. Lenson had expected.

His musings were interrupted as a nearly invisible beam from *Horn* boiled the air. It flicked from one flying shape after the other. They fell, spinning, drawing sketches of charred-plastic smoke against the blue. The needle-beam stabbed so rapidly here and there across the sea that he wondered if it was a laser at all. Hadn't Naval Research been working on a particle-beam weapon?

A pause, then Phase Two began. The old destroyer swerved east and accelerated to twenty knots, her max speed, as he recalled, on one screw. He lifted the glasses again. She still looked regal, even dangerous, with a white-foam bone gripped in her teeth. Driving over three-foot seas smoothly as a big Peterbilt down a Texas interstate.

Just as she had that day off the coast of Israel. . . .

* * *

Assigned to a barrier patrol, they'd intercepted a pair of incoming Osa/Komar attack craft. When he'd illuminated them with radar, the response was a salvo of Styxes. *Horn* had batted them down, and he'd sunk the Osas with Harpoons.

But the contact behind them had been a small trawler, looking as innocent as a fisherman could well be. But then, what had the shooters been protecting?

He closed his eyes, gripping the handrail as pain jabbed his neck like a hot needle. Fighting the old terror, suddenly just as strong as it had been for months afterward.

* * *

The German frigate reported a glitch, so the exercise coordinator called a two-hour delay. A helicopter appeared from landward, settled over *Horn*'s fantail, and figures fast-roped down. It moved off to hover a hundred yards away. Minutes ticked past.

A small craft he hadn't noticed before—likely lashed to the far side of the old destroyer's hull—emerged from behind it. The inflatable fell astern, then turned and motored for *Ffoulk*.

His former command turned away, accelerating again. Her wake broadened as she smashed into the seas, boiling the blue into a froth hearted by swirling pools of moss and lime and absinthe. An amber haze seethed above her stack. Caught by the wind, it streamed out over the sea until the horizon shimmered like a Gulf mirage.

Dan bent hunched over the splinter shield, binoculars welded to the shrinking silhouette. Ignoring the pain in his neck, his back, his legs.

Pain he'd carried ever since the blast.

* * *

He'd been looking away when it happened. Even so everything around him, sea, steel, uniforms, had blazed into the brightness of the noon sun. The lookout screamed, clutching his eyes. The dreadful, burning light went on and on, as if someone had opened the scuttle to Hell.

He lunged across the bridge, to shout into the 1MC, "Nuclear detonation, brace for shock!"

The deck jolted upward as he dove for it, whiplashing him into the air. An instant later the windows disintegrated with a crack like a bolt of lightning tearing an oak apart.

As the hellish light waned to a red glow, *Horn* inclined to port. A clamor reached him, a clanging racket like a boiler factory stood on end and shaken. Then water crashed down, the base surge, with shards and debris clattering on the decks.

With a massive groan, *Horn* staggered back upright. She rolled to starboard, then back to port. Sluggishly, as if trying to sense how badly hurt she was.

Dan pried himself off the deck. His hands came away bloody from his face. Something was wrong with his neck. The others hoisted themselves to their feet. The exec was on the phone, demanding damage reports.

When he felt his way out onto the wing, a queer beige fog hung above the waves. He swept the sea where the trawler had drifted seconds before. Waves rocked crazily, radiating from an inchoate jumble of boiling whitecaps. A column of dirty vapor towered from a misty base.

He turned, to look the length of his ship.

Horn had been blasted broadside, and the radar-absorbing tiles were peeling like sloughing skin. All her antennas were gone. Life rafts, davits, stanchions were swept clear or bent at strange angles.

With sudden horror he realized what the gritty mist on his face was, and what might be filtering into the ship with it. He slammed the door, dogged it, and roared at the dazed-looking boatswain, "Set Circle William throughout the ship. Commence water washdown."

Yet when he'd peered out again only a few nozzles spurted. Instead of being shriven in cascades of water, *Thomas W. Horn* had wallowed, scorched and flayed, as the radioactive rain pelted down.

* * *

Now, decades later, he blinked, gripping *Ffoulk*'s splinter shield. Hollow, as if he'd left part of himself back there. Some part that believed the worst could never happen.

"Recommence exercise, Phase Three," an overhead speaker intoned.

"Flash gear, Admiral. Going to the main event." A petty officer held out hood, goggles, heavy gloves. Dan accepted them reluctantly—they carried bad memories—but drew the hood over his head and snapped on the goggles. He had to grin then; the usually sweat-stinky hood had obviously been freshly laundered *for the admiral.* He drew the gloves on last.

The OOD poked her head around the wing door. "Setting Condition Zebra, Admiral. Did you want to come inside?"

"Surely we're far enough away. And upwind, right?" The target was a speck on the horizon.

"If you insist, sir. But I'm pulling everyone else in."

Dan nodded abstractedly. He fingered the glasses, torn between wanting to watch and fear he'd burn his eyes out. Then stepped inside.

The exercise circuit announced, *"Stand by for impact."*

The sea rolled under a clear sky. *Horn* was a pinpoint, barely distinguishable from the sawtooth shapes of the distant waves.

A prick of light ignited high in the blue. A white, perfectly straight line unrolled behind it, like the track of a skate on ice. Thin almost to disappearance, it drew with incredible rapidity downward, out of the heavens.

As if in response, that nearly invisible beam reached up again. Like those that had incinerated the drones, but thicker. Denser. It locked onto the descending point, tracking as it fell. Holding steady.

Yet the descending fire refused to alter. Faster than he could draw a breath, it completed its fall. Straight from the zenith down to the afterdeck of the fleeing destroyer.

A blinding flash, white-hot, swiftly expanding.

The ship seemed to swell, expand, rise slightly out of the sea.

Then it exploded, wiped out in a white cloud of smoke, steam, and vaporized metal. The cloud expanded, covering five times her length, blotting out whatever was happening within.

He realized he was gripping the binoculars so hard his hands cramped. After nearly a minute the fog thinned. The wind peeled it away to reveal a rocking, smoking, foaming sea, and amid it, the after half of a ship just slipping beneath the waves. The bow half, forward superstructure and hull, rolled in a strange nose-down attitude. Dan could see the interior. Whatever that had been, it had broken the old destroyer's back.

"Effective compartmentation," the junior officer muttered beside him.

Dan flinched. In his imagination he'd been aboard her, groping through canted, smoke-filled passageways, calling out for anyone still trapped below. He cleared his throat, blinking back a stinging in the eyes. "What *was* that?" he managed. "A hypersonic, I assume."

"A deorbiting kinetic energy weapon, Admiral," the JO said. Her tone both humble and a little proud, no doubt to be able to explain something to someone so senior. "A satellite-launched, gravity-powered, hypervelocity projectile."

"A contract with SpaceX," Blair added. "We put ten-meter-long heavy-metal shafts in circumpolar orbits. An onboard system calculates trajectories to the target, then fires braking rockets. The shafts hit at twenty times the speed of sound." She put her hand on his arm. "Are you all right?"

"Yeah . . . yeah." He nodded, sucking air. Even with the particle beam going all out trying to deflect them, the bolts had fallen as inexorably as the thunderbolts of Jove. They'd torn his old ship apart, probably less by the damage they did going through, than the bubble their impact created under the keel, as all that energy was converted instantly to steam.

And they could strike any point on earth or at sea.

"Continue exercise, Phase Four," the overhead speaker said. The coordinator's voice flat, as if even he had been sobered by the violent death of a ship. Not to mention what it boded for the future of the Fleet.

Dan accepted a chief's offer of coffee, and carried it out on the opposite wing. A torpedo slammed into *Horn*'s bow section. A few more seconds and that wallowing hulk slipped beneath the seething chop as well, gushing foam and veils of steam.

He closed his eyes, imagining her settling to the distant bottom. To be crewed only by groupers, the lurking moray, and the poison-spined lionfish.

Ffoulk approached warily. A mile. A thousand yards. The empty sea still smoked as crew members held up phones, videoing the end of what to them was a legend from the distant past.

At last the smoke and bubbles ceased, and the sea rocked on, as it had forever. Only a few patches of creamy froth swirled, to mark where a ship had died.

He stood alone, trying to suppress a nausea that wasn't only from the overcooked, too-strong coffee. Surely it was better this way. For her to make a final contribution. Instead of rusting away in some backwater, since she was still too radioactive to be recycled.

He straightened, shaking off the gloom. Was he projecting?

He still had work to do.

* * *

Blair called her staff. She'd overnight in Hampton Roads. After a sit-down in the morning with the NATO allied commander, she'd return to the Pentagon on the evening helo shuttle. Dan would have been happy to stay at the BOQ, but she'd reserved a room at the Cavalier, an old, beautifully landscaped hotel in Virginia Beach. They showered, changed, and took a dignified promenade on the boardwalk, her security detail trailing them a few yards back.

Back in their room, unchaperoned at last, she put her arms around him. Whispered in his ear, "Remember when we used to hole up in Bahrain?"

"I do."

"Remember what we used to do?"

"Uh . . . sort of."

"Guess I need to remind you."

He was pulling off his pants when his phone chimed. A glance at the screen sobered him. "Hold that thought. I need to take this."

She sighed. "Burke-Bowden?"

"Switzerland."

"Oh. Yeah, I guess you better." She pulled her blouse together, and gave him a final, rousing squeeze. "Put it on speaker, so I can hear."

"Lenson," Dan said into the phone.

"Mukhtar Corris here. Very sorry, I was not able to return your call until just now."

"No problem. What've we got?"

"Well, not good news, I am afraid. The high commissioner for human rights wants to move forward on your charges. He has just appointed your prosecutor.

"Dr. Amir Al-Mughrabi started his career investigating American

atrocities in Afghanistan. He's prosecuted civil war and genocide in Lebanon, Rwanda, Syria, and Ukraine. He specializes in Article Seventeen cases—where the state in question, that's the US in your case, is unwilling to prosecute. So that is like, as you say, two strikes out of four."

Blair touched his knee. Whispered, "Did he say 'Al-Mughrabi'?"

Dan muted the phone. She muttered, "I met him. Twice. In Zurich, setting up the UN monitoring team for the war. And in Singapore, at the peace conference."

He nodded. "Anything I need to know?"

"Probably nothing your attorney doesn't. The guy's definitely not pro American. But he's not the one who'll pass judgment."

Dan unmuted the cell. "Um . . . okay. And by the way, it's three strikes, not four. Before you're out."

"Thank you for the correction. Yes, it will make my defense, I mean, our defense, more difficult. And your chances, I am sorry to say, less sanguine. On the other hand . . . as we discussed . . . most likely one reason you are being indicted is to justify the prosecution of senior officers and political leaders of the former Associated Powers for more serious crimes. So the ICC does not look like it is levying victors' justice."

Dan nodded. Yeah, he could think of several people who belonged in front of a court. Or better, a firing squad. "Roger. What do I need to do?"

"Mainly, it is time for you to decide, Admiral. I know your country's policy. You will not be forcibly extradited. But the final decision, sir, is up to you."

Dan exchanged glances with Blair. She tucked her chin, looking away. The message was clear: *It's up to you.*

He drew a breath. Then said, as he pretty much knew he would all along, "I think I acted properly, Doctor. And if I didn't, I need to accept my punishment. It's a matter of honor."

A pause, a hiss on the line. *"Honor?"* Corris said at last, astonishment, or maybe incredulity, salting his tone. As if he'd never heard the word before, at least in a legal context. Blair put a hand on his arm, eyebrows raised.

He shook her off. Gently, but getting the message across. You left it up to me. So let me handle it.

At the same time wondering if, as he'd managed too fucking often in his star-crossed career, he was galloping full tilt down the wrong road.

Screwing it all up, from some misplaced sense doing it the easy way wasn't right.

He inhaled deeply. Ever since the Academy, some people had considered him a straight arrow. Locked on, as they said in Bancroft. Maybe *too* straight. Rigid? Unrealistic? Holier-than-thou?

But he'd accepted that, about himself. It was too late to change.

"I'll be there," he told the attorney. Catching one last horrified look from his wife; her shake of the head; and signed off.

8

On Worden Field

The drums tolled like the heartbeat of the earth. *Left. Left. Left, right, left.*

Up ahead, the Academy Band struck up "The Marines' Hymn."

Fall, a hot Friday afternoon, and the Brigade Dress Parade. In short blue high-collared padded jacket with gold buttons, black leather sword belt, high-waisted trousers, and white leggings, Dan marched at the head of the company. The dress sword, modeled on one presented to John Paul Jones, was welded to his right shoulder. His left hand, in a spotless white glove, swung six inches to the front, three to the rear. The other midshipmen officers kept perfect pace behind him.

Winston Door, the company commander, was sick in his room, down hard with flu. Can't fuck up now, Lenson . . . To Dan's left marched his roommate, Teddy Scherow, bearing the glittering guidon with the company number in gold on a blue field.

Stribling Walk. Above the marching columns resplendent with bright brass and glittering gold swayed the sparkling steel of bayonets. Polished boondockers swished through autumn leaves. Shouted commands drifted back from the lead companies. Dan centerlined on the starboard walkway, measuring his paces so the sandblowers—the short mids, at the rear of the company—wouldn't have to run to keep up. They passed the Midshipmen's Monument, dedicated to grads fallen in the Mexican War. Mahan Hall loomed ahead, towering above the hooknosed figurehead of HMS *Macedonian*, dismasted and captured by Stephen Decatur in the War of 1812.

Forget that. Concentrate. He eyed the turn point, counted the steps, and lifted his sword.

"Column lellft . . . *harch*." He snapped the blade down and pivoted smartly off his right foot. The company followed, each rank pivoting in turn, then realigning in a subtle shifting shuffle as each individual dressed and covered. To present, once more, a compact, aligned body, ordered, disciplined, in perfect step.

He squinted against the sun, centerlining himself on the pavement. In step with the drumbeat, at the regulation thirty inches per stride. Coming up: a column right, past the Museum and Preble Hall and the Barbary Monument, oldest in the Yard, a gleaming marble wedding cake, its bronze inscriptions eroding to green stains.

Downhill now, trees rustling overhead, the smells of mown grass, the high skirl of trumpets, the swish and stamp of a thousand boots. Past the brick bulk of Isherwood Hall, named for the engineer who'd dragged the Navy kicking and screaming into the Age of Steam. Tourists and families lined the route, dressed as if for church, smiling and applauding.

The field opened ahead. Named for the *Monitor*'s captain, blinded in the battle with the rebel ironclad but still fighting, until the monster retreated to its lair. Dan resisted the urge to hurry, keeping his interval with the company ahead. Sweat soaked the rubber-padded wool of his tunic. The high collar chafed his neck and his heels burned, but he couldn't do anything about that. Suck it up, Lenson, he told himself. Grit your teeth. The Brigade's unofficial motto: a hundred thousand dollars' worth of education, jammed up your ass a quarter at a time.

He glanced toward the river. A yawl was gliding past. His gaze yearned toward it. Was that a woman, on deck? A flash of tumbled locks, long, bare legs—

"Dan!" A warning from behind.

When he snapped his attention back, he realized he'd tuned out at exactly the wrong second. Delayed his column-left onto the field, placing them off track for their assigned position. Not just his company, but those following, as well. "Shit," he muttered. Then, aloud, "Column lellft" . . . sword raised . . . Scherow lifted the guidon, passing the signal back . . . "*Harch.*"

The band swung into "Anchors Aweigh." The steady multifarious tromp of boots behind and ahead dulls to a softer whoosh through the precisely mowed, meticulously fertilized grass. A milling haze rises. Shining motes dance in the sun, a golden mist that smells of haylofts and lawn mowings.

Dan nodded to Teddy, who peeled out and sprinted ahead, searching the turf for the bronze markers that spaced the companies across the field. Once some anonymous prankster had pried them up the night before. Battalions had wandered lost, formations countermarching into one another, disintegrating into chaos. Now the markers were screwed deep into the ground.

When Scherow halted fifty paces ahead, Dan grimaced. They were *way* off. He didn't want to try a half-left. Everybody had a different idea of what forty-five degrees was. The grading officers were scrutinizing them from the stands, binoculars aimed like gunsights. He bit his lip and corrected left two yards.

A mutter from behind: "You're not gonna make it drifting over."

Out of the side of his mouth: "I'll make it." He corrected once more, hoping the file guides picked it up. Then again.

Not great, but better. They were still about five feet off though. Scherow glanced back and took one surreptitious step right. Watching from the side, the grader might not even notice.

"Company . . ." Left, right, left, right; command on the left foot, execute on the right. "*Halt.*"

The company stopped, swayed, steadied. He imagined it from above: again the subtle microadjustments, as each marcher gauged and corrected dress and cover, the recalibration eddying back through the ranks. He lifted his sword and drawl-shouted, "Orderrrr . . . *harms*!"

A thunderous thud, as the butts of a hundred rifles slammed into the sod. "Paraaade . . . *rest.*"

A clatter as his company snapped rifles outboard, left feet outward, left hands whipped up behind the back. Dan dropped his sword tip to the ground and took the same stance.

The band halted, all at once, mid-beat. From the reviewing party, a knot of men and women before the stands, an officer stepped to a mic. The PA system crackled. "*Ladies and gentlemen,*" it intoned, "*the Brigade of Midshipmen.*"

Applause clattered off the brick façades of Captain's Row. Well, maybe it looked better from the stands. When you weren't sweating in ranks, breathing hard, watching some kind of insects boiling up from the ground a few yards in front of you.

Ground wasps. Shit! They whirled in short arcs, executing, he guessed, some sort of search pattern. Looking for whatever had disturbed their afternoon. The breeze wafted them back toward him. He began to sweat in earnest.

"*Ree . . . port.*"

Far ahead, the High Stripers marched and countermarched. Swords flashed in the air. Hoarse shouts floated back.

Dan flexed his knees, eyeing the wasps. More were swarming up, milling, joining in an ominous high-pitched buzzing. A subterranean nest. Good thing the company hadn't halted right on it. But the bastards were widening their search. . . .

A long pause. At last the order floated back, passed from the brigade commander to the regimental commanders, parroted by the battalion commanders. "Ah-ten . . *hut* . . . Pree-sent . . . *harms*."

Sword up from the ground, hilt at the face, arm half turned, extended upward at a forty-five-degree angle. A muffled shriek sounded from someone in the company to their right as he, or she, got a bayonet tip in the back of the head.

The band struck up the National Anthem. Elevated, rigid, his sword arm trembled. He set his teeth as behind him the rest of the company, holding eleven pounds of rifle in front of their bodies, grunted and sighed.

The last note echoed away to silence. He bit his lip, willing his arm not to fall, not to shake. How much longer. . . .

"Order . . . *arms*."

They stood for what seemed eons in the broiling sun as someone was awarded a medal. Not a mid, of course. The words *defense* and *heroism*. The rest was indecipherable. The wasps explored the air around him, then his face. He didn't move. Then, gradually, they drew back, rehousing themselves in their hole.

Dan eyed it apprehensively. When the company marched off, they'd track directly over the nest. He couldn't think of any way around it, though. Sidestepping would just slam his company into another.

Unfortunately, he had a youngster, a third class, who was allergic. Harrison had nearly died after a bee's sting in Chapel. He was on medical hold. Dan gritted his teeth, trying to think of how to save the guy.

Then had it. Maybe. If the wind . . . yeah. It was cooling the back of his neck, coming off the river.

"Hey. Corwin." He angled his chin just enough to mutter over his shoulder.

"Aye." The laconic, redheaded violinist was the tallest in the company, so he was in the first rank.

"Got a wasp nest up here. Harrison's gonna walk right over it."

A pause. Then: "What you wanna do?"

"Swap him out with . . . whoever's four places to his left."

"You kidding? That'll fuck up his whole rank."

"He steps a half pace back. Scoots to the left. The other guy, half a pace forward, then *he* scoots right."

"No way, José. The grader'll roast us."

"So Harrison gets stung? Just pass the word. But don't execute until my command."

Another pause; then, murmurs. He hoped the order didn't get mixed up on the way back. Like a game of Telephone, passed from mouth to ear to mouth.

The high-pitched, carrying voice of the brigade commander. Then, louder, passed back battalion by battalion: "Pree-sent . . . *harms*!"

The slap and clatter of palms on the loose wooden handguards of the old Garands. "Stand by," Dan said out of the side of his mouth.

A terrific bang went off somewhere behind them. The saluting battery, firing blank charges out over the Severn. As ever, someone in the stands screamed. Car alarms blared singy-songy along the seawall. The clap echoed away. Another bang. Another.

He called back over his shoulder, "Ready . . ."

White smoke drifted over the ranks, choking, sulfurous.

"Two," Dan yelled as the smoke filtered over them, blurring the outlines of the companies to either side. Also obscuring, he hoped, the vision of the officers with binoculars and grading cards.

The smoke thinned, drifted past. He eyed the nest again. Yeah, they were still hunkered down there. Probably holding a staff meeting, deciding what to do.

Finally, the command every mid on the field had been thirsting for. "Pass . . . in . . . *review*."

He lifted his sword. "Company. Forward . . . *harch*!"

With a thud and a jingle they surged into step. As he passed the hole he glanced down. The wasps were still milling down there, on edge, pissed off. They'd be out for blood at being marched over again. He just hoped nobody else was allergic . . . at least he'd gotten Harrison out of range. . . . He dismissed that and concentrated again on steering the company through the furrowed grass left like wakes in the green by the company ahead.

No howling behind him, no curses. Maybe they'd lucked out. The company could use a decent grade. Navy made a big deal about one big family, but everyone competed, every moment, from marching performance, to grades, to aptitude. Even if you avoided walking out Bilger's Gate, your final class rank determined everything. Your choice of service. Your duty station. How fast you got promoted, out in the Fleet.

Where he'd start over, at the bottom again . . .

He wondered if everyone around him felt the same. Like some kind of imposter . . . just an actor, like in his roommate's plays . . .

The reviewing stand loomed. Marines in green and black. Navy in blue and gold. Ranks of Old Grads in sport jackets and GO NAVY caps, wives and daughters in flowered dresses and straw sun hats, aiming cameras. He reeled his mind in and straightened his back.

And the band struck up "Stars and Stripes Forever," and the sunlight glittered off bayonets, and the same chill ran up his back he'd always gotten, ever since Plebe Summer.

Standing alone to the right of the line of march stood a slightly bent, gray-haired figure, with gold up to his elbows.

Dan lifted his sword. "Eyes . . . *right*!" and snapped his head around.

The Supe. His white-gloved fingers grazed a gold-encrusted cap in salute. For just a fraction of a second Dan caught a glance from under the visor, a blue-eyed, piercing perusal sharp as a stab from an épée.

Yeah. The old man had marched here, too, once, just like all the rest. And for one long second Dan wondered if it was even remotely possible that in some future alternate universe he, too, might stand there, like that.

Ha! He'd be lucky if he graduated at all.

The moment passed. He shouted, "Ready . . . *front*," and snapped his head back. Then his boonies rang on asphalt again, on the road back to Mother B, and a hubbub broke out behind him, cursing, joking, the discipline and unanimity of the parade evaporating, the tight cohesive machine shattering again into its individual shards.

Becoming, once again, all too human.

9

The Netherlands

The flight went smoothly. He'd put in for back leave, left Burke-Bowden in charge, and flown commercial from Washington direct to Amsterdam. In civvies, since he wasn't under orders. He'd treated himself to business class. Considering what might be in store.

At Schiphol he halted a few meters from the EU check-in booths. Beyond them, barely restrained by customs agents in gray-blue uniforms, a scrum of reporters surged like wind-driven swells against a stone breakwater. They held up cell phones and digital recorders. Somebody hot must be due in. Royalty, a celebrity, an influencer. But as his passport was being stamped he suddenly made out what they were yelling.

"Admiral! Admiral Lenson! Do you have a comment—"

Past the booth, and he was in it, like chum in a boil of bluefish. He fended off mics and hands, trying to elbow through. Resisting the temptation to cover his face. One guy yelled, "Are you pleading guilty, Dan?"

Another, in a German accent: "Are you sorry you left them to die?"

A less hostile voice, a woman's: "What made you decide to extradite yourself?"

Just . . . fucking . . . great. From the looks of things, his case, or maybe his self-surrender, was blowing up the internet.

They badgered him all the way out of the terminal, but he shook them at last at the taxi stand. In the cab, he canceled his dot-com reservation for the Ambassade, and asked the driver to take him to an inexpensive place near the train station. "And wait until I check in, please."

He ended up at a budget three-story on Weteringschans. Signed in, dropped his overnighter in a cramped basement room, then was off again. He'd scheduled an hour's sit-down with the historian and architect at the Scheepvaartmuseum, the Netherlands' primary maritime museum.

* * *

Dating from 1656, the five-story stone structure, only a little smaller than Bancroft, had been built on dredged spoil too. The historian told him the pilings had held up, despite seepage and fill creep from the surrounding canals. He also led Dan through the three-masted East Indiaman moored out back, where he barked his forehead painfully on a low beam in the cheese room.

It was good to have some at least semiofficial business to take care of. Still, it was hard to shake the gnawing at his gut.

The ICC could award prison sentences of up to thirty years.

* * *

The next morning dawned dark and raining hard. Of course . . . He borrowed an umbrella at the front desk. It came in handy on the way to the station, as water poured from a deck-gray sky.

After forty-five minutes on a sparkling-clean, extremely fast electric train, he debarked at The Hague.

Koninginnegracht 14H was an unobtrusive façade of opaque glass with a small brass CORRIS & PARTNERS sign. Beneath that, INCASSO EN JURIDISCH ADVIES. Which pretty much defined what he was here for, if he understood Dutch. Fortunately, the media seemed to have lost him. He touched a buzzer and the door clicked.

This was the first time he'd met his counsel, though of course they'd had phone and video conversations since Blair hooked him up.

Mukhtar Corris was slight and steel-spectacled in a gray suit with nearly invisible pinstripes. His tie, too, was gray, but in a slightly different pattern of . . . trilobites? Dan, in a travel-rumpled sport coat and slacks, suddenly felt underdressed.

In a book-lined study the attorney poured him hot tea and settled behind a desk. Facing him, yet some feet away. A fiftyish woman with severely bobbed gray hair set a recorder between them, then took a seat against the wall. Corris introduced her as Margaretha. The furniture was so modern and angular it looked painful, all chrome, leather, and weirdly bent wood. A framed quotation on the wall read *Every injustice committed against an individual is, in the end, experienced by all humanity.*

"Peter Kropotkin," Corris said, noticing him noticing it. "You know his work?"

"No. Sorry."

The attorney seemed wary. Dan doubted it was because he didn't recognize some writer. He wondered how many mass murderers, ex-presidents, and agents of genocide had warmed this same obviously expensive but acutely uncomfortable chair his ass now occupied. Corris shrugged. "Perhaps a bit dated by now . . . your forehead. You have been injured?"

Dan touched the bump. "It's nothing. Banged it on a low overhead this morning."

"Ah, that's good. That it is nothing. So. Let us review our situation." He gazed at the ceiling, as if speaking by rote. "The ICC hears accusations against individuals. In your case, Admiral, for a war crime. The US is not a signatory to the Rome Treaty, but you're here voluntarily, defending yourself in person. That's a point in your favor. It should count with the court."

Corris's Swiss-German accent was thick, but Dan could follow. "Okay." He crossed his legs, trying not to fidget. Really, the chair seemed designed to torment its occupant. Frankly, he'd rather be taking a ship into battle. And representation at this level didn't come cheap. A thousand bucks an hour . . . why was he doing this, again?

"Now, the process. The Office of the Prosecutor conducted a preliminary examination. What we call *proprio motu*—on their own initiative—but actually, at the request of the Berlin government. The OTP asks three questions: Does the ICC have jurisdiction; is the accusation not already being dealt with by a national court; and would a prosecution be in the interests of justice? They concluded all three tests applied in your case."

Corris blinked, then dug a finger beneath the spectacles. "The OTP interviewed the surviving victims and others relevant to the allegations. I submitted a statement in your defense and a plea for dismissal. I had hoped the prosecution would recommend against continuing your case, after the preliminary examination. Their advice is nearly always followed by the court. Unfortunately, they did not . . . Are you with me so far?"

Dan shifted on his seat, but his back and neck still protested. "Uh . . . yeah."

"The OTP gathered enough evidence, mainly from the officers and crew of the vessel in question, to conclude prosecution was warranted. Then things halted for a few months, since other cases were ahead of yours. Meanwhile, I took steps to identify your accusers, and interviewed three of them."

Corris paused, blinking again; turned away. "Excuse me." He slid open a drawer, tilted his head back, and applied eye drops. Margaretha edged the recorder closer.

Dan nodded. "The people you interviewed—did they include Reinhard Geisinger?" The tanker's captain.

The attorney blotted his cheek with a tissue. "Yes. That was a particularly painful conversation."

Dan nodded, swallowing. He didn't want to relive all that. But he'd have to, over and over again.

If he wanted to defend himself, and walk free.

* * *

He'd mustered a scratch force, Task Group 779.1, the Ryukyus Maritime Defense Coalition Task Group, at the start of the war. His orders were to close the Miyako Strait, north of Taiwan, and position USS *Savo Island* to cover Taipei until the *Franklin Roosevelt* strike group could arrive.

Savo had rendezvoused with GNS *Stuttgart*, a German-flagged tanker, to take on personnel, cargo, and fuel when the submarine struck. Out of the blue, despite Dan's dense and, he'd thought, well-positioned ASW screen.

He felt the strike as a thump against the soles of his boots, conducted through the sea and then the cruiser's steel. Black smoke burst above the replenishment ship's afterdeck. The hit was on the far side, away from him.

He shouted, "OOD: Breakaway, breakaway! Right hard rudder. All ahead flank as soon as the stern clears. Stream the Nixie. Helo control: Get Red Hawk back in the air . . . sonobuoys, MAD run. Boatswain: Sound general quarters! Set Zebra, Aegis to active, Goblin alert. Sea Whiz in automatic mode."

The boatswain put it out over the 1MC, adding, "*This is no drill*" as *Savo* heeled hard, accelerating.

When he'd looked back, the stricken tanker was on fire, smoke streaming in the wind.

"Ringmaster, this is Steel Hammer. Shortshot. I say again, Shortshot. Over," the tactical circuit announced. Dan was on the 21MC with Sonar when *Curtis Wilbur*, one of his screen units, reported that the torpedo had been fired from *within* their protective screen.

The enemy sub was inside the wire. It could even now be generating a firing solution on *Savo*, the only antiballistic-capable unit.

Then the radio crackled. *"This is Captain Geisinger. We have taken a torpedo. Flooding. Fire. Request assistance."*

Dan grabbed the mic. "We are prosecuting the sub that torpedoed you. Over."

"That is good but . . . I need help here. Fire's out of control. . . . Over."

He'd racked his brain. But lying alongside to render assistance risked losing another ship. "This is *Savo*. Nailing this guy takes priority. You're on your own, Captain. If you have to abandon, do so in a timely manner. Over."

" I protest this decision. You are running away. You can save us. All I need is help. Firefighters."

Reluctantly, Dan had released the Transmit button. Leaving the ship, and its crew, to their fate. Later he'd sent his helo back, and lily-padded the survivors to Okinawa for treatment. Most had made it. But not all.

The attacker had escaped, so skillful and stealthy they'd never laid a glove on it. But at least he hadn't lost any of his other ships.

He still thought he'd made the right decision.

But he'd always regretted not having had another choice.

* * *

He coughed into a fist, realizing both Corris and the assistant were staring. He forced a tormented smile. "Sorry. You were saying?"

Corris nodded. "The Pre-Trial Chamber made the determination to confirm the charges, and issued the indictment and summons to appear.

"Now, as I believe I told you before, the trial process begins slowly, then moves very expeditiously indeed.

"I will accompany you in this afternoon. Once officially surrendered, you'll be taken into custody. Not to a cell, but you will not be permitted to leave the city.

"Tomorrow or the day after will be your initial appearance. I will be there with my team. The proceedings will be conducted in your language.

The judges will confirm you are the accused and determine whether you understand the charges. Both prosecution and defense will make opening statements, our first chance to argue for exoneration.

"At that point I will introduce another motion to dismiss. Since the judges have already decided there's enough evidence for trial, I doubt that will succeed. But we should take every opportunity." Corris finished his tea, then refreshed both cups. "I presume we are in agreement thus far?"

"So far." Dan was half regretting he'd started this ball rolling. No, not him. Berlin had started it.

"Now, did you bring the documents I mentioned? Those governing your actions at the time?"

"I tried." He shrugged. "Unfortunately, wartime instructions are still classified. All I could obtain were copies of the ship's logs. That should help with any timeline questions."

Corris drew air through his teeth. He didn't comment further, but Dan didn't need an explanation. After the Nuremberg trials, claiming he was acting under orders wasn't a defense. But absent them, he could be saddled with deliberate mass murder.

Margaretha stood, and said something in German or Dutch. Corris smiled and rose too. "If you will excuse me . . . another client. You are welcome to stay here until we head over. Or take a lunch. It might perhaps be best to enjoy your noontime."

Dan rose too. Getting the message: it might be the last meal he'd eat in freedom for quite a while.

Maybe even, ever.

* * *

The rain had let up, though it was still drizzling. He found an outdoor café with an awning but the bratwurst and sauerkraut, though obviously good quality, seemed to wedge somewhere below his breastbone. He walked back to the office and he and Corris drove over to the ICC. Halfway there he realized his overnight bag was still at the hotel. Well, Corris had said he'd be back. He just couldn't leave town.

The ICC complex loomed ahead. Smaller buildings whose windows formed a checkerboard of black, gray, and white surrounded a central tower of onyx concrete and blue glass. This central block was clad in metal gridwork, as if the building itself were being caged.

Corris parked in a gated lot, slotting a passcard into a turnstile. Cameras stared down as they walked to the front entrance, past an enormous folded-steel sculpture that reminded Dan unpleasantly of the twisted metal left after the missile attack on USS *Hornet* in the South China Sea. A sign read COUR PENALE INTERNATIONALE/INTERNATIONAL CRIMINAL COURT.

The front doors were flanked by vertical stainless-steel panels that conjured another image: the bars of a cell. Corris squeezed his arm; apparently previous clients had balked here. *"Bon courage,"* he murmured. "You're doing the right thing."

Dan couldn't think of a response. Actually, he was feeling less and less sure that was really true.

And, suddenly, there they were again, the scrum and tumult of gleaming lenses, avid, flushed faces with open mouths, converging from the porticos where they'd sheltered from the rain. He tried to ignore them, but it was hard. A dark-haired woman yelled, "Will you compensate Gunter Hemler's children?" One of the dead crewmen, Dan assumed. Another shout, in an American accent: "Has the Navy abandoned you, Admiral? Letting you face the music alone?"

"I need to make a statement," he asided to Corris.

"I advise not, Admiral."

"It'll be short."

"I strongly advise—"

"A statement," Dan yelled. His tormentors backed off. Cameras focused. He swallowed. Yeah, maybe a bad idea. But he had to make a couple of things clear.

"I'm here of my own volition," he said. "No one's abandoned me. I've been called before a court of law. I intend to prove my innocence. Beyond that, no further comment."

They howled for more, shoving mics in his face, but Corris stepped between him and the mob and they retreated a few steps, aiming their phones up to take in the gridded façade.

The lobby held a colorful display of national flags. The signatories of the Rome Treaty, apparently. He looked in vain for the Stars and Stripes. Six men and women in business attire stood waiting. Corris announced, "Admiral Daniel V. Lenson is surrendering."

A tall, Scandinavian-looking blonde stepped forward. She didn't extend a hand, so Dan didn't either. She held out a clipboard. Corris signed it, then Dan. She looked him up and down, then leaned in, squinting. "You have injured your head."

"A bump. Yesterday. Nothing to worry about."

She gestured to one of the others, who stepped in to take a close-up with his phone. "Follow me please, Admiral," she said.

"Um, my attorney. Can he accompany me?"

She looked surprised. "Oh, yes, of course."

Staffers stared as they walked through the building. Outside again, they traversed a water-filled trench that seemed less a moat, though it might also serve that purpose, than an architectural decoration. The stone pavement was gray as the sky and slick with the rain. Why, in the movies, did it seem to rain every time someone went to prison? A white van waited at the end of the walkway. Two uniformed men stood by it, holding rifles muzzle down.

Dan halted. "What's this?"

"The detention center," the woman said, looking surprised again. She frowned at Corris, who seemed taken aback. *"Heb je hem dit niet uitgelegd, raadgever?"*

The attorney tapped his palm with a fist. *"Hij gaat niet vluchten. Is het detentiecentrum echt nodig? Ik dacht—"*

They argued for a moment, then she turned to Dan. "I am sorry. There was obviously a misunderstanding. The only possible place for you is the detention center. I'm not sure why your attorney thought otherwise. Your phone, please." She held out her hand, glancing toward the guards. One swung open the back door of the van.

Feeling like a condemned aristocrat mounting a tumbril, he climbed in.

* * *

The detention center had to be fairly close, judging by the brief ride, but he wasn't sure where. After debarking into a covered portico, he was marched down a long, brightly lit, white-walled corridor. The beautifully polished floors reflected his face. But the heavy-looking, evenly spaced gray steel doors made it perfectly clear what this place was.

His cell was equally immaculate. It smelled of disinfectant, and didn't look to have been used much. A desk, with a lamp. A wooden chair. A narrow, dorm-style bed. A sink, with a steel mirror, toothpaste, brush, soap, and towel. It reminded him of his old midshipman room, though Bancroft didn't have stainless-steel toilets. Or flat-screen TVs. Maybe a better comparison would be the hotel he'd stayed in on the North Slope last year. Unlike that, though, this room had a window.

Corris stood wringing his hands. “I am desolated, Admiral. I thought we had an agreement otherwise.”

“No, no. It’s okay,” Dan said, though he didn’t feel okay. He’d stuck his fingers into an alien machine, and now the gears were dragging him in.

“You may have twenty minutes with your attorney.” The blonde glanced at her smartwatch. “Then we will be closing the visiting hours. *Twintig minuten, niet meer.*”

Dan handed Corris the umbrella. “I borrowed this from my hotel. And I left my overnight bag there, with my meds. Could you see that—”

“Certainly. Certainly! But I will petition for you to be released to my custody after the initial hearing. You are not a flight risk, after all. There’s a legal library down the hall. Computer terminals,” Corris said. “And a gym. It is not a bad place for a short stay.”

Dan thought being released seemed unlikely. The door to his cell was open, though. Maybe that was a good sign.

After more reassurances, Corris left. No guards paced the hall. He closed the door gingerly. It didn’t lock. Another good sign? Giving him the privacy to slide off the bed and sink to his knees on the polished, exquisitely clean floor.

Bowing his head, he asked for help. For wisdom, to do the right thing. Unsure as always who, or what, he was addressing.

But strength had always been there, when he’d asked.

Was he doing the right thing? His own government said he didn’t have to be here. (Though not forbidding him to come.) Was he standing up for justice, or just being incredibly fucking naïve?

Once again, then, he thought of the mids. How could he teach responsibility, if he ducked being held to account? Or lecture about integrity, if he waffled and skated?

On his knees still, locked fists to closed eyes, he considered praying for a dismissal. But at last didn’t. It wasn’t in his hands. He’d just try to be content with that.

He climbed back to his feet. Examined his face in the mirror. Brushed his teeth. Then turned to his neatly made-up bed, tore it apart, and made it up again, the Annapolis way.

10

And the iron routine of the Academy ground on, like a mill slowly masticating everyone's youth. Uniform changes. Showers. Classes folding laundry the exact same way he'd been taught as a plebe. Another uniform change.

Now dusk was falling outside the windows. The chow callers' frenzied shouts were bouncing off the smooth blue tiles of the bulkheads. The plebes chopped past on their way to their rooms, chins rigged in, eyes in the boat.

Dan was still the acting company commander. Door and his roommate both had mono, quarantined at Hospital Point until they weren't infectious anymore.

When he strolled out, Scherow called the company to attention and reported all present and accounted for. Dan walked one rank, then the next. As usual, the plebes were braced up and sweating. The third class looked fidgety, as if they couldn't quite believe they were past being yelled at, and the segundoes were squared away. He nodded to his classmates, the other firsties, but didn't inspect them. He strolled back to the front of the formation, then broke everyone for evening meal.

Hell, what was all the fuss about? This leadership stuff didn't seem to be all that hard.

* * *

He was in his room that night, trying to study, when someone tapped at the door.

He opened it to Sheldon, the rotund, always-hungry third class. He wore the CMOD armband. The company mate of the deck stood watch manning the single phone in each company area, sorted and delivered mail, stayed alert for fires, and delivered messages. "Hey, Dan."

"Len. Whatcha got?"

"Lieutenant. Wants you in his office."

Dan sighed. Checked his alignment in the mirror by the door, brushed his shoulders off with the little brass-wire whisk broom, and headed over.

Their company officer lived out in Parole with his wife and two young kids. So what was he doing here at night? Dan knocked, entered, and squared away in front of the desk. "Midshipman First Class Lenson, reporting as—"

"Sit down, Dan." Oleksa was short and tubby, with a buzz cut the color of chewed gum and shoes polished as brightly as any of the mids'. He wore a submariner's dolphins but scuttlebutt had it he wasn't in the running for command. He looked tired. A folder lay in front of him, along with several desk toys. He pointed to the settee on which so many mids had been warned, counseled, praised, or given bad news about deaths at home. "Got a problem. At least, it might be one."

Dan eased himself down onto the worn leather. "Uh, yessir. What seems to be—"

Oleksa was also famous for never letting a mid finish a sentence, though he'd been observed to listen meekly and without interrupting to Major Bartranger, his direct superior. He tapped the folder. "Got a report of sexual activity."

Dan tensed. His night with Mignon? He said tightly, "Sir, if you—"

"*Criminal* activity, to be precise." Oleksa shifted in his chair, looking away. "Fortunately, not in our company, though I believe you know the midshipman involved. The batt officer tasked me with it, to avoid any appearance of favoritism. But before I shoot this up the chain, I want more details. Mr. Door's out sick, and you're our honor rep, right? Investigate. Fast, and make as few waves as you can."

Dan relaxed. So it wasn't about him. But whoever it was, it might be messy. "Aye, aye, sir." He tried not to sound reluctant. "If you—"

Oleksa spun the prop on a little model submarine. "I was at home. I can only hang on to it for twenty-four hours. So get back to me ASAP. By, say, 0800."

Dan glanced at his watch. Not much time. In fact, given it was almost taps now, no time at all. But when they told you to take a message to Garcia, you didn't ask who Garcia was, or where, or how you were supposed to get there. "Yessir," he said again. "I'll need to—"

"Dismissed." Oleksa was already reaching for his phone. Dan wondered who he was calling. His wife? He got to his feet. Came to attention, then let himself out.

The p-way was echoing with the slappy-slap of flip-flops as a giggle of towel-turbaned females headed for the showers. He leaned against the bulkhead and opened the folder. Two sheets. The first was the COMDT-MIDNINST 1610.2 Form Two, colloquially known as the Pap Sheet, the Fry Notice, the Form Deuce.

Propped against the tile, Dan surreptitiously checked out the girls' bare legs under their issue b-robes. A short segundo gave him a glare and he forced his attention back to the folder.

Mids could be papped, fried, zapped, or more formally, placed on report. Running his gaze down the paper, he tensed.

Accused: Mario Patterson, Midshipman Fourth Class. Created By: Midshipman Easton R. Davis, Midshipman Lieutenant. Level Awarded: Major Offense. Primary Offense: Article 04.03, acts of a sexual nature on the grounds of the Naval Academy. Secondary Offense(s): Articles 04.02, fraternization of a sexual nature; 04.05, disrespect and insubordination; 02.02, direct and intentional violation of oral orders. And finally, handwritten in on the side, *Honor Violation: Lying to superior officer.*

He puckered a whistle. Davis was throwing the book at the plebe. But the main charge . . . acts of a sexual nature? The incident summary lifted his eyebrows even farther.

Reporting midshipman entered shower area in MacDonough Hall after lacrosse practice approximately 1605 to find lights out in area. Turned lights on to find Midshipman Fourth Class Mario Patterson engaged in sexual intercourse with a second person, small in stature, apparently male, face not visible. Both were partially clothed. The reporting midshipman ordered both members to stand fast. Instead they attempted to escape in different directions.

Reporting officer having recognized Midshipman Patterson, he tried to pursue the other participant via an alternate exit from the shower area. Midshipman Patterson then grabbed reporting officer forcibly preventing him from pursuing. The second participant escaped.

Midshipman Patterson requested reporting senior not to report the incident. On an explanation being requested, he stated the activity witnessed was nonsexual horseplay.

Dan whistled again and flipped to the second page. The preliminary inquiry report. Blank. Obviously, Oleksa expected him to fill it out.

"Now taps. Taps. Lights out. Maintain silence about the decks," the 1MC stated. Back at the mate's desk, Sheldon was flicking off the overheads. Not to complete darkness—every third fluorescent still glowed—but gloom fell over the company area, the normally brightly illuminated passageways now tunnels bored through night.

Dan lowered the folder, staring at the bulkhead opposite as Muff and Donkey slunk past. Rates were off after taps. "Mister Lenson, sir," DuKay ventured. Dan ignored him, rubbing his mouth. "Shit," he muttered.

A passing youngster gave him a side-eye, seemed poised to stop, then didn't. Yeah, Dan would have preferred to drop this hot potato too. Unfortunately, it had just been jammed up his . . . up the usual place.

Davis had rung the bell on all three possible ways to screw his least favorite plebe.

And it wasn't going to be easy, coming up with a recommendation for what to do.

* * *

Back in his room, the desk light on, the window jacked for a breeze. A binder open in front of him, and Dan's head in his hands. Scherow was already snoring. Out like a light, the way he always slept. As soon as his head hit the pillow, nose turned to the bulkhead, he was zonked.

Every mid had a copy of the regs, also known as COMDTMIDNINST 1610, aka the Administrative Performance and Conduct System Manual, on his desk. Signed for, so ignorance could be no excuse for the scores of separate conduct offenses possible, from abuse of a public animal to murder. Well, not actually murder; that was punishable by court-martial. The Uniform Code of Military Justice applied to mids just as much as to the white hat in the Fleet.

But the real shocker in this report was the single sentence, actually just two words.

Apparently male.

Sexual activity, in and of itself, was a conduct offense, even if consensual. There were a few cases every semester since women had joined the Brigade. He actually knew one guy, over in 22nd Company, who'd nearly been separated over a drunken hookup. She was a plebe, he a second class, but the assault charge had been dismissed when she said it was mutual attraction. They both got Class As and she was transferred to a different company.

But *homosexual* activity . . . He cracked his red leather-bound copy of the Uniform Code of Military Justice, the textbook from his Military Law course. Article 125:

(a) Any person subject to this chapter who engages in unnatural carnal copulation with another person of the same or opposite sex or with an animal is guilty of sodomy. Penetration, however slight, is sufficient to complete the offense.

(b) Any person found guilty of sodomy shall be punished as a court-martial may direct.

The penalty was five years' imprisonment, forfeiture of all pay and allowances, and a dishonorable discharge.

Dan blew out, looked enviously at his roommate again—few things were as scarce and longed-for at Navy as sleep—and decided to start with Davis.

* * *

The nameplate on the door had the Chiquita banana sticker that meant, or at least claimed, the occupant had had sex inside the bounds of the Yard. "Yeah," a voice yelled. "C'mon in."

Davis was still up, klaxed feet propped on his desk, lighting a pipe. *The LOG* lay on his desk, open to the "Company Cutie" centerfold. The room was redolent with scented smoke. Against regs, to smoke in one's room. But no mid put a classmate on report, unless ordered to by an officer. The other rack was a bare mattress. Apparently the guy roomed solo. Uncommon, but not unheard of.

"Got a minute?" Dan said. "That Pap Sheet on Patterson. My company officer wants me to check it out."

"Not much more to it." The other firstie planted his feet on the deck. He moved a portable typewriter from his desk to the empty bunk and pulled over a pair of what were obviously his class shoes. He plunked them on the pinup, popped a can of Kiwi, licked a rag, and started massaging polish into the cracked leather. "Happened like I wrote. What else you need to know?" He nodded to a chair.

Dan sat, squared a yellow tablet on his lap, and clicked his issue Skilcraft. "I just need the dump."

"Told you. Read the Form Deuce."

"I need to hear it from you."

"Well, like I said. I left my towel in the shower yesterday. When I went back, the lights were out. I flip 'em on and holy shit, there's two fags going at it hot and heavy."

Dan wrote *Going at it.* "What exactly were they doing? Nuke it for me."

"I couldn't see a dick but it was obvious what was going down. Patterson's skivvies were at half-mast. The other guy, couldn't see his face. But he was into whatever they were doing, if you know what I mean."

Dan nodded. "Then what? You yelled for them to stop?"

"Yeah, 'halt,' and like that. I turn around to see if there's anybody else out in the locker area to back me up. A witness. By the time I look back the little guy's tearing ass out of there. Ha ha. Taking the back door. So to speak." He grinned.

Dan made another note. "Then what?"

"I had Patterson cold, so I run past him to try to catch the other queer. The moke grabs my arm and swings me into the bulkhead. Hit my arm on the shower handle." Davis pulled up his skivvy sleeve to display a bruise. "I ordered him to let go but he hung on. By the time he unhands me the other fag's gone."

Dan consulted the Form Two. "That accounts for the act of a sexual nature. And fraternization of a sexual nature. Grabbing you, that's the 04.05, disrespect and insubordination. Not letting you go, that's 02.02, violation of an order?"

"Roger."

Dan opened the regs, which he'd tabbed with a yellow tailor-shop chit. "How come you didn't charge him with 04.21?"

"What's that?"

"Physical violence."

"Well, I don't think he meant to hurt me." Davis winked. "Actually, you know, I might could've slipped on that wet deck and gone into the wall myself."

Dan noted that. "Finally, written in on the side, 'Honor Violation: Lying to superior officer.' That your handwriting?"

Davis nodded, working polish into the welt with an old toothbrush, its handle half melted off. "Correct."

"In what way did he utter a falsehood?" Dan smiled. That sounded pretty cool. Maybe he should think about being a JAG officer. No, maybe not.

"He said they were just farting around. Skylarking. When it was obvious it wasn't."

Someone tapped at the door. Cracked it and thrust in a foil-covered tray. "Hot dogs, guys? Relish, mustard, ketchup, and kraut. Dollar apiece." The two firsties yelled, "No," and "Get the fuck out."

With the door closed again, Dan said, "Just to point out, you can't pap somebody with both a conduct and an honor violation at the same time."

"No, they're two different charges." Davis set the first shoe aside and started on the other. "Sucking dick is a conduct violation. Lying about it's an honor violation."

Dan granted him that, but said it required a separate report. Davis shrugged. "Okay. Cross it out. I'll see our honor rep about the other. But, you know, I don't think Snowflake'll be around long enough for that. Once the gay stuff goes up the line."

Dan sat with a blank mind for a moment, watching Davis's fingers circle on the toe cap. Bringing it to a gloss. What else? Oh yeah. "You sure nobody else saw this go down, Easy?"

Davis looked, for the first time, evasive. He squinted at the sole. "Shit, this thing's got a hole. . . . Like I said, nobody. Just me and these two chocolate soldiers. Going at it right there. Open and shut. Right?"

Dan splayed his fingers, like *I guess we'll see.* He clicked his pen, tapped his teeth with it. "You really had it in for this kid. Out on the field. Remember? Said you were gonna run him out."

Davis snorted. "So I made this up, to get him booted? I may be a hard-ass, but I'm not that low. This fool wears his fucking name tag upside down half the time. A no-load. A shitforbrains nonperformer. He'll drag our company out of the Color Competition all on his own."

"Okay." You assumed a classmate was telling the truth. "Anything else?"

"You gonna talk to Patterson now?"

Dan nodded.

"He'll lie to you."

"Well, I still need his side of the story." Dan rose, flipping the folder shut.

The other firstie licked the rag again. The polish was making his tongue black. "You're gonna let me know where this goes, classmate?"

"Sure. I guess."

Davis set the second, finished shoe beside the first. "Yeah, you're right.

About me thinking we're better off without this guy. But I know what I saw, Dan. Believe me. I know what I saw."

* * *

The plebes had their door open, as per regs. They scrambled to their feet when he came in. A four-man room. The other three fourth-class had books open. Studying by flashlight. Which was nonreg after taps. Patterson was in his bunk. Dan eyed the others and jerked his head to the side. "The passageway. Or the head. Just not in here."

They grabbed b-robes and fled. Patterson slid reluctantly from his rack and perched on the windowsill, stick-thin arms crossed over his chest. Just as unattractive, pimpled, massive-nosed as ever. Well, no one looked good as a plebe. Behind him the glass of the half-open window was dark. A breeze cooled the room, rippling the sleeves of the issue white-and-blue-striped pj's, which no one but plebes ever wore. Dark circles rimmed his eyes. He said nothing.

Dan skated the folder onto the desk and grabbed a chair. "Guess you can figure why I'm here."

"Mister Davis. Sir."

"Yeah. My company officer tasked me with the prelim investigation. Want to tell me about it?"

"What's Mr. Davis say happened? Sir."

"I want your account, independent of his. So I can help Admin decide what to do."

The plebe uncrossed his arms, looking uncertain. "Do I get a lawyer? Or something. Coach?"

"So far it's just a conduct investigation." Dan didn't add, though it could go to UCMJ. "So no, you don't. Just give it to me straight, okay?"

"Yessir." Patterson ran his hands through dark half-inch stubble. "Davis—like I told you out on the field, Mr. Davis wants to run me out. Said so in front of everybody. Now he's making up this story, to get me discharged. I didn't do what he says."

"Okay." Dan kept his tone neutral as he leaned back, teetering the front legs of the chair in the air. "Let's have it."

"Like I told him, we was just horsing around. Slapping each other with towels, like that. There wasn't nothing—anything sexual about it."

Dan nodded. He wrote *horseplay*, more for show than anything else. He'd thought about the next question, how to pose it. "Sounds harmless. Who was this other guy you were horsing around with? Another plebe?"

Patterson looked away. "Just some guy, happened to be in there. I don't know his name."

Dan said, eyes on his notepad, "White or Black?"

"He was . . . I don't know. Sir."

"You don't know. Or a plebe, or an upperclassman?"

"No, sir. It was dark."

"So Mr. Davis said. Why were the lights off? Did you turn them off?"

No answer. The plebe's gaze stayed on the deck. He was hugging himself again.

Dan sighed. Really, he didn't have a dog in this fight. If the kid was gay, sure, it was a violation of the UCMJ. And a sin, at least they said so in church. But he remembered how his own firstie had damn near run him out. And something about the kid reminded him of . . . himself.

Regardless, innocent until proven guilty. Maybe he *had* just been farting around, and Davis had seized the opportunity to bilge him. Usually no one wanted to feed another mid to the meat grinder. Everyone in Bancroft regarded Admin as a malevolent and all-too-personal enemy. But the competition to be the lead company in the battalion, and in the Brigade, was cutthroat. One nonperformer could cost everybody extra liberty and color ranking.

He glanced at the door, to make sure no one was eavesdropping. "Mario? Listen up now. If you give me a name, and he confirms the two of you were just grab-assing around, that's two to one against what Mr. Davis says. Enough to torpedo a major charge. I can probably get you off with good judgment, failure to use. Or conduct prejudicial to good discipline. Ten or twenty demerits. You can walk off that in a couple weekends."

He sat forward, waiting. If the guy wasn't gay, he should have no problem naming his buddy. If he was, turning the other in won him nothing . . . it just meant they'd both go down.

The ineluctable logic of Navy regs. If the kid *was* gay, he had no good options. If he told the truth, it was a court-martial, five years in the brig, and a dishonorable discharge. If he didn't, Davis would take him before the honor board, and he'd be separated for lying.

Patterson looked away. "I told you, I don't know who it was. Sir."

Dan rocked back again, contemplating the downturned face. He had only one card left to push into the kid's hand. "Um . . . okay. How 'bout this: Easy, Mr. Davis, says he thought this person he caught a quick look at was a guy. 'Small in stature,' but a guy. But was it a female? One of your WUBA classmates, maybe? In which case it's a major conduct infraction. But, consensual, I'd guess, ballpark, eighty demerits. A D in conduct for the semester, and restriction until Christmas leave." It might be more than that, and the annual limit was 180 demerits, so the kid would be walking a razor blade the rest of the year. And he'd still have the problem of coming up with the girl's name, and getting her to confirm.

Patterson hesitated, obviously thinking it over. Finally he said, lifting that long chin with some remnant of dignity, "I would prefer not to answer that, sir."

Hopeless. Dan clapped his hands on his thighs, giving up. "Uh, okay. So. Easy, I mean Mr. Davis, says you asked him not to report the incident. That right?"

"Yes, sir. 'Cause it was just horseplay. Like I said." The lip came out, the downturned face grew darker.

"One last question. Again. Did you turn the lights off? Or did this other person?"

"They were off when I went in."

"You went in, in the dark, ran into this . . . individual . . . you didn't know, and started *wrestling* with them?"

No answer. Patterson looked resigned. Despondent. Dan gave him another five seconds, then sighed. He slammed the chair down and stood. "Okay, that'll have to satisfy them. Oleksa'll probably want to see you tomorrow. You and he can take it from there."

The evicted roommates were standing across the passageway. They glanced at Dan, then away. One looked as if he was about to say something. "Yeah?" Dan asked him. "What? Pipe the fuck up, you got anything to contribute."

"No excuse. Sir."

"Okay, then lemme ask *you* something. Your roomie, there. Anything interesting about him?"

They exchanged glances. Finally one said, "He helps us with our skinny."

"Oh yeah? He's good at math?"

"Except he keeps arguing with the prof," another said.

Not what he had in mind. He tried again. "Does he ever have visitors in your room? Like a she-mid? Does he have his Podunk girlfriend's picture in his cap?"

They exchanged glances. Averted their eyes. At last one said, “A girl?”

Dan waited. Another added, “Sir, permission not to bilge a classmate.”

“Granted,” Dan said. Reluctantly. Dead end, then. But Oleksa could circle back, if he wanted to. If he wasn't too busy with his wife and the twins, or agreed the Navy would be better off if this kid just got railroaded out.

He glanced back into their room one last time. Patterson was still slumped on the windowsill, head down. Was there something more he should do? Something more to suggest? He stood for a moment longer, rubbing his chin. Too bad. But Patterson should have known. The regs were clear, after all.

He sighed, and headed back to type up his report.

11

The Hague

Corris visited every day. Dan took his meals alone at a table in the detention center mess hall. The fare was heavy on meat and cheese, with freshly baked bread and sweet cream butter. He'd better watch his waistline. Twice a day he could walk in the chain-linked exercise area, or work out in the gym. He shot baskets from the foul line and pounded out laps around the court. Through the windows a church spire was the only building visible. Now and then the distant chime of a carillon floated on the heavy air.

In his cell, he studied the *Rules of Procedure and Evidence*, a thick tome dense with legalese and references to various articles that had to be traced out from section to section. There was a lot about protecting witnesses and affording the accused a proper defense, and who was responsible for punishment or imprisonment. But it said little about the trial itself. For a break, he allowed himself a few pages of a James Salter autobiography from the library.

The day of the hearing a guard woke him at seven. He dressed, shaved, and put on the clean white shirt and tie Corris had brought. The attorney had wanted him in uniform, but Dan had refused. He wanted to involve the Navy as little as possible. Actually, he was surprised not to have been relieved of duty yet. But officially he was still on leave.

Obviously, if convicted and sentenced, he wouldn't be returning to Larson Hall. Most likely he'd stay here, at Scheveningen Prison, but in another wing, a separate facility for those convicted by various international tribunals.

The same white van took him back to the ICC. He walked back over the water hazard, on the glass-railinged ramp, ahead of his guards. It wasn't raining this time, but the sky was still that threatening gray. At the far end waited the same blonde who'd checked him in. Mukhtar Corris stood beside her, carrying a leather briefcase. Without a word, she led the way to an elevator.

They emerged into a courtroom far bigger than the gym he'd shot hoops in. The ceilings were so high they were nearly invisible. He blinked, dazzled. Everything was white. So white. White panels on the walls. White tile floors. Awkward, sterile-looking ranks of stark white desks, each with screen and keyboard. Above, to left and right, glassed-in galleries looked down. No one was visible up there yet. "For the translators," Corris murmured. At the back of the room a beige curtain stretched from wall to wall. Fully a dozen cameras angled to cover every millimeter of the courtroom.

And in the front, on raised daises, two rows of seats, obviously for the judges. Not white, but pale wood. And so far, empty.

The blonde led them to places in the center of the front row. Margaretha was already there, in the same subdued pinstripes as her boss.

Corris patted Dan's hand. "Do not worry, Admiral. We have a strong defense. Let us see what they present. Then we will discuss our response. Here are your headphones. This dial selects the language you wish to use, to follow the proceedings."

Dan chose English, and tried them on, but no one was speaking yet.

Gradually the room filled. Men and women filed into the galleries, donned headphones. With a grinding hum, the curtain at the back of the courtroom retracted, revealing a high, glassed-in gallery. Filled, he saw, with spectators, and probably the fucking media too.

A swarthy man in dishdasha and ghutra, with a Mephistophelian beard, shuffled papers across the room from them. Dan muttered, "Is that the prosecutor?"

"Yes. That is Al-Mughrabi."

Blair had mentioned him, and an online search at the library had furnished more detail. Dr. Amir Al-Mughrabi was a former Appeals Division judge, International Criminal Court. From Morocco, though his family was Lebanese. He'd been involved in prosecutions for civil war and genocide in Lebanon, Rwanda, Syria, and Ukraine. Had overseen investigations into alleged Coalition war crimes in Afghanistan and Iraq. Studying his thin, dark face, overhung with thick eyebrows, Dan was reminded of Fahad Almarshadi—his wiry, nervous, birdlike exec when Dan had assumed command of *Savo Island*. And who'd taken his own life with a nine-millimeter bullet.

Their gazes met. To his surprise Al-Mughrabi inclined his head. A vanishingly faint bow?

"All rise," the blond woman announced. "The International Criminal Court is now in session." She repeated this in French and German, then in a fourth language Dan didn't recognize.

Everyone stood. He got to his feet as well, as the judges filed in. Of mixed ethnicities, four women and one man. All wore deep blue robes with lacy white jabots. "No wigs. I'm disappointed," he muttered to Corris.

The barrister forced a chuckle, clearly less in amusement than to humor his client.

When they were seated again, Dan turned the volume up on his headset. One of the female judges, gray-haired, the senior one, he assumed, read a statement. Slowly, so the translators could follow. Dan was getting it in English, in a monotonous German- or Dutch-inflected voice. She recounted how the charges had been brought and by whom, and that the preliminary prosecution had found evidence a crime might have been committed. The nonparty state not having commenced civil or military proceedings, the case had been brought to the ICC by the government of Germany.

Dan turned the pages on the printed copy of the charges Corris had given him.

The main allegation, stripped of legalese, was that international law, embodied in various treaties and conferences—listed at wearying length—specified a duty of mariners to rescue anyone in distress at sea. This applied in wartime as well. Dan had neglected that duty when he'd had the means and opportunity. Thus, he bore direct responsibility for the thirty-plus lives lost aboard *Stuttgart*.

A short recess. He stayed in his seat, discussing strategy with Corris.

Then it was time for the prosecution to open.

Al-Mughrabi rose. Dan leaned forward, centering his legal pad in front of him. Corris and his partners adjusted their headphones, looking expectant.

The prosecutor began, his English carefully enunciated but French accented. "Good morning. The sea, like space and certain other locales, is a venue of inherent danger to human life. International law is clear on a mutual duty to assist those 'in peril on the sea,' as an old Christian hymn has it. This duty to rescue is set forth in the international law of the sea, the maritime laws of various maritime countries, and international humanitarian law, including proceedings at Nuremberg.

"True, that duty is not unlimited in scope, duration, or applicability. The defense may attempt to show that the *Stuttgart*'s abandonment in the South China Sea falls under mitigating factors. Unfortunately, Admiral Lenson's actions showed a blatant disregard for the laws of war, of the sea, and even the traditional obligations of a military officer. For he left helpless mariners to die.

"The government of Germany asked that the responding state charge him with the crime. Since the United States declined, a complaint was filed with the ICC under universal jurisdiction. After investigation, a warrant was issued. Still Washington refused to acknowledge the responsibilities of a responding state."

The prosecutor turned toward the defense bench and inclined his head again. "To his credit, Admiral Lenson decided to appear in his own defense. This I praise. But it cannot be allowed to mitigate his guilt. That would signal to all combatants, for all time, that the duty to rescue no longer obtains in wartime. This case will set a precedent for generations to come.

"Finally, we will show that this is not the first time Daniel V. Lenson has committed this particular crime."

A nudge at his elbow made Dan glance down. A note from Margaretha. *What does he mean, not the first time?*

Dan closed his eyes. He'd nearly forgotten.

He'd left men to die before.

* * *

West of the Luzon Strait, many years before. The night had been black, impenetrable, blustery. The frigate formerly known as USS *Oliver C. Gaddis* was saber-sawing into ten-foot seas driven by an oncoming typhoon. Dangerously low on fuel, without orders, manned by a sullen and restive crew.

She flew no flag. To send a message to a shadowy enemy, while protecting US interests by making Dan's actions deniable.

They'd met that enemy. And sent her to the bottom.

Clinging to the gyro repeater, he'd stared down. Oil slicked the passing waves, gentling them. Limp, unmoving bodies, life jackets, and debris rose and fell on that anointed sea.

Here and there men gestured at the ship that slowly passed by. Some raised their arms in surrender. Others shook fists. Yet most simply regarded him silently as they rose and fell on the swells. His mind skittered, like an operating system hunting for a lost program.

A knot of the castaways slid down the frigate's side, thirty yards off.

An easy toss with a heaving line. Their keening came through the howl of the wind. They waved blackened oil-smeared arms. Holding up their hands to him. Pleading for rescue to *him*—

He'd dropped life jackets and rafts, but in the face of the oncoming storm it was only a gesture. He hadn't picked them up. He couldn't.

He blinked, recalled to the courtroom by a tug on his arm. Another note, this time from Corris: *What is he talking about?*

Dan scrawled, *Discuss later.*

* * *

Corris presented the defense's arguments in sober, measured tones. Speaking slowly, for the translators. He pointed out that a major exception to the duty to save life under the UN Convention on the Law of the Sea was a corresponding obligation not to endanger the salving ship and crew. The convention also granted an exception in Regulation 331: that if a ship receiving an SOS considered it "unreasonable" to act, it need not do so, though the inaction had to be logged.

"The defense will prove that Admiral Lenson's actions were consistent with both provisions, as well as the laws of war. However, as Dr. Al-Mughrabi asserts his responses were not in accordance with the doctrine of the responding state, I will introduce our first insider witness, Captain Cheryl Staurulakis, United States Navy."

Dan sat back, forcing an untroubled expression. He hadn't wanted to call her, but Corris had insisted. In the absence of printed tactical instructions, someone had to testify for him.

His former exec, later CO of *Savo* in her own right, appeared on screens before the defense and prosecution. The judges turned to their personal monitors. Dan glanced up; the same video flickered in the press gallery. Cheryl looked less haggard than she had during the war. He rubbed his mouth as Corris led her through her testimony.

"Exactly, counselor. The admiral's actions were in accord with doctrine at that time. There was an active enemy submarine in the area. We suspected it was actually inside our defensive perimeter. Going alongside would have placed the assisting ship in mortal danger."

Corris introduced a historical reference. In September of 1914, a German submarine had torpedoed a British cruiser in the North Sea, HMS *Aboukir.* When two other warships had approached to rescue the survivors, *U-9* had torpedoed *Cressy* and *Hogue* too, one after the other. "That lingers in the Navy's memory, does it not? That to render aid to a torpedoed ship, when the attacker is still at large, is suicide?"

Staurulakis looked thoughtful. *"I don't recall hearing that particular incident mentioned, but it's certainly in our doctrine. We avoid entering what we call the torpedo danger area, except to carry out an attack."*

Corris nodded. "But this torpedo came from the south, correct? Striking the other side of *Stuttgart* from your vessel, which was alongside taking on fuel. Meaning, if *Savo* had stayed to render assistance, she might have been shielded by the larger vessel, and thus safe from attack."

Staurulakis said dryly, *"Sir, a submarine operating in wartime tries hard to make itself difficult to locate. Yes, the torpedo came from the far side of the formation. My initial recommendation was to place our ship between what we guessed was the firing position, and the tanker.*

"We quickly thought better of that, for three reasons. First, the submarine could reposition at will. Second, it already had a firing solution on the tanker, and Savo *would have been exposed during the approach. Finally, it made more sense to send a lower-value unit, USS* Mitscher, *in to prosecute, with the help of our embarked helicopter."*

Corris nodded. Thanked her, and bowed toward the prosecution. "Your witness."

Al-Mughrabi got to his feet. His robe whispered as he paced back and forth. Then looked into what Dan assumed was the video camera, on a tripod centerlined between the benches. "So in essence, then-Captain Lenson placed a subordinate ship in the danger zone, while withdrawing his own; and taking essentially no action to assist the survivors of *Stuttgart.*"

Cheryl didn't blink. "Savo *was the higher-value unit."*

"You mean, the more expensive? Or with the most senior officer aboard? Please explain."

Cheryl said calmly, *"At that time,* Savo Island *was the only antiballistic missile–capable ship between Taiwan and Japan. Her loss or damage would have put hundreds of thousands of lives at risk. Both Navy doctrine and common logic meant standing clear was the only course a reasonable commander could take."*

The prosecutor studied his notes. "Is it true that your promotion opportunities depend on his evaluations?"

"No, sir. He is no longer in my chain of command and I am free to testify without concern for my career."

Al-Mughrabi shrugged, looking unconvinced. But finally murmured, "No further questions of this witness."

* * *

They adjourned for the day. The guards escorted Dan out and loaded him back into the van. Back in the prison cafeteria he slumped in his chair, wrung out. Depressed. And this was only day one.

"You the American? All right if we join you?"

When he looked up, two men stood holding trays. They were both in the gray prison jumpsuits. He nodded at the empty chairs. "Sure. Grab a seat."

The large, fiftyish, shaven-headed man said he was from the Democratic Republic of Ashaara. The slight, mustached Middle Easterner in sunglasses was from Syria. "Never before has an American been tried here," the African said. "Up to now, only Africans. And I think Yugoslavia. Serbians."

"*I* am not an African." The Syrian frowned. He kept shaking Dan's hand, his own very soft. "I am glad to make your acquaintance. You are the one who torpedoed the German ship and left them to drown, yes? It is good we can meet."

"Uh, not exactly." Dan felt uncomfortable. Their names were familiar. The African was a former prime minister accused of genocide. The Syrian had been a GRU-trained torturer for the Assad regime. And both were giving him the same depthless stare . . . the same . . . *vibes* . . . he'd gotten once from another mass murderer, in Srebrenica.

Speaking of which . . . he glanced around warily; wasn't Ratko Mladic imprisoned here too? But, yeah, in the separate wing. "Not exactly. The ship was already torpedoed. I had to leave the scene. Orders."

"Orders, of course." The Syrian nodded eagerly. "To duty we owe obedience, we military men, no? A strong defense. At least, *circonstances atténuantes* . . . ?"

"Mitigating circumstances," the African supplied. His big puffy hands closed and opened on the table, as if gripping reins. "Anyway, it is political theater. Being judged by the same Europeans who conquered and enslaved Africa in the first place. Oh, yes, very fair. If we are guilty, everyone is guilty. You play chess?" He sounded hopeful.

"A little."

"We must have a game! To pass the time."

A Dutch guard sauntered over. Dan expected him to break their conversation up, but he simply stood there listening. Maybe he was bored too.

"Would you like to play now?" the African said.

"Um, not right now, thanks. I really have to concentrate on my defense."

"Of course, of course. Forgive us for interrupting you."

* * *

The next day, back in court. This time, apparently, it was the prosecutor's innings.

Dan looked across the room at a face he'd only glimpsed at a distance, across a heaving sea.

Reinhard Geisinger.

Stuttgart's former captain was in a dark blue jacket with gold stripes, probably German merchant marine service dress. Geisinger raised his hand to be sworn in. "I solemnly declare that I will speak the truth, the whole truth and nothing but the truth."

Al-Mughrabi led him through the disaster. From the torpedo strike to the loss of power, the pumps going silent. Massive flooding had listed the huge replenishment ship to port within minutes. Midships had become an impassible inferno of fuel-fed flame, menacing the missiles and shells on deck to be transferred. The after lifeboats had been destroyed, trapping those survivors on the afterdeck.

The court hushed when the prosecutor asked, "To whom was your call for assistance directed? From whom did you request help?"

"From the task force commander. Captain Lenson." He pointed a trembling finger at Dan.

"And his response? Do you recall the exact words?"

Geisinger twisted in his seat to face Dan, cheeks blanched a pale ivory. "He said: 'You are on your own.' I protested this abandonment. But received no response."

Al-Mughrabi nodded. "I introduce the log of USS *Savo Island* on the day in question. At time 1338, 1:38 P.M. local time, the distress call is logged. Shortly thereafter the ship turns south, toward the stricken vessel. Four minutes later, it makes another turn, heading away. Can you explain this?"

Geisinger said, "The explanation is simple. The deck officer began to approach us, to render assistance. Then Lenson countermanded the order and fled."

"How many died as a result?"

"I would say . . . all twenty. On the ship, and afterward, when several drowned awaiting rescue."

The prosecutor let those words hang under the high ceiling, in the stare of the cameras. In their high loggia the translators' lips writhed silently. Dan sat with hands folded, staring at nothing as the judges impassively looked down at him.

* * *

Al-Mughrabi called the second mate from *Stuttgart*, who'd been on the bridge when Geisinger had pleaded for help, to corroborate. He added details, but the testimonies matched. As the mate stepped down, the prosecutor turned to Corris and Dan. "Your witness."

Corris rose, shuffled papers, and cleared his throat. Walked across to Geisinger, looking thoughtful, or perhaps regretful, and smiled. "Captain. I am sorry for your loss, of your ship and friends. No blame attaches to you, I am sure. But . . . a few questions, if you please. To elucidate."

"That is what I am here for," the German said stiffly, darting a glare at Dan.

"How many were lost, of your crew, again?"

"Twenty men all told. Nineteen crew members."

"Who was the one not a member of your crew?"

"A Dr. Schell, from *Savo Island.* He was returning to the US. We cross-decked him with a female naval intelligence agent. She made it across just before the torpedo struck."

"I see. Of the twenty, how many were killed in the initial explosion?"

Geisinger looked away. "We could not recover bodies. The fire was too intense. The danger of the explosives."

"To the best of your knowledge, then."

Geisinger said reluctantly, "Nine we lost track of belowdecks, operating the elevators and pumps for the replenishment."

"Nine. Of those, how many were still alive when you abandoned ship?"

The captain hesitated. He glanced at Al-Mughrabi, who returned a nod. Finally he said, "I had no way of knowing that."

"Did you send a search party to the pump room, the magazines, belowdecks? To see if they were trapped, and could be released?"

Geisinger shifted in his chair. "I . . . had no time."

"Yet you had time to retrieve your logs, deploy the forward lifeboats, and get your crew into them. Climb down into one, yourself."

Al-Mughrabi jumped to his feet to object. One of the judges waved him back down. *"Ga door met praten,"* she said. The voice in Dan's headphones didn't translate that.

Corris went on, forcing Geisinger to enumerate, step-by-step, what he'd done in the aftermath of the torpedo strike. Forcing him to list each act, and how long it had taken. Underlining, in the process, how he'd failed to search for those either killed outright or possibly still alive, but trapped deeper in the ship. The mild-mannered, even-toned attorney was slowly eviscerating the man on the stand.

It was unfair, of course. Hindsight was easy. Dan had been aboard other stricken, burning ships. You did what you could, amid severed communications, smoke, conflicting reports, and panic.

But the judges weren't mariners. Had probably never been to sea, except on a vacation cruise.

Corris said, "Let us proceed to the aftermath, in the lifeboats. How many remained at that point?"

"Fifteen, including myself."

"Including yourself. As you said, you were the last to leave the ship, yes? . . . at least, not counting those you left behind. In the midships section, and on the afterdeck."

Geisinger rubbed his nose. His face, pale at first, was flushed now. "Amidships . . . they were already lost."

"So far as you knew, yes? Though you did not send to make sure. And those trapped on the afterdeck?"

"I was unable to help them. The boats were filled to capacity."

"You were 'unable to.' Why, exactly?"

"As I said, the remaining boats were already filled. The sea was at the gunwales. I had no way of knowing if anyone would rescue us. Overloading and sinking them would have killed many more. I had to think of that."

"It would have killed many more," Corris repeated, addressing the court at large. "He had to think of that." He looked up at the judges. Bowed to the haunted, sweating man he'd left broken on the stand, and walked slowly back to his place.

* * *

That evening Dan asked the guard if he could shoot a few hoops, though it wasn't a recreational period. The woman looked reluctant, but finally shrugged.

The gym echoed emptily. He ran, dribbled, and shot, the tennis shoes he'd been issued squeaking on the varnished floor. On and on until he was soaked with perspiration, trying to shake the black dog following him since Geisinger's testimony.

But it didn't help.

That night new signs had been set up in the dining hall. They directed the defendants currently on trial to one side of the cafeteria. Another group, in blue rather than gray coveralls, was standing in line on the far side.

A single table was set on the ICC half. The dictator and the torturer were already there, arguing in French. Dan threw a few things onto his plate and carried it over. He was cutting into the breaded veal when a shadow loomed over him.

"You are Lenson, yes?"

He glanced up, frowning. And after a moment, recognized the intruder.

The bulky body was even heavier now. The gray hair now white. But the very small, very pale blue irises, the thick peaked eyebrows, and slabbed doughy cheeks were the same.

Back then this man had worn a utility uniform, a soft cap, expensive-looking leather gloves. He'd laughed jovially, and his breath had smelled of fruit brandy.

Dan had faced terrorists. Had been tortured by Saddam's Mukhabarat. But the aura of pure evil that had emanated from General Ratko Mladic had outdone them all.

He'd ordered his thugs to take Dan 'where the wolves fucked.' Srebrenica still played in his mind's theater whenever he heard the lazy buzzing of fat spring flies. They'd shot his escorts, Jovan and Zlata, in front of him. Then, for whatever reason, had left him alive, to find his own way back to NATO lines.

He remembered what Zlata had told him about the siege of Sarajevo: *If you run, you hit the bullet. If you walk, the bullet hits you.*

Now the premier and the torturer stared up as Mladic shook Dan's shoulder. His other hand was shoved into a pocket. "Lenson, yes? The one who denounced me."

"I'm Lenson, yeah. " Dan meant to add all he'd done was report what he'd seen. What Mladic had intended him to see, to say "fuck you" to NATO and the US president.

But the concealed hand was coming out of the pocket. And with it, a gleam of sharpened metal.

Dan managed to thrust a lifted arm between his throat and the descending blade. But he was trapped in his chair, gripped by the shoulder, though he strained upward against the downward pressure of Mladic's still-beefy arm. The guy was much stronger than he looked. Maybe they had a gym on the prison side of the complex as well. With his free hand Dan grabbed for the guy's balls, but with his attacker turned sideways most of what he got was a handful of jumpsuit.

Mladic bellowed, twisted free, and attacked again, slashing downward with what looked like a sharpened screwdriver. Shouts rose. Guards ran toward them, drawing nightsticks and Tasers. Too far, though, way too far off. Dan kicked the chair away and dropped to his knees, hands up, searching for a grip on the descending weapon.

From two sides, bodies crashed into his attacker. The Serb grunted as the African planted a heavy fist in his midriff. The Syrian clutched Mladic's knife arm, twisting and locking it up in some fighting maneuver Dan had never seen before, until the weapon clattered to the floor.

Then the guards were on them, shoving the others away, pinning Mladic's arms, dragging the condemned mass murderer off as he shouted insults, threats, in Serbo-Croatian and mangled English. Still struggling, he stamped on a guard's foot and nearly broke free again.

A Taser sizzled. Mladic crashed to the floor, convulsing, glassy eyed. The guards grabbed his legs and towed him away across the polished tiles.

The premier dusted off those big hands. "That is the trouble with life sentence," he said, as if lecturing in a classroom. "It is better to leave no one to seek revenge. You must kill him first, Admiral, if you are sent to the UNDU. There is no other way."

Dan grabbed the table and hoisted himself off the floor, gasping. Noticing for the first time a gash on his arm where the shiv had slashed skin. Blood stained his shirt, dripping onto the deck. A quarter second's hesitation and Mladic would have buried it in his neck. Aimed down through the clavicle into his heart. The classic close-quarters killing stroke. Caught from behind, Dan hadn't been able to defend himself.

"Thanks," he said to his two defenders. "You saved my life."

The Syrian grinned mirthlessly. "Oh, we are all innocents together, yes?"

The premier leaned in, dropped a hand on Dan's shoulder, and muttered, "Perhaps, since we are friends now, you can find a way to repay us."

* * *

The infirmary. The sting of a local anesthetic. Stitches. Bandages. Antibiotics, and a glass of cold water to take them with.

Back in his cell that night, with the door closed and the desk chair wedged against it, he stood in front of the mirror. Staring into his eyes.

Not a good day, though Corris had defended him. Tried to lessen his culpability by accusing Geisinger of the same acts of omission. And, yeah, the German probably didn't feel great about his actions either.

But that didn't mean Dan was less guilty.

The fact, hard as a blood diamond, remained: he'd left men to die.

On the other hand, he'd survived a knife attack that could have easily been fatal, thanks to a defendant just as murderous as Mladic and a torturer for the Assad regime.

Not inspiring company. But his peers, now.

He looked up, at the topmost row of window bars. A horizontal chunk of steel anchored them, probably to prevent them being pulled from the concrete. This room might resemble one in a budget hotel, but he was definitely in a cell.

If found guilty, he'd be held in the UN Detention Unit population with Mladic. It would be kill or be killed, then. As the premier had said.

He touched his belt. Usually his escorts took it away after bringing him back from court. But today someone had slipped up. His fingertips slid over the braided leather. Stout enough, probably, to take a considerable weight.

He looked at the chair, by the desk.

A cold sweat broke, and he shivered.

He unbuckled the belt and slid it through the loops until it dangled free in his hand. He looked up at the window again, judging if the height would leave his toes off the floor, once he kicked the chair away. Yeah. Probably rip the stitches in his arm open again, as he clawed at the wall while he strangled. But it would work.

He stared up.

Then turned abruptly away and crossed to the door. It held a steel flap to slide a meal tray through. He fingernailed the access open. Stuffed the belt in, until it uncoiled, clattering to the floor outside.

He washed his face, brushed his teeth, took his meds. Then lay on the narrow bunk, staring up into the gathering darkness.

12

The hieratic hush of the Rotunda, and the Friday night watch squad inspection. The colossal bronze doors wall off the evening outside. Above the ordered ranks of uniforms the huge mural of USS *South Dakota* at the Battle of the Santa Cruz Islands unrolls like a vision of a naval Valhalla.

Dan stood front and center of the offgoing watch section. For the previous twenty-four hours he'd been responsible, at least on paper, for the whole regiment. Though nothing had happened of note.

And firsties rated weekend liberty. The officer of the watch and the midshipman OOW paced slowly along the ranks, inspecting for smiles in cap covers, dull shoes, loose spiffys, dandruff on lapels, trousers that didn't break six inches above the shoe, patchy shaves, Irish pennants, hair over an inch and a half long, or any other deficiency out of dozens.

They paused in front of him. He stared ahead, motionless, gaze fixed as the cold orbs of the fourth batt officer scanned him head to toe. Then, with a step to the side, the inspector moved on.

"Atten-hut . . . dismissed!" echoed. He relaxed, shaking out his arms, and unbuckled the sword belt. Jogged back to his room . . . a quick change into civvies, slacks and shirt, a jacket for the cold; and he was out the door and headed for the gate.

* * *

He'd called Mignon, but she couldn't make it. Behind on her assigned reading. And her last letter had sounded . . . detached. It was hard to tell what girls wanted. Unfortunately, it didn't seem to be the same thing he was after.

The taxi dropped him off at the old guy's house. His MG was in the driveway, top up, keys on the seat. He debated knocking on the door, saying thanks, but got in instead. He only had a few hours off. Better make every minute count.

Benny's was packed. Cigarette smoke drifted in layers. He waved it away and fought his way to the bar. The first beer went down like penetrating oil into a cracked casting, the sweating glass chilling his fingers, the cold brew numbing his throat. God, it was good. He finished it in five long gulps and pushed it across for a refill.

Turning his back on the bar, he surveyed the room. Oddly, none of the guys from the team were here. Had they convened somewhere else, without him? Since he wasn't varsity now? No, that was paranoid. They'd show later. Or were just holing up in Bancroft studying for midterms.

He grimaced, remembering Mrs. Colson's warning. *Otherwise, you might want to consider other options than graduating from this institution.* Yeah, he should sign up for extra calc instruction.

Or . . . ask Patterson? The gawky plebe seemed to have a gift for skinny. And he'd offered.

He drained the second glass. The alcohol was hitting now, lifting his spirits. Still, no way could he ask a plebe to tutor him. Especially not while investigating the same plebe for . . . whatever the final charges turned out to be.

The bartender looked over, and he signaled for a pitcher. No point paying glass by glass, and sooner or later someone would come in to split it with.

He carried it to a table overlooking the lanes, where the haze seemed thinner. The rolling thunder of the balls competed with the chatter and shouting from the bar area. Someone fed the jukebox, and Three Dog Night blasted over the hubbub.

The pitcher was half empty when someone said, "Need help with that?"

He glanced up to alert brown eyes behind black plastic-rimmed glasses about as sexy as a French prime minister's. A serious expression, freckles. Her hair was longer than regulation and more brown than blond. A tight sweater. Jeans.

He frowned, trying to remember where he'd seen her. No way a guy could know everyone in a thousand-mid class, but when you ricocheted off each other often enough most faces were at least vaguely familiar. He tried, "Steam?"

"Excuse me?"

"Aren't we in Lieutenant Bitchey's thermo class?"

"Oh, you're a mid. No. I'm a Johnnie."

He couldn't help a double take, a wary glance around. St. John's, not far from the Academy, was a notoriously left-wing liberal arts college. Most mids' closest interaction with Johnnies was when the students threw bottles and firecrackers at the columns of mids marching to the stadium. And occasional fistfights out in town. "Uh . . . okay."

"Licia."

"Alicia?"

"*Licia.* Licia Shalayev." She pointed at the pitcher. "Want to share?"

He stole a glance at her chest. Mids didn't date Johnnies. Or talk to them, except at the stiffly formal annual croquet match that dated from God's first birthday. Still, whatever . . . He shrugged. "Why the fuck not." He flipped a hand at a chair.

She topped off her glass and slid in opposite him. She held her left leg out stiff, sliding it under the table with a grimace. Dan said, "Uh . . . I'm surprised to see one of you here. Thought it was a mid hangout."

She scowled into her glass. "We drink beer and eat pizza too." She glanced over one shoulder. "I came with some friends. But we had an argument."

"Sorry to hear that. What . . . I mean, are you in pain? Your leg."

"Apparently I've got some kind of thing where your body eats your joints. . . . I don't want to talk about it, okay?" She drained her glass and eyed his. Then refilled them both.

They talked for a while, about what they were studying, mainly. "I'm in Non-Romance languages. Classic Greek, Russian, and modern Slavic. Right now I'm translating Clement of Ohrid. He's, like, the Preslav Literary School. Where the Cyrillic script developed from the Glagolitic."

"Gee, that sounds . . . what can you do with that kind of degree?"

A sardonic smile. "I *wanted* to be an epigrapher. A kind of archaeologist, specializing in inscriptions. But now, with this disease . . ."

He kept drinking, unsure how to respond. Not much course choice at the Academy. You were an engineer, first, last, and always. This woman sounded brilliant. A fucking intellectual. She probably thought he was some kind of militarist idiot.

But she was still sitting with him, wasn't she?

* * *

Sometime later he found himself staggering out to his car. The night had turned chilly. Cloud cover glowed saffron from the lights of DC, miles to the west. East sprawled the utter darkness of the Chesapeake. Shalayev limped along beside him, by what agreement or invitation he didn't quite recall. When they got far enough from the lights, he took her hand.

It was a long, deep mouth-to-mouth kiss, tasting of Budweiser and Lay's. When they broke she exhaled. "Wow. Do they have classes for you guys in how to do that?"

"Yeah, and dancing, and drinking tea," Dan muttered, fumbling with the keys. Now he remembered. He was driving her back to her dorm. Wherever that was, since he'd never been on the St. John's campus.

"Damn, it's cold. Why didn't I bring a jacket?"

"There's a blanket in the trunk. Lemme, uh . . . lemme get that out for you."

They climbed in. When they kissed again the night reeled. Damn, he was wasted. She was too, judging by her glazed eyes, the whites glowing in the neon from the Benny's sign. The bass beat from the bar made something in his dashboard buzz like a cicada.

His hands found her breasts. She unbuttoned with her free hand, breathing hard when their mouths parted. How far could he push this? "Uh . . . this is great but . . . how about a hand job?"

But she was already unzipping his pants. A mock-malevolent smile in the faint light. *"Ne vursha ruchna rabota,"* she said into his ear. A tractor trailer whined past on 50, the engine blatting as the engine brake kicked in.

He sneezed. "What?"

"Old Church Slavonic. 'I don't give hand jobs.'"

He threw his head back as her mouth molded around his dick. "Fuck," he gasped. Mignon had never done this. Maybe there was something to be said for a liberal arts education. He squeezed his eyes shut and came almost instantly into the soft warmth, the flicking caress of her tongue.

She wiped her lips with the back of one hand. "Jeez. You're on a hair trigger tonight."

"I didn't . . . that was the first time anybody ever—"

"Yeah, I got that impression. Don't you have a girlfriend? Or, wait . . . what do you call them . . . class girls? Grease girls?"

"Class caps" and "class shoes" were good enough for class. "Grease caps" and "grease shoes" were kept spotless and ready for inspection. Where had a Johnnie picked up Yard slang? "Uh, sure, yeah, I do. But she doesn't . . ."

"Put out? I used not to either." A shadow shaded her eyes. "But now . . . Aw, fuck it. You good? Ready to take me back?"

"You don't want me to, like, do anything for you?"

"Nah, fuck it." She sat back, buttoning her blouse. Looking away as another truck blatted past. She fished out a big silver pocket watch. "Better get you back to the Yard. Before they lock the gates on you."

Yeah, he wasn't her first mid. He tucked himself back together, zipped, and started the car.

On the trip back everything seemed very dark and far too fast. It was starting to snow, which didn't help. He kept drifting off to the right, yanking the wheel back when the tires grated on gravel. Fortunately there wasn't much traffic, except for the semis. "Where are all these fucking trucks going?" he muttered. "And they're all driving like fucking maniacs."

"You're the one driving too slow."

"Want me to go faster?"

"Fuck no! You're only half on the freakin' road, anyway." She cranked the window down and stuck her head out. Coughed, then retched. "Oh, God . . . I just got the nasty all over the side of your car."

The stench of stomach acid and used beer goosed his own nausea. A glowing yellow diamond whipped past, then a red octagon. "Christ," he muttered. He'd just run a stop sign. If the cops were out . . . he slowed even more, until the needle hovered at twenty-five. Almost out of gas too. For a little car, the MG seemed to burn an awful lot of high test. And shit, the temperature gauge was in the red! He turned the heater all the way up. That might help cool the engine too. Maybe.

"Eleven-fifty." She pushed her hair back, peering at her watch. "We're not gonna make it. Look, forget about dropping me off. Just let me out here."

"We'll make it. Only a couple more blocks."

She squinted out, shading her eyes. "Do you . . . d'you even know where the fuck you are?"

"Yeah, comin' up on State Circle . . . take East down to the main gate." But as he neared the floodlit loom of the State House he saw the circle was parked solid with cars. He managed to make the turn without sideswiping a Caddy, but he was white-knuckling it now, unable to judge distances, feeling like he was peering through some viscous medium. Shalayev gasped as they narrowly missed a gray sedan backing out. "Fuck, did you even *see* that asshole? You gotta— We're gonna get killed—"

He felt for the brake but hit the gas instead. The roadster shot forward. A terrific jolt popped the hood open, obliterating sight. The car hurtled a curb and branches whipped at the windshield. He stamped frantically for the brake and the engine coughed and stalled. But they still charged on, narrowly missing trees. Shalayev screamed. Dan yanked at the emergency brake and at last they crunched to a halt, with another scraping bang that whiplashed their skulls bobblehead-doll fashion.

Silence, with a crackle from the engine. Snaps and creaks from behind, where they'd crashed through the shrubbery.

"Fuck me," Shalayev muttered. "Are we still alive?"

Dan wrenched free of his seat belt, then tried to fling the door open, but after two or three inches it banged against concrete, or stone. Someone was shouting in the distance. In the movies, crashed cars burst into flame and exploded. "Get out," he yelled. "Right now."

"Fuck. My goddamn leg—" A snapping metallic creak as her door came open.

She tumbled out and started crawling away. Ahead, around the popped hood, flashlights bobbed, searching over a clipped lawn, past pollarded trees. More lights came on, illuminating white columns. A mansion.

He slammed the door out again, something gave way, and he lunged out. A length of wrought-iron fencing protruded from the grille like tusks. He tripped over the shattered remains of statuary and was sprawled full length in a patch of vinca, watching the world spin, when flashlights approached from the house. The beams transfixed him like a B-17 over Berlin. Three dark forms stood behind them. One reached down and hauled him to his feet. "Shit, you believe this?—We're gonna need ID, kid. Know where the fuck you are?"

"Uh . . . Annapolis?"

"In the governor's front yard, dickhead. God, smell the booze fumes . . . you alone? Any passengers?"

When he glanced over, there was no trace of Shalayev. Just a crushed path through the underbrush, already erasing itself as the shrubbery straightened. He fumbled out his wallet. "I'm a mid. Naval Academy. First class."

"A first-class *drunk*," one of the voices announced.

Someone else joined them from the big house. Dan wondered if it was the governor. One of the men put his arm around his shoulders. "Ain't like none of us ever got shit-faced, amigo. But you might wanna think about not drivin' after puttin' this much away.—You call 'em, Mike?"

"On their way."

"'They' being who?" Dan asked. But a sudden revolt in his gut doubled him over, and the men stepped back as he vomited into the vinca.

* * *

When the cops arrived they took him to Taylor Avenue, where he drank powerful black station coffee sitting on a hard bench in one of the cells until the nausea passed and he began to realize how much trouble he was in. Aside from missing expiration of liberty and wrecking his new car.

* * *

The town cops turned him in at the Main Office, red-and-blue flashers strobing across T-Court as lights winked on in Bancroft. Yeah, it'd be all over the Brigade by morning meal. His head felt like 2,250 psi air was being injected directly between the left and right ventricles.

He slumped in the duty officer's cramped little pookah as the cops recounted the details. The OOD logged them, stone-faced, and handed Dan his copy of the Form 2.

Blinking desert-dry eyeballs, he scanned the carbon. Article 02.04: *Violation of MIDREGS with major effect.* 02.09: *Good judgment, failure to use.* 04.11: *Destruction or damage of government or private property.* 04.17: *Carelessness in operating a vehicle.* 05.01: *Irresponsible drinking.* 05.12: *Drunk driving or driving under the influence of alcohol.* And 05.07: *Being under the influence of alcohol in a nature that brings discredit upon the naval service.*

At least four Class A offenses. Not to mention, the cop had said something about how he'd have to pay to relandscape the mansion's garden. Add towing fees and repairs . . .

"That about cover it?" the Marine said, expressionless.

"I was back late over liberty. Sir."

"You were in police custody, so I cut you a break on that one. Since Lieutenant Oleksa's a friend of mine."

Was that Marine humor? Dan tried to look equally stoic. "Roger that, sir."

"Go to bed, Lenson. Sleep it off. Tomorrow you can put the word out, see who wants to buy your uniforms."

"Aye, aye, sir." He came to attention, almost fell, about-faced, and staggered off down the passageway.

* * *

He was deep under at last when someone shook him. It was Muff. "Get the *fuck* off me," Dan muttered, fending the plebe off with a straight-arm thrust. "It's nowhere near reveille."

"Sir, no, it isn't, but you need to come."

A confused hubbub percolated through the doorway. Muff shook him again, harder. Dan threw the covers back, furious. His window stood wide open, funneling in a freezing draft. As usual, Scherow, in the bunk opposite, was snoring like a band saw. "Do not lay hands on me," Dan snapped. *God*, his head hurt. His mouth tasted like seagulls had crapped in it.

"It's Patterson. Sir."

Fuck. "What about him?"

"You're the company commander, right? Since Mister Door's sick."

Dan blinked away sleep crusts to see other fourth class in the passageway, some in b-robes, others in skivvies. Actually, a lot of plebes. He swung his legs out, accepting the inevitable, grabbed his bathrobe off the chair, slid his feet into klax, and stumbled out.

A knot of underclass milled outside the head, wearing sweat gear. Uniforms, shoes, caps littered the deck. A midnight 'plebe ho.' One of those wonderful customs that entailed rousting the fourth class out of their racks in the middle of the night and tossing the entire contents of their rooms into the passageway. After running them back and forth through it, they'd be dismissed, with threats of room inspection in the morning.

Odd, though, that no one spoke. Pallid, shocked faces turned as he came up, his klax slapping on the freshly waxed blue tile beneath the litter of T-shirts, skivvies, socks, jockstraps. The crowd parted for him.

The head was silent. The overhead lights blazed. The restrooms, at night, offered the only privacy in a plebe's life, a resort for bullshit sessions, memorizing rates, and whacking off into wads of toilet paper. A couple of years before, when females arrived, bulkheads had been hurriedly built down the middle of each company's head, dividing them in two. The women had turned the urinals into vases for plastic flowers.

Now, on the men's side, the stall doors stood open. Dan staggered past, dreading what he'd find.

The frosted-glass window at the far end was up. A frigid wind gusted in. Snowflakes whirled between the urinals. Two plebes stood near it. One tall, one short.

"It's Mario," the tall one said, voice shaky. "Sir."

Fearing the worst, Dan crossed to the window.

The body lay far below, four decks down. The light was dim, just a bleed from the first-deck rooms and the lampposts over toward Tecumseh, but a yellow halo seemed to surround its outflung legs and arms. After a moment Dan realized the halo was the bricks of the pavement. The impact had blown the snow cover from around the body. As if Patterson had been making a snow angel down there.

When he pulled his head back in he felt dizzy, vertiginous, nauseated again. He shuddered. "Uh, were you two here when he went?"

They shook their heads. One offered the belt of a USNA-issue bathrobe. The other held out two hands: a klax in one, a slip of paper in the other. "He used to come in here to smoke. At night. We found these. On the deck, there. The paper was lying in the drain."

Dan accepted the belt, the flip-flop, then the half sheet, which was damp from where it had come to rest. A few blurred lines showed through.

He leaned out again, looking down once more. Had no one down there seen the plebe fall? T-Court still glowed empty. The lamps shone on as if nothing had happened. He pulled his head back in and scanned the half sheet of bond. The typed lines, in all caps.

MOM DAD
I'M SORRY
I'M NOT WHAT THEY SAY
SOME UPPERCLASS WANT ME TO DO THINGS TO THEM
I SAID NO THEN THEY LIED ABOUT ME
IM NOT GOING TO MAKE IT HERE AND I DON'T FEEL LIKE TRYING ANYMORE. FUCK MY CLASSMATES, FUCK THE SYSTEM, FUCK EVERYBODY. SORRY. MARIO

"Dan." A low, confiding voice. Easy Davis leaned over the sill as well, looking down. Then straightened, shaking his head. "Shit. *Shit.* Can you believe it? What a pussy."

"Excuse me?" Dan set the note, the klax, and the belt carefully on top of one of the stainless-steel shaving shelves over the sinks. "What did you just say?"

"It's the coward's way out. But, you know, we're better off without him. Just between you and me."

Dan felt too angry to respond just then. He asked the plebes, "Did anyone call Medical? Or Main Office?"

They exchanged glances. "We'll find out, sir."

"So you didn't. Call them now. I'm going down to . . . to check him out. Post a guard at the door. Keep everybody out. Until an officer gets here."

They nodded, looking frightened.

* * *

The snow sparkled like rock candy. Fresh fall, only an inch deep. He shivered, bare-legged in bathrobe and skivvy shirt, crouched beside the splayed-out form. By now voices were approaching from Main Office.

Patterson's neck was twisted and the side of his skull was caved in. A little blood was sprayed dark on the snow. His right arm looked broken. Dan felt for a pulse but couldn't find one. He felt separate from himself, as if someone else was out here with the kid. He turned and yelled, "Anyone call Medical?"

"On their way. Who're you?"

"Lenson. First Class. From the company next to this guy's."

He hesitated, knowing he shouldn't disturb anything, but then grabbed the slack shoulder and rolled the kid over. The face was a bruised mass. The outstretched hands were bloody claws. From fighting? The bruises, from a beating? No, probably just from the fall, or maybe from scrabbling at the bricks as he died. Some kind of reflex. The dark eyes were open but glazed. Like a drunken girl's, in the buzzing lights of Benny's . . . He shoved that image away and started administering CPR. Yeah, the Academy taught you everything you'd need. From how to roll your socks to how to save a life.

Except how to revive the dead.

A sword clanked as someone took a knee beside him. With the yellow MOOW brassard. "What happened? Who's this?"

"A plebe." Dan tilted his jaw to indicate the lit square of window far above. "He jumped from the head."

"Fuck. *Fuck.*"

"Yeah. I'm not getting a pulse. Still administering CPR, though, I guess. Can you make sure sick bay knows—?"

The MOOW sprang up and left. Dan bent again and fitted his mouth around cold slack lips. He still felt detached, but the horror was starting to penetrate.

A yell from the curved ramps leading up to the Rotunda. "Sick bay answered up. Corpsman's on his way."

When he lifted his head, the body gave a faint bubbling that made him feel sick to his stomach again. The lungs weren't holding the air he was pushing into them. He accepted defeat. Rocking back on his heels, he backhanded bodily fluids off his mouth. "We're supposed to be leading them. Not driving them over a cliff," he muttered.

"Move, guy."

Two corpsmen, one male, one female, shouldered him aside. Enlisted, older than the mids. They moved swiftly, economically. "Epi," one said, readying an injection, while the other positioned herself at Patterson's head. Cradling his skull, she began feeding a tube down his throat. Within seconds they had a respiration bag attached and were pumping air into the lungs. The male medic flashed a penlight in the open eyes. "Fixed and dilated."

"He's gone," the woman said. "Already cold." She fixed Dan with a stare, then dropped her gaze to his bare legs. "You the one found him?"

He explained, while they worked away with gradually slackening effort. Finally he said, "Uh, do you still need me?"

"No, we got it from here," the woman said.

* * *

Back on the fourth deck, breathing hard from sprinting up the ladder. He shoved his way into the head again, through the crowd still thronging the p-way.

The scared-looking pair, tall and short, stood to one side. He recognized them now: Patterson's roommates. Another enlisted, apparently another corpsman, was talking to them. "Sure you guys are all right?" They mumbled subdued responses.

The medic looked at Dan. "Who's senior here? You?"

"No. From down the hall. But I guess . . . I guess I'm senior on deck. Acting company commander. From next door." He wondered where the dead plebe's own firsties were.

"Somebody's gotta make a report." The corpsman had a flat Pittsburghy accent. "Ya know that, right?"

"I was just down in T-Court. The midshipman officer of the watch, he saw—"

"An *official* report. We'll do the medical side, but you gotta call it in."

Dan rubbed his mouth, wondering why telling the MOOW hadn't been enough. But whatever. "Yeah. I'll do it."

He dialed from the mate's gray steel desk. *"Main Office, Bancroft Hall, midshipman officer of the watch, may I help you sir or ma'am,"* a voice answered.

"Need the officer of the deck. It's urgent."

The same hard Corps voice that had welcomed him back from his disastrous night out. *"Captain Slayne."*

He took a deep breath and closed his eyes. "Sir, this is Midshipman First Class Lenson."

"Lenson again. What is it now?"

"Sir, I have to . . . I have to report a death."

* * *

It was only now sinking in. How bad this was going to be. After making the report, and answering Slayne's rapid-fire questions, he called Lieutenant Oleksa's home number. A sleepy voice answered. The lieutenant said he'd be right in, and would call Patterson's company officer.

Dan hung up. He sat for a few seconds, mind blank. Then sighed, got up, and walked slowly back toward the head.

The crowd was thinning. Even after a tragedy everyone valued sleep. When he looked out the window again the medics were pushing a gurney across the courtyard, leaving tracks in the snow. The body was covered with a sheet. Dan stared until the little cortege vanished inside the archway between the second and fourth wings.

What now?

Oh yeah. Preserve the evidence.

But when he went back to the sink, the note wasn't there. The single flip-flop was, and the b-robe belt. But not the damp, typed-on half sheet.

He searched the deck, presuming it had blown, or been kicked, under the stall partitions. It wasn't there either.

When he came out, the same two plebes were waiting. He snapped, "You guys here the whole time I was gone?"

"Yes, sir."

"Where'd the note go?"

Startled looks. "Note, sir?"

"The *suicide* note, ploob. The last words your roommate wrote. On a half sheet of typewriter paper."

Patterson's roommates exchanged glances. "Don't you have it?" the short one, with a red, zit-pocked face, said. "Sir?"

"You were looking right at me when I put it on the shelf. Who else came in while I was gone?"

"Well, the corpsmen . . . and some other . . ."

"Upperclass? Plebes?"

They exchanged another glance. Then, simultaneously, an ignorant duet, "We'll find out, sir."

"Just a lot of people going in and out, sir," the tall one added. "We didn't know you wanted us to keep a list."

Dan closed his eyes, shaking his head, and went back in. Searched again, in every stall and corner. Even up on the tile bulkheads, though he didn't see how it could have ended up there.

"Sir?" The tall plebe. "Maybe that corpsman policed it up? And took it with him? Sir."

He nodded reluctantly. Yeah, the Medical department. That was probably it.

When he went out again, everyone else had gone back to his or her room. The passageway lay empty, the fluorescent overheads humming and flickering, the only sound aside from that was the water-torture ticking of the hall clock. Someone had decorated it with a Mickey Mouse decal, sticking Mickey's white gloves at the end of the clock's hands.

He stood pondering in the gloom. Yeah, the kid had been in a dark place. And there'd been times in his own plebe year when he'd looked down four stories and thought about never doing another push-up ever again.

Sure, it could be hell. Especially when you had a bastard for a firstie riding your ass, determined to run you out. But suicide? Plebe year only lasted nine months.

It was a tragedy. But worse, and the reason he felt this helpless rage, was that he'd turned away. The kid had asked for help. Asked *him* for help.

Sure, Patterson hadn't been his assigned responsibility. But Dan had been his coach. The guy the kid had turned to.

He resolved never to look away again.

13

The Hague

He was shaving in his cell, getting ready for court again, while the news played in the background. The large screen had cable, but only certain channels. From the US, it carried APN, CNN, CBS, Fox, and several new channels debuted since the war. Plus European media. He tuned in France 24 from time to time, to freshen his language skills. He couldn't follow the Dutch programs at all.

His scar itched, which meant it was healing. Another for the collection. Since Mladic's attack in the cafeteria, the court had heard from three more witnesses. One was the wartime commander of USS *Mitscher*, the screen unit Dan had tasked to prosecute the contact in place of *Savo*. The other two were expert witnesses, one for the prosecution, the other hired by Corris. Dan hated to think how much that would cost.

Then they'd adjourned for several days, for one of the astonishingly frequent Dutch state holidays. He'd spent the break rehearsing his testimony, playing chess with the indicted president of Ashaara, working out, researching comparable cases, and emailing Blair, Nan, and Burke-Bowden to keep up. Blair had apologized again for not being able to fly over, but said she had a surprise for him when he returned.

His Academy deputy insisted everything was under control. Dan hoped so . . . but surely the place could run without him for a few weeks. If not, there was something wrong with his staff.

Also, he'd asked Corris if there was anything he could do, in a legal way, for the president and the Syrian. Corris had looked askance, but said he'd investigate.

He was rinsing his face when someone mentioned Beijing on the news. He went over, blotting his cheeks with a towel, to listen.

Live from the capital, read the chyron scrolling across the bottom of the screen. *A spokesman today said the government was considering the turnover of General Huan Pei and Admiral Bohai Lianfeng to respond to a recent summons from the ICC. Pei and Lianfeng were prominent in the Zhang regime. China has never signed the treaty establishing the Court. But there still exists a mechanism for voluntary rendition of individuals to face trial for war crimes and crimes against humanity.*

One American is standing trial at the moment, establishing a precedent. The Executive Yuan and Justice Ministry will consider the matter in the days to come. Former head of state Zurong Zhang is reported ill in Russia, where he fled after the military revolt that ended the war.

He pulled on a shirt, straightening the wounded arm carefully, and stood buttoning it, staring out the window toward the church tower, which was obscured by fog. The weather was still drizzly. Had never really stopped since he'd surrendered himself. Now and then the tolling of its bells reached him, as if freedom itself could float through the humid autumn air.

He couldn't help dreading what was about to happen.

Today he was taking the stand. To relive it all again.

And no doubt Al-Mughrabi had prepared something much worse than simply a forced recounting of events. Accusing him of dereliction of duty, of abandoning drowning sailors . . . It pulled the square knot tighter in his gut.

A discreet tap; his guard. Dan to-blocked his tie, shrugged his sport coat on, and followed him down the hall, past all the other gray steel doors.

* * *

"You heard about the Chinese," Corris murmured, as they sat waiting to reconvene.

Dan nodded. "One general and one admiral."

"That was the main reason you surrendered yourself, was it not? To pressure the Chinese?"

"Uh, right. Sure." Dan cleared his throat, which threatened to close up. He'd have to start carrying an inhaler, if the damaged airway got any worse.

"I think it is praiseworthy," the attorney said. "However your case may go, I believe you have acted ethically. Which I cannot say of all my clients."

Dan smiled, unsure how to respond. According to his new prison buddies, his colorless little attorney had defended some devils incarnate.

As if thinking along the same lines, Corris added, "I looked into the charges against your . . . friends. Their crimes were serious. Their attorneys are appealing, but I fear there's little chance of release. However, we can prepare an amicus brief, if you feel so inclined. Arguing for a reduction of sentence."

Dan nodded. Most mass murderers, responsible for genocide, mass rape, and mutilation, were never brought to justice. Not to say the ICC was useless. Its very existence was probably a deterrent, and it might help shame national courts into prosecuting. In the end, no human institution would ever be perfect.

Nevertheless, he was here. Though not purely for the reason Corris had mentioned.

Mainly, it was so he could live with himself.

"All rise. The International Criminal Court is now in session," a woman announced, then repeated it in several languages.

The older judge, with the graying hair, read another preliminary statement. This time in English, but slowly, so the translators could follow. At last she nodded to Al-Mughrabi.

He stood. "The prosecution calls Admiral Daniel V. Lenson."

Corris laid a hand on Dan's wrist. "As I told you, it would be better if you declined to testify."

"I know. But they need to hear from me."

"Then keep it short. Yes or no answers. Admit no guilt. Stick to what we agreed on!"

Dan pulled his wrist free, and walked, as steadily as he could manage, to the witness stand.

* * *

The prosecutor started off in a friendly voice. He smiled. Said he understood it was wartime, that the attack had come as a surprise, and, of course, that Dan had been under enormous pressure. "In point of fact, you were responsible for the defense of a great city, were you not?"

As Corris had advised, Dan didn't answer right away. Trying to think ahead, plot, like an advance reckoning, or maybe more like a chess defense, where his adversary was headed. "Defending Taipei. Yes."

"Your ship had suffered an outbreak of legionellosis. A crew member had been abducted and raped. A military detective was aboard, investigating that case. Meanwhile, your small force was expected to guard a strait in place of an entire carrier battle group. Correct?"

The guy had done his homework. Dan gave it a beat, then said, "Substantially. Yes."

"Much responsibility. And you had not slept for . . . how long, at that point?"

"I don't recall."

"Would you say you had maintained your normal sleep pattern?"

Dan forced a slight smile. "A skipper at sea learns to do what he has to."

"I see." Al-Mughrabi turned to the judges. "In point of fact, as best we can tell from the logs, then-Captain Lenson had slept perhaps two hours in the preceding three days. Attesting to a definite diminishment of capacity."

Dan kept his features noncommittal. Was the guy acting for the prosecution or the defense? Obviously he was driving toward some point. But what?

The prosecutor turned back. "So, Admiral. Is it possible your capacity to understand and react to events was reduced by sickness, lack of sleep, multiple conflicting and overwhelming responsibilities?"

Okay, now he got it. It was a zugzwang, a classic chess move. If Dan answered "yes," he'd move a square toward admitting he'd erred. If he said "no," that underlined his possible guilt.

The courtroom was silent. He cleared his throat. "US Navy personnel are trained to make rapid decisions under conditions of extreme stress. From the beginning of our careers. I was fully capable of making the calls required in that situation. Had I not been, I would have turned command over to my executive officer."

The sleek-haired attorney nodded, smiling. "If you are satisfied with that answer, Admiral, so am I. Now, to the events on the day in question. How, precisely, did you learn of the torpedo attack?"

He couldn't help flashing back on the memories. Couldn't help tensing in the witness chair and doubling his fists. He spoke as evenly as he could. "The first indication was a shock conveyed through the sea. Second, a report from my sonar gang. Followed by one from the lookout, and my own visual confirmation."

"Your initial actions, please."

Why did they have to go over it all again, again, again? To break him, force him to make a misstep, obviously. He took a slow breath, let it out. "I ordered the officer of the deck to initiate emergency breakaway. All ahead flank, as soon as we cleared. I streamed the antitorpedo noisemaker and ordered our helicopter back into the air. Gave an initial vector and orders to localize and prosecute. Sounded general quarters."

Al-Mughrabi nodded, lips pursed. "And after that?"

"I ordered Sonar to go active."

"Captain Staurulakis has testified that she recommended, from her post in the CIC, that *Savo Island* maneuver so as to block a second torpedo. Is this correct?"

Keep it short. Yes or no. Dan said, "Yes."

"How did you react?"

"I assigned *Mitscher* to prosecute and stood off to assist."

"So you did not follow her advice and block a second attack?"

"No. We repositioned to assist in the prosecution."

"To 'assist.' Why not 'prosecute,' as you put it, yourself?"

"*Mitscher* had a more capable ASW—antisubmarine—suite. The assisting ship stands off and relays cross bearings to help localize the target. Once it's localized, it can be attacked from a safe distance."

The courtroom was silent except for the murmurings of the translators. Dan rubbed his chin. Al-Mughrabi rubbed his too. Was the guy mirroring him?

"Then you received the distress call," the prosecutor prompted.

Dan coughed into a fist, resisting an urge to blot his forehead. Was the courtroom growing hotter? "Actually two calls, several minutes apart. I think in his testimony Captain Geisinger conflated them. But there were two separate exchanges."

With exacting patience, Al-Mughrabi led him through both conversations. By the time they were done Dan was sweating in earnest. Loosen his tie? Mop his brow? Better not. He kept taking slow deep breaths. Really, he'd been in far tighter situations. *Calm, Mr. Lenson. Pretend to be calm, and you will be,* a voice from somewhere in his past said.

"Now, to the turn away from the burning vessel." The prosecutor folded his hands before him. "At what point did that occur?"

"You have the log. You know the time."

"I mean, what made you decide to abandon the burning ship? Which was helpless, as a result of your negligence."

The first time he'd heard that word here. "Negligence?"

One of the judges stirred. Al-Mughrabi shook his head. "This is not a conversation, Admiral! I will ask the questions. Your principal duty was to protect the tanker, is that not correct?"

"No. It was to protect the populations of Taiwan and Japan that lay within the radius of my antiballistic coverage."

"So you considered the safety of your ships and crews secondary?"

Again, he was being herded into a trap. Like buffalo being urged toward a cliff. He said cautiously, "In wartime, sometimes there's no absolutely safe course. You have to juggle risks."

The prosecutor cocked his head. "'Juggling.' I see. But at that stage of the war, had any missiles actually been launched? Toward Taiwan, or Japan?"

He forced a reluctant "no."

"In point of fact, hostilities had not yet commenced. Except for a few shoot-downs of unmanned surveillance machines. Correct, Admiral?"

Dan exchanged a look with Corris. "Correct. But the war plans—"

"So in the absence of actual war, if one of your own ships were attacked, would that not take precedence? A real emergency, rather than one that might not occur? Helpless human beings dying, burning, drowning, rather than a theoretical threat?"

Now Dan saw where he was going. Toward the idea that the hot war, the missile bombardment and invasion of Taiwan and the Marianas, now history, could not have been anticipated then. He glanced at Corris again, but his attorney was looking down, not at him. He said, "We actually had three missions. One: defend Taipei and southern Japan against missile strikes. Two: close the Bashi Channel to surface and subsurface passage. Three: support counterstrikes if the war went hot. Of the three, the ABM mission took precedence."

Al-Mughrabi nodded. "Let's proceed to your decision to neglect your imperative duty of providing assistance at sea. In the face of not one, but two calls for urgent assistance. And in fact, not just refusing help, but effectively fleeing the scene. How can you justify that, Admiral?"

Dan cleared his throat again, feeling the dozens of eyes on him. The glare of overhead lights. The glassy Cyclops focusing of the cameras. "As I said, my primary mission was to protect civilian populations. *Savo Island* was the sole ballistic missile defense unit in theater. That she was my flagship was immaterial. Strategically, she was the highest-value unit in my task group. As the log shows, I vectored Red Hawk 202, my shipboard helicopter, to assist Captain Geisinger."

"Just a moment!" The prosecutor cocked his head. "That is not precisely true, is it? You first vectored Red Hawk out along the torpedo firing bearing. Only later, after repeated requests from the stricken ship, and after your aircraft had returned to refuel, did you *grudgingly* divert it to the rescue mission."

He sucked air, feeling gut punched. One misspeaking, and Al-Mughrabi had pounced. "Uh, right. I had the order of events wrong. Red Hawk wasn't reassigned to rescue until after it had refueled. It was already close to bingo fuel when—"

"So in reality, you took *no action* to assist whatsoever. Until so much later, so belatedly, the effort was useless. Is that not correct?"

"No. Doctrine was clear. I had to—"

But the attorney cut him off again. "One question remains, Admiral. How do you live with yourself, sir? After leaving all those men to die?"

Corris rose at last. "I object. Counsel is traducing the witness. Rather than stating objective facts."

Without waiting for a response, Al-Mughrabi turned to the dais where the judges reigned, motionless, aloof. "If I did so, overtaken by emotion, I apologize. No further questions." The prosecutor's tone conveyed regret and disappointment at a high officer's malfeasance, his poor judgment.

And, in the final analysis, his sheer and shameful cowardice.

* * *

Another interminable recess. Dan fidgeted in a greenroom off the courtroom proper. Two guards sat with him, the same guys who escorted him back and forth from the detention center. Caspar and Ruben seemed neither friendly nor unfriendly, but Ruben was always ducking out, then coming back reeking of smoke. Dan had tried conversation, but they either didn't speak English or weren't supposed to engage.

So he just sat jiggling his foot, stewing over the morning's testimony. The prosecution had accused him of diminished capacity, then caught him in a misstatement that might appear to be a lie. He'd tried to rebut, and Corris had objected. But their effectiveness . . . who knew. A jury might have been easier to read.

But an ICC trial wasn't a jury process. More like a court-martial, with a small bench of expert judges rather than a larger group of the defendant's peers. Or—an unpleasant memory—like an honor board, at the Academy.

His attorney came in. "A postponement."

"Crap," Dan said. "Another holiday?"

"Oh, no. Just until this afternoon. I will have Margaretha order in. Is there anything special you would like?"

He waved a hand, too apprehensive to care. "Whatever."

* * *

He was finishing his stroopwafel when Corris returned. The counselor looked disturbed. "You okay?" Dan asked.

"Oh, certainly . . . It is just . . . something I did not expect." He glanced around the room. "There will be another witness."

"For us? Or against? I thought we had to be told in advance about any new prosecution witnesses."

"They're not appearing for the prosecution." Corris held up a hand. "Nor for the defense."

He explained. Witnesses could be called by the prosecutor's office, the defense, victim representatives, or by the judges themselves. "An overview witness called by one of the judges has just arrived."

"One of the *judges* called a witness?"

"It is not like your procedure in America, I know. It is more inquisitorial."

"I'm getting that impression. Okay, what's an 'overview' witness?"

"We have already heard from two. The professors we and the prosecution called. They assist in establishing the context of events, or other matters to give the court insight."

Dan was getting a bad feeling. Less about this new witness than that his attorney didn't seem pleased at the prospect. The word *inquisitorial* wasn't encouraging either. "So we don't know who he is, or what he, or she, is going to say?"

Corris nodded somberly. "Procedure here is like the continental system. Judges have more power to investigate. In this case, I assume, one decided he needed more information than the current witnesses could provide."

"Is there anything we can do? Or need to? Like, maybe, block his testimony?"

Corris looked horrified. "That would not be well advised. Such a motion would be denied. And it would not be a good look. We simply have to see what is said, and react accordingly."

A tap at the door. Ruben put his head in, accompanied by a strong smell of cheap tobacco. He spoke in Dutch to Corris, who stood.

"It is time for us to go back in," he said.

* * *

The court seemed more crowded this time, with more faces up in the press gallery. Dan took his place, fitted the headphones, and looked around.

And locked gazes with a small Asian gentleman a few seats away. One of the translators? But he didn't have a mic.

In his headphones: *"Captain Jianhua Cai is called as a witness."*

Corris, sotto voce beside him: "Do you know this man?"

Dan shook his head. But he was starting to guess who he might be.

The Asian took the witness stand. The same tall blonde who'd checked Dan in—an officer of the court, Dan assumed—confronted him, apparently administering an oath. Dan snuggled the headphones tighter, concentrating on the translations. They came from alternate voices, disconcertingly gender-switched. Apparently the Chinese-to-English translator was female, the Dutch-to-English male.

"State your name please."

"I am Cai Jianhua."

"What was your role in the recent war between the Opposed Powers and the Allies?"

"I began it as *hai jun zhong xiao*. The equivalent of a navy commander. Later promoted."

"And your post or position."

"Early in the war I commanded the Yuan-class attack submarine *Renmín Fangwei-17*. I then oversaw submarine production in the Wuchang Shipyard until its destruction in an Allied raid. I served on the staff of the Eastern Theater Navy Headquarters. I was at the submarine command staff in Beijing when a victorious peace was declared."

Dan exchanged glances with Corris and Margaretha. Both looked puzzled. He mouthed, *This might be okay*, and returned his attention to the testimony.

The blond ICC attorney said, through the translator, "Please describe the events of the day you encountered Admiral Lenson's task group."

The witness shifted on the stand, as if composing himself. Or mustering memory.

"We had set sail the day before from Ningbo. Our assignment was to break through the strait north of Taiwan and south of Okinawa. You call it the Miyako Strait. I was to transit to a patrol area three hundred kilometers east of the island. Once in position, the plan was to block any help sent to that separatist province. Our forces would cut them off from their allies and convince them to rejoin the mother country. Reunifying China and returning the world to peace and stability."

The interrogator nodded, urging him on.

He lifted his head. "On the morning of the tenth, my sonar reported the noise of many ships from ahead. I reduced speed and changed course to evaluate. We were able to distinguish the signatures of several United States and Japanese warships, plus one unidentified low-sound propeller. Over the next two hours I closed on the formation. We set up a firing solution on the low-sound unit, evaluating it as an aircraft carrier, helicopter carrier, or other large warship."

Dan frowned. The translator was obviously fumbling, trying to cope with both naval terminology and prewar political vocabulary. "Reunifying China" meant invading and conquering Taiwan; "low sound" probably meant "low frequency," which made more sense in discussing a long-range passive detection.

"What were your orders then? When war had not yet been officially declared?"

Cai shook his head firmly. "At that point we *were* under wartime orders. My instructions were clear. If I detected an enemy carrier in the strait, expend all efforts to sink it, up to and including the sacrifice of *Renmín Fangwei-17.* Only if attacking merchant ships was I allowed to place crew safety in consideration."

His interlocutor gestured to continue. Cai said, "As we later learned, the American carrier was never in the strait. Our intel was wrong. Instead, they blocked the passage with other forces.

"Regardless, I had to proceed cautiously. We knew their detection capabilities were high. We had already identified an outside guard. I could not use the periscope. I found . . . heat layer . . . and approached underneath it. The outer guard did not detect us.

"When in range, inside formation, I fired three torpedoes. Then quickly altered course to the south. At . . . slow quiet speed. We heard two explosions. I still could not use periscope, but rose closer to surface. We heard noises. A large ship was breaking up. At this point we still did not know what ship this was.

"At that time my sonar teams continued a . . . following . . . of three other ships. They identified one as a US Arleigh Burke–class destroyer. Another, farther off, Japanese. We identified this as JDS *Kurama*. I directed the crew to plot a course to intercept *Kurama*. This was a large helicopter ship. Its loss would deeply hurt the enemy.

"Then, beyond the noise of the ship which was sinking, we detected the . . . handwriting . . . of a US cruiser of the Ticonderoga class. Its . . . sound song . . . indicated that it was approaching our position. As this was also valuable, I selected it as our next target."

Dan sat riveted, hardly remembering to breathe. He could see it so clearly. The sub running deep and silent on its air-independent Stirling propulsion. Approaching the barrier Dan's Ryukyus Maritime Defense Coalition Task Group had flung across the strait, to intercept any attempt to reach the open sea.

But the hunted had become the hunter.

Cai had used silence, skill, and courage, hiding under the layers of heat and salinity difference to bypass Dan's outer screen unit, USS *Curtis Wilbur*. He'd targeted *Stuttgart* because of the deep slow beats of its screws, mistaking the tanker for a carrier. He'd followed his attack by repositioning, searching for the next victim.

And Dan had been heading west, directly across his bow. A perfect target for one or more of the advanced wake-homing torpedoes the Chinese had licensed from the Russians. It would have sidewinder-weaved up his wake and detonated in his screws.

Directly beneath the aft missile magazine.

Savo Island would have vanished, transmuted instantly into hot gas, smoke, flame, and high-velocity shards of steel.

Cai was staring at him across the courtroom. "Go on," the interviewer prompted.

"I fired two Yu-6 torpedoes at the cruiser, setting them at slow quiet so they would not be detected. But seconds after their departure, my sonar team reported the cruiser made a hard turn and increased speed. Departing the area. The torpedoes followed but exhausted fuel before reaching their target."

The Dutch woman nodded. "And then?"

"Then Sonar reported helicopters overhead. We broke off and retreated to reload torpedoes. I intended to return for *Kurama* but lost contact. I resumed my transit to the patrol area and carried out my instructions throughout the beginning of the war."

The court official turned to the defense table. “Do you have questions for this witness?”

Dan stood, shaking off Corris’s restraining hand. “I do.”

“This is not the way to proceed,” Corris hissed, trying again to pull him down. The guards, up to now leaning against the walls, straightened. Dan hesitated, then forced himself back into his chair. He murmured, “Ask him about his navy’s policy. A ship dead in the water to rescue survivors. Would he attack it?”

Corris stood. “Captain. If *Savo Island* had stopped to rescue survivors, what would you have done?”

Not a moment’s hesitation. “I would have attacked and sunk it.”

“And if another had stopped for the survivors of the first two?”

Cai said, “We would have torpedoed it as well. Also, as to survivors, we were instructed to surface, and use our machine guns.”

The room was quiet. Dan looked down at his notepad. He scrawled *machine guns.*

Corris sighed, as if confirming something he’d suspected. Waited, as if to let the witness’s statements sink in. Then said, very softly, “I have no further questions.”

* * *

In his closing argument, Al-Mughrabi hammered on Dan’s turn away from the stricken tanker. This, he said, was the crux of his violation of the laws of war. He dismissed the testimony of the submarine commander. “All beside the point, since Lenson could not have known these things.”

He also quoted from Senator Sandra Treherne’s remarks in Congress, citing Dan’s failures later in the war, in the central Pacific and off Hainan. “I do not accuse him of crimes in these instances, though his actions led to thousands of unnecessary casualties. They do not lie within this court’s jurisdiction. But they form a pattern of malfeasance, poor performance, and violation of his own country’s regulations, as well as the customs of civilized war.”

Dan forced himself to sit immobile, keeping his expression neutral. Though he couldn’t help jotting a protest, now and then, and showing it to Corris, at least.

A second address came from an attorney representing the victims. She spoke in German, reading a statement from the relatives of those who’d died aboard *Stuttgart* and in the water. Dan wanted to object. He wrote angrily *How am I responsible for those killed in the torpedo attack?* Corris shook his head. *Court will realize this*, he jotted back.

As in an American trial, the defense spoke last. Corris rose, holding a single sheet of paper.

"As has become obvious in the course of testimony, Admiral Lenson played no role in the commission of any war crime," he began. "The defense has shown this, based on three facts.

"First: The whole formation was under attack from the moment the initial torpedo detonated. As its leader, his responsibility was clearly not limited to those few survivors in the water. It extended to the hundreds of men and women in his task group.

"As the testimony of Captain Cai made clear, if Lenson *had* gone to the rescue of the survivors, rather than taking other action to assist them—which he did—hundreds more would have been injured, died, or been lost at sea.

"Second: His obligation extended even further: to hundreds of thousands of innocent civilians. *Savo Island* was the sole unit with the ability to intercept missiles aimed at the cities he was assigned to protect. As such, he had the clear duty to preserve her, beyond any other ship under his command. This is clear both in logic, in law, and in his military's doctrine.

"Now, as to that doctrine. The defense agrees that obedience to an order to commit a crime is never an extenuating circumstance. The relevant precedents are clear. However, Admiral Lenson did act in accordance with US Navy wartime instructions. This is further evidenced by the fact he has never been subjected to American court-martial or other judicial processes for those actions.

"Thus, we must conclude that Admiral Lenson obeyed international law, maritime law, and the laws of war. He acted in accordance with his responsibility to the civilian populations he was charged with protecting. Finally, he directed effective rescue efforts as soon as it was clear the attack had been driven off, and persisted until all the survivors had been succored.

"More than that, it would be difficult to ask of anyone."

He turned to Dan. "Did you have anything to add, Admiral?"

Corris had prepped him for this little act. He stood. Cleared his throat. Looked, not at the cameras, but up at his judges.

"Honored Justices. I sincerely regret the loss of life, both in the Miyako Strait and throughout the entire conflict. The laws of war are simple: protect the innocent; rescue the shipwrecked; use only proportional force. I was trained in those laws, and consider them part of the code of a military officer.

"Bearing those responsibilities in mind, even after intense reflection, years after the incident, I believe that given the situation, there was no other choice for a prudent mariner than to act as I did."

He remained standing, as if for any questions, but the judges simply stared back down at him, or studied their screens and papers. Corris tugged his sleeve; and after a moment more, Dan resumed his seat.

After a pause the judges rose, one after the other. Everyone else remained standing until they had filed out.

Dan blew out and slumped. He turned to Corris, feeling like he'd just run half a marathon. He rubbed his face, which the attorney had advised him never to do on camera; it made a defendant look guilty. "Okay. Now what?"

"We wait. For the verdict."

There certainly was a lot of waiting involved around here. "Which will be . . . when?"

"Difficult to say. It could be later today. Or in a week. Once rendered, we will have the opportunity to appeal. That process, though, could take much longer."

Dan nodded grimly. His fellow detainees had been found guilty. Both were still awaiting the outcome of their appeals. "Which means I could be here for months."

Corris gripped his arm. "Do not anticipate what hasn't happened yet! Let's see what the Court decides. Meanwhile, stay optimistic. I think we presented a strong defense. And Captain Cai's appearance, whoever arranged it, was very effective. I would say we have a good chance of exoneration."

Yeah, who *had* gotten the judges to ask for Cai? And getting the Chinese to let him attend couldn't have been easy either.

He had his suspicions, though. Was Cai the "surprise" Blair had hinted at? The US secretary of defense had to have some pull with Beijing.

* * *

Back at the detention center, a depression so bottomless he could hardly think mastered him. Burke-Bowden had left a message. The deputy supe wanted to know how the trial was going, when he'd be back, but Dan didn't feel like returning the call.

In the detention unit's common area, he tried to watch the news. But his brain kept shunting off into worry. Let's say they give me ten years. Most likely in a German prison, since the plaintiffs were German nationals. "We may petition the court to let you serve it here, however," his attorney had said. "Rather than in Berlin, or Munich."

Just . . . fucking . . . *great.* Either purgatory or hell. Although Scheveningen was more like limbo. It wasn't *unpleasant* here. A physical therapist, a library, a gym . . . and he'd stayed in BOQs with less comfortable beds.

But he could get an even longer sentence. Though he didn't think it would be life, like Mladic, Charles Taylor, Slobodan Milosevic, and the Ugandans and Congolese who'd been found guilty of genocide. Or Bosco Ntaganda, convicted of murder, rape, sex slavery, and recruiting child soldiers.

But whatever his sentence, he'd have to deal with Ratko Mladic. Sooner rather than later.

And he'd have to resign, both his superintendency and his commission. He hadn't looked into it yet, but conviction might cost him his retirement benefits, depending on how the Navy interpreted the law. He'd only see Nan, and Blair, briefly, through reinforced glass, for years.

And why? Because he'd turned himself in. He'd turned *himself* in.

What a bonehead move. The black tide rose again. He put his head in his hands.

He was sitting like that when the guard came for him. He had a visitor.

"Is it a woman?" he asked hopefully.

"No. Your attorney."

* * *

The judges were already seated when he was led in. The court seemed to be back in session, but without the full appurtenances of the daytime proceedings. Only a scattering of faces looked down from the gallery. Only a few staffers sat at the computers. And only four out of the five justices occupied the dais.

His guards led him in front of the bench; Corris stood beside him. Dan wasn't in leg-irons, but felt like he ought to be. He straightened his spine and waited.

The eldest judge cleared her throat. She began to read, in English, very slowly. She began with the charges and a description of the alleged crimes, then proceeded to establish that the events lay within the court's jurisdiction, having taken place on the high seas against citizens of a state that had ratified the Rome Treaty. She cited the preliminary prosecutor's investigation, and its recommendation an indictment be issued. "The accused rendered himself up voluntarily," she added. She continued with the number of witnesses called and where from, and noted, "In accordance with Article 68.3 of the Rome Statute, victims have also been heard in full."

Dan threw Corris a puzzled glance. It sounded as if she was trying to justify whatever sentence was about to come down. Which couldn't be good . . . Corris patted his shoulder and leaned in. *Only a little longer*, he mouthed.

"The evidence has established that Admiral Lenson was indeed in charge of the task force in question and issued the orders constituting the alleged crime. The defense argued extenuating circumstances, including the combatant nation's doctrine, the usage of the sea, and the exigent demands of wartime. These were rebutted by the prosecution and countered by the defense in final arguments."

The judge raised her gaze from her screen, to look directly down on him.

"This chamber has established beyond a reasonable doubt that Daniel V. Lenson was in charge of the force in question; that he gave the order abandoning the stricken vessel; and that he was aware of the consequences.

"In extenuation, he did subsequently arrange for the rescue and succor of those survivors later recovered.

"The chamber has also concluded after review of witness and expert testimony, including by the commander of the attacking submarine, that further extenuating circumstances existed. In view of an imminent and potent threat to the other ships in the force, as well as his mission to defend civilian populations, Lenson's actions in temporarily abandoning the survivors of GNS *Stuttgart* most likely resulted in significant saving of life."

She paused again, long enough for Dan to take a deep breath. Corris gripped his arm.

"Although the judges have written separate and in some respects dissenting opinions on relevant issues, the chamber has reached its final decision unanimously.

"The chamber concludes that the prosecution has *not* proved, beyond reasonable doubt, that the defendant is guilty of the crimes of abandonment on the high seas, murder, and other violations of the laws of war. An order relating to his release will be issued immediately.

"That concludes this hearing."

The judges rose, together, bowed to him, and filed out.

III

THE STORM

14

Annapolis

The Larson Hall staff burst into raucous song as Dan opened the door, startling him. His first day back, and his subordinates lifted glasses of sparkling apple juice to chorus "For He's a Jolly Good Fellow."

"Speech, sir!" cried Burke-Bowden, big and bluff and hearty, and looking at his open, guileless face Dan knew he had to respond.

He lifted a plastic tumbler and cleared his throat. "Thanks so much for the welcome. I missed you all, and . . . I'm really glad to be back."

Handed a saber, he sworded slices of vanilla-and-lemon faculty club cake piped with the legend INNOCENT. Valerie Marsh was there, looking prim. Master Chief Abimbola, for some reason in casual civvies instead of blues. Amarpeet Singhe, lithe and crisp in blue and gold; was that a subtle wink as she accepted her cake? Gupta, the athletic director, refilling his glass with sparkling juice as if his budget depended on it. Burnbright, Dan's PAO, with circles under her eyes . . . in her last trimester now and probably not getting much sleep. And Dan's fresh-faced aide, Lieutenant LeCato.

He didn't see Colonel Stocker or Dean Mynbury. He started to ask where they were, but didn't. The remark might make it seem like he was offended. Sometimes wearing stars was more about what you shouldn't say, than what you should.

* * *

At his office window, licking lemon icing off his fingers, he gazed down at the Yard as the ships' bells rang the hour from the Mahan Hall tower. The trees, the carefully tended flower beds were so beautiful. He was lucky to have this assignment. Lucky to be free. Lucky to be alive. He had to force himself to turn away, back to his desk.

Valerie had a sheaf of calls and emails to return, and Burnbright had media requests to respond to. After that he had meetings stacked back-to-back all morning, to catch up.

He sighed and turned to.

He returned the official calls in order of rank, per protocol. The SecNav's office, then the CNO. He'd leave N7 for last, then think about the requests for interviews and quotes. Yeah, he should release some kind of statement, though The Hague had announced the verdict.

Blair, of course, had welcomed him back the night before. He closed his eyes, recalling it. They'd coupled like cats, snarling and biting. They knew each other's buttons, and how to push, and lick, and stroke to maximum effect. There were signs of age, of course. Loosenings. Wrinkles. Subtracting nothing, rather, adding to the pleasure of being together still. Youthful infatuation might be great, but spending decades with someone you loved beat it all hollow.

The CNO's office asked him to hold. He busied himself looking over the minutes of the governing board meeting Burke-Bowden had held in his absence. When Hlavna finally came on, though, she sounded upbeat. "*We had our doubts, about your rendering yourself,*" she said.

The use of the plural confused him for a second. She and who else? But he waited for the rest of his sentence. If she was going to impose one.

"*Like I said, we weren't sure that was smart. . . . In fact, a couple folks here thought you were just plain nuts. But Dick Enders—he's your classmate, right?—said you knew what you were doing. And I have to admit, turning yourself in made us look twice as good and the Chinese twice as bad. Getting acquitted's just the icing on the cake.*"

Dan cleared his throat. "Yeah . . . but that wasn't why I did it."

"*Why, then?*"

"It seemed like the honorable thing. To respond, when you're accused."

A pause, then, "*Yeah, Dick said you were like that.*" She chuckled. "*You know, if it wasn't for that woman in Congress, I'd think you were angling for my job.*"

Dan had to snort. "Believe me, Admiral, I have absolutely no desire to be CNO. Not after seeing what it did to Barry Niles."

They discussed the former chief of naval operations for a few minutes—he was still fighting cancer, and to everyone's astonishment, still alive—before her tone turned serious. "*Have you had a chance to see what they're saying on social media? About your white power club?*"

He sucked air. "No. Not yet. And it's not really a—"

"It's gathering visibility fast. Saying Midshipman Evans's death wasn't an accident. That a white male had to be gotten rid of, so a female Jew could be brigade captain."

Why hadn't Burnbright mentioned it? "Ridiculous. I didn't even know Oshry was Jewish. And the autopsy was definitive. He slipped and fell."

"That doesn't matter. It's all part of the plot, to them. Most of the noise is from the fringe, Xchan, Loofah Delight, but keep a close eye on that club of yours. Before it tars us the way religious intolerance at Colorado Springs did the Air Force." Hlavna's tone sharpened. *"This is one Navy, Dan. Male. Female. Gay. Whatever color. Whatever religion, or none. Make sure everyone knows that the second they take the oath, we're all equal. It's not just right. It's what we* have *to do, these days, for recruitment and retention."*

Valerie, at his door. "Sir, the commandant's here."

Dan waved to send her in. He thanked Hlavna again for her support and ended the call. Wondering what or who had triggered the trolls, about Evans. Was there something he didn't know? Could it have come from inside the Yard?

He swiveled to face Stocker. "Colonel. Good to see you. Relax, have a seat."

She nodded. In impeccable greens, as usual. "First, congratulations, Admiral. On being exonerated."

"Thanks. What've you got for me?"

"Several emergent issues, I'm afraid. First up, we might've made a mistake. Permitting the Anglo ECA."

"I just got an earful about that from the CNO." ECAs were extracurricular activities, like drama, or the Glee Club, or the French Club. Dan restrained an impulse to remind Stocker *she* had recommended permitting it. Since Evans's accident, the club had been led by a tall, intense firstie with a West Virginia twang, Midshipman Galadriel Stewart. He seemed to know her from somewhere, but so far had never nailed down where. He added, keeping his tone neutral, "What's the trouble?"

She explained, expression grim. More racist graffiti. Abuse scrawled on a Black player's locker during baseball practice. "Most worrying, one of Seventeenth Company's plebes was beaten up last night."

"What?" Dan went to full alert. "*Very* not okay. Who by? We'll expel him . . . or exile them to the oldest, crummiest tugboat in the Fleet, if they're upperclass."

She grimaced. "They were masked, and it was dark. Behind the fourth wing."

Dan wondered what a plebe, any plebe, was doing back there after lights out. But whatever the reason, he didn't rate being assaulted. *"Masked?"*

"The blue NF95 masks we issue. She was masked too, apparently."

She? Oh, great. Worse and worse. "She wasn't—"

"She says not. Trans, by the way, but she identifies as female. Yelled at, beaten with fists, according to the report. No sexual assault."

That was a relief, at least. Still . . . something sounded not quite straightforward. The Brigade had a long, though officially discountenanced, tradition of settling disagreements one-on-one. Sometimes that had been semiofficial, in the boxing ring beneath MacDonough Hall. But at other times at night, in private, with seconds to keep things fair. It was nonreg, of course, and those involved rated major demerits if caught.

But never in a back alley, with several assailants beating on one victim. If that's the way it had been in this case.

He said cautiously, "Uh, who reported the assault? The victim?"

"No, sir. Yard employees. The cleanup crew from the Drydock."

The pizza-and-sandwiches joint next door, in Dahlgren Hall. He sat back, considering. The victim hadn't reported it. Which could mean she might not be a victim at all.

"I recommend a full-court press on this one, sir," Stocker said. "Get the NCIS in. Identify 'em and dismiss 'em."

As usual, she favored the nuclear option. "Uh, Colonel, before we do that, I'd like to talk to the mid involved," Dan said. "Believe me, if it was a racist attack, or gender-based, we'll crack down. And declare a brigade-wide stand-down, to get the message to all hands. But I'd like to make sure we're making the right assumptions first."

Stocker looked as if she wanted to disagree. But finally nodded. "And there's the cheating issue," she said.

Dan looked at his watch. "We'll meet about that later this afternoon, right? Let's just hold that thought, for now."

* * *

Commander Singhe's Sexual Abuse and Suicide Prevention Action Group met in his outer office. As ever, he found it hard to look away from her. Gleaming dark hair, and eyes like an Indian deity's . . . The same sandalwood perfume that had nearly taken him down, alone in his stateroom with her aboard USS *Savo Island*. . . . He blinked back a guilty fantasy as she introduced the brigade medical officer. Maybe it was good she was married now. A marine aviator, a test pilot out of Pax River and a prospective astronaut, no less.

The doc said, "Our takeaways: Depression and anxiety are normal for students in their teens and early twenties. Probably more here, since expectations are sky-high and failure seems catastrophic. Another thought: that population lost a lot to COVID, the C flu, and the war. Also, due to gaming, their focus is online, not on personal relationships. They struggle to ask for help, or communicate their feelings." The medico recommended assemblies in every company, led by the company officers. Also, a visit to sick bay, or a psychological consultation, should no longer result in a record entry. A talk with the chaplain didn't, after all.

Stocker, also attending, had remained silent. Dan asked her, tearing his eyes away from Singhe's casually crossed legs, "What do you think, Colonel?"

"I hesitate to say, Admiral."

He waved a hand. "This is a free-fire zone."

She sat forward. "Frankly, Admiral, if they can't stand the pressure here, they'll be useless on the battlefield." She paused again, then went on, obviously controlling emotion. "We had this discussion earlier. About Midshipman Second Class Court."

"The paralyzed girl."

"Right. If they can't meet standards, they don't belong here. We should be hardening these people. Preparing them to endure. Coddling them isn't a favor to them, or those they'll lead. We'll pay for it in blood."

There it was again, the everlasting dilemma: separate or nurture, reject or develop. He was about to respond when Mynbury lifted a hand. "I also disagree," the dean said.

Dan nodded reluctantly. The provost tented his fingers, and Dan braced himself for a numbing discourse. "We're making progress with this program. But it only scratches the surface."

Dan forced a smile. "How do you mean, Grant?"

"These all-hands meetings should include other issues than suicide prevention. I heard about the attack behind the fourth wing last night. Punishment just drives bad behavior underground. We need serious gender and diversity training. Role-playing. Trust exercises. Self-criticism sessions."

"Self-criticism," Dan repeated. "Like in the Red Guards? Wear a dunce cap, and confess your errors?"

Mynbury smiled condescendingly. "We've seen what prejudice-reduction initiatives can do in the Ivy League. Deep discussion. A multicultural curriculum. Challenging myths and stereotypes. And personal contact with the subjects of prejudice. There's a paper on contact theory I'll send you—"

"Please do," Dan said, desperate to get back to preventing suicides. "Meanwhile, I like the commander's idea about getting professional advice. Grant, you mentioned the Ivy League. Let's reach out, see how they've addressed this issue. We're a service academy, but the demographic we draw from can't be that different. Okay, Commander . . . what about your work on sexual assault?"

Singhe skated a single sheet across to him. "My recommendations. For one thing, we should hire a civilian professional to design and run our response. He, or she, can administer the training program, and serve as a resource for the alleged victims during the investigation process."

She cocked her head. "But it's not a cure-all. I won't point the usual fingers. Sure, it's unnatural, in some ways, to put people this age cheek to cheek and expect them to act like they're eighty.

"But we have to draw red lines. You don't hit on shipmates. You treat everyone with respect. When somebody steps over the line, bystander intervention; you call them out. And if they persist, you refer them to the disciplinary system."

She brushed her hair back and flashed him a glance. "Sexual attraction . . . it exists. Sexual misconduct . . . we'll never drive the incidence to zero. But that doesn't mean we stop trying."

Dan smiled. "Thanks, Commander. We need a road map and milestones. A system everyone can trust. And on the mental health issue, keep pushing the ball down the field on that too. I want every mid, and our staff members too, to understand that if things get too dark, it's okay to seek help."

He closed the meeting, and took a head break before the next one. Mynbury was still holding forth in the conference room as Dan washed his hands. God, the guy never stopped.

Back at his desk, he reached irritably for his inbox.

And pulled out the inaugural issue of the revived *LOG*. For the comeback, the editors had assembled a "Greatest Hits" issue, collecting the funniest articles and graphics since its first issue in 1913. He started to flip through, in a foul mood, then chortled at a ridiculous cartoon.

Minutes later he had to set it aside, choking with helpless laughter. Yeah, bringing it back had been the right idea.

* * *

The cheating inquiry brought him down with a bang. Twenty-three upperclass had been caught sharing a pony to an online engineering exam. The reviewing AI had flagged the identical answers.

Mynbury, Gupta, Burke-Bowden, and Stocker sat silently as Dan strode back and forth, hammering a fist into his palm. "We do not *lie.* We do not *cheat.* We do not *steal.* We teach every plebe that! So what's not taking?"

They glanced uneasily at one another, but no one answered. He raged on. "What burns my ass is, this happens over and over! I was an honor rep when I was a mid. For a while, anyway. And we saw the same thing then.

"I think the majority of our grads value honesty above personal interest. But every ten years or so, we get these massive violations. The honor system's supposed to be a deterrent? Obviously it isn't enough." He rounded on Gupta. "And guess what? Eight of them are on our basketball team."

The athletic director blinked. "Well, not to excuse them, Admiral, but fifteen of them *weren't.* Also, that's a notoriously difficult exam. If we could administer something more reasonable—"

"Just for the team members, you mean?"

The director shrugged, holding his gaze. As if to say, *Why not?*

Dan said through his teeth, "That's *unacceptable*, Virjay. How about when they're on a flight line, or conning a boomer under the ice? The sea doesn't accept liars. It kills them. Along with their crews." He picked up the briefing folder, then slammed it down. "What frosts my ass is *no one throws a flag.* They all just . . . go along."

"That'd be ratting their classmates out," Stocker said.

"We're not West Point," Dan snapped. "A mid can confront a cheater without reporting it to us. Nobody did that either! We're doing something very wrong."

He slammed the folder down again. Burke-Bowden winced. Dan snarled, "I'm going to recommend to SecNav we discharge them. Every damned one. Maybe mass expulsion's the only way I can get the point across."

They regarded him in shocked silence. Gupta actually went pale. He spluttered, "Admiral . . . these are varsity athletes. NCAA champions. Our win percentage—"

"I have more priorities than our win percentage," Dan snapped, knowing instantly *that* sound bite wasn't going to make him popular. "I'd rather have honest athletes on a mediocre team than dishonest players on a winning one. Do I make myself clear?"

Burke-Bowden cleared his throat. "Sir, we had this discussion with Admiral Cree. Do we base the honor concept on fear, or on the desire to do the right thing? You're going straight back to fear. Counsel, punish, but you're going to reap the whirlwind if you separate that many N-star athletes."

Dan rounded on him. "You too, Jack? I can pay out some slack for a mid if it's a minor violation of the regs, or he comes in a little low on aptitude or academics. But I can't give way on honor."

He jerked a thumb over his shoulder, bringing the meeting to an end. And hoped, as they filed out in silence, he was making the right call.

* * *

Hanover, the mid who'd been beaten up, reported to Dan's office at 1300. A beefy, truculent-looking third class, she still had bruises around the mouth. She refused to identify who'd given them to her.

"What we need to know, Ms. Hanover, is, was this a prejudicially motivated assault? Or was it prearranged? A grudge fight?" To help out, Dan had his legal advisor sitting in the corner of the office. "I'm not pressuring you either way. I just want the truth."

Hanover sat wordlessly, face averted. And didn't answer.

Dan touched his nose. Remembering from long ago a body in the snow. A lanky form silhouetted against a fresh snowfall on T-Court. And a previous interview, where the real issues could never be fully voiced. "The truth's always the safest course," he told her. "If it's a question of demerits for fighting, maybe I could ask the colonel to suspend those. This time. But if we've got guys beating up on a woman, that's different."

She said, reluctantly, "He was calling me things. You know . . . tranny. Shemale. Dickless freak. That kind of stuff."

"Verbal harassment's a conduct offense. Put him on report."

"Yes, sir. It's just that . . . getting the administration involved . . ."

She trailed off, but Dan got it. The eternal war. Added to that, the blowback for a mid who turned in a classmate . . . he knew about that. "Fine, but I'm going to need an answer. Was this a challenge fight?"

She bit her lip, hesitating. Finally said, "Sort of?"

Dan side-eyed the attorney, who inclined her head. "Good. That clarifies things. Now: Do you want me to proceed with an investigation? Or end this here? I hope no one promised you the Academy wouldn't suck now and then. Actually, pretty often, if we're honest.

"But if we proceed, it'll be UCMJ charges. Possibly federal prison time, for a hate crime. For him, I mean. For you, a Class A conduct charge."

She said, in a low voice, "I'd really rather . . . you didn't. Sir. Proceed, I mean."

"I can draw something up," the legal officer said. "She names the other participant in the fight. We award them both ninety demerits, for a challenge to physical combat. Then you suspend the forty-five-day restriction and walking tours, subject to good behavior for the rest of the ac year."

Dan nodded, trying not to look relieved. One less problem, and maybe all parties would learn something. He turned back to the mid. "But this is a one-off, Hanover. Understood? Any more trouble, you're both going down. Big."

The third class ducked her head, studying her swollen, bruised knuckles. At last she nodded. "Yes, sir."

* * *

Standing in Halligan Hall that afternoon, he still wondered if he'd made the right decisions that day. Maybe he should leave more of them to the commandant. Or to the NCIS. Maybe more accurately, though, by the time a decision got to his level, there were no right or wrong answers, only trade-offs.

Hell, maybe he could play bad cop this time. Let Stocker and Mynbury talk him down. He already knew, now he'd cooled off, he wasn't really going to discharge all twenty-four cheaters. Whoever had stolen the answers, yes. Whoever passed them on, sure. The others . . . well, he'd wait and see what the honor board recommended.

He dragged his attention back as Jerry Bonar, the public works supervisor, laid out the results of his preliminary study.

"Basically, sir, we only came up with three viable options to the sea level rise slash subsiding fill problem. Move across the river. Block the water on the Lower Yard with levees, seawalls, and pumps. Or abandon Annapolis for a higher location, farther inland." He paused. "Apropos of that, are you tracking Olaf?"

"Olaf?" Dan blanked for a moment, then remembered. "Oh, yeah, the hurricane. Weather has it headed up the coast well out to sea. No problem for us."

"I hope so." The engineer still looked worried.

Dan straightened. "Okay, enlighten me. And I know you can't provide hard numbers, but a ballpark would help. Also, let's forget about option three. We're not leaving here."

Bonar called up the holographic projection Dan had seen before. The scene it projected this time was different. Dan studied it as the supervisor said, "Here's what it looks like if we move the Brigade and our academic plant across the river. We leave the Chapel, the Supe's House, and Admin where they are, since they're above the floodplain."

Dan crossed his arms, frowning. The projection showed Bancroft and the academic and athletic facilities relocated to new sites. That wasn't really possible, obviously. Uproot the most massive dormitory in the world, built of granite on ten thousand pilings, and move it across a river? "We'd, uh, need new buildings."

"Yes, sir. This is just a placeholder, you might say."

"At how many billions?"

"I ran an order-of-magnitude estimate. Remember, it took over a hundred years to build out what we have now. The cost of reconstructing everything across the river . . . at least seven hundred billion over ten years. Not counting teardown, remediation . . ."

Dan rubbed his face. The numbers, in inflated postwar dollars, were mind-numbing. Congress would shut the Academy down before appropriating a fifth of the entire defense budget to move the campus a mile across the water. "Shit . . . I mean, okay. Option two?"

The holograph changed. Now the Yard looked much the same, except that high berms, or levees, had replaced the riprap seawalls along the Bay and river. Four new buildings were outlined in red.

Bonar dwelt a laser marker on them. "The dikes block most of the water as the Bay level rises. But they can't stop it all. Like I told you before: the water percolates up through that old fill.

"So we build an underground drainage system. At high or storm tide, these four pumping stations pipe the water up to a reservoir on Strawberry Hill. We release it when the surge passes. A bonus: as it runs back downhill, we spin hydroelectric turbines to recover the power. Not quite net zero, but close. I'm assuming we build this over ten years."

Dan grimaced. "You mean, where the cemetery is now?" Disinterring, moving, reburying nearly two hundred years of coffins and bodies . . . "How much would that cost? A wild-ass guess."

"A hundred billion."

He sucked air. Steep . . . but maybe affordable, over a decade. "Uh, and how long will it buy us? Before we have to figure out a more permanent solution?"

Bonar studied the water-stained ceiling. "Will President Holton's administration meet our Paris Agreement commitments? Will the EU? Will Russia, China, Africa? What are the Antarctic and Greenland ice caps going to do? And how bad are the hurricanes going to get? This season was supposed to break the records. So far it hasn't, but there's a couple tropical lows down there that could be headed our way after this one." Bonar shrugged. "Just too many variables, Admiral. This could give us thirty more years. But after that, we'll have the same problem all over again."

"Thirty might satisfy Congress," Dan told him. "They don't think any farther ahead than the next election, anyway."

He rubbed his chin again, staring at the image. He was tempted to set the problem aside. Let the next supe worry about it. But that was what every previous occupant of his office had done.

He sighed. "Okay. I need a more detailed presentation of both plans, okay? Both moving across the river, and the levees-and-reservoirs concept. If I can present the Budget Office with a ridiculously expensive permanent fix, and a second-best but cheaper Band-Aid, they might approve number two, at least. I don't know about relocating the cemetery, though. . . . See if we can figure out a way to avoid moving Arleigh Burke."

Bonar nodded. "I'll need help. Architects. Engineers. Environmental lawyers. I don't have the budget—"

"I have that discretionary account." Dan sighed. "If it isn't for long-range planning, I don't know what good it is."

His phone chimed. A text from Blair. *I want to take you to a movie.*

The public works director closed the hologram. It shimmered for a microsecond, like a vision of what might be; though Dan had a hollow feeling it might not. Then it vanished, leaving him feeling bereft. Cheated of a future that could have been, in an empty room that smelled of damp mold and ancient paint.

* * *

Walking back to the Lower Yard, he stopped on the bridge across College Creek. Leaned on the railing as a rowing shell stroked toward him. A chill wind whipped off the Severn. He shivered despite the bright day. Each varsity boat was named after a former team member, usually one fallen in combat. The coxswain, perched in the stern, spotted him and ventured a salute. Dan saluted back. As they passed beneath, he yelled down, "Beat Army!"

"Beat Army, sir!" the rowers roared back, twisting on their benches to look up.

Dan grinned ruefully. Their faces were so bright. They looked so young. . . .

His phone chimed. It was Mynbury. "Yeah?" Dan said, resuming his walk. "What you got, Dean? Something break on the wires exam?"

"Sir, do you recall our tour? When you first reported in?"

What fresh hell was this? "Yeah. Why?"

A pause as Mynbury spoke to someone else. Then, *"Where are you right now, Admiral?"*

"Uh, on the College Creek bridge."

"Excellent. Excellent. Can you meet us at Hopper?"

Dan bared his teeth, not liking the dean's tone. Was it the nuclear reactor? Or had the Astrophysics Division picked up a Manhattan-sized asteroid headed their way? "Shit, fuck," he muttered, getting a startled response from a passing tourist. He started to break into a run, then checked himself. The supe, in uniform, a decorated combat veteran with steel nerves, sprinting through the Yard? It would incite panic.

He made it a brisk walk instead, praying that whatever it was, it wasn't as bad as he could imagine.

* * *

The conference room was high in Hopper, overlooking the river. Looking out and down, Dan caught a YP making a cautious approach to the seawall.

He turned back to the three stern-faced men, and one very scared-looking mid, at the table. Dean Mynbury. The Cyber faculty head, Dr. Jason

Schultz. And, rather unexpectedly, Master Chief Donnie Wenck, from Dan's own staff.

The mid, reed-thin and ashen pallid, bit savagely at his lips as he stared down at his lap. Twisting his hands. "Okay, what's this about?" Dan asked them. "Master Chief?"

Wenck nodded to Mynbury. "I'll let the dean start with the big picture, sir."

The provost looked nearly as stressed as the mid as he explained.

Midshipman First Class Zachary Franklin, a twenty-year-old cyber/electronic operations and warfare major and a member of the USNA cyberwarfare team, had been cruising the Web the night before. To his surprise, he'd discovered what appeared to be a weakness in the operating software for the electrical grid in Kazakhstan. A back door into all the electrical systems across that Central Asian country.

"Unfortunately, and unknown to Midshipman Franklin at the time, Kazakhstan is intent on propelling itself into the big leagues. Improving their economy, converting to renewables instead of coal, and so forth. Moscow sold them new software to upgrade their grid."

The provost looked at Schultz, the cyber prof, who took over. "But their engineers lacked the expertise to integrate that new programming. One tweaked the control program a little. But he got careless in the access credentials. Didn't engage the full suite of controls. Left a hole in their security."

"Open access to the power grid in Kazakhstan," Dan mused, not seeing a problem yet and still hoping Mynbury had gone to general quarters over some nonissue. "Okay . . . you're Franklin, right?"

The mid didn't meet his gaze. "Yessir. Admiral . . . they must have just done the patch and neglected to engage all the security protocols. And no one else must've noticed. Yet."

"Okay," Dan said. "So why's it our problem?"

Wenck said, "So Mister Franklin here, after he noses around in their software last night, realizes the gravity of the situation."

The mid looked up pleadingly. "I wanted to help, sir! Anybody could have just gone in there and crashed their system. Install data-wiping or some other destructive malware . . . wreck their generators . . . overload their high-voltage substations . . . make the whole country go dark."

Wenck said, "So he fixes it, then locks the door behind him as he leaves. He masks his entry to avoid detection, and heads back to his rack in Bancroft. Whistling, probably."

"I wasn't *whistling*, Master Chief," Franklin said.

Dan passed a hand over his hair. "Uh, so far, I still don't see the problem. Is there one?"

Dr. Schultz said, "The next morning, he calls me and explains what happened. When I realized how serious this was, I called Dr. Mynbury. We convened to decide what to do."

Dan sat down. "I still don't get it. Franklin here fixed their problem. I agree, he shouldn't have screwed with their security, even if it needed it. But why do *we* have to do anything?"

Schultz looked grave. "This is serious, sir. It has potentially global implications."

Dan looked to Wenck. "Donnie. In words of one syllable?"

Wenck said grimly, "The way he locked the door . . . it still allows him access."

Dan sat back, instantly transitioned from puzzled to appalled. "Which means, if Franklin here wasn't totally perfect in his masking—"

"Right. The fucking Russkis can trace it back to our server here at the Academy."

Dan shook his head as they all stared at him. He'd anticipated surprises from the mids, sure. But this wasn't getting drunk in town, or even conspiracy to distribute drugs. Screwing with a Russian client? On the other hand, looking at the trembling kid across the table, he had some sympathy. "You didn't intend to cause any damage," he told Franklin.

A violent shake of the head. The mid's eyes shone; he was close to tears. "No, sir. I just thought, if somebody doesn't fix this right now, bad things could happen. People could die."

"But it *wasn't your responsibility*," Mynbury snarled.

Dan held up a hand. "Okay! It's done. What I want to know is, can we sneak back in, somehow, and get our prints off this?"

"*Not* gonna be easy." Wenck sighed. "Any attempt to go back in could trigger a trap. So when whoever finger-fucked with them came back in, they'd nail him. The Kazakhstanians might not be up to that, but the Russkis sure would. Being batshit paranoid, as usual."

Mynbury said, "Is that what you want us to do, Admiral?"

Dan scratched his scalp. Several nasty avenues, decision chains where he could really step in it, were opening ahead. "Uh, we probably need to inform Cyber Command. Unless you already have."

They exchanged glances. "So far, we've kept the lid on," Schultz said tentatively. "Are you ordering us to tell them?"

Dan sat back, taking just a few more seconds before committing himself. If this shitstorm went up the line, heads would roll. And the first to be lopped would be that of a bright young officer who'd only meant to prevent a disaster.

The way, now and again, Dan Lenson had bent the rules to serve a larger good.

But . . . was it dishonest? After the lecture he'd just given his people, that same morning?

It didn't seem exactly the same.

Especially if he laid his own head on the block, instead of Franklin's.

"I'm ordering you not to," he said. "You recommended, unanimously, that I pass this up the chain of command. I overruled you. Understand?"

Mynbury, of course, was first to comprehend. The dean smirked conspiratorially. "We recommended reporting it. You ordered us to stay quiet."

"Exactly. Meanwhile, we bust ass. The PhD and the master chief here see if there's a way to sneak in." He glanced at Franklin. "Maybe you can help out. At least, learn what you did wrong."

But for the first time in the years Dan had known him, the master chief looked uncertain. And suddenly, old. "I'm, uh, not sure I can, Admiral. To be totally fucking honest."

This wasn't good. "Well . . . when will you know?"

"I can take a look . . . but this code, it's in Kotlin. It's hard to fix bugs and I don't know that code. Then the Kazakhi twidgets installed other patches on top of it. So if we fuck up, the whole country could lose power." He shook his head. "I can't promise I can fix this, Admiral. And if we fail . . . See, this system isn't isolated. It's connected. There's a chance, like . . . If it crashes, we could take the whole Russian grid offline along with it."

No one spoke. Dan wavered, uncertain. This could go down very badly indeed. For himself, the Academy, the Navy, the country. Could start a cyberwar. Or even a hot one.

So, what should he do? Wait for the shit to hit the fan? Tell Wenck to check it out? For how long? And meanwhile, what? Run it up the flagpole to cover his own ass? Which would crucify Franklin. Or maybe go to the State Department, come clean, tell the Kazakhs we were like some kind of white-hat hacker?

No, that would sacrifice the kid too.

Finally he said, "Well, check it out. Fast! Then get back to me, ASAP, and I'll make the final decision."

He swiped wet hair back again as they sat down to keyboards. Belatedly, guiltily, he remembered he had another commitment too. Speaking of reporting up the chain of command.

He was scheduled for dinner and a show with the secretary of defense that very night.

15

Snow slicked the terra-cotta tiles of the colonnaded terrace beside Bancroft Hall. It had just started falling, heavy wet flakes clumping down from a sky darker than it ought to be at 1630.

Dan blinked icy crystals off his lashes. Head erect, chest out . . . ten more paces to the wall of MacDonough . . . he reached it and halted. A long count, then a smart about-face.

Another silent count, *two three four*, and he set out again, boondockers clicking on the tile. To his left and right other miscreants marched, mouths set and faces blank as spring-powered automatons. Most were plebes, with a few third class. He was the sole firstie.

Marching tours. Back and forth. Speaking was forbidden. Not the most rigorous of punishments, but the most boring. The very pointlessness made it doubly infuriating. The trigger guard of twelve pounds of Garand and bayonet gnawed his shoulder. He was in blue works delta: wool trou, wool shirt, black tie, combo cap, and tightly laced white canvas leggings. Black gloves, blue reefer jacket, and polished boonies, with two pair of socks against the chafe. They were already damp in the now swiftly falling snow.

His drunken drive into the governor's garden had netted three Class A offenses and a plethora of minor infractions. Qualifying him for the mythical Black N . . . if he managed to stay. From time to time an officer would poke his head out to check on them. Inattention, talking, lollygagging, skylarking, or grab-assing would pile a new sack of shit on top of the ton he was already lugging.

Halt.

About . . . face.

Forward, march.

He passed a waddling girl plebe with cold rosy cheeks and nose, expression blank as a china doll's. Their eyes met for a fraction of a second. Then the fourth class's jerked away.

Well, marching a tour gave a guy time to think.

About the rank he'd just lost, for instance. Bill Door was back to resume his place as company commander. Haley, the redheaded violinist, had been moved up to take Dan's place as assistant. Leaving Dan at the bottom of the pecking order, and dealing a mortal blow to his grease.

Or he could think about girls. Mignon had written. Saying she'd enjoyed Washington, but apologizing she couldn't give him what he wanted.

On the other hand, a blow job wasn't anything to feel down about. Unfortunately, he wouldn't rate town liberty again for the rest of the semester. And he hadn't gotten Licia's number before the crash, though it wouldn't be that hard to call St. John's and ask for it.

Shit, he was getting a boner just remembering it. Though it wilted as his dick rubbed the cold wool of the trou.

Halt. About-face. Forward, march.

The plebe's face wasn't rosy anymore. Her nose and cheeks were pale as wax. A pleading glance this time as they passed. What the fuck did she expect him to do?

Shit, it was *cold*.

Another image intruded now. A thin, agonized face, suffused with dark bruises. Blood on the snow. A bare foot, twisted on the icy brick of T-Court. Scuttlebutt had it the medical officer had filed his report. Concluded it was suicide.

But that didn't fix anything, did it?

* * *

Over the next hour he stewed about those and related issues as phase-changed H2O accreted on the tiles, as a blanched, barely visible thermonuclear orb declined toward the dome of the Chapel, as his steps wore a slushy path to and fro and his face froze. Whoever was in charge was supposed to secure the punishment detail if weather conditions got too savage. But no one had. He and the other marchers were probably doomed to trudge on until the bell rang for evening meal formation. Unless they toppled over, too frozen to keep going.

He darted a look at the others. Unless *he* secured them . . . after all, he was senior here.

Take the initiative? Or suffer on? An easy decision.

Think for yourself? Not at the Chesapeake University of Naval Technology.

* * *

The sun vanished, but they marched on. Darkness blanketed the Yard when finally a figure stepped out onto the terrace. It was Door, back from the hospital. Compact, punctilious, he gave the impression of careful listening before he spoke. He frowned at the fat plebe, who was limping badly now. "Extra duty squad: Halt. Order . . . arms." Then, "It's almost time for evening formation, Dan. Didn't anybody secure you guys?"

"Guess they forgot us."

"Uh-huh.—Fall out!" he yelled. To Dan, "If anybody has a problem with that, tell 'em I secured you."

The plebe staggered over to collapse against the balustrade. Her rifle clattered to the tiles. Ten more demerits, but no one said anything. Dan grunted a reluctant "Thanks, classmate," and headed in, cursing himself.

He could have given that order. Taken responsibility.

Like he could have done the right thing by Patterson.

When *was* he going to start figuring things out?

And if he couldn't, did he really belong in the Navy, at all?

* * *

Evening formation. Evening meal. Then back to their rooms.

He and Scherow had just cracked their textbooks when someone yelled down the passageway. "Pep rally! Spontaneous pep rally. T-Court!"

He and his roommate exchanged glances. "Fuck," Scherow muttered.

They pulled on sweats and watch caps and jogged down the passageway. Ahead surged a howling, jostling tsunami of plebes in camo paint and bathrobes and sweat gear, each brandishing a roll of toilet paper.

Tecumseh Court was lit so brightly with floods he had to shade his eyes. The very bricks glowed, swept free of snow by hundreds of running feet. The fourth class, liberated from bracing up, rioted and screamed like a medieval mob. An unseen band struck up "Up with the Navy."

And so it's up with the Navy, boys!
And down with the foe,
Good old Bill will triumph today!
And the bray of the mule
Will be heard from the field
As the Army line begins to yield!

Dan bellowed it along with the rest, flashing back on Plebe Year rallies, singalongs, buildups, all the forced enthusiasm and mandatory fun. To lose to Army was a disaster. To beat the Black Knights, a transfiguration.

Back then it had felt like liberation, losing himself in the tumult as his classmates screamed their throats raw.

Now he felt cheated. How had he fallen for this hokum? Maybe the graffiti in the head, the only uncensored expression possible, was accurate. *USNA: marking time for four years in the P-rade of Life.*

The cheering swelled to a window-rattling roar as the team trotted out, to be introduced, one by one, to renewed storms of applause. The players raised clasped fists, grinning down at their leaping, dancing acolytes. Streamers of shitpaper unspooled in the air. Paint-daubed faces grimaced like gleeful demons, stop-actioned by camera flashes in the falling snow. Torches of toilet paper, soaked with lighter fluid and held aloft by immobile attendants, lit the bleak bronze visage of Tecumseh. The God of 2.0 stared down, face painted half dead black, half stark white, and the flickering made his eyes seem to shift in their shadowed sockets, his scowl expand in a sardonic smile.

Dan cheered with the rest, half his heart still with them, while his other self regarded it with passionless detachment.

An alien observer, marveling at a grotesque and unfathomable carnival of the damned.

* * *

He paused on the way back to his room to watch a gang of plebes bricking up the door of the Army liaison. Inside seethed a multicolored maelstrom: hundreds of balloons, packing every cubic of the office. The mortar would be hard by morning.

The black cloud that had descended during his extra duty was closing down to zero zero. He trudged back toward the company area, glumly pondering his shortcomings. Why did he only realize he'd fucked up after the fact, when it was too late to do anything about it?

He passed Davis's room. Then halted.

He couldn't bring the dead back.

But maybe he could clear their name.

"Yeah," came the response to his knock. Dan poked his head in.

Davis was in his rack. Apparently he'd bagged the rally. The firstie frowned into the distorted rectangle of light from the open door. "Bed check? I'm here."

"Lenson."

"Lenson." A falling note. "What do *you* want?"

"A word." Dan glanced back into the passageway. Two plebes were eyeing him from a nearby door. Patterson's roommates, Tall and Short. They ducked back in as soon as they caught his look.

Davis sat up in bed. Grunted, "Make it fast. It's already past fucking midnight. Turn the light on. And close the goddamn door."

Don wondered again why the guy didn't have a roommate. He turned the desk chair around and straddled it, facing Davis.

The other firstie frowned. "'Fuck's this? Friendly visit? I didn't know we were such good pals."

"Informal counseling," Dan said. Wishing he'd brought his notebook, to add at least a little formality. Being in sweat gear and a watch cap didn't help.

"Counseling," Davis echoed. "For what?"

"For the honor violation you filed. About Patterson. The instruction says both the accuser and the accused have to be counseled, before the case goes to the committee."

Davis's brow cleared. "Oh . . . that. Isn't that OBE? Since the kid's dead. Sorry as hell, but why bother now?"

OBE, "overtaken by events," meant the universe had moved on, leaving previous plans bobbing in the wake. Dan cleared his throat, wondering now what he *was* doing here. "Yeah, but I . . . still got to submit a report. To close things out."

"I don't think so." Davis swung his legs out, feeling for his klax with bare toes. He was wearing skivvy bottoms but no top. A muscular chest, nearly hairless, though tufts of darkness showed at the pits. Past him, through the window, a shower of orange sparks clawed the night, then detonated with a *pop.* The plebes were still on the rampage. "You got a hair up your ass? Submit a Hurt Feelings chit. Now gangway, I might as well piss, now I'm up."

Dan kicked his chair over between the desk and the rack, still sitting in it, blocking Davis's exit. "There was something missing from the head."

Davis cocked his head, listening.

"Patterson left a note. Only when I went back up after I checked on the body, it was gone. I thought the corpsman took it. But when I called down to sick bay later, they said no. You were in there after me. Did you take it?"

"There wasn't any fucking *note.*" Davis curled his lip. "You're dreaming, classmate." But his gaze flicked to the door.

"I saw it."

"Well, if you did, you were the only one. So what did it say? If there was one."

Dan glanced at the door too. Still closed. "That some upperclass were lying about him. He wanted his parents to know he wasn't what we were saying."

"We?"

"His firsties, I guess. The Academy." Dan remembered the faces of the other plebes, staring down at their classmate's corpse. "Maybe, his own classmates."

Davis sighed and stood. "You gonna get out from between me and the door?"

"Not until I get a straight answer." Dan forced iron into his tone. They eyed each other. Could he take him? Davis was shorter but more muscular.

The other seemed to change his mind. He sat down again. "Sure, I'll tell you. Here's something you should know, Dan. You were his coach, for what, a week, right? But you didn't see what was going on, in our company area. We were close. I even spooned the kid."

This Dan could not believe. *Spooning* meant shaking hands, rates were off, no more "sirs" and "misters" but first names; friends instead of senior and junior. "Why would you do that? Maybe after Hundredth Night. But why that early?"

"I just felt sorry for the kid. He was trying, out on the field. There might've been promise there, if I could toughen him up."

Dan rubbed his mouth. Davis had said he hated Patterson, intended to run him out. Why this new story?

The guy was lying to his face.

He took a moment to think, trying to work it out. Patterson's note had mentioned an upperclass trying to force something on him. Maybe Davis had groped the plebe? Or made a verbal offer? Been rejected, so he made up the story about the encounter in the showers to smear him. Or make it seem as if the plebe was lying, if he reported him.

Patterson's note had denied the accusation. But he'd addressed it to his parents, something they could take comfort in.

By now Dan figured the kid probably *had* been gay. But did that matter? What mattered was that Davis's hazing, along with probably the threat of being thrown out, had driven him to climb on a toilet, push the window open, and step out into thin air.

So where *was* the note? Obviously Davis had taken it. Scooped it off the shaving shelf in the confusion. Squeezed it to a wad of damp pulp. Then, probably, just flushed it down the nearest commode.

Dan's heartbeat thumped in his ears. He clenched his fists. "Did *you* make a pass at him?"

Davis looked away. He said softly, as if addressing the darkness outside the window, "What exactly are you accusing me of, classmate?"

"I think it's pretty obvious."

Davis faced him. "Fuck you, Lenson. That shitforbrains had it coming. We're better off without him, like I said. That's the point, isn't it? To flush the no-loads who can't hack the program?" He got up again, narrowing his gaze. "Just forget it. Leave it alone! Now you're gonna get the fuck out of my face. Or we're gonna take it to the mat, right here."

Dan hesitated. Then got up, admitting he'd hit a stone wall. In a way, he could understand: a mid admitting he'd propositioned another male would be instantly expelled. Maybe Davis was as trapped, in his way, as Patterson had been.

There was still the lie.

But why did it seem so murky, like there were no right answers after all . . . ?

While he stood dithering Davis snorted and shoved past. Then, at the door, turned back, shaking his head. "Hey. Like I said, too bad he took the coward's way out. I get why you're mad. But that's how the fly shits, Dan. Nothing you can do about it. Unless you want a whole new shitload of hurt. And believe me, it's ready." He slammed the door open. "Now get the *fuck* out of my room."

* * *

Dan padded back to his room. To find the lights on, and Scherow sitting in the Air Force b-robe he'd won on a bet with a zoomie, chair kicked back. Behind him hung a chain-mail tunic with a lion's head rampant. His costume for the latest Masqueraders production.

Two plebes, one tall, the other short, stood with spines pressed to the sliding doors of Dan's locker.

"Fuck's this?" Dan said.

"Mutt and Jeff here woke me up." Scherow yawned. "Come to tell you something."

"Sorry, Ted.—Whadda you want, ploobs?" They looked half familiar, but it was hard enough recognizing the freshmen of one's own company. Shaven heads, goofy, scared expressions, chins pulled in like turkey gobblers.

The tall one's Adam's apple worked. "Sir, we're . . . we were, Midshipman Patterson's roommates."

Sure. The duo who'd scoped him out going into Davis's room. "Okay," Dan said. "So what?"

The short one cleared his throat. He said, "We, uh, heard Mister Davis yelling at you. Was it about Mario?"

Dan shrugged. "Upperclass business. What've you two dipshits got to do with it?"

The taller one swallowed again and glanced at Scherow. "Whatever it is, you can say it in front of my roomie," Dan said. "He's silent as the tomb. Except when he's asleep."

" ," said Scherow, mouthing words but not uttering them.

Dan waited, curbing an impulse to drop them to leaning rest. Finally the pimpled one whispered, "Sir, we want to give you something we found. But in confidence."

"In *confidence*?"

"Yessir. Like, just between you and us."

Unorthodox, but he was starting to guess where this might be going. He dropped into his desk chair. "Carry on, turds. What have you got that's so fucking important?"

"Sir, this, sir." The tall plebe extracted a copy of *Reef Points* from inside his trou and from it a half sheet of wrinkled paper. He hesitated, then held it out. "We found it on our desk when we came back from class."

For a moment Dan hesitated too. Did he really want to . . . ? But at last he accepted it.

It looked like the same note. Stained. Typed in all caps. A ragged tear at the left-hand upper corner, where the salutation had been. He read it again, then turned it over and looked at the back. Then looked at the front again.

It *was* the same note. But someone had added, in pen, in careful block letters, at the bottom, THE LACROSSE COACH.

An overwhelming sense of threat prickled the back of his neck. "Where'd you say you found this, again?"

"In our room. After class. Day before yesterday."

"Not in the head? Where Mario . . . uh . . . Mr. Patterson—?"

"No, sir." The short plebe widened his eyes. "That's the truth, sir."

Scherow looked interested, but said nothing. Dan gave it a moment, then prompted, "Did you see anyone going into your room? Or leaving?" The doors in Bancroft had locks, but no one ever used them. Plebes had to leave theirs open between reveille and taps. Except for the females, while changing or showering.

They exchanged worried looks. "No, sir."

Dan pulled at his lip. What the fuck, over? He'd put the note on the shaving shelf. Then it was gone. He'd checked with sick bay but no joy. And now it was back? With those three words tacked on at the end. Did these idiots realize just how deep a shitpond they were diving into? And dragging him in too . . . "You two geniuses sound off to anybody else about this?"

They shook their heads so hard he could hear the marbles rattle. "No, sir," said the tall one.

"Okay. You did that much right, anyway. So don't! Not your classmates, not your upperclass. Don't write home about it. Just dummy the fuck up, copy? I'll deal with this."

"Are you gonna pap Mr. Davis, sir?" said the short one hopefully.

"Shut up and get the fuck out. Shove off! Assholes and elbows, maggots!"

When the scramble was over and the door banged shut, Scherow stretched and whistled. "Is that what I think it is?"

Dan laid the slip carefully on his blotter. "It's not exactly a nail in his coffin. But it might substantiate the accusation."

"What accusation?"

He halted in mid-pace. Oh . . . yeah. There hadn't *been* any charges against Davis. The ones he'd been assigned to investigate had been against Patterson.

"You're gonna have to file a new case," Scherow said. "If you think there's something not kosher. Against a classmate. Not gonna make you real popular. Is it worth it?"

"The guy lied through his teeth," Dan said. And was still lying; obviously it had been Davis who'd added the line in pen. But it made doing anything about it a risk for Dan. It was clever as hell.

"How do you figure?"

"Filing the accusation when it wasn't true."

"How do you know it wasn't?"

"Because Patterson says so. Right in the note. Like he's—like—"

Scherow frowned. "Speaking from the grave? Like Banquo's ghost?"

"Something like that." Dan resumed his pacing, waving the note. "Doesn't he deserve to have his say?"

"And *you're* the guy to give it to him."

"Well, nobody else's lining up to, are they, Teddy?"

His roomie tapped his lips with steepled fingers, like some kind of defense attorney. "Is withholding evidence an honor violation?"

"I don't see how it couldn't be," Dan said, but at the same time he wondered if it really was. Maybe he should have paid closer attention during the briefings for the honor reps. The instructions talked about "integrity" and "honorable behavior," but never defined it. In fact, now he'd lost his stripes, *was* he still an honor rep?

Get real, Lenson! It was nice to think about. As if he could make up, even a little, for not helping the kid. But if he brought charges, his roommate was right. He'd be lower than whale shit. A bilger. What would happen to a firstie who turned in a classmate? Not just at the Academy, but after? That kind of rep followed you.

And what was even more dangerous was that now Davis had figured out a way to put it back into play, but this time make it work even better for him. Making it impossible for Dan to bring charges, or even reveal the paper's existence, without implicating himself.

With a sinking heart, he plunked himself down at his desk. Cracked a pack of Wolf Brothers, lit one, and took a deep drag. "Fuck," he muttered, coughing, sensing the walls closing in.

Maybe this wasn't the kind of situation a guy should make up his mind about, without thinking long and hard about it first.

16

Pentagon City, Virginia

Their evening started on a down note. In her E ring office, Blair sat him down. "Some things we have to get out of the way first." She pursed her lips, looking out the window. "Daniel . . . I have to say, your institution is being called into question. From numerous quarters."

He nodded. "I see the stuff on social media."

"The accusations of murder, and some kind of antiwhite conspiracy? That's ugly, yes. You can assure me there's nothing to it?"

"The brigade commander slipped and fell. That's what the autopsy concluded."

"Then that's the story we stick with."

"I could issue a statement, but my PAO said not—"

"They're right. No comments, no rebuttals, no *press conferences*. Anything you put out there, they'll use to trigger another round of coverage. Ignoring it's hard. But it's the best thing to do." She fingered her misshapen ear. He'd never thought it looked that bad, but she seemed to obsess about it. "But that's not all. The Russians noticed the intrusion. In the power grid controls."

Uh-oh. He studied the carpet. On which, apparently, he was being called. "Did they . . . trace it to us?"

"'Us' being your little computer club? No. *Very* fortunately. I don't pretend to understand the technicalities, but our people at Cyber Command scrambled their top team and managed to rewrite the—um, software—to mask the entry, so they couldn't trace it back." She eyed him sternly. "You did the right thing, calling them in. They just barely got our scent off it before the Russians ran the trail. But we, I mean DoD, got a really stern warning from both State and Homeland Security. Your errant cadet—I trust an appropriate level of discipline was exercised?"

Dan nodded. "I counseled him personally. Got the message across that if the word got out, he wouldn't be commissioned. He's off the access list, and we pulled his clearance, at least until he goes to his first duty station."

She looked away. "I'm afraid that won't be enough."

Uh-oh. "What do you mean?"

"Homeland wants him discharged. And so do I." Her lips whitened. Not a good sign.

He gave it a moment. "You want him expelled?"

"Believe me, there were those who wanted a court-martial and prison too."

He tried a grin. A coaxing tone. "I'm not sure that's . . . Look, Blair. His intentions were good. And when it went south, he let us know right away."

"That doesn't cut it, Dan." She swung back to face him. "This went all the way up to the Oval Office. I had to explain it to the president! If M'Elizabeth asks about it again, I've got to be able to show we cracked down."

"I *have* cracked down," Dan insisted. "Losing his clearance, that's a huge issue for somebody who wants to go into cyber. But anybody with that much talent, we need him inside the tent pissing out, not outside pissing in. Franklin could have held the Kazakhstanis to ransom, or crashed the whole Russian grid on his own. We fire him, ten to one he becomes some kind of disgruntled black-hat hacker. A cybercriminal, with a grudge against us. A thorn in our side from now on."

She swiveled back and forth, swinging one high-heeled foot. Obviously trying to gauge whether Homeland, the White House, the president would agree. "And what *exactly* did you do to make sure this never happens again?"

"No mid goes on the system now without a faculty member sitting in. No after-hours access. More stringent security checks. I'm satisfied that'll prevent another incident. No matter how smart someone is." He halted there, giving her time to think. Hoping he'd argued her out of it.

She glanced at her watch and sighed. "All right, let's leave it at that." She rose with all the grace of the teenaged ballerina she'd once been. He got a brief, conspiratorial smile. "Now, I think, we've got a movie to go to, Admiral."

* * *

The moment she ushered him into the lobby of the mall complex he sensed something in the air. The other theatergoers looked their way, whispering and taking photos with their phones. He stepped off the escalator and took her arm. "What the hell is this, anyway? What've you got set up this time?"

She grinned mischievously. "All in good time, my pretty. We're in theater eight. But you have to buy me popcorn first. With extra movie butter, yum!"

When they walked in, his hands full with Diet Cokes and an extra large popcorn, the audience rose as one, applauding. He blinked, astonished at familiar faces, friends from the past, from former commands. Wenck was there, and Monty Henricksen, from TAG. Cheryl Staurulakis was wearing the iconic olive-and-black shemagh, now very faded, he'd bought for the crew in Dubai. The subdued guy beside her must be her husband, who'd spent most of the war as a POW. Amarpeet Singhe, in a dress cut heart-stoppingly low . . . Blair greeted her coolly, obviously still nursing suspicions. Ollie Uskavitch and "Red" Slaughenhaupt. A scattering of his classmates: Dick Enders, Andy Mangum, even Tim Simko, who apparently was no longer holding a grudge. Aisha Ar-Rahim, swathed in a flowered daishiki. She looked happy; a husky man beside her held a child's hand. Jenn Roald, his old Situation Room supervisor, accompanied by a slim brunette whose smile beamed like the sun. And others . . . Dan's daughter was there too, accompanied by a bland-looking guy she introduced as Harry, or maybe she'd said Larry; he wasn't sure, he'd caught it in the hubbub.

And many more. He was glad to see the ones still in uniform, as they stepped up to shake his hand, had advanced in rank with time and the war. They wore many more ribbons than when he'd served with them.

He tried not to think about those who weren't there. Lost in fires, in battle, in accidents. They'd written their nation a blank check, and honored that signature.

He asided to Blair, "What the hell *is* this? It's not my birthday. I'm not being retired early, am I?"

"You'll see in a minute." She smirked, as the house lights went down.

* * *

The film was titled *Pacific Victory.* A credit line read *Based on the book* Task Force 91 *by Linwood Naylor.* Dan remembered him, a reserve historian attached to his staff for Operation Rupture Plus. The guy had been Mr. Invisible then, but obviously had taken notes.

He couldn't dodge this bullet any longer. He settled into his seat, wishing he had a shell, like a turtle, to pull his head down into.

The film opened with the thermonuclear attack on the USS *Franklin D. Roosevelt* strike group. It was rendered in apocalyptic CGI so intimidating the audience gasped. Most had seen war firsthand. They identified with the burned, blasted crews of the ships bursting into flame, exploding, capsizing, going down. He had to slow his breathing, gripping the arms of his seat.

Blair laid a steadying hand atop his. "It's only a movie," she whispered.

Cut to *Savo Island*, guarding the Bashi Channel. And on her bridge, a tall, iron-jawed actor Dan realized, with a sinking heart, was supposed to be himself. But shorn of any doubt or nuance. Lacking the second-guessing, the self-questioning that had always dogged him. Maybe it showed the man he'd always tried to project. The stoic, all-knowing commander who never suffered fear or uncertainty.

But it wasn't the Dan Lenson *he* lived with.

On the screen, torpedoes slammed into a tanker. Castaways waved imploringly from an oil-slicked sea. Shadow Dan rushed to throw them a life ring.

When what he'd actually done was steer away, and leave them to the mercy of a fiery sea.

Faces turned to regard him in the darkened theater. He steeled himself for snorts of derision. Mutters of astonishment. None came, as far as he could tell.

The next scene: action in the Central Pacific, against a massive wolf pack of enemy submarines. Single-handedly, Dan shattered the blockade. The Fleet charged westward. Marines raised a flag on a tropical beach. Again, no mention of his mistakes, or his agonizing over how many lives to trade for those victories.

In the film, Justin Yangerhans clipped glittering stars to actor Dan's collar, who returned a jut-jawed salute . . . even though they were indoors. The audience tittered; Dan closed his eyes in disgust as the commander in chief, Pacific, gave him a suicide mission.

But as Blair said . . . it was only a movie.

It made him wonder. Was all history as simplified, as one-sided, as this? Stainless heroes, or blackhearted villains? He clenched his fists, nauseated by the oily stench of fake butter.

Then, the invasion of Hainan. Troops stormed ashore, all in US uniforms, though actually most of the landing force had been Indonesian. Chinese jets spun smoking from the sky as ships' crews cheered. The intrepid admiral, snapping orders on the bridge of his flagship, shamed fearful staffers counseling retreat. No mention of the tactical AI that had also recommended aborting. Dan hadn't been on the bridge, either, but down in CIC, skull clamped in the heavy, stinking, helmet-mounted display. But obviously that wouldn't make a very dramatic visual.

The moon rose. A multicolored glow like burning rainbows glimmered and flashed above blasted, burning ships.

And an idealized, film-star Dan Lenson grimly issued the order Naylor recorded in his book, that was now apparently Navy lore. "Victory or death, gentlemen. Victory or death."

"Oh, fuck me," he whispered, sliding down in the padded seat, covering his eyes. Torn between sardonic laughter and tears. It would be ridiculous, if it weren't so tragic. It would be tragic, if it weren't so ridiculous.

But beside him a rapt spouse covered his hand with her own, fingers greasy with coconut-oil spread. And when the final credits rolled, the audience rose as one, applauding and cheering. He forced a smile and a tepid wave, steeling himself not to howl aloud, or bark a harsh, bitter laugh that once begun, might be impossible to halt.

* * *

The next morning, he went to the Pentagon, accompanied by LeCato. The sky was overcast. He checked his weather app again before leaving, just for reassurance. Hurricane Olaf was following the predicted track, bowling along off South Carolina. Though it was still a Category Five and nothing to be dismissive of, NOAA predicted it would keep curving east, like most tropical storms in the Northern Hemisphere. It would weaken on the way, to make landfall in Boston or Cape Cod as a Cat Three.

The stand-up breakfast was informal, a get-acquainted mingling of the superintendents and senior staff of the five service academies: Annapolis, West Point, Colorado Springs, the Coast Guard academy at New London.

And, often forgotten, the Merchant Marine Academy at Kings Point. Dan chatted with its leader, a pleasant woman of Native American descent from Wyoming. During the war, the Merchant Marine had manned the makeshift "jeep carriers," converted from container ships by roofing them with flight decks and mounting National Guard self-defense missiles. They discussed integrating tactical training, and Dan promised to push for two more Navy instructor positions on her faculty.

The business of the day was "The Way Forward for the Service Academies," chaired by the undersecretary for training and readiness. The superintendents occupied the sole conference table; aides and deputies, as usual, ranged the walls.

The first agenda item was standing up the new Space Force Academy. The Air Force Academy supe argued that Colorado Springs was the natural location. The undersecretary brightened when he said that would save money. Yeah, Dan could see where this was going.

"Shared faculties makes sense." The undersecretary made a note. "I like that approach. As long as we're thinking about merging air and space, what if we applied that to the other facilities? West Point and Annapolis, for example. The first two or three years of joint training at one location, then specialization to land and sea, space and cyber in the senior year. Responses?"

Dan knew the man in Army greens. Major General Randall Faulcon's prominent cheekbones were almost fleshless, his already-thin hair had receded even farther, and he looked only slightly less tired than he had as Dan's senior as deputy Pacific commander. Both Dan and the superintendent of West Point started to speak at the same time. They exchanged looks, then each gestured for the other to proceed.

Just then Blair let herself in, and all stood. "Madam Secretary," the undersecretary said respectfully. "I believe you know everyone here."

She smiled at Dan. "I would say, some better than others."

A low chuckle and whispers. Apparently not everyone had known they were married.

"Please, continue." Blair accepted a seat and waved them on.

Dan mustered his thoughts again. He defended the separate academies first, basing his justification solely on the needs of each service. When the undersecretary's knitted brows signaled he wasn't getting through, he went to his fallback position. "It would make more sense, if we're being forced to cut costs, to merge New London and Annapolis. Or New London, Annapolis, and Kings Point. The three sea services have far more in common than the Military Academy and the Naval Academy."

A few nods around the table. "But above all, let's not take precipitate action. There are a lot of stakeholders who need to be heard from." He looked toward Faulcon. "General?"

The rival superintendent smiled coolly. "I think that's everything that needs to be said at this point, Admiral. Especially about the . . . outside stakeholders."

Blair tapped the table. “Mr. Undersecretary. If I may?”

“You have the floor, ma’am.”

She leveled a glance at Dan, and her tone turned less accommodating. “Annapolis is the most threatened location of all our training facilities. Considering sea level rise and that installation’s limited room for relocation. Why maintain five separate faculties, parade grounds, athletic facilities? Especially when most of our accessions come from university reserve programs? Really, it’s something we here in the Building struggle to justify to our masters on the Hill.”

Dan felt torn. She was the woman he slept with. But she was his civilian boss too. “Yes, Madam Secretary, I hear you. And it’s clear times are hard, as we all struggle to bring the country back.”

He took a breath. “Closure, consolidation . . . those options have been debated since the academies were established. Generation after generation, Congress and the public chose to keep them. The most pressing reasons, I think, are less quantifiable. Things like esprit de corps. Specialized education.”

“You may use the T-word, Admiral,” Blair said. “If that’s where you’re headed with this argument.”

Dan forced a tight smile. “Tradition has its place, sure. But it’s no reason to stand in the way of progress.”

“Yet it’s always the default appeal. For those who want things to stay the way they are. Sometimes, for not very admirable reasons.”

“Well, I’m not one of them.” Dan gave her the same direct stare he would have given any superior. “Excellence. That’s what I’m defending.”

A moment’s suspended pause; then Blair nodded. “You may want to polish your defense on that issue, Admiral.”

She seemed about to say more, but rose instead, and left.

* * *

He stood out in the parking lot, disturbed. Blair had gone back to the E ring, without inviting him along. Of course, that would have looked like favoritism. Though she hadn’t shown any when she’d cross-examined him.

“That was rough,” LeCato muttered, tentatively, as if feeling he needed to break the silence.

Dan glanced at a sky that now looked even darker, more ominous, than earlier that morning. A chilly mist was falling, not quite rain, not quite fog. “Well, that’s her job, Vince.”

"Yessir. Still, she really came after you."

Couldn't he leave it alone? Dan snarled, "There are bigger issues at stake than us here, Lieutenant. The Fed's broke. The Midwest and Seattle have to be rebuilt. All we've got is the little keyhole picture."

The aide looked stricken. "Sorry, didn't mean to snap at you," Dan muttered. When you screwed up, best to apologize at once. Waiting only made it harder.

But Blair was right. He did need to sharpen his arguments. . . . "Where's our car?" he murmured as the rain began in earnest. LeCato pulled out his phone.

They were retreating toward overhead cover when a vibration trilled in his pocket. From Burke-Bowden. *Olaf speeding up and backing west. Estimated landfall Norfolk. ETA Annapolis 0300 tomorrow.*

Dan tapped the NOAA app and stared horrified. Four to eight inches of rain. Winds of up to a 150 miles an hour.

Worst of all, the system had indeed swerved. Instead of tracking up the coast twenty to thirty miles offshore, as per earlier predictions, it would head smack up the middle of the Chesapeake.

The biggest storm to hit the area in decades, with the most powerful winds. But it wasn't really the winds he was worried about. They'd wreak damage, but the Yard would be battened down. Wind-whipped seas would threaten, but the massive granite boulders of the seawalls would shatter their green hearts into sprays of harmless foam.

No, the greatest threat was storm surge. Driven by hurricane-force winds, it would stack on top of existing tides and flooding from massive amounts of rain. Driving water levels, if the timing was right, to heights that would overwhelm their safeguards.

A new text pinged on his phone: Jerry Bonar. *Prepping for major high tide, flooding, winds.* Dan texted back *When is high tide* but got no response. Probably the public works supervisor had his hands full.

Burke-Bowden again. *Implementing emergency flooding power and high winds bill. Suggest u return ASAP.*

The rain picked up, pelting harder, colder, carrying an ominous tang of high-altitude ozone. Head bent against the rising wind, Dan texted back *On my way.*

17

Philadelphia

The snow had eased off. That morning's sprinkle had barely frosted the grass where the Brigade waited for the march-on. Idling after the four-hour ride up from Annapolis, the big blue-and-yellow buses the mids called Milk Cartons rumbled clouds of monoxide. Three thousand upperclass milled about beefing, joking, and smoking in the cold. The plebes stood at parade rest, biting their lips. If Navy won, they'd get carry-on until Christmas. If the Big Blue lost . . . shit ran downhill, and they huddled at the bottom.

Dan shivered as the icy wind gnawed his throat. No rifles today. Just calf-length wool bridge coat, white scarf, then more wool under that: sweater and service dress. But he was still cold, and they'd be out here all afternoon. He clapped his arms like too-short wings, trying to warm up.

The Army-Navy Game had been played here since 1936, with one interruption for a world war. He stamped his boondockers, crunching the cold, crisp grass. Ahead, Midshipman Lieutenant Door was conferring with his new assistant company commander. No doubt, about the revised march positioning they'd been handed as they jumped down off the bus.

Not his problem. He was just another doofus now, demoted to the ranks. . . . The segundoes were chattering excitedly, discussing their expectations for the night. The Brigade had Cinderella liberty after the game. Most had laid plans, either for dinner at some local restaurant or meeting their drags—girlfriends—out in town.

Unfortunately, he was still on restriction. He'd left a phone message at Mignon's dorm, asking her to meet him after the game, if only for a few minutes. But hadn't heard back.

And . . . Licia? He smiled, hands deep in his pockets, watching chill clouds of breath drift away on the wind.

As for the Patterson thing, he was still puzzling over that. Where the note could have gone, who'd resurfaced it, and why.

He'd called a pal on watch in the battalion office, and gotten him to look up the dead plebe's hometown. And called there from the phone bank in the basement. Rattling quarter after quarter down into the box. *Ding. Ding.* Dreading speaking to the kid's parents, but had his explanation ready. Waited, as first the AT&T and then the local operator had searched for a Patterson family. And come up empty-handed.

No one by that name lived in Lake Fork, Ohio.

He stamped his feet, blowing more clouds of white vapor into the air. Shivered, as his forebrain puzzled over it like a dog with a rubber bone.

* * *

At last Scherow lifted the guidon. The company drifted into ranks. Somewhere ahead a band was playing. Cheers echoed back, concrete-penned, ghostly in the chill air. More flakes drifted down, and the mids studied the sky. "It's not really gonna dump on us again this year," Enders muttered, beside him.

"We can have another snowball fight with Army," Haley offered.

"Brigade! Atten . . . *hut*," the command came back, barely audible over the grumble of diesels. The buses would idle all night, until the time came to gather up their drunken cargoes for the retreat to Mother Bancroft.

"*Company* . . ." yelled Door. Dan wiped his nose with the back of his glove and tuned his ear to the distant drums.

"*Harch*," yelled Door, and the company stepped off.

But as they turned a corner a line of tie-dyed and jeaned people blocked their path. A woman pushed a soldier in a wheelchair. In Army fatigues and an olive-drab battle jacket, he looked no older than Dan. His face was drawn in pain, or maybe hatred.

The motley barricade lasted only moments as cops waded in, shoving the protesters out of the way. Dan's gaze locked with the amputee's, who lifted a clawed hand, one finger extended.

In loose step, the Brigade filed past television vans and roach coaches, parked limos and ambulances. Finally, like cattle resigned to their execution, they tramped down a dim concrete ramp lined with overflowing trash cans.

Then, suddenly, light. "*LADIES AND GENTLEMEN*," a stentorian voice thundered, "*THE BRIGADE OF MIDSHIPMEN*."

The stands stretched to the sky, filled with thousands of surging spectators. Colorful chyrons flickered. Camera flashes speckled the crowd. The stands opposite were a block of cadet gray. The noise was deafening, concentrated by the enormous ring of concrete. As they steered out onto the field, the company's ranks tightened, meshed, welded. Dan stepped out, centered on the man in front, gaze on the guidon. No one would hear an order in this tumult. When it dipped . . . there. Right, left, *halt.*

He stood planted, shivering, until the order came to break for their assigned seats.

* * *

Everyone stood for "The Star-Spangled Banner," those in uniform at the salute, those in civvies—the alums and fans and guests—with hands over hearts. Dan held the salute a moment after the last note faded. The Flag. He still believed in what it stood for. Maybe it was just an ideal. But it still felt *real.*

Or maybe the truth was, he wasn't sure *how* he felt. Everything was so fucking *contradictory.* Your parents told you one thing. The church, another. The Navy, that honor and duty were what truly mattered.

But which could you count on? And why should you believe any of it?

He shook it off, annoyed. Nobody else seemed to wonder. And settled in on the cold metal of the bench seats, to watch the game.

Navy won the toss. The players crouched, and the whistle blew for the first play.

Dan was perched halfway up the Navy section, huddled between Haley and Scherow, trying to stay warm through the first quarter. Below them the plebes were screaming. Now and then, in the breaks between 4-N cheers and fight songs, an answering roar from the gray-clad ranks opposite rolled back over the field, past the struggling figures locked in panting toil below. Bill the Goat, the Navy mascot, bucked and butted, nervous at the noise, yanking at his lead. Probably freezing *his* ass off too.

Both sides started with long drives that petered out with turnovers. Both tried field goals when they got in range, but had them blocked. Then the Brigade leapt to their feet, mad with glory, as the Blue kicked a twenty-five yarder.

* * *

The snow began to fall in earnest during the second quarter, the brisk, icy wind driving it into the mids' faces. The churned-up field grew muddy. A snack vendor slipped on the slush-slick steps, tumbled to the bottom, and was carried off by the corpsmen.

Army pushed a long drive back from their nineteen after a Navy fumble marked by despairing boos and groans from the plebes. Then, even worse, the Mules tried a thirty-yard field goal with ten seconds left in the half. To the mids' horror, it sailed over the dead center of the goal posts.

Then the numbers flashing on the huge scoreboards in the end zones were even.

* * *

Halftime. Some of the parents and girlfriends had brought blankets. Their mids huddled with them off to the side. Others streamed back under the stands to buy hot dogs, snacks, coffee. A hot chocolate vendor was doing land-office business. Dan got a cup and drank it standing near a gaggle of Old Grads. He side-glanced lined cheeks, bald pates, age spots, shaking hands. Leg braces, canes, wheelchairs. He'd never get that old. Nope.

Two haggard-looking geezers caught his eye. One extracted a pint bottle from his coat. "Hey there, firstie. Want a drink?"

Dan eyed the bottle. After crashing the governor's garden, and the horrific morning after, he'd sworn off alcohol. But it was so fucking cold. . . . At last he nodded. "Sure."

It burned all the way down. He coughed as the oldsters chuckled. "Go ahead," one said. "Pour some in your chocolate, there. Then you can take it up to the stands."

He handed the bottle back reluctantly. Yeah, he felt warmer already. He swirled the chocolate and brandy and muttered, "Thanks."

"Sure, kid. Beat Army." They grinned and turned away.

* * *

He was in line in the stinking dim underground restroom, awaiting his turn at the troughs and taking an occasional hit off the concoction, when someone poked him from behind.

He turned to confront Easy Davis, with two of the other firstie's company mates. Big guys, name tags hidden under their bridge coats. He nodded. "Hey."

They grinned back. "Classmate."

"Thought we should talk," Davis said.

Dan looked around. Suddenly they were in the center of a cleared space, there in the piss-stinking, barely lighted concrete labyrinth. He balled a fist in his pocket, wishing he had something else in there than a dress glove. Like, brass knuckles. "What about?"

"Just to reinforce our class solidarity," Davis said. "You know, how you never bilge a classmate?"

"We know *you* wouldn't," said one of the others. Not the biggest, but a guy with a bad reputation. Dan remembered him now: wealthy parents and a major sense of entitlement. "Just wanted to underline the message."

"You're out of line. Threatening me? You think that's smart?"

"You'll find out who's out of line, Lenson," said the biggest. He shrugged a shoulder, as if to point out the thin gold stripes on his boards. "Your rep follows you, classmate. My dad made sure I knew that."

Dan snorted. "Your dad?"

"Let's just say, as a two-star, he should know." He plucked the still-warm half-full Styrofoam from Dan's fingers and sniffed it. "Drinking on duty. Oh, yeah . . . you got a problem with booze, don't you?"

Dan didn't answer. The striper two-pointed the cup into a trash bin. "You don't want to find out what happens to somebody who thinks he's greasier than his classmates."

"If I see an honor infraction—"

"Then you use your head," Davis finished Dan's sentence. He glanced around as an announcement crackled. Halftime was ending. "Hurry up and take a leak, Lenson. Before somebody decides to beat the piss out of you instead."

* * *

The third quarter lasted forever. The temperature dropped at least ten degrees. The snow drove down so hard at times they couldn't see the field. Dan stayed on his feet, more to keep his ass off the cold metal than to cheer a flagging team. They trotted to and fro on the torn-up sod, pursuing a ball Army seemed to control by telekinesis. Whenever it squirted out of scrums, or a Navy runner fumbled it, a black-and-gold player was there to take it. Still, the defense held. Like a tiring but still-stalwart shield wall holding back a barbarian horde.

As the crowd alternated between screaming curses and passing wave-cheers back and forth, he weighed the threat. He didn't believe it, about a beating. Prison rules didn't go at USNA. But they could make life unpleasant. Maybe calculus wasn't his biggest worry.

He had to decide. He still had the note, padlocked in his lockbox.

But he couldn't hold on to it forever.

* * *

The fourth quarter was a cliff-hanger. Army kept making gains on the ground but somehow never made it across the goal line. Navy nearly scored on a twenty-yard run but was stopped short on fourth down at the one-yard line. The mids groaned and booed. Answering howls rose across the field from the WooPoos.

The last minutes. Navy ground forward again. Quick plays: a yard here, a yard there. The mids screamed. Dan screamed with them, lost for a few minutes in the mass, the collective, the mob.

Then suddenly it was over, the clock run out with the ball still short. Shocked silence fell over the stadium. No one had expected a tie. No one, apparently, knew how to respond.

The mids came to attention for the alma mater.

Four years together by the Bay,
Where Severn joins the tide,
Then by the Service called away,
We're scattered far and wide;
But still when two or three shall meet,
And old tales be retold,
From low to highest in the Fleet,
We'll pledge the Blue and Gold.

He joined in, but without enthusiasm. Who gave a crap? The sense of being part of something bigger faded along with the chocolate-and-brandy glow. Fuck it, he thought. Fuck it all. Whatever he decided, it wouldn't make any difference.

Across the field, the gray tide broke, spreading to meet a blue wave as the fourth class from both sides mixed and mingled in center field. Dan stepped cautiously down the metal steps, which were even slicker now with slush and spilled drinks, and paced along the empty benches. As he neared Bill, the shaggy Angora snorted. Tossing its horns, it nailed him with a baleful yellow gaze. The mascot's handlers stood to either side, a wary eye on the cadets. Each year they tried to kidnap the mascot.

He'd asked Mignon to meet him under the Navy goalposts. He strolled that way, toward several drags who'd obviously gotten the same directions. But she wasn't there. He stood watching as mid after mid found his girl, furtively pecked a cheek, and led her off the field.

At last he stood disconsolate, shivering, sleet piling on his shoulder boards. He turned slowly, surveying the empty stands. His classmates were headed out for parties in town. He considered joining them. Just saying fuck it and going out in a blaze of alcohol and glory.

But he was still on restriction. He trudged glumly across the field, through the gate, up the ramp. Threading the ranks of trash cans, battered and spilled now, their contents of empty cans and bottles and wrappers half trampled into the snow, back to the bus.

* * *

The plebes stood around behind the stadium, looking stunned. They jerked their hands from their pockets as he neared. "You guys don't have liberty?" he asked.

"No, sir. Word from the 'dant's that a tie doesn't rate fourth class liberty."

"That's tough titty."

"Yessir, we're pretty bummed. Sir," a girl added.

A firstie with a brassard came down the line of buses, waving the unfortunate to board. Navy protocol: juniors first, seniors last. He let the plebes go ahead, then put his head down and climbed aboard.

They were rumbling down the highway when, glancing back along the aisle, he spotted a pallid, pimply face. Patterson's roommate. The plebe looked away as soon as their eyes met. Dan crooked a finger. Pointed at him, then at the seat beside him.

The plebe stood swaying in the aisle, looking apprehensive. "Mister Lenson, sir. Permission to come aboard?" He gestured to the empty seat.

Dan frowned. "Yeah. Come aboard."

The plebe sank onto the vinyl as if not fully trusting his weight to it. He whispered, "Sir, did you decide what to do with, you know, with the note?"

"I'm still thinking about it."

The kid looked as if that was the wrong answer but he was afraid to say so. Dan shrugged inwardly. But after a moment added, "Do you remember who it was addressed to? Before whoever had it tore that part off?"

The plebe paled. “Uh, no, sir. I don’t.”

“I think you do. Consider your answer. You saw it. You read it. Out with it.”

He struggled for a moment. Then the duty to tell the truth won. “It was—Mom and Dad, right?”

“Right. But, know what? I tried to call his parents. And there aren’t any Pattersons in his home of record.” The plebe looked confused, but Dan persevered. “Were you guys his Plebe Summer roommates too?”

“Uh, us two were. Yeah. Yes, sir.”

“Okay, who’d he write to? Your cadre made you do letters home, right?”

The plebe’s eyes widened. “You didn’t know? Mario was an orphan. Sir.”

Dan frowned. “Uh . . . okay. But, he didn’t have, like, a stepfamily? Or foster parents? Anybody who came for Parents Weekend?”

“He never wrote letters, sir. Not the whole summer. The first set cadre kept riding his ass about it. Since we were supposed to, every week. But he just said there wasn’t anybody.”

Taken aback, Dan muttered, “Uh, no. I didn’t know that. Thanks for telling me.”

The plebe half rose. “Permission to shove off, sir?”

Dan waved his hand. “Yeah, whatever. Dismissed.” Gripping the seats against the jolting of the bus, the plebe made his way back, trailed by the curious gazes of his classmates.

Leaving Dan alone, running the logic, like on the Academy’s big mainframe you had to program with stacks of punch cards.

It took a day or two to get the results. But when you did, the printout showed clearly where you’d gone wrong. Exactly where, when you thought you’d had it all figured out, the code suddenly froze.

And then you had to go back and start from the beginning. Making sure, this time, you got everything right.

18

Between Washington and Annapolis

Damn, Admiral," his aide said. "This isn't going anywhere. Should we get out and walk?"

Dan shook his head. "I'm tempted. But my maps app shows it loosening up ahead."

LeCato and Dan sat stalled in traffic. It seemed as if half the population of the Coastal Plain and Eastern Shore were stampeding west, for the fall line or even farther inland. He tried to phone Bonar, then Burke-Bowden, but both calls went to voice mail. He steamed in the back seat while his aide blew the horn and inched forward.

By the time they reached Parole the rain had turned to sleet. High-altitude popcorn hail clattered on the hood. When they rolled through Gate 3 at last, the sky was black, though it was only a quarter to five. All he could see beyond the trees was a gluey haze of fog. The lamps illuminating Stribling Walk were globes of wavering light in the driving rain. He wanted to head down to the seawall, see what kind of seas Olaf was driving in on them, but decided to get the big picture at his office first.

The Admin building glowed in the fog like a great lantern. He jogged toward it, soaked to the skin in only the few yards from the car to the door.

His conference room had been converted to an ad hoc command center. The screens didn't show enemy concentrations, but currently flooded areas, the track of the storm, and the tide and surge predictions. Chiefs, officers, and civilian employees had brought in folding chairs. A queue stood at the coffee maker, and Marsh was setting out sticky buns. She looked up. "Admiral's here!"

"Carry on." Dan waved them back to work. "Where are we on the storm bill?"

The public works director handed him a marked-up paper copy. "Eye's passing over Virginia Beach now." Bonar looked apprehensive. "Most comms are down, but Norfolk Naval Base reports major flooding throughout the Hampton Roads area. Winds over a hundred and fifty knots. Gusts to a hundred eighty. City power's out. Highways out. Bridges closed. Underpasses flooded. This one's hitting hard."

Dan rubbed his chin. Nan was out of town, presumably safe on higher ground. And Blair ensconced at the Pentagon . . . he hoped. He asked Burke-Bowden, "Did they get the Fleet out of Norfolk?" Usually ships were safer at sea than bashing themselves to scrap alongside the piers.

The deputy supe shook his head. "SOPA thought sortieing would put them smack in the path if the storm passed offshore, like it was predicted to. So he kept them in port. This last-minute swerve took everybody by surprise."

Bonar scrubbed his face with both hands. "It's bad, Admiral. NOAA's discussing making this the first official Category Six. Isabel, in '03, peaked at seven feet above mean low. This is worse. Higher sustained winds. More flooding."

Dan remembered seeing pictures of that storm's impact on the Yard. "Up to now, the season was easier than expected."

"This'll make up for it. Like it's stored up all that energy that used to be dissipated in two or three storms, and packed it all into one monster."

Dan patted his shoulder. "Take a breath, Jerry. We'll get through it." To Burke-Bowden, "What're we doing about our people? Mids? Staff? And dependents, over in post housing?"

The deputy said the Brigade had been relocated to Bancroft's second and third floors. "High tide plus storm surge could flood the basements, maybe the first deck, and the roofs are vulnerable to wind damage. Housing should be safe, they're on high ground. But we opened the Exchange as a shelter, for those who want to go."

Dan studied the maps. "The Chapel's on the highest ground. Should we evacuate Bancroft now? Before the surge hits?"

As if this had been argued over before, the two men stared at each other. "They'd be safer in the Chapel, Admiral. I agree," Burke-Bowden said.

"Too risky getting them there," Bonar said. "Those old oaks, the root systems are shallow. Once the ground soaks and those gusts hit, they'll start coming down."

Dan weighed the choices. "What's Colonel Stocker's take?"

The deputy said, "The 'dant wanted to keep them in Bancroft. I deferred to her."

"Okay, Jack, I guess that makes the most sense. Where is she?"

"Main Office. Supervising. She's got the mids sandbagging the basement entrances."

Dan nodded. "Fine. We'll shelter them in place."

More hail clattered on the windows. Beyond the shivering glass it was full night now. The wind was still rising. Its daunting howl chilled his bones, evoking atavistic memories of huddling in caves as the sky exploded. The lights and screens flickered dark, then lit again. Flickered again, and stayed on.

"Emergency power, from our generators," Bonar said.

Dan bent to examine a live feed with the latest predicted track. A chill harrowed his spine. Yeah, Olaf was boresighted up the middle of the Bay. The screen froze for several seconds before updating again. How long would they have connectivity? Another screen displayed current air temperature, wind velocity, and sea level. He frowned. It read zero wind, zero tide. "Uh, where's the data from our weather station?"

"The one on Santee Pier blew away an hour ago," Master Chief Wenck told him. "We can still get Brewer Point and Thomas Point Light." Leaning over Dan, he called up the one at the mouth of the Severn. "High tide'll be a little after midnight."

Which, as far as Dan could deduce, would be just about when Olaf passed over. He closed his eyes. The heavy, drenching rain thundering down outside would only add to the flooding. Now he understood why Bonar looked so stressed.

Dan led him into his private office and closed the door. Valerie had set several small battery lamps around the room, preparing for loss of power, but giving it a haunted-house vibe. "Level with me, Jer. Just how bad's this gonna get?"

Bonar shook his head. "This is our worst-case scenario, Admiral. Eight to ten inches of rain, a spring tide, and a hurricane surge. When they stack, we could see fifteen feet above mean sea level. Maybe more."

"Fifteen?"

"Yessir. Twice what we saw with Isabel, when the whole Lower Yard flooded. Way more than we're set up to handle."

Dan nodded, dismayed. Most of the Yard was only three or four feet above mean sea level. In his previous talks with Bonar, he'd tried to think fifty or sixty years ahead. Well, tonight they'd see what every day would look like, then. "Gotcha . . . but what we have to think about now is how to preserve lives. Should we evacuate? Into town?"

Bonar looked torn. "If we'd done it earlier, maybe. Too late now. The trees, flying debris."

The wind's roar had risen to a shrill note not far short of a shriek. The lights occulted again. The windows of his office bulged inward slightly, creaking audibly, like a sub's pressure hull as it neared crush depth. Marsh rushed in and rattled down the blinds. In case one of the panes shattered, Dan figured. "I asked Admiral Cree to install shutters," she said. "But he never put in for them."

Just . . . fucking . . . great. He raked his hair back and tried to compose himself. Once again, he'd have to pretend everything was in hand. That he knew they'd come through okay.

But he had no such confidence. Fifteen feet, and gusts nearing a hundred and eighty . . . only one response remained. They were reduced to the last resort of the ancestral hominids, before fire, before houses, before technology.

Hunker, and try to endure.

* * *

Back in the conference room, he held up his hand. As the buzz quieted, a gust smacked the building so hard the walls shook. He shouted over it, "Listen up, everybody! We *will* come through this. There'll be damage, but we'll survive.

"Right now, let's concentrate on keeping everyone safe. Captain, have Colonel Stocker secure her sandbagging parties. Everyone take cover. Windows in Bancroft at half-mast to lessen the pressure. Mids, bunked down in the passageways, with mattresses and blankets. Secure power at the master breakers, to avoid fires when the water shorts things out." He glanced around. "What else, people?"

"Cars, parked along the seawall. The firsties' cars," someone said.

Dan chuckled grimly. "If they haven't moved those by now, they're toast. I want our people on the middle floors of the most solid buildings. Hopper. Bancroft. The Chapel. Here." He dragged a hand over his hair again. "Any other suggestions? If not, I'm going out." He looked around. "Need a volunteer."

A heavyset man stepped forward. The command master chief, Kareem Abimbola. He said nothing; just inclined his head.

* * *

Bundled in rain gear, hard hats from one of the Yard crews clamped on their skulls, he and the master chief hiked, bent into the rising wind, toward the river. A handheld two-way was clipped to Dan's belt. The wind drove the rain nearly horizontally, stinging their downturned faces. It was mixed with icy sleet. The Yard lights flickered, but he could still see a few feet ahead. The branches of the massive old oaks whipped wildly, like the dancing inflatables that advertised used-car lots. Now and then a limb crashed to earth, pulping the carefully tended flower beds. But so far the trees' roots seemed to be holding.

The bandstand was missing half its roof, which lay wrapped around the granite phallus of the Herndon Monument. Dan gave it a grim acknowledging glance. Scaling that obelisk's smooth greased height, to perch a cap at its apex, had been the high point of Plebe Year.

They plowed on. Dan mounted the steps to the plaza between Michelson and Chauvenet Halls, remembering how impressive they'd looked when new. Now the concrete pavers were canted and crumbling. The 1970s hadn't been a good time for architectural permanency.

When he halted on the balustrade overlooking the Severn, his mind refused for a moment to make sense of what he saw. Ingram Field, where he'd played lacrosse: gone. Dewey Field, beyond it: vanished. To his right the river lapped the great granite entrance of MacDonough Hall. Its lofty arch had once admitted sailing craft. A shallow-draft boat could have entered now, could any have lived in this wind . . . the newly risen river surged past nearly at his feet, turbulent, wind-tormented, roiled gray-brown with sediment. Branches and driftwood swirled past, then a sodden blue-and-gold life jacket. Dan glanced toward the basin, but saw nothing except blowing rain and gathering darkness.

A crackle; his radio, turned all the way up. *"Where are you, Admiral? Are you all right?"*

It was Burke-Bowden. Dan clicked a response. "We're at Michelson. Ingram and Dewey are at least three feet deep."

"Sir, please, get back here. Or to high ground. You're at risk too."

Dan double-clicked an acknowledgment, then added, "Back shortly. Going to check out Bancroft next."

Three-foot waves were driving across the rising water, crashing apart against the slanted walls below him. Dirty spume leapt high. The keening wind caught the spray, mixed it with rain, and drove it into his teeth. He backed away and jogged toward the dormitory as a violent gust picked up one of the visitors' benches and hurled it sailing across T-Court, to crash into the windows of the first deck.

Behind the first wing a group of sodden mids and Yard personnel were filling bags from a sandpile, passing them hand to hand, and stacking them in the entrance of the Mid Store. Obviously they hadn't gotten the word to secure. One glance told him their efforts were futile. The rising water was swirling around the makeshift barrier, waves sloshing through the shattered doors into the store.

Dan closed on them, grabbed two, and pulled their heads toward him. He pitched his voice above the wind. "*Get inside!* Anyone else you see, get them under cover. Nobody should be out here."

One of the civilian workers yelled, "*You're* out here, Admiral."

Dan ignored that. "Let's try to work our way over toward Santee," he shouted to Abimbola.

After a halt to check in on the radio—the storm was still tracking up the Bay, the surge prediction unchanged—they climbed to the first deck of Bancroft. Paced through spooky abandoned passageways and out onto the colonnade to MacDonough. He remembered marching punishment on these terra-cotta tiles, now slick with rain and pocked with hail. Through that vast hall, the steel roof supports knitting the dark together overhead, and out the riverside exit. Descending to ground level, they waded through cold water up to their waists around Luce Hall and out toward where a gonging clamor from the mist told him the basin lay.

With the largest collegiate sailing program in the country, Navy hosted several big-boat regattas each year. He had thirty keelboats for basic training, a small fleet of forty-four footers, and even larger donated boats. The mids raced them to Canada, Bermuda, and more distant ports. Millions of dollars' worth of fiberglass and wood and metal.

But what loomed out of the rain-fog and blown spume was sound rather than sight. The jangle and clang of halliards against reeling masts, and the deeper, more unsettling booming of hollow hulls into concrete.

The noise set his teeth on edge. The basin held nine large sailing craft, ten to fourteen 44 yawls, thirty Colgates, and a mix of others, skiffs,

EdgeWaters, and Zodiacs. Thirty intercollegiate dinghies had been stowed on the hard. He waded through swirling water, trying to remember where Santee Road ended. "Know where the edge is? I don't want to step off into deep water," he yelled to Abimbola.

"No idea, sir," the senior enlisted yelled back.

The wind was driving huge waves out of the darkness. He grabbed a stanchion, bracing himself as the surf foamed around them, waist-deep, chest-deep. The wind struck him full in the face, so strong he couldn't inhale. A heavier wave blitzed in at throat level, and he staggered backward. When it was past he crouched, cupping his mouth to draw a breath, but the wind blew even harder. Gusts to a hundred and eighty?

"We should get back to the office, sir," Abimbola shouted.

"Just a quick gander, Master Chief," Dan shouted. "Then we'll head back."

The wind slacked. He waded a few more yards, trying to make out what he thought might be mooring pilings ahead. Then he caught faint shouts, the flicker of handheld lights.

When he reached the basin, he drew a horrified breath. The seas were roaring in out of the darkness, white-maned, driven to eight and ten feet even in the short fetch of the river by the gale. The protective mole was submerged. Several of the larger boats were loose, blown in among the twenty-four footers. There, hung up by their keels on the shoaling bottom, they rolled and plunged like rodeo bulls, wreaking havoc on the smaller boats and grinding themselves against the now-submerged inner seawall. Tearing metal and breaking wood crunched and snapped, deafening even amid the howl of the wind. He searched the maelstrom for his own boat, but it was lost in the clanging welter of clashing masts and plunging hulls.

Anyway, that was the least of his concerns. . . . He waded around the basin, bent over, toward the sailing center. Its windows, which looked out over the river and bay, were dark. But he'd seen lights. . . . He slipped and went down, soaking the rest of his clothing, but regained his footing and plowed on.

Halfway to the building he came across a small party of Yard workers and older civilians. In the wavering flicker of flashlights, they were furiously trying to bend additional lines to the remaining undamaged boats. As Dan and the chief came up, one shadowy figure tossed him a coil of line and pointed to a piling. "We need this fast on that piling, guys. For *Zaraffa*. If you're here to help out." Belatedly, Dan recognized Virjay Gupta, the athletic director.

"Sir, we really need to get back," Abimbola yelled into the storm.

Dan nodded, but hesitated, looking at the huge sleek white hull as it plunged and reeled against its remaining lines. Several dangled loose, snapped or abraded until they gave way. Each time the hull surged, the braided rope wept water as they snubbed it up short. Nylon was elastic, to a degree, but clearly it wouldn't stand the strain much longer.

Zaraffa was the pride of the Academy's sailing fleet, an enormous Reichel/Pugh racer-cruiser. Built to world-class standards, the sloop had taken a second place in the Fastnet and raced Newport Bermuda four times, winning a Lighthouse trophy, as well as taking firsts on the North Atlantic Challenge and the Transatlantic. It would be impossible to replace her, if she were damaged.

He eyed the piling Gupta had pointed him to. The basin was normally sheltered by a seawall, but that bulwark was submerged. Each wind-harried wave crashed into it, then showered down on the workers as they struggled with the lines. A narrow finger pier led out to the piling, but repeated poundings were smashing it upward, like an opening drawbridge.

"Admiral, we should leave," his companion urged again.

"One second," he yelled.

He coiled the wet line around hand and arm, boatswain style, and swung his body around the inboard piling. The structure shuddered under his weight. For a moment he wondered if it would be smarter to just let everything go. Then, hearing the others cheer him on, he mustered his courage. Letting go of the piling, he ran four quick steps out along the canted, jerking pier to the outboard one. He tried to flip a tugboat bowline, but the wind destroyed his knot. Instead he leaned into the piling, clinging to it as a wave slammed into him, and made the line fast with a round turn and a couple half hitches. Done.

He was turning back, left arm still around the piling to anchor himself, when a white hull drove in out of the mist and spray and caught him between boat and piling. The snap of breaking bone echoed in his head.

Suddenly the chief was at his side, tugging him away. The finger pier flexed under their weight. Just as they reached the hard, stepping off into what looked like the river but yielded solid footing underneath the surface, the cruiser crashed into it again. The whole pier gave way, collapsing into the foaming surge as more spray rained down.

He glanced back, cradling his crushed arm, grimacing as the pain arrived. Rearing, then dropping precipitously, the huge craft parted its remaining restraints. Shaking itself loose, it began to drift down on the line of snarled, surging twenty-fours.

Abimbola and Gupta led him away, slogging through the water back toward Bancroft. The chief was on the radio. "The admiral's broken his arm," he yelled into the transceiver. "*Broken his arm.* Need immediate assistance. Over." To Dan he yelled, "We'll get you to sick bay, sir."

"No. Back to the office," he shouted, as the wind drove cold rain down his throat.

"What? Sir, we need to—"

"They can meet me there. I have to get back." Belatedly, and not just because of the injury, he was realizing he'd gotten sidetracked. Abimbola and Burke-Bowden were right. His post was on the quarterdeck, in charge. Not showing off in the teeth of a storm. He'd screwed up, coming out here at all.

He cradled his arm, which was already swollen and seemed deformed. He was thinking, At least I'm not losing any blood, when the darkness seeped into his mind, at first just at the very edges, then, suddenly, came down over his head like an abductor's black bag.

* * *

He came to being jostled on some kind of litter. The night was still dark but bright planets were drifting by. Was he . . . in space? Then the orbs resolved into emergency bulbs. He was being carried into Bancroft.

Sick bay was an organized chaos. Water was creeping under the doors, pushing aside a dike of wadded towels. Corpsmen and techs were hustling gear and records up to the first deck. A portable X-ray machine buzzed. The doctor examined the screen. "You've got a fracture in the ulna, Admiral. The large bone on the outside of the forearm." She readied an injection. "A local. This is gonna hurt. When we reduce the fracture. But not for long."

He couldn't help looking down as she gave him the shot. His whole lower arm, from wrist to elbow, was swollen and purpled.

She readied another needle. "To make you more comfortable, afterward—"

"I'll pass on the general. Do what you have to," he mumbled, looking away as she called a corpsman over to assist. She planted her feet and placed one hand firmly on his wrist, the other gripping above his elbow.

The pain jerked a shriek out of him. He bit his lip, hoping the sound hadn't carried far. She wound a splint, then looped a sling. "That should do for now. Come back tomorrow and we'll make sure everything's staying in place. If you feel pain when you move your fingers, though, call me right away."

Dan adjusted the sling with his right hand. "We done?"

"Not yet. Take these." When he started to object, she said, "They'll help with the pain. Though you really should stay here, sir."

He sat up and swung his legs down. Swayed, fighting nausea, but stayed upright. "I had on rain gear, coming in here—"

She told the corpsman, reluctantly, "Get him his raincoat."

* * *

Back at Larson, Bonar updated him. The rain had overwhelmed the drains that channeled precipitation to the river. The Lower Yard was flooding as the Severn backed up through the drains and the storm surge overwhelmed the seawalls. Farragut Field was four feet under. Both field houses were inundated. Looking at the screens, Dan realized the route he'd walked an hour before, to the basin, was now impassible. Only the raised terraces between buildings remained above water.

And the tide was still building.

Burke-Bowden sighed. "Basement of Bancroft's filled, and the first deck's flooding too. Stocker's staging the mids up to third and fourth decks."

Dan adjusted his sling, then flinched. It was really starting to hurt. Maybe he should've accepted the shot. But he couldn't risk being impaired, possibly making a bad call. "Yeah, I saw that in sick bay. How's it going across the river?"

"Localized flooding, but everyone's safe."

"The YPs?" The Yard Patrol craft, training vessels for surface tactics, were docked in their own basin on the far side of the river.

"The north bank's in the lee. Tripled mooring lines should keep them secure."

"How about injuries?"

The deputy averted his eyes from Dan's arm. "We have a few storm-related ones, yes, sir. But we kept everyone—almost everyone—under cover. Mostly, it'll be property damage."

Marsh called, "Sir, DoD on the line."

It was Naval Facilities Command, asking for a status, and whether he needed assistance. Dan was outlining the situation when the line went dead.

He stared at the phone, then put it down. They had other channels—SIPRNET was still up—but he couldn't think of anything anyone could do to help. The Academy should have been either moved or flood-proofed decades ago. In the end, you couldn't conquer the sea. It would keep rising, and the Academy, like every other coastal installation, would have to find a way to cope.

* * *

The dark hours went by. Slowly. The winds backed as the eye passed over, but the tide kept rising, as did the flooding.

Dan stood gnawing his lip, wishing he could mentally force the steadily increasing water back down. The video feeds throughout the Yard had all either blown off their mounts or gone dead from water intrusion, so the only way he could learn what was going on was through verbal reports. But he was feeling more and more tired, woozy, out of it. . . .

* * *

Dawn began to break. He woke from a groggy daze, head cradled in one arm on his office couch. Started to rise, then caught his breath at a jab from the broken arm. "Shit," he hissed. Staggered to his desk, found naproxen in a drawer, and bolted two tablets dry.

His secretary. "Admiral, you're awake . . . sorry to disturb you, but you have a call from the SecDef."

"Landlines're up again?"

"No, sir. She's on my cell." Marsh held out her phone.

Where was *his* phone? Oh yeah . . . wet and out of commission. He reassured Blair he was all right, aside from some bruises. "A sling for a few days, that's all . . . Yeah, I know, not my smartest move."

"And the Academy? I understand you're completely flooded."

"Uh, still working on a damage report. But, yeah, this is pretty clearly the worst this place has ever seen."

"We'll need to talk soon, Dan. About your long-range plans."

"Absolutely," he assured her, and ended the call.

Sighed. And stood, cradling the arm.

In the conference room Bonar was staring at a screen, red-eyed. Dan called, "Jerry, let's take a look. See how bad it is."

"Sure you're up to it, Admiral?"

He didn't answer, just searched out his still-wet rain gear. Someone had pulled his sodden shoes off while he napped. Stepping into them, he wondered who.

Only barely dawn, and still raining, but enough leaden light oozed through the still-streaming clouds that they could see. The chill breeze smelled dank. Dan tested the law he'd learned as a mid: that when you placed the wind at your back, the eye of a circular storm lay behind you to the left. Yeah, it still worked.

The floodwaters began downhill from the Chapel and stretched south toward Bancroft and east toward the terraces of Chauvenet and Michelson. Random zephyrs stirred the surface, as if the hurricane hated to go. The curving walks were all submerged. Oaks lay toppled, their discoid, surprisingly shallow root systems poking twisted juts of soil and bark above the water.

His ears pricked up at the purr of an outboard. An inflatable, probably from across the river, nosed this way and that as a seaman in the bow pushed debris aside with a boat hook. Dan hailed it, and he and Bonar clambered in.

Threading amid the fallen trees, whose wind-stripped branches formed spidery hemispheres above the surface, they trolled toward Bancroft. As they purred down Stribling, Dan borrowed the boat hook. When he sounded, it clicked on brick five feet below. The landscaping was ruined. The flowers, scorched with salt, would die. Possibly all the grass too.

T-Court was flooded. Shit-brown, greasy-looking liquid lapped halfway up the steps to the Rotunda. Mids were dropping paper boats like white butterflies from the windows. Caught by the wind, they scudded past him as the inflatable turned.

They cruised out onto the river. Rain still misted its surface. Shattered trees, boards, the debris of wrecked piers, and other trash drifted Bay-ward. The storm tide was receding, and the scale of the destruction left him shaken.

"Your reservoir and pump system. Would that have prevented this?" he asked the engineer. Bonar responded with twisted lips and a shake of the head.

"How *do* we prevent it, then? Levees? Dikes?"

The public works supervisor shrugged. “We don’t. It’ll flood like this again, and more and more often. There’s no way to completely stop it, Admiral.”

They turned and motored back into the Yard. As they neared the Main Office Dan made out Stocker on the steps, waving. He jerked his head to the man at the wheel.

When they were close enough, Dan bent awkwardly, favoring his arm, and tossed her a line. The Marine made it fast around one of the Spanish trophy cannons. Her camo trou were muddy; dirt smeared her blouse; drops of water sparkled on her hair. She’d obviously lent a hand with the sandbags. She glanced at his sling. “Heard you had some trouble, down at the basin.”

“My own fault,” Dan said, a little sheepishly. “I got too enthusiastic, trying to save one of the racers. Should have just let her go.”

He followed the colonel up the stairs, out of the rain. The Rotunda looked untouched except for muddy trails across the slick cream-and-rose marble deck. He gazed up at the massive murals decorating the barrel vaults, at the dome high above. “Wish that was the only damage, Colonel. How’d we fare here?”

“Basement’s flooded. We’ll lose everything there—rifle range, barber shop, Mid Store, medical, tailor shops.” Stocker sighed. “But all hands pitched in to move the most valuable items to the upper decks. And Memorial Hall was above the high point of the flooding.”

“Good. Good.” He rubbed his chin, debating whether to assess the damage himself. No, he could work with the commandant’s report. So, where next? He glanced out the massive bronze doors. The water swirled ominously, carrying branches, bright orange plastic traffic cones, pallets, a green bench torn loose from its base, a sodden dark object that made him start—the arched back of a drowned body?—until he realized it was simply a wad of sodden clothing. Was the level dropping yet? Hard to tell. He looked around for Bonar, but the engineer had gone off somewhere.

A first-class mid rendered a sharp salute. Brunette, small-boned, with a touch of New England in her voice. “Admiral. Midshipman First Class Oshry. Did you want to address the Brigade, sir?”

Juliane Oshry . . . the new brigade commander . . . the mid the trolls said Dan had murdered Evans for, in order to promote in his place. His arm throbbed with a deep ache. He wanted to lie down, and maybe accept a pain pill at last. But she was right. A bracing word was in order, after the night just past.

He followed her to the office. Another striper handed him a microphone. Dan cleared his throat, and the raw growl echoed in every corner of the two-thousand-room dormitory.

"Good morning. This is the supe speaking.

"It's been a hell of a night, for all of us. First, let me thank everyone. The 'dant tells me how we saved valuable gear, merchandise from the Mid Store, equipment from sick bay. The X-ray machines and other . . . stuff."

"Other stuff"? Was he getting woozy?

"I mean . . . important gear. Medical equipment. Probably several million dollars' worth. In the days to come we'll be clearing debris, maybe helping out, out in town. They've been hard hit too.

"It's no news this is the worst flooding event ever to hit the Bay area. We've lived through a historic night, and we've all come through safe. For that, let's offer thanks, everyone in his or her own way.

"We'll pass work parties tomorrow. Meanwhile, steer clear of the basement, first deck, and other damaged areas. Bunk down and try to get some sleep." He clicked off and glanced at Stocker. "Colonel, anything to add?"

She swept a mock bow. Close up, she looked exhausted too. "You nailed it, Admiral."

He clicked on again. Still thinking of Evans, and Oshry, and the outsiders who were trying to tear the Brigade apart. Setting them against one another. *"The commandant told me how everyone in Mother B turned to. I'm proud of you all, and how well you worked together. Just a sample of how much we can accomplish, when we're united.*

"So then, good morning, and everyone, again, try to get a couple hours' rack time. Tomorrow—that is, today—will be a busy day."

He resocketed the mic, sighed, and turned away. He'd tried to search for encouraging words. But they just hadn't come.

* * *

He lingered on the steps, looking down onto T-Court. The rain had stopped, though gray clouds still drove across the sky and the wind refrigerated his sodden clothing. Tecumseh, no, he was Tamanend now, scowled back across the brown water that swirled and eddied between them. To judge by the watermarks on the statue's pedestal, it was finally receding.

The damage would cripple the Academy for years, even if Congress approved funds for repairs. Which seemed unlikely. Merging the academies . . . that might make sense financially. But it would weaken the nation. Outsiders could scoff at tradition. But stories of how others had suffered, died, but ultimately achieved victory—that was what welded units together when all seemed lost.

He rubbed his face, suddenly bludgeoned by fatigue. Mixed with depression, and something akin to fear. He'd hoped for a new beginning. Making the Academy more inclusive, more forward-looking. Embracing new technologies and new ways of thinking.

Instead he might preside over its demise.

He eased out a sigh, staring out over toppled trees, debris, and wrack. Water lay many feet deep between him and the academic buildings. They, along with a few ancient oaks and the tops of the lampposts, were all that remained.

Gray and grand, those stone constructions had endured a century and more, secure on pilings driven deep into the solid earth beneath.

An idea stirred in a dark corner of his bewildered brain.

Driven not into the fill. *Into the solid earth beneath.*

Bonar had explained what lay down there. Glauconitic sand. Clay. Dan had seen its shells and fossils exposed along the Chesapeake's western bank. The strata shaded from greenish-brown to greenish-black, weathering to a rusty hue as the iron oxidized. It dated to the Paleocene, sixty million years before.

The idea wavered, retreated, dissolving instead of solidifying. He frowned, passing a hand over his hair, trying to coax it back into the light. Oshry and Stocker, at his side, were trying to tell him something, but he waved them to silence. Closing his eyes. Chasing the thought.

He coughed into a fist, gasping as anguish jolted up his shattered arm.

Could it be possible?

He'd have to find out.

19

T*was the week after Army, and all the good mids*
Were prepping for Christmas, while Dan's on the skids. . . .

The doggerel echoed in his tired brain as he slogged back and forth. On the terrace again. Rifle digging into his shoulder. With the plebes and third class, marching off their venial demerits. With his lips freezing, cheeks and toes numb. He hadn't slept well either. Dreaming about being late to a thermo test, out of uniform, no pencil, without a clue.

At this rate he'd be out here until the day he graduated. If he *did* graduate.

It wasn't snowing this afternoon, but the wind off the Severn was razor cold, the empty sky the off-white of cracked ice. Where did the gulls go in the winter? Grimy heaps of dirty snow barricaded the entrance of the Mid Store. Past that the playing fields stretched muddied, tracked-up. Rimes of ice ridged the green slow-moving river. To the east, glimpsed for a moment as he about-faced, the sailing craft lay frozen, immobile in their sheltering basin. As if locked into a stasis field by invading aliens.

No one knew how to react to a tie with Army. The plebes, missing the preholiday carry-on they'd so eagerly anticipated, were restive, like serfs denied emancipation. The upperclass had different issues, like finals, but the depressed mood was everywhere. As if the Dark Ages, the legendary abyss that riveted a clinical depression on everyone between Christmas and spring leave, had arrived early.

The leather sole of one boonie skidded on a frozen patch, and he nearly went down. Barely catching himself before the rifle hit the deck, he came to a sloppy attention. About-faced. And began trudging back.

* * *

He was peeling sopping socks off, changing for evening meal, when DuKay knocked on his door. The plebe bulged, a gray planetoid in multiple sets of sweat gear, face streaming with sweat. "Yeah," Dan snapped. "What is it, Donkey?"

"Sir, lieutenant wants you in the company office."

Scherow raised an eyebrow from his rack. Dan hesitated, one sock on, one off. The discarded one lay limp and wet on the tile deck. "Now?"

"Yessir. ASAP."

Oleksa probably just wanted one of his little chats. Dan kicked the socks under his desk, pulled on fresh ones, jammed his feet into his class shoes, and headed out.

* * *

In the passageway he threaded between howling second class and frantic, sweating plebes. Walloped in the ass with an atlas, a fourth class shot down the hall, leapt into the air, and belly flopped onto a row of mattresses. Carrier landings . . . Dan knocked at the door of the company office, entered, and sounded off. "Midshipman First Class Lenson, reporting as ordered."

"Lenson? Come in. Close the door." Oleksa rose from his latest hobby, a hulking dull-silver computer he was trying to transfer USNA forms to. Plopping behind his desk, he flicked another toy. A shiny steel ball smacked a row of similar spheres, and another on the far end sprang up. Then the process repeated . . . The company officer was in blues, white shirt, black tie. His blouse hung behind the door. The room smelled of coffee and ozone. Probably from the computer. "Siddown."

Dan perched on the edge of the chair, then forced himself to slide back a couple of inches. Trying to relax. *Click*, went the balls. *Click. Click.* What did the guy want? But you couldn't ask. Just wait for him to get to it.

The submariner drawled, "So, how's restriction treating you?"

"Uh, all right, sir."

"How we doing, marching off all those demerits?"

We? "Uh, we're making a dent in—"

"But we have a ways to go, right?"

"That's right, sir. Just . . . do it an hour at a time, I guess."

Click . . . click. The thing was hypnotic. Watching it made you believe in perpetual motion.

Oleksa lifted a paper, then dropped it. "I'm concerned by what Mr. Door's been telling me. About the bad blood between you and our neighboring company. Stemming from the, um, death last month. Though finding the body must have been a shock."

"Yes, sir. I—"

"I know I'm not, um, privy to everything that goes on around here. But I hear you think one of your own classmates was responsible in some way."

Dan swallowed. He'd typed up the honor violation report on his old Royal, but it rested still in the combination-locked desk safe that was the only place a mid could call private, along with the note Patterson had left.

Once he turned them in, he'd be a bilger.

The lesson was hammered in from the first day in the Yard: you looked out for your classmates. Back in the dim mythical past, one Richmond P. Hobson had fried two full pages of his peers for smoking, being late to formation, and improper uniforms. For two years no one had spoken to Hobson, looked at him, or acknowledged his existence. Dan didn't think a formal Coventry still existed, but there was no doubt he'd be in shit city.

Click . . . click. Oleksa cleared his throat. Dan sat up straighter in the chair, which seemed to have turned slippery under his ass. "Sir, you read my, um, my prelim investigation. I think he *was* responsible. At least, for pushing too hard." He hesitated, wondering if he should mention that the note had reappeared. Then decided to hold off just a little longer.

Oleksa nodded, pursing his lips. Then got up and peered out his window, parting the blinds. Looking down, as if he expected to see something interesting in the alley between the wings. Though usually it held only dumpsters and maybe a laundry truck. "Mind if I offer a little advice?"

Dan worked his shoulders surreptitiously. "Yes, sir. I mean, no, sir. Maybe I *could* use—"

"I looked over your peer evaluations, Dan. All the way back to Plebe Summer. You have a rep as somebody who's kind of . . . more uptight than the average run. Convinced he's always right."

"Sir." Dan blinked. "I don't get to see those."

Oleksa waved it off. "I know, all you see's the rankings. And it's not necessarily a bad look, to be locked on. Even if you believe you're more righteous than some of your classmates."

More *righteous*? While he was spending every free minute walking off multiple Class A offenses? "Uh, sir, I don't see myself that—"

"Well, maybe not. Still, there's such a thing as getting along. Both in the Navy, and the world at large." The lieutenant glanced at his watch. "Due home for dinner. Just thought I'd offer that to you, for what it's worth."

The steel balls leapt, fell, rested, leapt once more. Dan blinked as invisible energy shuttled back and forth. Would the fucking thing never run down? "Uh, thanks, sir, but I'm still not sure exactly what you're telling me."

Oleksa looked weary. He ran his thumbs around his waistband, where his gut had pulled the shirt out. "Okay, lemme try again. You're gonna see some things in the Fleet, sometimes, that might not seem exactly in line with the way they should be. Or are supposed to be. Or are advertised to be.

"I'm supposed to guide you guys, but there's only so much I can do. You know? Just a little around the edges. A nudge, here and there."

Dan frowned, bemused. Oleksa was still speaking to the window, so close his breath frosted the cold glass. "I guess what I'm tryin' to say is, when we start out, everybody wants to think he's special. A hot runner. The top one percent. But the reality is, most of us aren't. We're just someplace in the middle of the pack. Where the pack goes, we go. And that's about the best we're ever going to get."

Fuck was he talking about? Dan nodded, faking comprehension.

Chow call went out in the passageway. A plebe two doors down, bellowing as loud and fast as he could: officers of the watch. Menu for evening meal. The movies out in town. Ending with, "Time tide and formation wait for no man. Five minutes, SIR!"

Dan stood. "Ah . . . permission to shove off, sir?"

Click . . . click. Yet Oleksa still stood looking down into the alley. At last he muttered, as if to himself, "Get out of here."

* * *

The overhead lights in King Hall seemed dimmer than usual. The windows, black. Meatballs, gravy, mashed potatoes, and mushy, overcooked peas and carrots. Dan let the third class harass the plebes a little, then suggested they let them eat. "In fact," he added, "why don't we just give them carry-on."

After an astonished moment the fourth class unlimbered their jaws and slid back in their chairs. They looked suspicious, as if they didn't deserve to eat normally. Muff shot him a silent glance. Gratitude? Or resentment? Dan didn't care.

"Going home for Christmas, Dan?" Teddy said suddenly.

He helped himself to more potatoes. Confront his dad again? The violent, angry ex-cop, wallowing in his resentment of a town that had wronged him? Then remembered, actually with relief: he'd still be on restriction. For better or worse, Navy was his life now. Was that what Oleksa had been trying to tell him? He still wasn't sure.

"Dan?" Scherow prodded.

He flinched. "Uh, sorry . . . Fuck, I'm gonna be marching tours. You?"

"Zusana's invited me to meet her folks."

"Sounds serious."

"Maybe. I'd stay at a hotel, but I'd spend Christmas with them." His roomie looked conflicted. "But it'd be the first time I . . . y'know . . . wasn't home for the holidays."

Dan nodded. Remembering what Oleksa had said, he forced the words out. "That's a real dilemma, Teddy. But I know you'll make the right decision."

* * *

That night in their room, Dan waited until Scherow was rehearsing again, staring at the bulkhead and emoting about the slings and arrows of outrageous fortune, before bending and spinning the dial of his safe. He reached behind the confidential codebook they were supposed to memorize for tactics, and laid the now-crackling, dry note on his blotter. Outside, in the passageway, someone screamed, "Plebe ho!" at the top of his lungs.

"Not fucking *again*," Scherow muttered. He jumped up and slammed their door. "This is my big chance. I gotta nail this soliloquy."

Dan smoothed the note flat, wondering again what to do. Let it go? Or do what was right, regardless of the consequences to himself?

He examined the edge of the tear, where the upper corner had vanished. If only he could figure out where it had come from. There was something there he just didn't grok.

Okay, Dan. Let's assume for a moment that the bruises on Patterson's face, the blood on his clawed fingers, hadn't been from the fall. That someone else—say, Davis and his two buddies—caught him there in the head that night, maybe taking a smoke break, like his roomies said he did, shoved him through the already-opened window, and left a fake note.

But why would they then *steal* the note? It proved Patterson had jumped on his own.

And once vanished, why the *fuck* would it reappear?

He teetered back in his chair, almost to the point of going over backward. Faintly through the door came hollering and cheering as the youngsters urged the plebes on in a crab race. Jeez, he was getting sleepy. . . . He slammed the chair down and went to the window. "Mind if I?"

Scherow frowned over his script. "We got somebody on window-closing detail?"

"Yeah." Dan cracked it just enough so a chill breezed the room. Half an hour before reveille, a plebe would ease his way in and silently seal the windows. So everything would be toasty when his seniors woke.

Wait a minute. He'd seen a typewriter in Davis's room.

He thrust the report chit back into the safe and twirled the dial. Picked up some bond paper and folded it around the note. "Back in a sec," he muttered.

Scherow shrugged, lips moving silently as he struggled with Hamlet's eternal equivocation.

* * *

The plebes' door was open, their room empty. Dan found a black typewriter case beside the shower, along with a B4 bag. The tag read M PATTERSON MIDN 4/C. He set the case on the desk, opened it, and cranked the blank bond around the platen. Sat, and set the caps lock. Looking at the note, he typed the longest line.

> IM NOT GOING TO MAKE IT HERE AND I DON'T FEEL LIKE TRYING ANYMORE

He held the original beside it and compared the scripts.

Both were in elite font and equally dark. Registration, then. The *H* was slightly elevated on the note . . . and on the line he'd just typed. The upper enclosure of the capital *R* was dark, crammed with lint and carbon from not being cleaned. The same as on Patterson's note.

Struck by another thought, he lifted the bail, pulled out his sheet, and flipped up the cover. Hit a key, to test which way the spools revolved, then reached in and pulled out a few inches of ribbon. The letters he'd just typed showed plainly, very slightly discolored on the black ink-impregnated fabric. And ahead of them . . . very faint now . . . *FUCK EVERYBODY. SORRY. MARIO.*

He zipped the ribbon back into place and snapped the cover down again. Certain, now, that the doomed plebe's note had been typed on his own machine.

But did that prove *Patterson* had written it?

He couldn't think of any way to test that. As his own presence showed, any upperclass could have come in and done it, when the occupants were out. As they often were, for classes, pep rallies, and formations.

But assume Mario had typed it and stepped off into eternity all on his lonesome.

Then where had the note gone after that?

If Davis had seen it there in the head, why not leave it in situ, to forestall any doubt?

"Fuck," he muttered, stymied again. Mind blank as a sheet of fresh cotton bond.

The door opened. The two plebes, one tall, one short, stumbled in. They were shaking, red-faced, stained with sweat. "Bastards," the short one muttered, before catching sight of Dan. He snapped to attention and started to sound off.

Dan silenced him with a finger to his lips. He pointed to the gear by the door. "That his stuff? Your roomie's?"

"Yes, sir. Nobody knew where to send it."

Right, he was an orphan. "And this typewriter?"

"That's his too, sir." They exchanged glances. "Do you want it? We were going to keep it, sort of to remember him—"

"Oh, that's not—no, I don't want it." He got up. "Look, did you, um, ever see any other upperclass using it? Coming in, like, to type something?"

They shook their heads. Dan eyed the open door. "Okay. Well. Don't tell anybody I was I here. *Capisce?*"

They nodded again, expressions blank. "Good plebes," he said. Thinking, as he left, *Shit, what a stupid thing to say.*

* * *

Halfway back to his room he halted, in the suddenly empty, echoing passageway. Frowning down at the note again.

At the upper corner, where a piece had been torn off.

"Crap," he muttered. Now it made sense. What had been nagging at him all this time.

Like his roommate had just said: nobody knew where to send his personal effects.

Patterson didn't *have* a family to write to.

But his note had begun *DEAR MOM AND DAD*.

The note had been typed on his machine, sure. But *he* hadn't typed it.

Whoever had, hadn't known the plebe was an orphan. But he must have realized his mistake shortly after the plebe's death. And figured he had to make the note disappear.

Then, later, had figured he could have it both ways: make it look like a suicide. *And* throw suspicion in another direction. On another first class.

On Dan.

* * *

"*Taps, taps, now lights out*," the 1MC announced. Scherow was still emoting on his side of the room. Dan flicked his desk lamp on, trying to concentrate on partial integrals. But he couldn't conjure what the symbols stood for. His mind kept slipping off into fantasizing about Mignon's tits, Licia's lips on his dick. Anything to evade thinking about what he should do now.

At last he got up and pulled on his b-robe.

When he looked into the company wardroom, the TV was still on. It was supposed to be off after taps, but since Oleksa was out, and no midshipman officer of the watch would pap his classmates, it was blaring. Coke cans and Lay's bags from the basement machines littered the deck. His classmates' faces were slack, lit by the flickering tube. He hesitated, then walked on.

The elevator was off-limits for mids. He pushed the button and got on, feeling a sudden sense of liberation from all restraint.

Maybe you ever only really appreciated freedom when you didn't have it.

He strolled out onto an empty T-Court. The wind was icy on his bare ankles. He halted where the body had sprawled. The windows of the Main Office were brightly lit. Considering his demerits, getting fried for being out here would put him over the limit.

Maybe this was how Patterson had felt.

Slipping by submerged, pretending to be someone you weren't.

Anyway, what mattered was that someone, and he was more and more certain it was Davis, had lied, fabricated evidence, and, maybe, committed murder.

It was obvious what was right. Not because the regs, or the honor code, said it was.

This wasn't just about Davis, or Oleksa's advice on going along to get along. It felt more like, how was he, Daniel Valentine Lenson, going to live his life from here on out.

He wondered if Patterson was looking down. Watching him. Probably not. He wished he'd done better by the kid. Whatever he did or didn't do now, it wouldn't bring back the dead.

He stood there for quite a while shivering in the thin bathrobe. In all that time, no one crossed the windswept expanse of frigid yellow brick.

* * *

He stood at the door of the battalion honor rep, tapping the formal report of an honor offense against his lips. Making sure he was ready to go through with it.

Finally, he lifted his hand and knocked.

20

Back at the Supe's House, he tried to catch a couple of hours of sleep. But the broken arm, splinted and slinged, stabbed him awake every time he turned over. He lay worrying in the dark. Nan still wasn't home. Nor had she answered his texts. Still, she was an adult now. . . .

At last he sat up, clicked on the bedside light, and checked the news on his phone. Olaf had strewn destruction all the way up the Chesapeake and into Pennsylvania. Whole neighborhoods were flooded. Saturated banks had given way, plunging homes into the sea. The eye had passed directly over Phillips Island, a low-lying community in the middle of the Bay. The storm surge had forced five hundred residents from their homes, to shelter at the highest point.

He turned the phone off and lay back again. Trying not to think about taking another of the little white pills.

* * *

Dawn, at long last. He peered out at a hot, curiously inappropriate sun baking the raw silt covering the lower half of the Herndon Monument into a flaky chocolate crust. Steam rose from toppled trees. Dirty ponds dotted the Yard.

When he ventured out the mids were at work in cammies, turning to alongside the ground crews. They were clearing brush and trash, pressure-washing benches and cannons, filling holes, replacing sod, replanting toppled trees or chainsawing those too damaged to save.

The Severn glittered in the brightness. At the basin Dan contemplated a sad tangle of wrecked piers and sunken boats. Crews from across the river were shoveling debris into trucks. A crane beeped a warning as it slowly hoisted a broken-backed 24-footer from the steaming asphalt of Santee Road.

His own sloop lay bottomed and covered with mud, mast canted, hull gored by a piling like a horse by a frenzied bull. A total loss, most likely. He perched on a bollard to rest, adjusting the sling to ease his arm. He should call his insurer, file a claim . . . but more concerning were the dozens of Academy craft wrecked, sunken, driven ashore. He didn't want to think about how many millions he'd have to beg the alumni for, to replace them.

It was clear Congress wouldn't. Not if Blair might abandon Annapolis altogether, as the installation most threatened by rising seas. Sure, Olaf was a five-hundred-year event. But history didn't seem to be a trustworthy guide anymore.

His phone, and St. Audrey Larkin's Maryland accent. "Mrs. Mayor," he said, stepping back as a forklift trundled past with a mangled IC, trailing a propane smell and dragging a shroud wire. "Did the town come through all right? What can I help you with?"

"Admiral. I understand you were injured last night. Not badly, I hope?"

"Busted my arm. But not too bad. Are *you* okay?"

"I'm fine, but as you know, a tornado touched down in the city limits. During the worst of the storm."

"Uh, no, ma'am, heard a lot of noise, but didn't know it was a tornado."

"I surely can imagine the Academy had its own worries. But we could use some assistance. The governor says he can't send anyone until the roads are cleared. And you're right here."

Dan nodded, cupping the phone as he jabbed a note to himself in one of the succession of green GSA wheel books he'd kept since *Reynolds Ryan*. "We're still digging out here. But tell me what you need and I'll see what we can do."

She said the tornado had plowed through several older homes between Porter Road and King George Street. *"There still may be bodies in the wreckage. We need to get them out, and start clearing the streets. Also, there are gas leaks, so we have to be careful what equipment we operate. Can you spare some strong young men who aren't afraid to work?"*

Dan said he'd see about sending help. Then headed back toward Bancroft, sidestepping several of the lighter boats that had broken free and been blown inland. He hiked through T-Court, where Yard crews were hosing slime off the bricks. Past his house—looking for, but again not seeing, his daughter's car. He returned the startled salute of the guard at the gate and headed into town.

The flicker-flashes of ambulances, fire trucks, emergency response vans strobed ahead. The seesaw whine of sirens, and the nasal purrs of chain saws and generators. They were clustered west of College Avenue. He watched long enough to gauge the damage. Then phoned Stocker and asked her to consider sending over two or three companies, commanded by their firsties, in hard hats or helmets. Larkin had said "men," but she was going to get some hardworking midshipwomen too. He called the NSA security det and asked for a team, if they could spare one, as well. "Where there's damage, there'll be looters," he added.

Back in his office. The makeshift command post was still operating, though his staff tottered about like coffee-animated zombies. Most had been up all night. He told Burke-Bowden to get them relieved.

At his desk, he answered emails and returned calls from NAVFAC and the O-6 level liaison the Navy kept on the Hill. NAVPERS was scolding him for missing the comments deadline on the revised Navy-wide grooming standards. The DoD inspector general audit was faulting his sexual assault prevention office for lacking an ISO 9000–compliant process to document interactions with victims who chose not to file an official report. He also had honor board recommendations to review, the verdicts on the cheaters from the wires exam.

A quick perusal made him shake his head. Eleven were recommendations to dismiss. Only one urged exoneration. And Stocker wanted her fired too.

"Wow, Danelle. Sure you're not being too easy on them?" he muttered, looking out the window. The hurricane had stripped the leaves off the remaining oaks. He had a clear view all the way across the mucky, rubble-strewn Yard. He didn't like to overrule her. But there were gray areas. Sometimes remediation was better than simply disposing of men and women who'd probably, aside from one lapse, done their best.

On the other hand, he didn't have the time to reinvestigate every case.

Each time he signed off on a verdict, it would redirect a life. A second chance, or iron justice? Mercy, or spare the Navy from an individual who had, when it came down to it, put self before duty?

Sometimes it was a difficult choice. He set his teeth in his lip, propped his head on his good arm, and forced himself to read through them again.

* * *

He went out again that evening, walking the boundaries of a stinking Lower Yard as the sun declined. Bonar had reported progress now and then throughout the day, as Dan had to his own superiors. Wreckage was being cleared, residual floodwaters pumped out, this or that building returned to operation. Naval Facilities Command kept demanding a dollar estimate of the damage. Which he had no idea of yet . . . To judge by the news, the bases and airfields in Norfolk and Virginia Beach had been hit nearly as hard, though without quite as widespread flooding. Their new drain systems and elevated piers had brought them through.

He should check on the rest of his command as well. Acre-wise, the bulk of Naval Support Activity Annapolis lay across the river. He shaded his eyes, searching the far shoreline, but of course couldn't see anything significant.

Reluctantly, he called for his vehicle.

* * *

He stopped at each tenant command for a walk-through. The Exchange, the YP basin, the YPs themselves, and the Navy Lodge were intact, except for minor wind damage. He listened, nodded, and handed out "well dones" and "attaboys" as seemed appropriate.

It was dark again outside his windows when he convened his leadership team back at Admin. Gupta, Dean Mynbury, Colonel Stocker, Captain Burke-Bowden. Jerry Bonar too, of course.

Dan eyed the dean. "Grant, I asked everyone for a preliminary damage report. I haven't seen yours yet."

Dr. Mynbury smiled. "I assumed that would be included in the facilities report. By Mr. Bonar."

"Jerry has a shit ton on his plate right now, Grant. I expect your report by opening of business tomorrow."

Mynbury spread his hands. "That may not be possible, Admiral. We'd have had to do a thorough canvass of the Maury, I mean Carter, complex, the library, Rickover Hall, Hopper, all the academic buildings and labs—"

"Then what *have* you been doing, Dean?" Too sharp, but damn it, everyone else had managed. "Turn your profs to. Assign each an area. Damage, time to repair, and a plan for reopening, in alternate spaces, if necessary. On the bleachers of the field house, if you have to, but you *will* resume classes day after tomorrow."

Mynbury shook his head, looking down, as if unable to credit the patent inanity of his boss's demands.

Of course, that was the real problem. The dean had never really considered Dan his boss. Rather, an annoyance who interfered with the serious business: education.

Unfortunately, Dan couldn't do much about it. Theoretically he could discipline or even fire the dean—if he wanted to rip the lid off a can of maddened dragons. The headlines would blare about academic freedom, and his civilian profs would resign or go out on strike. Dan eyed him. "Will you need *assistance* to do that, Dean?"

"No, I . . . we'll have something to you," the provost said reluctantly.

Dan moved on. The athletic director said the main loss was the sailing squadron, with additional damage to MacDonough, Wesley Brown, and Ricketts halls. The playing fields would need drainage, topdressing, and overall refurbishment.

Dan listened with a sinking heart. When Gupta got to the cost estimates, he held up a hand. "Uh, I'd rather not forward a number up the line until we have a firm one. From your contractors. Until then, I'm just going to say, 'Somewhere in the neighborhood of fifty million dollars.' Okay?"

Gupta raised his eyebrows. "That was just for the fields, Admiral. The basin, the boats will be far more. We'll have to—"

"Go to the alums. Right." He took a breath. The lack of sleep, and the ache in his arm, was honing his temper. Where had he gotten the idea his twilight tour would be spent relaxing, sailing, catching up on his reading? Cree had pictured parties and receptions catered by the house staff, and everything else on autopilot. Yet so far it was the same pace and pressure as an at-sea command. Though, to be honest, it beat wartime.

Bonar's brief was ominous as well. "Worden Field was completely submerged. No P-rades there for a while. Senior officer housing, basements and first floors. Captain's Row's needed rebuilding for a long time—"

"Why? The houses look great."

"On the outside. Since they're on the National Register. But they haven't been updated inside since aught-seven. *Nineteen* aught-seven. Warped floors, rot, mold, insects—"

The litany continued, depressing him, though he tried not to show it.

At last he closed the meeting, reminding the dean, "Don't forget, damage report. ASAP."

As they rose he suddenly remembered his vision, or insight, on T-Court that morning. He caught Bonar by the shoulder. "Jerry. A minute?"

"You wanted estimates—"

"This'll just take a second. I wanted to run something past you."

As Dan explained, Mrs. Marsh hovered at his door, eyebrows raised. Her signal, he'd learned, that whatever she had shouldn't wait. "Valerie?"

"Sir, bad news, I'm afraid." She held out her phone.

He grabbed it, fearing the worst: Nan was injured. In trouble. Or someone had taken a shot at Blair. But it wasn't.

Admiral Barry Niles, four stars, his former CO and on-and-off mentor for so many years, had passed. The funeral would be at Arlington.

Marsh took back the phone. "Will you be going, Admiral? Should I make reservations?"

He nodded somberly. It wasn't a surprise. Niles had looked gray as death at their final interview in the CNO's office.

He sighed, acknowledging the passing of someone who'd always fulfilled his threats and kept his promises. He wouldn't have made vice admiral without Niles. Or even, in all likelihood, stayed in the Navy. "Absolutely," he told her. "And let Blair know I'll be there."

He was turning back to Bonar, getting ready to explain what he'd visualized, but the engineer was riveted to his cell. "Shit," he whispered. "Sir . . . check your phone. Do you have a weather app?"

"I have NOAA. For the upper Chesapeake—"

"Take a look. I don't like what I'm seeing."

When the map came up Dan stiffened. "Not again," he whispered.

"It turned *around*," Bonar muttered. "Headed out to sea, so it looked like we were okay. Now it's starting a loop. A three-sixty."

Dan toggled to the Olaf live feed. Sure enough, the fucking storm had its rudder hard over in a clockwise turn. The track updated as he watched. Clicking around a few degrees farther. Back toward the Maryland coast.

"I've heard of this happening," Bonar said. "Not often, but . . ."

Dan wished he could unsee what he was seeing. "When they come back, do they get stronger or weaker? Pick up energy again, over the open sea?"

Bonar shrugged. "Probably depends on . . . Well, I don't know."

His secretary again. "The governor, Admiral. Your private line."

The knot in his gut grew tighter. He started to reach for his desk phone, but the injured arm lanced him with a sudden jolt so fierce he gasped.

Bonar laid a hand on his good arm. Gingerly. "Sir? You okay?"

"Get us ready, in case this bastard heads for us again," he told the engineer. Then, to Marsh, "I'll take the next calls at my desk."

21

Aboard USS *YP-703*

The diesels growled at full throttle, with a pounding, thrusting roar that shook and buzzed everything on the little bridge. Dan stood on the wing, cradling binoculars in his good hand and fighting flashes of sea memory. The Arctic wastes north of the Greenland-UK gap. The massive rollers that had battered old *Reynolds Ryan*, and the screams that had haunted his nightmares since . . . how many thousands of hours he'd passed this way, on so many bridges: bored, sleepy, brain goosed into weary half alertness by endless cups of joe.

And here he was again. Wind and sea conditions: five knots from the northeast, waves one to two feet. The calm before the storm. No one else was out on the gray emptiness of the upper Chesapeake, though the squared-off fill site of Poplar Island was visible to port.

Tucking his binoculars under his arm, he felt in his pocket. Thumbnailed the milled edges of a quarter. Glanced around, making sure no one was watching, and dropped it over the side. Hearing again the youthful, confident tones of the man who'd taken him under his wing so many years before. *Sailors used to offer silver to Poseidon at the beginning of a voyage.*

You believe in that? Dan had asked. Naïve. Trusting. The greenest of green ensigns.

Believe? Hell no, I'm a devout atheist.

Retrieving the binoculars, he examined the withered shrubs dotting the dikes. The sky was a crystal blue, with only the faintest blur of cloud on the horizon. The winds, light since they'd set out, barely ruffled the surface. As yet.

Three more gray-hulled mini-destroyers followed in *703*'s foam-speckled wake, each spaced an exact hundred yards astern of its predecessor. Inside the little glassed-in pilothouse stood three figures. Galadriel

Stewart; he'd been surprised to find the chair of the Anglo-Saxon Culture Study Group was also commodore of the Academy's training squadron. A taller shadow: a Black firstie, Merwin Dearborn, was this YP's captain. A third class stood behind the wheel, gnawing her lip as she matched the gyro needle with the ordered course.

From the yardarm streamed Dan's flag, the three stars of a vice admiral. Most likely, the last time he'd ever fly it at sea.

He grinned unwillingly, appreciating the irony. Not much of a force, compared to those he'd commanded before.

Though to those he was tasked to rescue, they'd be the answer to a prayer.

* * *

The four Yard Patrol craft had gotten underway three hours after the governor's phone call. They served as the Academy's training fleet for maneuvering, formation steaming, tactics, and shiphandling. Fortunately, the orientation of their basin across the Severn had sheltered them from the worst of the wind.

Unfortunately, they just weren't that fast. Even all out, they could barely make fourteen knots. Maybe sixteen max over ground, today, with the current behind them.

They'd barely reach their goal in time.

Before the war, the Coast Guard and Navy would have carried out such an evacuation with response boats and LCACs. But those had been sent to the Pacific, where they lay either sunk or wrecked. And according to the governor, an air evacuation was out of the question.

The islanders' lives depended on him, the mids, and the Academy's own mini fleet.

* * *

A voice behind him startled him from his reverie. "Admiral, current ETA is 1827," Midshipman Stewart reported. "We're picking up a southerly tidal set, one point seven knots. Chief Yarborough's ready to brief the entrance and exit plan."

Dan nodded. Their destination lay halfway down the Bay, nearly to the Virginia border. The two Caterpillar C18s were pushing all out, fifteen hundred horses total, but they'd reach the entrance channel almost exactly at sunset. And as he recalled—having visited the island once, a weekend with a girlfriend between wives—that access was narrow, tricky, and poorly marked, with shifting shoals and barely more water than his flotilla drew.

He glanced at Stewart. Her pinched face and sharp chin reminded him of someone, but he wasn't sure who. He cleared his throat. Maybe he shouldn't broach the subject. It was jumping so many levels of command. But what the hell. "Mind if I ask you something?" he ventured.

She drew her eyebrows together. "Sir?"

"About your club . . . your ECA. You're that Stewart, right?"

"Yes, sir. Anglo Studies. Did you care to join?"

What? "Uh, no! I wanted to ask . . . I keep getting reports of racist graffiti in Bancroft. Does your ECA do anything to prevent that?"

She looked away, and once again she looked familiar, only not quite enough to fire whatever neurons held her image. "We're not a racist organization, sir. We actually have several nonwhite members. And we discourage the kind of thing you're talking about. Pride in our people, our culture—that's it."

"Is 'white' a culture?"

"Is 'African American'?" She looked skeptical. "Sir? Respectfully. If they can have a club, if there's an Asian Studies Club, why can't we?"

"That's what Colonel Stocker said. I'm suspending judgment, myself."

"Come to a meeting, then, sir. See what we're all about."

Yeah, right. Just what he needed—to be seen at a whites-only gathering.

All at once, out of nowhere, he recalled where they'd met. The day he'd taken command, running his old cross-country loop at dawn. She'd stopped and asked if he was all right. Then, when she found out he was the incoming supe, muttered, *At least we got one of our own this time.*

He smiled grimly. "Midshipman Stewart. I'll warn you now, off the record. Or on, if you prefer it that way. I gave in when the 'dant recommended we approve Mr. Evans's application. Reluctantly. But if I hear one thing linking you or your members to threats, or graffiti, or racist social media postings, or promoting rumors there was some sort of conspiracy or cover-up around Evans's death, I'll jerk your permission that same day. *And* a note will go in your personal record."

Her face set. "Heard and understood, Admiral. But I can go you one better, sir."

"Excuse me?"

"I can give you my word: if I, or we, hear of any such activity, you and the 'dant will be the first to know."

Was she taking his warning aboard? Could he trust her?

A midshipman does not lie. He had to believe that. He set his teeth against more angry words and turned away. "We'd better go over the plan."

Back in the little tight compartment behind the bridge, the chief in charge of the YP fleet, BMC Truman Yarborough, had set out a tablet with NOAA charts, sailing directions, and a copy of the *Waterway Guide.* The YPs had been slated for updating with digital navigation and vessel management software, but it hadn't happened yet.

"Sir, it'll be tricky getting in," the chief opened. He was about five four, with a prominent nose and a buzz cut. Also, he looked dauntingly young. Once the chiefs, E-7s and 8s, had seemed grizzled to Dan, even grandfatherly. Now they looked like kids.

Dan turned to the craft's captain. "Mister Dearborn?"

The Black mid leaned with the deck's slow roll, hands behind him. "The *703* class draws seven and a half feet, sir."

Yarborough scrolled the chart. "About a foot and a half more than the wood-hulled 676s you trained on, Admiral. The two channels into the island, west and east, meet at a basin in the center. That's the town proper, the highest point."

Dan adjusted his sling to lean in, noting wrecks to the south—*Texas*, *Alabama*, and *Indiana*—sunk as targets a century before, but still dangerous rusting reefs—and on the island, the symbol for a water tower. Usually the highest location. He set his finger on it. "Where the evacuees will be gathering?"

"At least, where they're supposed to. Them island folks . . . they can be a fractious bunch."

Dan nodded. "Which is why they didn't evacuate. Governor says they said they'd pray the storm away." It hadn't worked; the island's own fishing craft had been wrecked or blown so far into the marshes and mudflats they were useless. And Olaf was aiming straight for them on this second go-round.

"Yessir. Now, the western channel here, it's rated at six feet. Eastern's charted at seven, with a tidal range of a foot and a half." Yarborough consulted his phone. "High tide . . . it might just work."

Dan massaged his face. If it didn't, if the chart soundings were outdated, or a YP veered out of the channel, he'd end up with the flotilla bottled up, stranded. Right when the hurricane arrived for a second bout.

But if he *could* get there . . . he could save four hundred lives.

Stewart said, "Sir, I had a confab with my captains on the radio. Suggest we go alongside two at a time. Once a YP's loaded, we head it out to the east."

Dan looked to the chief. Yarborough said, "Sounds like a plan. Then, as we get clear, head into the sound for a lee. Set two hooks and lay to 'til this motherfucker—sorry, ma'am—'til this mother blows over."

Dan nodded. "Do we have enough fuel to run engines while we're anchored?"

"We should," said the chief, at the same time Stewart said, "That depends."

He eyed her. "On what?"

"How quickly the hurricane goes over."

Dan looked at the chief again, who made a wry face. "We *should* have enough, Admiral. To run one kicker at low rpm, anyway."

He checked his Seiko again, then the navigation app on his phone. Then he toggled to the storm track, and grimaced.

It was going to be neck and neck.

* * *

The island hove in sight four hours later. The water tower and the spire of a church. The blue sky had been replaced by a black whirl of approaching storm. The wind was rising. The anemometer stood at twenty-five knots, and ribbons of white spray laced the parkerized waves. NOAA kept updating Olaf's track, but it was still barreling down like a bowling ball aimed for a strike.

Even worse, it was tracking slightly east of the island. Since the wind speeds at its front would be the algebraic sum of its eye's forward speed, plus the rotational velocity, this meant the strongest winds, plus any tornados the cyclone might generate, would hit shortly—at most, two hours—after he reached the piers.

He had to be loaded out, free of the island, battened down, and securely anchored before then.

The lookouts, plebes huddled in reefer jackets against the chilling wind, were calling in marks over their sound-powered phones. "These channels're always shoaling on this side of the bay," Yarborough said past raised binoculars. He was double-checking the channel markers. Up close the boatswain looked even younger. Another marker of Dan's own age, though he didn't feel *old* yet. . . . He remembered again how intimidated he'd been by the senior enlisted as a fresh ensign. The barely suppressed contempt some had shown, the fatherly advice others had given. It was a cliché, but they made the Navy run.

"There he is," the chief said.

Dan one-handed his own glasses up to catch a small whaler fighting its way out of the channel. A tiny figure in bright orange slicker and life preserver. The mayor had said he'd send his son out to lead them in. As it reached open water the boat turned bow on to the incoming seas, pitching wildly, tossing curtains of spray that blew back along its length. "All right," Dan told Dearborn. "Head on in." He glanced at the third class. "That your best hand on the wheel? They're gonna have to hold her against a stiff crosswind, when we come left to go in."

Dearborn nodded. "She's good, sir."

As the prow came around, *703* caught the wind full force, sagging away. Recovered a few degrees, then shuddered as a sea broke over the bow, blasting spume into the air. Dan bent his knees, ducking as icy spray blew past.

"Bottom's comin' up," Yarborough yelled. "Surf's building."

Dan didn't like the looks of these seas. Nor of the increasing wind. It was ripping the foam off the waves, smearing white across the surface. It buzzed in the housing of the wing searchlight like a fistful of hornets.

"Visibility degenerates any more, we'll lose our marks," the chief yelled.

Which would present a nasty choice. They couldn't dawdle out here. But the channel was too tight, the terrain relief too low, to thread it on GPS or radar. He glanced inside again; the young faces so rapt, engrossed, backs ruler-straight. The diesels were growling all out, but the channel markers were taking their damn fucking time getting closer.

Another sea slammed them, shouldering the whole craft over. He grabbed for a handhold as more spray showered down. Yarborough beckoned him inside. Dan nodded, and ducked in.

The pilothouse was close, hot, cramped, smelling of fuel and electronics and maybe a little . . . fear? Stewart and Dearborn stood close together, clinging to an overhead cable, both staring out as the pilot boat tossed and yawed, evading capsizing or pitchpoling by the merest of increments. "That fucker's really an ace boathandler," Yarborough muttered.

Another heavy sea. *703* reeled, then dropped, leaving Dan's stomach behind.

A solid *thud* from below shuddered every instrument on the bridge. Yarborough grabbed Dan's shoulder to steady him. Stewart half turned, pointed face paling. "What was *that*?"

"Striking bottom," Dan and the chief both said at the same time.

"Sir . . . should we turn back?"

"No. Keep pushing," Dan rasped. They should have at least a foot beneath the keel . . . but they were surging so much, with these heavy swells, they might strike again. Foul a prop, bend a shaft, even snap the keel.

He bit his lip and waited, every cell dreading another slam, then the sudden deceleration as they ran hard aground.

But it didn't come. Did not come . . . A green light flashed through the blowing spray atop a black steel pole. He binoculared its base to gauge the state of the tide. High, which made him wonder again why the keel had touched. Then shoved it out of his mind. They were in the channel. Now to just keep the prow in the wake of the skiff. It was churning inland. Past low banks of marsh, only dimly visible to port as dusk advanced.

A tight little harbor came into view. Its banks were littered with wrecked boats, perched high on riprap or with bows jutting from piles of torn fiberglass. The wing of a small plane stuck up incongruously from the roof of a gray-shingled building. No wonder air evac had been ruled out. Beyond, inland, a steeple poked up. He glassed the shore, fearing to see bodies, but unable to pick out anything clearly identifiable as such.

A voice from the overhead speaker. "*Yankee Papa Leader, this is Yankee Papa seven zero niner. Report we are hard aground. Over.*"

Stewart, holding the handset of the bridge-to-bridge radio. "Sir, *709* reports—"

"Heard it," Dan snapped. He wheeled to stare astern. Sure enough, a gap had opened between the penultimate and final craft in line. Then a blast of rain wiped both from view. "Tell them to make best effort to get free. They won't be punished for going aground. I'll assume responsibility. Dearborn, stay in that wake."

They plowed ahead. Floating debris littered the water: congeries of fishing floats, timbers, the peeled-back roofs of demolished crab houses. The Black mid glanced at him; Dan shook his head. The steel hull nudged the flotsam aside with slight bumps.

"Bend to port coming up . . . five hundred yards to town landing," the chief said.

Stewart was biting her lip. "Admiral. We can't leave *709* out there. Not with the storm bearing down."

"I know that, Ms. Stewart. What do you suggest we do about it?"

"We should . . . go back for them?"

"Ten souls on *709*. Four hundred we need to get to safety before the storm hits. Sure that's the right answer?"

He let her chew on that while he glassed ahead. Piers to starboard. Buildings. Rice-grain hail was starting, clacking onto the windscreen. He asked Dearborn, "Where will you lay alongside? Captain?"

"Harbormaster, on VHF, wants us alongside that bulkhead."

Dan followed the skipper's pointing finger to a pier, or landing, jutting out into the thoroughfare. In the deepening gloom lines of people stood in brightly colored rain gear, carrying suitcases, duffels, backpacks. Families. Kids. Below them, along a riprap breakwater, smashed boats lay capsized or half sunken. A slick of petrochemicals greased the water, and the smells of gas and diesel welled up.

Dearborn said over one shoulder, "Right ten degrees rudder. Make turns for three knots."

Dan looked aft, ahead; checked the anemometer; thought about the pivot point and the turning radius. It looked like the mid had the approach in hand. A bustle out on deck; the rest of the crew, third and fourth class, were flemishing out mooring lines.

"Back two-thirds," Dearborn said quietly. "Rudder amidships . . . back full . . . engines stop." *703* coasted to a stop. "Lines two and four."

Islanders in stocking caps and bulky jackets lunged to catch heaving lines, then bent to haul them in. *703*'s haze-gray hull kissed the pier, rebounded, rocked to a halt. Someone blew a whistle. "Moored. Brow over to port," Dearborn yelled down.

"Nicely done," Dan said. He swung down to the main deck, careful of his arm, and headed aft. A grizzled man stood on the pier, fists on hips, watching as the townspeople lined up to file aboard. He saw Dan and lifted a hand. "Admiral?"

"Dan Lenson," Dan said. "Mayor Crocker?"

"Town manager. Yeah." They shook hands over the lifeline. Crocker jerked a thumb toward the queue. "How many on each of your ships, there? Somebody said you could overnight fifty?"

"Fifty belowdecks, yeah. I hope they brought food. I was able to get some MREs aboard, but not enough for this many." Dan shaded his eyes against the blowing rain, surveying the crowd. "There's not four hundred here."

"No, sorry. 'Bout half decided not to come."

"Decided not to . . . ? The governor ordered an evacuation."

"I know. But we don't take kindly to being ordered around. I'm not going either."

Dan put a hand to his head. "So . . . where are they sheltering? *Is* there a storm shelter?"

"We'll wait it out in the church," Crocker said. "With Reverend Michaels. God's taken care of us so far. I don't think He'll let us down now."

Dan glanced at the clouds, which were taking on an ominous Gatorade greenish-violet. Debating whether to just let them live, or die, with their decision.

But, no. His daughter had put her life on the line to help people who didn't believe in vaccinations, or sanitation, or science. She didn't just shrug, and let a pitiless universe deal with them.

The passengers were humping their luggage aboard from the catwalk. Stewart was looking down from the bridge. Dan waved to get her attention. "Going up to the church," he yelled.

She looked startled. "Sir?"

"Some of 'em don't want to leave. Stand by for me, but not too long. If I'm not back in fifteen, you and Dearborn know what to do." He mimed speaking into a radio, and she dropped him one of the handhelds. He waved to the second craft in line, hove to now off the pier. Pressing the Transmit button, he told them to come alongside forward of *703* and prepare to load.

* * *

He commandeered a golf cart standing empty and drove down the one-laner main drag as the rain continued its steady cold drizzle, rattling against the zip-on plastic screen of the cart. The houses were small, one story, with microscopic yards. Most stood deserted, windows plywooded.

The First Methodist was white clapboard with the looming steeple he'd glimpsed from seaward. In the deepening darkness its lights shone out welcoming bright. The strains of "Abide with Me" swelled from the open door. He waited cap in hand until the end, then went in. Walked up the center aisle toward an elderly man who stood as if expecting him, Bible in hand. The congregation coughed and murmured.

"Admiral," the pastor said as Dan neared. "Welcome to our worship service."

Dan looked around at families, older folks, a scattering of kids. They seemed subdued but self-possessed, except for a few wailing babies. The air smelled of candle wax, wet wool, and floral perfume. "Reverend Michaels?"

"I am."

"I understand you and these good people are thinking about staying put for this storm."

"'From whence cometh my help?'" Michaels said mildly. "'My help cometh from the Lord, which made heaven and earth.'" He nodded to Dan's sling. "You're injured, sir?"

"'He will not suffer thy foot to be moved; He that keepeth thee will not slumber,'" Dan said, ignoring his inquiry. "Psalm 121. May I have a word with your congregation?"

Not a moment's hesitation. "Of course, Admiral. But I don't think you'll shake our faith."

"Believe me, that's not my intention, Padre. At all."

He turned, picking out faces to speak to. A young woman. An elderly man. A toddler, thumb fixed in her mouth, eyeing him gravely. "My name is Daniel Lenson. Your governor's tasked me to provide evacuation for everyone on this island. I command the ships alongside your bulkhead, uh, downtown.

"We have room for everyone. But we can't stand by long. The storm will be overhead in"—he checked his phone—"an hour and a quarter. Just enough time to load you, get underway, and take you to shelter. I promise I'll get you back to your homes as soon as it's safe to return."

He paused, but no one moved. Or spoke. Michaels stood with head lowered, fingers caressing the book. Dan cleared his throat. "Please. Follow me, and let me take you to safety."

A grizzled fellow in the front pew said, "Admiral, sir, I'm ex-Navy myself. *Independence*, on Yankee Station. Thank you for coming. But we have a more powerful savior."

"Thank *you* for your service. But I'm not sure you all understand." Dan raised his voice. "No point on this island is over three feet above sea level. The predictions are for a twelve-foot storm surge. You'll experience massive overwash flooding and winds of over a hundred knots. I've already cast off one craft with evacuees. We need to board the rest of you now."

A stirring in the back, a murmuration. Another voice: "We've been here for three hundred years. We're not going anywhere."

Someone else, a young woman's voice: "God protects us here. He'll bring us through this piddlin' storm just fine."

Dan looked to the pastor. "Sir, this is no 'piddling storm.' This island will be demolished. If you add your voice to mine, we can save lives."

Michaels said mildly, "I'm not a jailer, Admiral. Anyone who wishes is free to go. But those who trust in the Lord will stay."

"And you, Padre. Will you lead your people out of Egypt?"

Michaels smiled. "Thank you, again, but the Lord will provide."

Dan sensed he wasn't winning the theological debate. Still, the stir in back, the occasional bang of the door letting in the wind, meant a few were slipping out. Probably whoever'd brought the babies, since the wailing had ceased.

The lights flickered. Michaels gestured, and a woman began lighting candles. One last try, then. "Sir, the Lord *has* provided. He dispatched the US Navy. We're not angels from on high, but we definitely were sent to rescue you." He looked at his phone again, making it ostentatious. "Let's join hands, and all get out of here before it's too late."

More voices in back, muffled protests; the door banged again. Little by little, the back pews, probably those already less committed, were emptying. The front ranks, though, with the older parishioners, stood firm. They met his eyes without doubt or question.

Michaels stepped forward. "Perhaps you had best return to your duty, Admiral.—Hymn One Hundred."

Dan stood irresolute a moment longer, then accepted it. A partial victory. A partial defeat. He started to leave, then turned back. Plucked the sleeve of the Vietnam vet. Muttered, "I need your help aboard, Chief. And bring your family."

A moment's wavering, as the grandfather eyed his pastor, then Dan again. At last he bent, whispering to his wife, his daughter, his grandchildren.

They set down their hymnals and filed out.

As Dan walked down the aisle, the aged voices swelled behind him. "*A mighty fortress is our God, a bulwark never failing. Our helper he amid the flood, of mortal ills prevailing.*"

He only hoped they were right.

* * *

When he got back, *710* had loaded and left, as had the third in line. *703* was still waiting, engines idling. Dan lingered on the pier as the rain became a torrent. The town manager had vanished. To the church with the other diehards, probably. The temperature was dropping. The rain turned to hail again, so stinging he had to retreat under the eave of a crab shed. Over his handheld, Stewart relayed that the *709* boat reported free of the shoal and heading in. He acknowledged, heart lightened a little. He'd hoped that would happen as the tide rose.

That last YP loomed out of the night, too eagerly. Its diesels howled, backing full. It slowed, but too late, and lurched into the pilings so hard they groaned and creaked.

As the remaining families trooped aboard, the tide lapped the bottom of the decking. The wheels of the brow squealed as the boat rocked. Dan kept checking the app. Less than an hour until the storm hit in earnest. Already the wind was shrieking like a revolutionary mob.

They had to leave . . . but a few more islanders were still straggling down the lane. He waved them aboard peremptorily, then shaded his eyes back up the main drag. No one else showed on the path. The overhead lines swayed in the wind. The few lights left on in the homes flickered violently, then all went out at once.

He gave it two more minutes, then pulled himself aboard. Yelled up to the bridge, "Cast off, and let's get the hell out of here."

* * *

They ran out of the channel at full speed and turned north, racing the storm to the cove he and Yarborough had picked out. The bottom was mud and sand, which should be good holding. Land cupped it on three sides. His other craft were already anchored, line abreast to the anticipated winds, engines running to ease the strain. If a tornado hit they'd be in trouble, but short of that, he felt, peering through the hail-clattering windscreen into the roaring dark, they were set up about as well as they could be to ride it out.

Buffeted by the gusts, *YP-703* snatched at the bitter end of its rode. The anchor set hard and suddenly and the deck lurched, slamming his bad arm against the helm console. He grunted involuntarily.

"You all right, sir?" said a voice from the dark.

He muttered a reassurance, and turned.

Two faces were bent flickering green over the radar scope. Dearborn and Stewart. He sagged against the console, watching. Half catching their low tones as they recorded initial radar ranges and bearings, to determine whether, during the long and doubtless nerve-racking darkness to come, they'd be dragging anchor.

Working together.

He knew then that—at least for tonight—they would come through.

IV

A CODE OF HONOR

22

Arlington

The sky was cloudless, the air chill. Skeletal trees stood motionless as if cast in black resin. The carefully groomed grass between the serried gravestones was free of weeds, even of fallen leaves. Olaf's rage hadn't stretched this far inland.

Downhill lay the somber ramparts of the Pentagon. Beyond it, past the Potomac, rose the slim white obelisk of the Washington Monument, and the distant floating moon-dome of the Capitol.

Winter was passing. They'd survived the semiorganized madness of Army-Navy. Weeks of pep rallies, then the Gala Ball in Philadelphia. Blair had been busy, so he'd dragooned Nan into service as his hostess, both forcing smiles in the receiving lines, pressing flesh as hundreds of grads and donors filed past, each with a request, a compliment, a suggestion. After a video summary of the season, he'd addressed over two thousand people. Realizing anew just how much the tradition meant to them, and how much the Academy owed them.

And after that, the game itself. Former governor, now President M'Elizabeth Holton had been the guest of honor. Dan and General Faulcon had chatted with Holton before walking her out to center field for the ceremonial coin toss. (Army won.) Holton seemed polite but distant, and addressed herself more to Blair than to Dan.

Army led at halftime, but to Dan's relief Navy won, maintaining their series lead. When the alma maters had been sung, the mids and cadets mingled on the field, seeking out friends and letting the rivalry go.

He was proud of them all.

* * *

Today featured a less joyful ceremony. In service dress blues, he held a salute as Barry Niles's burial detail slid the flag-draped casket onto the caisson. They stepped back, saluted, and he snapped his own hand down.

He and Blair had attended the service at the post chapel. He'd greeted his old mentor's family members and nodded to faces he half recognized, older now, but after a moment familiar again. Many were African American, senior officers who'd followed in Niles's well-broken trail. Allied diplomats. Members of Congress. Retired service chiefs and combatant commanders. The current service chiefs, including Niles's replacement as chief of naval operations, Shaynelle Hlavna. Those the Old Man had worked and quarreled with, in peace and war, over a forty-year career. Even the ambassador from a newly united, still-struggling China. He and Blair had had quite a little confab on the chapel steps.

Now a distant drum tapped a low, leaden beat. The head of the column swung into motion. An escort platoon of Marines and Navy, followed by the Navy Band. The chilly, distant sun flashed off trumpets.

"Shall we?" He offered his arm to the secretary of defense.

They fell in behind the caisson, walking at a sedate pace. Her security detail kept close behind them. The wagon was all black save for one adornment—a studding of silver stars—and drawn by six perfectly matched black Friesians. The only sounds were the *clop-clop* of hooves, the hiss of rubber tires, the jingle of harness, the nickering of the team.

The grave yawned amid an Astroturf aproning. Other tombstones surrounded it, all alike, all uniform, their scrubbed shining marble glowing in the sun. The southern extension had been opened for the veterans of the Pacific War. Dan remembered the old Navy Annex standing here, a nondescript crumbling "temporary" from another war. He'd reported there now and then from Crystal City.

How long ago that seemed . . . and how old it made him feel.

How had his own career measured up? He'd faced challenges. Fought. Worked. But had he been as good a mentor to those he led? Promoted the careers of those who deserved it? Guided, led, consoled, advised, encouraged?

He lowered his head, feeling guilty for not having done enough. Or maybe everybody felt that way, faced with mortality.

Yet he still had a chance. To do the best he could.

The burial detail stepped up. As the casket slid off, as six marines and sailors carried it to the graveside, the military members of the audience rendered honors once more. Dan held his own salute, blinking back a haze, remembering.

They'd met when the older man had commanded Destroyer Squadron Six. Later, Dan had been headed for Op-03 when the freshly minted Rear Admiral Niles had tapped him for the Joint Cruise Missile Project Office.

Back then, an Air Force colonel had shared the secret to a successful military career. "Find a boss who rewards loyalty and competence. Stay on his wing, and match his climb rate."

Not that Dan had done that. Not exactly.

The bearers lowered the casket into position over the grave. Ushers led the official party to green-felt-covered chairs. They seated Dan and Blair in the second row. Behind them stood a cluster of other mourners, too many for the available chairs.

She tweaked his sleeve. "You're deep in thought. Is it about Nan?"

He roused himself. "Huh? Uh, no. She got home all right."

In truth he *was* worried about his daughter. He hadn't seen much of her the last couple of weeks, after the game and the holiday social events at the Supe's House.

As if she was hiding something . . . or avoiding him for some reason.

An early wasp buzzed past, swerving among the seated guests, and out of nowhere he recalled steering around the ground wasps on Worden Field. So many years ago . . . The wind gusted, bringing the rich loamy scent of fresh-turned earth. "It does seem like we've been going to a lot of funerals," Blair whispered.

"Yeah."

"Niles, and Bankey—"

"I know you miss Senator Talmadge."

"Not entirely. Bankey *was* a bastard. But overall . . ."

"You miss him," he finished her sentence. "It's part of getting older, I guess. Losing old friends. Mentors. People you respected, who helped you get where you are."

She closed her eyes and sighed, and he looked close, really seeing *her*, instead of the placeholder your mind carried of those you loved: idealized, younger, happier. The fine lines had deepened around her eyes and lips. The once sharp, clean profile of her jaw had softened. She was still lovely. But like everything and everyone, she was sea-changing . . . in the ever-ebbing tide of time.

The chaplain stepped back. "Please rise for military honors," a cemetery rep called.

Everyone stood. Blair placed her hand on her heart. Dan, and the other men and women in uniform, held the salute. The rifle detail cycled their actions. Blanks cracked out a volley. Once. Twice. And once more.

The long sad notes of taps lilted over the hill.

Dan squared his shoulders and walked to the head of the grave. With metronomic, almost robotic movements the burial detail folded the flag and passed it to him. Still favoring his recovering arm, he left-faced, took five deliberate paces, and knelt to present the tightly wrapped cloth to Vera Niles. Regal in a black dress, she looked more angry than sad. "I'm so sorry," Dan murmured. "He was the greatest man I've ever known."

He wasn't sure, but he thought she whispered back, "You have no idea."

* * *

The ceremony concluded, condolences extended. They strolled back downhill toward Memorial Avenue and Blair's car, her protective detail a few yards behind. The reception was at Fort Myer, but she said she was due at the Defense University for a conference on synthetic bioweapons. "Go without me, if you want to," she said.

The wind gusted. She shivered and he draped an arm around her shoulder. She touched her lips with a clenched fist. "So . . . I suppose you want to be buried here?" she said abruptly.

He grimaced, startled. "Uh, I'm not really sure." Jeez, he wasn't even retired yet, and she was planning his funeral? "I haven't thought about it. But I guess it's that, or burial at sea, or the Naval Academy Cemetery." A blink of memory; standing exhausted at the top of a hill in winter; frost-stripped branches clicking in a dark wind. Though considering Bonar's plans for the Upper Yard, maybe that last wasn't a great choice.

"It isn't morbid, to ask what someone might want."

"I wasn't upset. Just not ready to think about it, I guess."

"Well, I already had to. During the war. If something had happened to you."

He shook his head. If he'd died then, there wouldn't have been a body to worry about. He'd have lain entombed in steel, deep beneath the sea.

Like so many others.

"Well?" she urged, giving his arm a squeeze.

"I told you, I don't know." He softened his tone. "How about you?"

"Wherever you are, that's where I want to be. I don't have much other family left. You and Nan, and DoD, and my old friends from the Library of Congress . . . wherever you are."

He felt uncomfortable with where this was going. "So, join up later for dinner?"

"Sure, where?"

"Remember that Vietnamese place in Georgetown? That we used to go to, when I was in the West Wing . . . wait a minute." He halted, remembering too late there'd been trouble in their marriage then. He was still ashamed of the way he'd behaved. Accusing her of sleeping with the president—not good. Though De Bari *had* propositioned her. Dan had gotten drunk. Smashed dishes. One of many reasons he'd quit drinking.

But she'd forgiven him. "Sure, if you want," she said mildly. "Text me, and we'll meet up. Bye." They'd reached her sedan; her driver was opening her door. She kissed his cheek and slid in.

* * *

Suddenly and unexpectedly alone, which actually felt welcome, he strolled the grounds. Called up the app, and located several graves. He took a contemplative knee by each. Remembering, rather than really praying.

The reception was more upbeat than he'd expected. Everyone he talked to had glowing reminiscences of Niles. Unfortunately, a lot of what Dan himself had done under the former CNO's orders was still classified. He could only offer generalized praise, and a few tongue-in-cheek observations on the admiral's quirks, like needing his Atomic Fireball candies always at hand. Still, he enjoyed working the room, a chore he usually loathed. At 1400 he glanced at his Seiko. Time to go.

* * *

Madison Burnbright had set up the interview. *Navy Times* was a respected voice in the military community. The mainstream media picked up its articles. Unfortunately, since the public affairs officer was nearing her due date, she couldn't accompany him, as the PAO usually did to outside interviews.

He met Gordon Shrekeli in the lobby of the Graham. Shrekeli was in his late twenties, casual in a black T-shirt under a sport coat. "Call me Shrek," he joked, holding out a fist to be bumped. "Only I'm not green."

Dan chuckled. The guy had a British accent. No, wait—Australian.

"Basement bar okay? I checked out the rooftop terrace, but it's a bit of a chilly bin up there."

"Sure."

The bar was an uneasy mix of mid-century modern and industrial chic, with exposed overhead pipes that reminded Dan of his first destroyer, and brick walls, and polished teak flooring. "Good, not crowded, but it will be later," Shrekeli said. They found a corner table and ordered coffee. The journalist set a digital recorder between them. "Okay? Echoey in here, but I've got noise canceling. Ground rules: if you don't want something published, say 'that's not for attribution' or 'off the record.' Otherwise I can use it. Cool?"

Dan nodded, but Burnbright had warned him: whether on the record or off, the mic was always on. "Yeah, uh, cool. Will we, uh, get prior review?"

The reporter frowned. "We're not part of the military, Admiral. Despite our name. But I wouldn't attribute anything to you that you haven't actually said."

"Of course. I trust you on that." Dan sipped coffee and sat back. "Okay, shoot."

Q. Admiral, first of all, you're a famous name, after the film. *Pacific Victory.* Any comments on that?

VICE ADMIRAL LENSON. Linwood was on my staff during the action off Hainan. I respect his right to his interpretation, but the credit belongs to the soldiers, sailors, airmen, and marines, including our Indonesian and Vietnamese allies. They're the real heroes.

Q. Well put, sir. You've been at the Naval Academy for some months now. What are your primary concerns there?

VICE ADMIRAL LENSON. First of all let me say it's the most personally rewarding tour of my career. I enjoy working with the mids. My primary concern is to coordinate the team; work with the academic staff, the athletic department, and the other departments. Look ahead, anticipate challenges, ensure we continue to deliver the best possible leaders to the nation.

Q. Let's refocus. The Academy seems to have tolerated institutional racism, sexism, for far too long. Why do you think it's been so slow to move with the times?

Dan cinched up on the bat. He could imagine how this was going to look in print, if he made a misstep, or lost his temper.

VICE ADMIRAL LENSON. Well, Shrek, I'm not sure that's accurate. Right now our student body's nearly forty percent Hispanic, Black, multiethnic, and Asian. Also, thirty percent female. I won't deny there are hard spots, but we're addressing the remaining problems.

Q. Is it true you approved a white power chapter at Annapolis? And that they have a Faceline and Twaddle presence?

VICE ADMIRAL LENSON. Not quite. There's an extracurricular activity, the Anglo-Saxon Culture Study Group. Actually, the Commandant tells me some of its members are minorities. Blacks. Asians. Hispanics. I trusted its president to keep things aboveboard, and so far she has.

As to online presence, we have to bear in mind every student still has First Amendment rights. On the other hand, what they post reflects on the Navy. And I won't say we always get that balancing act exactly right.

Q. A recent study reported that sexual assault is prevalent at the Academy. The survey showed twenty-three percent of female mids reported being assaulted and seventy percent stated they knew of a friend or fellow mid who had. The figures are even higher for transgender or nongendered individuals.

VICE ADMIRAL LENSON. I agree, those numbers are disturbing, and we're moving on the problem. We hired a dedicated specialist and directed education efforts at the company and battalion level. The Fleet has no place for sexual offenders.

Q. Also, the numbers seem to show minorities are being dropped for grades, honor violations, and physical fitness failures at higher rates than white students.

Dan took a slow breath. The guy was trying to nail him to the wall. *The facts, Dan, just the facts.*

VICE ADMIRAL LENSON. Those numbers include voluntary resignations, right? Some mids realize military service isn't for them. Separations for academic failure, PE, or medical deficiencies are ruled on by the academic, athletic, or medical boards.

However, we also have the R&R Program, Reevaluation and Reappointment. That lets me take a second look at mids whose performance points to a potential for good service in the future. First, we send them to the Fleet in an enlisted status. If they perform there, I reappoint them.

Q. Taking off on that question, is it true you and the current commandant have a contentious relationship? That she tends to crack down harder on minor misbehaviors than you think wise?

VICE ADMIRAL LENSON. I have the greatest respect for Colonel Stocker. She deals much more closely with the Brigade than I typically do.

That said, there's a larger rank gap between the supe and the 'dant at Annapolis than at other service schools. That means part of my job is to mentor her. That includes the concept of shades of gray, versus by-the-book decision-making.

Q. About your faculty. Is it true the percentage of people of color and non-cis individuals has actually fallen during your tenure? Does hiring favor conservative and ex-military faculty?

VICE ADMIRAL LENSON. That's two questions, right? First, yeah—we're lagging in terms of broadening our faculty. But faculty composition takes a while to evolve due to tenure. In some cases, decades. We're trying to freshen the pot, but it takes time.

As far as favoring retired military, that's true, especially in the tactics, engineering, and professional development realms. Do we give preference to veterans, especially disabled vets? Guilty as charged.

Dan decided to stop there. Explaining more would make him sound defensive.

He tented his fingers, playing for time. (Jeez, maybe that was why Mynbury did it so often.) He knew where these questions—or rather, accusations—were coming from. Shrek had been primed, most likely by the Rowdy Twins. Or "New Reformers," as they preferred to call themselves. The far-left professors' latest target was John Paul Jones, on the grounds he'd been a mate on a slave ship.

Abort the interview? No. Part of his job was to defend his actions. Not hide behind "no comment." And if stating an inconvenient truth now and then was going to get him relieved, he'd faced that possibility before.

He cleared his throat and signaled for a refill. "Uh, are we gonna discuss anything else? Or just beat these unfounded allegations to death?"

Q. Okay, next question. Your application figures keep falling. Some say the problem isn't the Academy, it's today's youth. Are they too accustomed to lowered standards? Or is your regimen, or rather Colonel Stocker's, just too hard?

VICE ADMIRAL LENSON. That's a tough one. It goes back to how we deal with those who are having problems with academics, or mental pressures, or who just don't conform to whatever the current model of an "Academy grad" should be. Do we help them? Or just kick them out, like bad parts on an assembly line?

Q. So what's your answer?

VICE ADMIRAL LENSON. There is no one cut-and-dried answer. I can attest that the bottom five percent of the Brigade takes up eighty percent of my and the 'dant's time. But at times, we've been too quick to bottom-blow those who were struggling. Often it's those who don't shine in our structured environment who become stellar leaders later in life.

Sure, some say today's youth are softer than those of generations past. I hear that from a significant minority of our alumni. Well, I don't agree. The mids I meet, and I meet a lot of them, strike me as intelligent, dedicated, honest, and hardworking.

For example, two thousand mids volunteered to clean up debris and repair damage in the town of Annapolis after the recent hurricane. Half the Brigade gave up their weekend to stay and help.

I can't argue that we place immature people under enormous stress. The flip side is that when fragile kids snap, we should have some kind of safety net, instead of the humiliation and sense of personal failure that conduces to self-harm. We need to provide counseling, reassurance, and a well-lit glide path to what will hopefully be a less stressful civilian environment.

Q. Thank you, Admiral, for that revealing interview. We'll probably follow it up with a piece on the academic side, and maybe an interview with a recently separated midshipman. To get the less official side of things, as it were.

VICE ADMIRAL LENSON. My pleasure.

The recorder clicked off, and Shrekeli stretched, easing his back. Grinning. "Sorry if I came across like a prosecutor. But somebody's gotta ask the hard questions."

Dan didn't like that grin. "I welcome the opportunity to set the record straight," he lied. Realizing that the "academic side" would probably be the Twins, and some disgruntled ex-mid still steaming over his or her separation.

Being the supe seemed to be as much about managing the public as it was about actually doing his job.

And now, with the Yard basically in ruins, he'd have to work twice as hard to get more money out of the alums.

* * *

He met Blair at the Miss Saigon restaurant on M Street. An intimate place. It didn't look like much had changed since he'd been there last. She looked more tired than he liked. She sat back, fingering her damaged ear, and he said, on the spur of the moment, "Is that hurting? Your ear? I mean, couldn't you get a plastic surgeon to fix it, if it bothers you?"

She shrugged. "I suppose so. But, you know, I'm kind of used to it now. It's sort of like . . . sort of a wound badge, I guess. Like a Purple Heart."

He chewed that over. It sort of made sense. Maybe it was even an advantage, for a politician.

She said, "So, have you had time to look at any houses?"

He cleared his throat. Plead The Hague, Olaf, the press of business? The bare truth was easier. "Uh, I haven't. Sorry. How about you?"

The waiter came, and they ordered. She said, "I've looked online. There's one place. Beautiful views. It's got a pier and deep water, for your boat. Which I'm really sorry about."

The marine surveyor had taken one look as it lay broken on the seawall, keel and shaft crumpled sideways, bow holed, mast buckled, and declared it a total loss. Dan had insurance, but he'd miss her. "Send me the link. I swear I'll look at it."

"Stand by. As you would say." She grinned and flicked it across from her phone.

He examined the pictures. "Is this upriver or downriver of the bridges? For clearance. For the mast."

"What? I don't know. I'll leave that up to you."

He got to the price and swallowed. "Whoa. It's nice, but—can we afford this? I know you had to pay off the loans from your House campaign—"

"You let me invest your back pay, remember? Plus, after I finish as SecDef, there'll be board offers. IT firms. Defense. Policy. I could get you something, if you liked. When you retire . . . We'd be selling the house in Arlington too. Or rent it out, if we wanted cash flow."

He didn't want to have this discussion right now. And he'd never liked the revolving-door idea, government to industry. "I'll break some time out, go over and check it out."

"Don't wait. Homes that nice go fast."

Their main courses arrived. For her, pad thai. For him, lemongrass chicken. Dan stirred it with a chopstick. For some reason he felt repelled by it.

She eyed him. "Is your arm still hurting?"

He grimaced. "Just not all that hungry right now."

She set down her fork. "Are you still taking your antirads?"

He nodded, but she persisted. "Should I not have mentioned retirement? Or was it the interview? Your text said he gave you a hard time."

"Some hardball questions, is all."

She shot a knowing glance across her plate. "But you coped."

"Yeah, but I felt like I was just shoveling the same old chickenshit. The kind of nonanswers I used to hate to hear from Higher."

"Well, there's a lot of that at our level." She smiled. "Remember the old days, when we could just say whatever we thought? Then complained because nobody was listening?"

He had to chuckle. "Right. Guess there's no pleasing us."

"Uh, look," she said after a few more bites. "I have to go over to the Hill next week. The supplement for your repairs, and . . . other stuff. It'd be good if you were there." She blotted her lips with the napkin. "I'll have someone call Valerie. I also . . . begged an early draft of a CRS study. I'll send you that too."

"Any, um, hints? Anything I should be ready for?"

She eyed her plate, suddenly somber. "I didn't tell you this, Dan. But, considering everything that's happened . . . start thinking about how to justify having a Naval Academy at all."

The savor disappeared, leached from his meal as if he'd lost the sense of taste. "Oh. Appreciate the heads-up. I'll try to be ready."

They finished their dinners in silence.

23

Late afternoon. Like any other winter evening, yet different. He was sprinting all out, pushing it as hard as ever he could. Leaning into the uphill, weaving between heaped-up snowbanks as salt and sand grated beneath his trainers. His thighs burned. His calves felt like they were wrapped with hot wire. The wind rasped his throat like a chilled-steel file. But he kept going, pumping his fists, swerving to skirt the onyx gleam of black ice. The only way to build stamina was to slam yourself flat against that invisible wall, again and again.

And maybe, if he spent every bit of energy, he'd feel less angry and scared.

The honor hearing was tonight. And he'd be the chief, and possibly the only, witness for the prosecution.

Cemetery Hill still rose ahead. The asphalt snaked between ranks of tombstones. Skeletal oaks arched over it. Their winter-stripped branches swayed and clicked in the wind like the knitting needles of unrelenting Fates.

Deep winter, and he was finishing his workout with repeated sprints up the only real elevation the Yard offered. This was his tenth set. Dusk was falling and he was out of oomph. Just a few more yards . . . He grunted, digging deep, pushing through the exhaustion, fighting for the top.

At last the salt-gritty road leveled and he slowed, easing to a jog. Panting and coughing through the breath- and snot-wet scarf as the shadowing Yard below opened between the trees. The old green wooden bridge over College Creek. The power plant. The Isherwood complex. Beyond that, Mahan and then the brooding granite octopus of Bancroft. A chill dark-smelling wind hit full force as he came over the top. It sliced through the baggy sweats, the uniform gloves, the wool watch cap, the blue-and-gold scarf over his face.

He'd started running alone, since no one else would work out with him. Or answer when he spoke to them.

Coventry wasn't dead after all.

He slowed to a loose-limbed amble, shaking out his arms. Glancing at the tombstones. Admiral this. Lieutenant Commander that. Captain and wife. Names he remembered from *Reef Points* and plebe indoctrination.

One huge cairn was topped with a cross draped with stone carved into snow and icicles. He stopped to read the inscription. USS *Jeannette.* An Arctic expedition in the 1870s. What had happened he didn't know, but it had obviously been tragic.

The wind clicked and rattled in the bare branches, moaning like an incoherent voice. He turned slowly beneath the trees, shivering, studying the stones. Some were weathered, eroded, their granite or marble stained black with mold. Others gleamed pristine white, freshly carved.

Each stone recorded a life. And doubtless many marked empty coffins. Lost, buried at sea . . . He hesitated between awe and mindlessness, and the world seemed to rotate around him while he stood, for a moment, on the other side of Time.

He shook away reverie, suddenly angry at himself. Dreaming again, Lenson? Dusk was falling. Lamps popped on, buzzing salmon light over the snow. Pushing weary shaking legs once more into motion, he slogged downhill, back toward the Yard. The last place he wanted to go, or be.

But only those who lay still and quiet behind him were beyond the call of duty.

* * *

No one spoke to him at evening meal. Nobody had since he'd turned in the honor report on Davis. He occupied a seat, but he was invisible. No one met his eye, though the plebes darted surreptitious glances, as at some horrific, freakish malefactor. Even Teddy Scherow was giving him the cold shoulder in their room. A few days earlier, when he'd gone into the company lounge, his classmates turned off the television and sat mute, stone-faced, until he left.

He'd anticipated something like this. But it still felt . . . *unjust.* He wasn't the one who'd pushed a plebe to suicide, maybe even murdered him, then tried to cover it up.

He picked at his meat loaf, brooding. Maybe he should resign. Serve out his obligation in the Fleet. Or maybe in the Corps? The thought of going into a hot war as a foot grunt was both attractive and frightening.

"Pass the butter down, please," he said.

But not one hand moved at the table.

* * *

He'd anticipated tonight's hearing with dread like Jupiter-grade gravity weighing in the pit of his stomach. The honor board convened late, after taps. In the dead of night, as if such deliberations were best shrouded in darkness and anonymity. As if no one wanted to be held responsible for destroying a reputation, career, and future.

Davis wouldn't be the only one on trial tonight.

The board convened in a warren of low-ceilinged, sparely furnished, badly heated, and nearly inaccessible cubicles high above the Rotunda. Dan climbed the narrow steps slowly, up and up, above the empty echoing chill air of the vast space, until the inlaid mosaics dwindled far below and the world seemed to reel around him again. He paused on the fifth deck, steadying himself, right hand to the railing. Felt in his pocket with the left, to make sure what he'd prepared was still there.

Maybe it would work. Maybe not. But it was all he could think to do.

* * *

A second class met him at the door. "Name?" Dan scribbled it on a form, and she seated him in a small, bare anteroom without another word. It was very cold. Crap, he should've brought a reefer, or at least a sweater. She closed the door, leaving him alone with a side table, a wall clock, and his thoughts.

"Fuck," he muttered, shuffling his feet on the worn carpet to warm them.

The Brigade policed itself in terms of false reporting, theft, lying, and cheating. As a company rep, he'd served on juries, and as usher and recorder. One case had been open and shut, a guy from 18th Company accused of fondling, fingering, or raping—the testimony was contradictory—a third class during a drunken snake-house party out in town. The rape charge was a police matter. It was the accused's lie about not being at the party that brought him before the board. The verdict, after the jury examined photos of him in the drag house: unanimous for expulsion.

Another case. A second class stole a copy of a chem final from the prof's desk and circulated it to her buddies in the Glee Club and Gospel Choir. That board had taken weeks to interview everyone. In the end, Dan's jury had cleared two, reprimanded eight, and recommended three to the supe for discharge.

Yet another charge had been against a third class for copying movies, then selling the videotapes room to room in Bancroft. Instead of waiting to be disenrolled, he'd resigned. Last Dan had heard, he was in prelaw in Albuquerque.

Every defendant came in on a hair trigger: angry, cowed, defiant, frightened, occasionally fighting tears. And each case consumed many hours, and often multiple sessions—probably why they were scheduled for after taps.

The accused had the right to remain silent. He, or she, had the right to counsel, though not a civilian attorney. Usually his own company rep sat beside him. The stumbling block in most cases was proving intent to deceive. Intent wasn't necessary to convict, but most jurors saw its lack as an extenuating circumstance. One defendant had filled out a false muster, but insisted he'd misread a note from the mate of the deck and thought the missing man was sick in his room. After pondering the scrawl, the board had acquitted on reasonable doubt.

He'd seen up close what worked and what didn't. Admitting guilt or error right off the bat seemed to help. Juries also tended to give plebes more leeway, recommending reprimands or warnings instead of discharge. They came down harder on second and first class.

Now and then, through the heavy varnished door that led into the hearing room, he could hear the murmur of voices. Never clearly enough to make out what they were saying, though. He hugged himself, shivering. Thought again of going back to his room, getting a jacket. But they could call him at any minute. . . .

* * *

He flinched, coming awake. Dozing off any, Lenson . . . The hands of the clock ticked over. 2340. So much perfectly good rack time wasted. What the fuck, over? Were they ever going to call him in?

At midnight the inner door cracked an inch. He started out of the seat, but the latch clicked again. He sank back, then rose and stretched, pacing back and forth. A worn trail in the carpet testified he wasn't the first.

The door opened again and the usher stuck her face in. "Mr. Lenson? They're ready for you now."

* * *

The layout was like that of a court-martial. Five mids, three of whom he knew, at the battered and rickety wooden table he remembered from his own jury duty. He nodded to them, but no one met his gaze. Outside the one small bull's-eye window, the night was black ink.

"Please be seated," the chairwoman said. A short, oval-faced blonde, with the four thin gold bars on her collar of a midshipman lieutenant commander. Her name tag read CHUGH.

Ionet Chugh, the Brigade honor rep, was an Olympian-level gymnast on the parallel bars and a Masqueraders drama lead. She wore the collar stars of an academic standout. She was a fast burner everyone figured for a Rhodes Scholarship, admiral's aide, and eventual flag officer material.

To Dan's left, Easy Davis slumped at another smaller table. His counsel sat beside him, back straight, jotting something on a yellow legal pad with a black Skilcraft. Davis glared at Dan, arms folded. Yeah, he'd be one of the defiant ones.

The chairwoman said, "Mr. Lenson. First, as you may be aware, we are not bent on punishment here, although we will recommend it if deemed necessary. Our first duty is to establish the facts. Only then can we consider what if any action may be necessary.

"Let's start with your version of the events following the discovery of Midshipman Patterson's body."

His version? He eased himself into the witness chair, across from Davis, who looked away. A gust rattled the panes of the bull's-eye, and a cold draft iced his cheeks. There was no swearing of oaths before the board, since mids were presumed to tell the truth. Dan bit his lips to force himself awake. "I covered it in my report."

One of the jurors, an Asian, nodded. "We read. Of course. But we want to hear from you." Dan made him as a Korean or Japanese exchange, there were a few in each class, from allied countries.

"It was after taps. I was asleep. Muff, I mean Midshipman Fourth Class Herzog, reported the . . . discovery to me. When I got to the head, Patterson's roommates were already there. They handed me a klax, a b-robe belt, and a note. Cotton bond, like what you use to type term papers. A half sheet."

Chugh tapped something on the table. "This note. The one you submitted with your report of violation. Typed, but with a handwriten addition."

"Uh, correct. But the corner wasn't torn off that night."

Expressionless gazes. No telling what they felt. "Go on, please," one juror said.

"Uh, I looked out the window. Mario . . . Midshipman Patterson was lying down there, on the bricks of T-Court. My first action was to make sure someone called sick bay."

He shivered again, both from the chill in the high little room and from images he couldn't help seeing all too vividly. An angel's outline, in the snow. Splayed bare, hairy legs, one foot twisted inward. Clawed, bloody hands. He forced out, "I set everything they gave me on a sink shelf and went down. When I got to him I checked his pulse, cleared his airway, and administered CPR. But he was already dead. The corpsmen got there a few minutes later."

Another juror, a guy Dan recognized from his European history classes: "Why'd you conclude it was suicide? Initially, I mean, the way you reported it to Main Office?"

"Mainly, from the note."

Was Chugh frowning? Another juror lifted a finger. "Was there any blood on the sill, any sign of struggle?"

"No. Just the kicked-off klax and the belt. The body was pretty . . . banged up. His fingers were bloody, but I figured that was from scratching at the bricks. At the time, anyway."

Davis snorted, shifting in his chair. His counsel shot him a reproving look.

The Asian mid again. "What else you see?"

Dan went over it. How when he'd come back up to the company area, the note was gone. "The plebes said they didn't see who took it. A corpsman had been there; I assumed he had it. I only found out later he didn't."

"And no one saw it again," Chugh asked, "until these same two plebes found it in their room?"

He had to admit, it sounded fishy. But that was what had happened. "That's correct, ma'am," he said. Why the hell was he calling her ma'am? Anyway . . . "That's how it went down. His roomies'll back me up. If you want to call them."

Davis's counsel cleared his throat. He said mildly, "Mr. Lenson. I'd like to give you the chance to reconsider your testimony. Isn't it the case that you typed this note yourself, and brought it forward to settle a personal grudge against Mr. Davis?"

The jurors looked to him. Dan said carefully, "No. The plebes will testify to the sequence of events. I was in my bunk when they came to get me with the news. I only held the paper for a moment. But they both saw it. And if I typed it, why would I add something that incriminated me?"

Chugh resumed. "Just to clarify. Your interpretation is that someone other than Patterson actually typed it, then removed it from the crime scene, and later added the note at the bottom and resurfaced it again."

"Except in between, someone tore off the part at the top. The salutation."

"And to your recollection, what was on it? The part that's missing?"

"It said, 'Dear Mom and Dad.'"

The defense counsel said, "The plebes say they caught you typing something. In their room. On Midshipman Patterson's typewriter."

Dan blinked, taken aback. He'd thought they were headed down the right avenue, but now . . . yeah, that looked bad. "I was trying to find out whether or not it was written on that machine. They should also have testified that I came to their room, to do that, after they'd already found it and turned it over to me."

He thought that was a decent answer, but the defense counsel sat back, looking satisfied, as if he'd delivered some kind of telling blow. And two jurors nodded, as if they agreed.

To his relief, Chugh got them back on track. "So, if we believe the missing piece said something about his parents, and we know Patterson had no one living to address such a note to, who do you think actually wrote it? And why?"

"*He* wrote it." Davis glared at Dan. "The plebes just said so." His counsel laid a hand on his shoulder.

"No, I'll answer." Dan shifted in his seat. Despite the chill, he was starting to sweat. "Over time, thinking it out, I came to believe Patterson didn't jump. He was in the habit of going in the head after taps, to smoke, by an open window. He was forced, or pushed out that window. Or beaten up, then pushed. Leaving a forged suicide letter meant it was a premeditated action."

He expected the defense to object, but he didn't. So he went on. "Davis showed up right after we found the body. He was in the head when I left. I believe he typed the note, before either cornering, or maybe even inviting, Patterson into the head that night.

"But then he remembered, or realized, the mistake he'd made." The counsel raised a hand, started to object; Dan hurried on, speaking over him. "So he fixed it, or thought he did, by tearing that first part off. Then added the line at the bottom and slipped it onto the plebes' desk, while they were out, for them to find and turn in."

No one said anything. In fact, no one met his eye. Dan sagged in his chair. What was going on?

Unless they'd backed down, or been intimidated, into a don't-rock-the-boat, don't-bilge-your-upperclass denial.

In which case, not only would Davis get off, but Daniel Valentine Lenson, midshipman first class, would be subject to prosecution himself, for uttering false statements and submitting false reports.

He swallowed with a dry mouth. Rubbed his lips with the back of a hand. Fuck it, he'd told the truth.

He fingered the scrap of paper in his pocket. Maybe he wouldn't get the chance to drop his little bomb after all.

Right on cue, the defense counsel said, again in a friendly tone, "Is it fair to say there was history between you and Mr. Davis? That you'd argued before over this plebe?"

Argued over him? Was that an insinuation? Dan said, "I coached batt lacrosse. Patterson came to me as his coach, seeking guidance. Davis was riding him. Pushing the boundaries of the indoctrination system."

One of the other jurors: "Hazing him?"

"He didn't get specific . . . but it was clear the kid was under a lot of pressure. Sure, that's what the system's for. But then Davis turned him in for sexual activity."

The jurors turned their gazes away; some looked down at papers, which he assumed was his investigation report of the encounter in the shower room, Davis's accusation of homosexual activity, and Patterson's denial. The Korean, or Japanese, grunted something under his breath.

Yeah, it was messy.

Still, the kid had died, and Davis had been involved. Of that, he was sure.

One of the jurors glanced at his watch. He muttered to Chugh, who nodded. "Let's go back to this suicide note," she said.

A heavier gust rattled the panes of the bull's-eye, making everyone glance that way. Dan shivered as a new draft made the room even more frigid. He said, "May I show Mr. Davis something?"

They regarded him doubtfully. Finally Chugh said, "Defense counsel?"

The straight-backed guy shrugged. "No objection."

Dan got up. He pulled the scrap from his pocket, holding it on the right side of his body, shielded from the defendant, but visible to the jury. Their gazes followed as he crossed the room. He set the torn-off corner in front of Davis, then stepped to one side, so the jurors had a clear line of sight.

And asked, "Is this the missing piece?"

Davis barely glanced at it. His lip lifted in a sneer. "No," he said. "That's not—"

He halted in mid-denial, mouth still open. Beside him, his counsel drew an audible breath.

Silence. After a moment Davis added in a rush, stumbling over the words, "*You* typed this. Those . . . words. But it doesn't fit the note. Try it. You'll see it doesn't—"

"How would you know it won't fit?" Dan glanced back at the jurors. Chugh was already nodding, as if she got it, so he aimed his words at the Asian guy. "Yeah, I typed this scrap. And no, the edges won't match the original. But how does Mr. Davis know that? Because *he* tore it off. He flushed it, or burned it! And put the rest of the note where somebody would find it, and turn it in."

He could see them struggling with it. He understood why. How much neater, simpler, if there were no questions left. Just some poor fucking plebe who'd cracked under the weight of the system. Not the first, not the last. Just another . . . *failed part*, broken during manufacture.

But he couldn't say any of that. Or sound off about what a waste it was. That would just sound bitter. It wasn't a *fact*.

The pane rattled again, sounding as if it was going to break. But probably it wouldn't. The glass had held for nearly a century. Dan waited a moment more, then went back to the too-hard chair. Shit, he could see his *breath* now.

"He's lying!" Davis sounded desperate, addressing not Dan but the jury. He flicked the scrap to the deck. "He just *admitted* he typed this—this *forgery*—himself. He's lying to get back at me because he feels *sorry* for the pussy who killed himself. Or maybe for some other reason, I don't know. The two of them were pretty fucking chummy. Think about that."

Beside him his counsel sat silent, gazing at the floor, bent, as if all the starch had leached out of his backbone.

Chugh tapped a pencil on her notepad. "Thank you, Mr. Lenson. That will be all."

Dan hesitated, frozen. Had he convinced them? If not, they'd be calling him back. To face charges himself.

"You can wait outside," Chugh said to Davis. She turned to the secretary. "We'll be going into closed session now."

He forced his legs to push him upright, inclined his head to the jury, and walked out.

24

Washington

Taking a seat in a side chamber in the Dirksen Senate Office Building off Room SD-G50, Dan was struck by a dizzying sense of déjà vu. He'd cooled his heels in rooms like this before over the decades. At the Academy, before an honor board hearing. Here on the Hill, with then–Rear Admiral Barry Niles, about cost overruns and test failures of the prototype Tomahawk.

He couldn't help smiling. The aviators had fought it tooth and nail. But for a long time now, no air strike had launched until those same missiles had hammered down the opposition.

"What goes around, comes around," he muttered.

Seated next to him, Blair lifted an eyebrow, but didn't look up from her tablet. With them sat Jerry Bonar, the Yard engineer, and Leslie Stocker, who'd just pinned on her first star. (He'd left Burke-Bowden in charge back at the ranch.) The public works director looked uncomfortable in a suit and tie. The newly minted general was in Marine greens, with an impressive display of combat decorations. Dan wore blues; his own ribbon rack was topped by the blue and white of the Medal of Honor. The witnesses from the other academies waited opposite, accompanied by their staff.

Outside it was nearly spring, though cold rain had spattered the windshield on the way up from Annapolis. The Yard had lain spookily empty, the Brigade still out for Easter leave. He corrected himself: *spring* leave. The lawns were still soaked, the once-glorious plantings masses of churned, stinking mire. Like rescue crews in a shelled city, contractors toiled on the basements and first floors, running dehumidifiers, rewiring, patching plaster.

He blew out, jiggling his foot. According to the study Blair had sent him, this hearing could be an inflection point.

Or even the end of the Academy.

Beside him Bonar cleared his throat. "We set up for this, Jerry?" Dan asked him.

"I think so, sir."

"I hope your tech managed to get those last—"

A very young page in a blue skirt suit stood in the doorway. "Miz Titus? Our other witnesses? You may go in now."

Blair snapped her tablet closed, stowed it in her briefcase, and stood. Dan stood too, straightening his tie. Flashing back, again, to previous hearings on the Hill.

He'd sat behind the principals then. Handed up notes, or dug out a paper if they needed it. Part of the supporting cast.

This time, he'd be the star.

Or rather, the quarry.

* * *

High ceilings, wine-colored carpets, and a lot of pale green marble and walnut paneling and bronze sconces. The witnesses filed into chairs facing a semicircular dais. The Great Seal hung on the wall above. A large video screen loomed behind the senators, but at the moment it was dark. He was briefly grateful this room, this building, this whole city even still existed. During the war, it could easily have been vaporized.

Instead of still hosting the rumbustious hot mess Americans fondly called democracy. Shrill, flawed, and unanimously damned as dysfunctional. Yet somehow it still seemed to creak along. More or less.

His heart fell as he noted one face among the dozen occupying the red leather senators' chairs. He'd known she was on the committee, of course. But he hadn't anticipated seeing Sandra Treherne, junior senator from Tennessee, wielding the gavel. In a bright scarlet blazer, she tracked him with a frown as they took seats at the witness table.

"Uh-oh," he muttered to Blair.

"I'm surprised too. But I heard Bill Mulholland's ailing," his wife murmured. "This could make it interesting."

No lie, Dan thought. He'd known Sandra Treherne—back then, Sandy Cottrell—at George Washington U years before. With her flushed cheeks—she tended to perspire even in winter—her over-the-edge manner, and her spacey laugh, he'd always suspected she was on something stronger than the hand-rolled Douwe Egberts shags she chain-smoked. Also, she wasn't above sleeping with professors for an A.

He'd put her in danger, and she'd neither forgotten nor forgiven.

Elected to the House, she'd married up, inheriting Senator Reverdy Treherne's seat when he died. These days she looked smooth, lustrous, as if sealed over with clear plastic. Her far-out press conferences, outrageous posts, and spectacularly public political feuds made her a perennial on news feeds. For vehemence, weirdness, and caustic divisiveness, the latest podcast of *Treherne for Truthism* was de rigueur for thousands of followers.

To her left and right the other members arranged papers, settling in. Blair was up at the dais, chatting in low tones with a white-mustached, lordly looking gentleman in a crested blazer. Hollister Peache, from Maryland. One vote, at least; she'd said he was on their side. Behind the witnesses, the seats for the public were largely empty. Since the pandemic and Antiwa riots, the Hill had been closed to visitors. A few members of the credentialed press sat in back, where a pilot light glowed on what he guessed was the C-SPAN feed.

Treherne tapped her gavel and the room quieted. "Next, a hearing on future plans for the military service academies," she announced. "We're running a little late today, since all the patriotic members of the House and Senate assembled for a picture. I see staff and support still coming in. Take your seats at once.

"This meeting will come to order. I am Sandra Treherne. I will chair this subcommittee on military personnel. I welcome our witnesses and members of the audience."

She greeted Blair and "the superintendents and senior staff of our national service academies." Then smoothed back a coiffure so lacquered it barely moved. "I must preface our proceedings by confessing I was disturbed to read the briefing materials submitted by today's witnesses. They neglected important shortcomings at their various institutions. Apparently they plan for business as usual while asking for ever larger appropriations.

"That approach won't satisfy this committee, or the public who pays for these out-of-date, hidebound institutions. They've learned nothing and forgotten nothing from the conflict just concluded.

"Also, my good friend Senator Lisabeta Maldonado-Ortega"—she nodded to a young woman in a mauve headscarf, who looked startled at being addressed—"is concerned about the dismaying incidence of sexual assault at these institutions, and the inadequate response to her repeated statements of concern.

"With that, I'll ask for opening statements from our . . . *distinguished* witnesses."

Dan read his opener second, after Faulcon, from West Point. He kept it short, skipping several paragraphs he figured would do as well on the printed record. He ended, "As the members are aware, Navy suffered major wind and flooding damage from recent hurricanes. The appropriations required to restore grounds, buildings, and facilities are itemized in my report. We request that line item be included in the next National Defense Authorization Act, in addition to the normal operating expenses. This includes—"

Treherne had limited herself to sighing and looking skeptical, but now interrupted. "Does that conclude your remarks, Admiral?"

It didn't, but he got the point. "I can stop there, Senator," he said. "If you prefer."

Treherne lifted her chin, glaring down. "You were responsible for our near disaster in Hainan. Three times more than anyone expected in killed, wounded, and missing. A bloody failure that many say was your direct responsibility."

Yeah, she was on the warpath. He said, as evenly as he could, "The enemy had a say in that battle, Senator. And with all due respect, it wasn't a failure. We prevailed, and ended the war."

"At a huge cost." She cut off his attempt to respond. "I'm very concerned about what I hear about your institution. Many people say it actively advances a radical woke agenda."

Whoa. The first time he'd ever heard USNA described as "radical." "Not true," Dan said. "Senator."

"We'll see. You also submitted to trial in the International Criminal Court. In defiance of national policy."

One of the other senators murmured an inaudible objection. Treherne half turned. "Yes, I know. But in my opinion, it *is* germane to institutional leadership.—So, Admiral. Can you be so good as to explain your rationale for disobeying orders, and subjecting the United States to an alien judiciary?"

Dan leaned into the mic. Delicately, he reminded himself. Respectfully. "Ma'am, if you think it's germane, it's germane. I will object, though, in that I was never ordered not to go. Only advised that I need not attend. Which is different."

She opened her mouth to interrupt again, but he plowed on. "As to why I went, I felt I had to clear my name and the reputation of my country. How could I advise the leaders of the future about integrity, if I took the easy way out and evaded judgment? It was a question of honor. If I can use that word here."

Beside him, Blair hissed an intake of breath. The disbelieving stares, the thunderous frowns from the senators warned him he'd made a misstep. "Um, sorry, that's not to imply that the Senate isn't—"

"Oh, your meaning was quite clear, Admiral," said one senator frostily. A craggy-faced, shaven-headed Black man. "My own service was in Afghanistan." He held up a prosthetic hand. "So you don't need to lecture us on honor."

Shit, Lenson, you're really stepping on your crank here. Dan rubbed his mouth as another member bent to his mic. "The point being, you violated national sovereignty by appearing before an unrecognized court. Our country must stand alone."

Dan bobbed his head. "With respect, sir, ma'am. A country with worldwide interests can't stand without allies. And my appearance led to the rendering up of notorious war criminals by the new Beijing government."

Treherne glanced at the others, but no one else seemed to have anything to say.

The kerchiefed woman pressed some invisible button. Treherne smiled at her. "Senator Maldonado-Ortega."

She cleared her throat and began reading what apparently was a prepared question. Dan tried to look attentive as she attacked the Naval Academy as being secretive and elitist. "I've visited the place, and was not made welcome," she said scathingly, eyeing him. "I was stopped at the gate and interrogated. Once inside, I found myself in some kind of right-wing theme park. Everyone was obedient, everyone was patriotic, everyone looked the *same.* The taxpayer doesn't need these pampered robots I saw parading around like windup dolls. We need thinking leaders. If we need a military at all."

Okay, he got it now. Treherne was firing from his right flank, Maldonado-Ortega from the left. Fixing him in the kill zone. Dan started to respond, but the senator went on. "That scrubbed, everything-is-wonderful face you present to the tourists hides moral decay and leadership neglect. Over the past two years, the records show four separate cheating scandals and too many reports of sexual assault to tabulate. Assault and battery. Breaking and entering. Numerous drug charges, including eight fentanyl-related overdoses. Shall I continue?"

Dan leaned to the microphone again. He said as deferentially as he could, "I apologize that you were not immediately admitted to the Yard, Senator. A call to my office ahead of time would have secured you instant access and an attentive escort.

"As to the statistics: We do not and never have had a spotless record. In the cases you cite, the miscreants were identified, punished, and often separated from the service. Wouldn't it be more concerning if such crimes were never reported? I think it speaks both to our transparency and our rigorous enforcement of the relevant laws and regulations."

He sat back, and at last got a respite as Treherne called for statements from the other superintendents. But he didn't like the way she kept eyeing him. With that little smile that meant *You are on my shit list, you self-important prick bastard. And you're going to pay for what you did to me.*

The next attack came from the handless vet. "This is for Admiral Lenson. I'd like to follow up on the senator from New York's point about elitism. I was enlisted, myself. How do you answer charges that your graduates are overwhelmingly white and overwhelmingly from the upper middle class?"

Dan nodded to the commandant, beside him. "If you don't mind, sir, I'll ask General Stocker to field that. She has the latest numbers." As well, of course, as being living refutation of the charge.

Stocker came in on cue. "Only nine percent of young Americans are interested in serving in the military. Even fewer meet our stringent eligibility requirements. This is the pool we have to recruit from. Our accession figures show increased diversity—more female, minority, and economically disadvantaged accessions—year over year. True, they don't perfectly reflect the general population. But I'd suggest that isn't the goal. We want young men and women we can form into the defenders of our nation."

She paused, ramrod-straight, the very picture of a tough Marine. "Also, true, we extend preference to children of former prisoners of war, those missing in action, and holders of the Medal of Honor. If you think that's unfair, sir, please tell us how you'd restructure it."

She got a muttered thank-you, barely loud enough to hear. Dan jotted *DIRECT HIT* on his tablet and tilted it so she could see. He got the tiniest half wink back.

Treherne tapped her gavel. "General Stocker mentioned producing defenders of our nation. If that's our goal, why are we teaching critical race theory, gender studies, pardon my French, *horseshit* like that at a military institution? If we really need professors of queer theory in the Navy, can't we get them somewhere else a lot cheaper?"

A titter rose behind them; phones were being held up. Yeah, that would be all over the Web this afternoon. Sandy was a media genius. Dan smiled, gave it a beat, then said, "We don't graduate 'professors' in any subject, Senator. We're not a postgraduate institution.

"As to why we have those studies: naval officers have always needed to know more than how to lay a gun or fly a plane. We teach history, economics, and foreign languages and cultures because they're crucial to understanding our allies and fighting our enemies. We also need to understand what it means to be gay, bisexual, asexual, agender, or transgender, because those who identify as such will be among the sailors and troops our graduates will lead.

"I personally have served with personnel of all ethnicities and preferences, and learned one very important truth: courage and dedication are not the exclusive preserve of straight white males."

A disbelieving grin from the woman seated above him. "'Not the preserve of straight white males.' I see. But they do still have some value, do they not?"

What was she driving at? He frowned. "Of course they do, Senator."

"Then answer us this, Admiral. Of your six battalion commanders, your brigade commander, and her deputy, two are Black, two are female, one Korean, a gay Ukrainian, and two are Latinos. Do you deny this is a conscious, deliberate, and sustained program of replacement?"

He sat still for a moment, reviewing the billets. Crap, she was right. But . . . "Those positions are filled by a well-defined selection process, Senator. The fact none happen to be, um, straight white males at the moment is purely a coincidence."

"Purely a *coincidence*," Treherne repeated sardonically. The words hung in the air.

Belatedly Dan remembered both *regimental* commanders were white males. But he wasn't going to play that game. "If I may extend?" he added.

The senator from Maryland waved him on. "Go ahead, Admiral. You have the floor."

"Yes, sir. Ma'am. As I said, we have a process, but we don't select by quotas. The sole criterion is demonstrated and potential leadership.

"I believe no ethnicity, or race, or gender, or religion, is inherently superior to any other. The Navy, and our other armed services, need to welcome all who want and are able to serve our country. Into the highest ranks."

Peache was frowning; shaking his head slightly. Dan took that as a signal he'd said enough. He closed, "That has been my opinion throughout my career, and that is how I am running the United States Naval Academy."

Treherne scowled, obviously trying to figure a way to flay him some more, but finally lifted a folder. "Let's go on. I have here a report from the Congressional Budget Office, in coordination with the SecDef's office. It's interesting reading.

"One of its options calls for shutting Annapolis down. All Navy officers would then come from the hundred-and-seventy-some civilian colleges and universities that currently host reserve officer programs. Given the cost of rebuilding large portions of your physical plant, that would seem a better . . . *husbanding* . . . of taxpayer dollars." She grinned down, obviously relishing her pun. And just as obviously, hoping to see him squirm.

He tensed. The report had come through Blair's office? "If I may, Senator. That's an old idea, broached many times in the past hundred years. Each time, Congress opted to retain the academies. It's also been said that after a few months of active duty, the source of one's commission doesn't matter. And yes, the reserve programs significantly broaden our talent pool.

"But when you look at retention over the course of a career, the numbers change. At the Academy, mids internalize leadership, integrity, self-discipline, and academic rigor twenty-four seven. That immersion has to have an effect.

"Our grads constitute only thirty percent of all entering ensigns. But a recent survey shows they comprise over forty percent of all Navy captain and Marine colonel grades, over sixty percent of all two-star selects, eighty percent of vice admirals, and upwards of eighty-five percent of four-star-level full admirals.

"I'm not putting down our other sources. Many outstanding officers hail from those colleges. But I think we're doing something right when we provide the majority of our most senior leaders."

Treherne was clutching her gavel, giving him the *time to shut up now* glare, so he hurried to finish. "It's often said one strength of the American armed forces is our cadre of professional noncommissioned officers. I think another is our senior leadership. They're often criticized, sometimes rightly so. But they're the ones—I have to point out—who led our country, and our alliance, to victory against China, Iran, Pakistan, and the other Opposed Powers."

A graying older senator, who hadn't participated thus far, twirled half-moon glasses, flourishing a document in his other hand. "You may have a point, Admiral. However, it's by no means clear how we're going to fund even the current budget. The cost of rebuilding you cite—it's just too high."

Maldonado-Ortega lifted a hand. "Madame Chair? May I call on Dr. Rinaldi, of the Congressional Research Service."

Treherne waved permission. "Have at it."

Rinaldi introduced herself, a nervous-looking young woman. Sending graphics via her phone, she presented what she called "the optimal solution, where the objective function reaches peak value": a single joint undergraduate military college.

Dan massaged his chin as she added, "Modern campaigns are joint operations. Doesn't it make sense to train cadets to think joint from the start, instead of forcing them to learn Air Force or Space Force or Navy-speak much later in their careers?

"As they specialize, the logical place for Space Force and Air Force pre-commissioning programs is at Colorado Springs, and for the Navy and Army at West Point. Both are on high ground, with much larger acreages than Annapolis and dormitory and educational facilities already in place. Making additional appropriations unnecessary." She halted, looking both exhausted and triumphant.

"Admiral. Your thoughts?" Treherne smirked down.

This was the study Blair had sent him an early draft of. Dan shuffled paper and located the response he'd drafted. "I respect Dr. Rinaldi's analysis. Her numbers seem solid. I can't speak to Colorado Springs. However, courses of study at West Point and Annapolis, and thus to a large extent the facilities required to host them, are simply not the same. Classrooms, athletic and drill fields—okay. Model test tanks, small-arms ranges, artillery ranges, cyber operations facilities, sailing and power craft training, a nuclear power plant to train submarine officers—quite different."

He cleared his throat. "I understand the budgetary stress. However, if any installations have to be . . . closed, or abandoned, the most rational course might be to merge the Naval, Coast Guard, and Merchant Marine academies into a new United States Maritime Services Academy."

Peache, the senator from Maryland, piped up again. "Where would that be located, Admiral?"

He hated to weasel, but . . . "Uh, I'd decline to register an opinion without further study. So I'm not advocating that. Only pointing out another option."

Treherne looked to Dan's left. "We've yet to hear from the secretary of defense. The *Honorable* Blair Titus. Ma'am?"

Dan sat back, trying to feign disinterest as Blair read her statement. But it wasn't easy. She had to cut costs, with the country desperate to rebuild in so many other ways. Contaminated cropland to be remediated. Transport infrastructure rebuilt. Hundreds of thousands of demobilized veterans to reeducate, care for, and find jobs for.

But the world was still a dangerous place.

* * *

Blair took her time, arranging materials in front of her. Adjusting glasses she really didn't need, but they made her look more credible. At last she looked up. "Gentlemen, ladies, Ms. Chair, thank you for the opportunity to testify. Are we accessing and training our military leaders in the best possible way, at the least possible cost? Let's review the statistics."

She traced accession rates, retention rates, and referred again to Dan's point about senior officers. The senators listened, but the kerchiefed woman fidgeted impatiently. Finally she burst in. "This background's interesting, Madam Secretary. But what are your recommendations going forward?"

Blair laid her binder aside. Removed her glasses. "I'll leave the remainder of my prepared remarks for the printed record. As you wish, Senator, I'll proceed to my recommendations.

"DoD, and the country, have a considerable amount of sunk costs in these facilities over the decades. In some cases, such as Quarters 100 at West Point, over two hundred years. Not an investment to be lightly discarded.

"Still less to be lightly set aside, though, are the immeasurables. The traditions our academies transmit from our past into our future. In peace and war, these expectations of service, honor, and courage are the reason we've never had a traitor or spy in the ranks of our senior armed services. We take this for granted. But it would be hard to find such a record in the ranks of our global competitors."

The veteran tossed his head. "You're whitewashing a lotta history there, Madam Secretary. We had traitors, all right. At the highest levels."

She nodded. "The Confederacy. Granted, Senator. But since then, I'll place our record against any other country's."

"You credit the *academies* for this?" Maldonado-Ortega raised an eyebrow.

"I do, ma'am. They set a standard the others strive to emulate. And I believe they're making a good faith effort to erase prejudice of all kinds in their ranks.

"That battle may never end, since we recruit from a society that's not always perfect, either. But our military's the most inclusive institution in America. When it falls short, that calls for more effort. Not abandoning the battlefield." She smiled. "My recommendation: we stay the course with all four academies and seek savings elsewhere. You'll find that position in our budget submission.

"Thank you for your attention."

* * *

A scowling, red-faced Treherne announced a recess. She retreated through a door behind the dais, followed by most of the other members. Peache stayed, chatting with Blair again. Dan sat reviewing his numbers.

The recess ended. A comptroller reviewed current appropriations for building and maintenance at each academy. Dan pretended to study his handout as the bean counter droned on.

When he yielded the floor at last, Treherne tapped her gavel. "Time for a vote. I move that this subcommittee cut to the chase, and recommend the disestablishment of at least one of these expensive, obsolete institutions. Whichever would require the largest expenditure to continue operations. If someone will second?"

The disabled vet said "second" at the same time Maldonado-Ortega did.

"Moved and seconded," Treherne said. "Any discussion?"

She meant, obviously, by the committee members, but Dan lifted his hand. "Before the vote, may I make a further statement? With a short video presentation."

"We've given you more than enough time, Admiral," Treherne snapped. "You and your . . . spouse. Who's obviously in cahoots with you."

The senator from Maryland cleared his throat. "Madam Chair? I'd like to hear what he has to say."

"So would I," drawled the twirler of glasses.

Dan could see his time would be brief. He nodded to Bonar, who'd been busy to the side with one of the room's supporting technicians.

"First of all," Dan said, "I'll speak to the central purpose the national academies, as well as other military colleges, including VMI and the Citadel, were meant to serve.

"The founders realized the real security of our country lay in the hands of its citizens. Our major wars have been fought with mass armies, mostly volunteers and draftees.

"But they also realized a mass levy would not suffice on its own. A stiffening cadre was essential. A nucleus around which to rally, and that could hold the line until reserves and volunteers mustered and trained. A steel core of professionalism.

"Annapolis serves that purpose. Our graduates have carried the Navy to perseverance and ultimate victory through the darkest hours of American history.

"But to continue to succeed, our institutions must adapt to a rapidly changing society, while still providing leaders in case of war.

"Some say we have to harden our graduates against adversity. That's true. Others say they need broad views, to anticipate the future. They're right as well. But above all, we have to emphasize integrity. Without that, we won't produce graduates our citizens will trust.

"To continue that mission, let me present a model."

He nodded to Bonar, and a three-dimensional planform leapt to existence on the big screen. Several senators twisted to look up before realizing they had the same display on the monitors before them.

Dan said, "Our engineering faculty developed this model. Instead of relocating or merging, we'll move some operations to higher ground, demolishing or relocating aging officer housing along Porter Road." They vanished from the screen. "Replacing them with modern homes across the river."

The image evolved. A blue tide rose, first probing, then infiltrating among the remaining buildings. "Meanwhile, instead of fighting the rising sea, we welcome it in. Retaining Bancroft and most of our current plant by removing the failing fill between Stribling and other roads, and using that material to elevate the walks." The lowest areas vanished, replaced by a rippling blue-green. "The result will resemble Venice, with canals and short bridges. Floating structures may also prove useful. In fact, the Academy once had what were called station ships—*Constitution, Santee, Reina Mercedes.* Mooring a retired destroyer or frigate in the river adds the opportunity for hands-on instruction on shipboard systems."

He took a millisecond to sweep the faces on the dais. They seemed to be following, but who knew if they agreed. He plunged on. "Most buildings in the Lower Yard are set on deep pilings. They'll be fine as the water rises, if we reconfigure the lower floors.

"At the same time, we'd convert the entire installation to a zero carbon emission facility, erecting solar panels between buildings and above athletic fields. Those will do double duty by providing shade during summer training."

They winked into existence on the screen, a glittering array between buildings and covering the roofs.

Dan pressed on. "This plan, Naval Academy 2100, will be cheaper than relocating and building anew. It will keep us at our historic location, and let us survive predicted storm tides and sea level rise up to the end of this century."

There, that should do it. Congress loved to kick the can down the road? Put off major decisions as long as they could? He'd done his damnedest to give them the opportunity.

He glanced along the row of what felt like fellow defendants. The other superintendents. He got back cautious nods, but no offers to back up his testimony. The senators' expressions yielded no clues. Save for Peache, who shot him a covert thumbs-up, they seemed bemused.

Had he just sealed the Academy's fate?

"Perhaps we don't need our witnesses for the vote," Treherne said icily. She smiled down. "Thank you all for your service. And for your very *imaginative* testimony."

Bonar shut down his projection. The witnesses and experts rose. And departed, as a heated discussion erupted behind them.

* * *

He was standing on the steps outside, checking his emails on his phone, when one caught his eye. *You might want to see this.* From: Jason Schultz.

He puzzled for a moment before he remembered. The cyber prof. Schultz had mentored the mid who'd nearly crashed Kazakhstan's electrical grid. He opened the email.

One of our Cyber majors scraped this off a post, Schultz had written. *While we were researching the Future Academy project for Jerry Bonar. We had to work on it a bit, but this is what we found.*

Dan clicked on the video.

It rocked crazily, obviously shot on a speeding boat. He recognized Annapolis harbor. Audio cut in. A rowdy bunch of teens, high schoolers, the guys in trunks and the girls in bikinis. They were passing beers around, laughing, careening through the anchorage, pumping air rifles and shooting them *pop, pop* at other boats as they passed.

"What is it?" Blair asked him.

"Just a minute." Dan moved aside, to let others pass on the steps, and held the phone closer to his eyes. A tinny voice tinkled above the snarl of three hulking Suzuki outboards.

"Hey, how 'bout that asshole." A pointed finger followed a figure leaping rock to rock along the seawall.

The video halted. *Used AI image enhancer here*, Schultz wrote in a tag. *Cleared and recovered detail on four sequential frames.*

The first wide angle showed three of the teens aiming their rifles. Then the picture zoomed in on the upper left corner.

The next frame, blown up, caught the runner in midair. The next showed the figure stumbling. The last frame showed him down, rolling, tumbling toward the water with arms flung out as the shooters' heads swung away, not even seeing what they'd done.

He lowered the phone, horrified, but at the same time . . . *relieved.*

That's what had happened to Evans. Where the curious sting marks had come from.

No deep state plot. No antiwhite conspiracy. Just a bunch of drunken, thoughtless young civilians, shooting air rifles. They'd hit the brigade commander in his leap from one boulder to the next. The sudden unexpected lashing stings had startled him, made him miss his footing, strike his head, fall to his death.

Dan stood contemplating it. Then forwarded the clip and email to St. Audrey Larkin, mayor of Annapolis, to send on to her chief of police.

25

Spring at last, after a hard winter. Along the walks the tulips bloomed like tiny explosions of scarlet and yellow. Dan shifted his books to the other hip, walking faster, then slackened again. Why bother? The sooner he got to Bancroft, the sooner he'd be back in the shit. Might as well smell the flowers, enjoy the sunlight, as long as he could.

A hole yawned beside the Mexican Monument. The diggers and fillers had torn everything up, scattered bricks around, then abandoned the site, leaving a pit everyone had to skirt. Dirty water gleamed around a rusty pipe. Scuttlebutt claimed an abstracted mid had once stepped into just such a trap, and vanished, leaving only his cap floating atop the puddle.

Dispirited, disconsolate, he shambled along. Contemplated just throwing his fucking textbooks into the hole. But that would be Article 05.02: *Government Property, Destruction Of.*

He'd expected to be called back to the honor board after his appearance opposite Davis. But hadn't. Days had passed. At last he'd run into Chugh, sitting with two other midwomen over shakes in the Steerage. He'd asked, but gotten only a cold stare. "Honor deliberations are secret," she'd told him. "You know that."

"Yeah, sure, but—"

"But nothing. If there's anything official, I'll make sure you get the word." And she'd turned back to her friends.

Since then . . . nada. Weeks had turned into over a month. And since the hearing, he hadn't seen Davis around. When he encountered Easy's buddies in class or in the passageway, the pair who'd threatened him in Philly, neither said a word. Even the usually noisy deep-channel scuttlebutt had gone dark.

Leaving him frustrated and anxious. When would the other shoe drop? And what would happen to him, when it did?

* * *

Back at his room, though, he found a note taped to his door. From the brigade honor rep. *Come by my room before evening meal*, it read.

He tapped at Ionet Chugh's door. "Come in, and leave it open," she called. Added, to her roommate, "Can you give us a minute?"

His heart sank. This was how bad news got delivered. Privately, before the official notification. To give you the chance to resign, before being booted out.

Chugh looked even slighter and blonder by daylight, her skin even fairer. She was in gym gear, her cropped hair damp and spiky from workout or shower. The ammonia tang of Brasso tinted the air, along with a floral note of deodorant. She was polishing a belt buckle on a spread-out copy of the *Sun* sports section. The rest of her desk was occupied by laundry, each piece precisely folded. She jutted her chin at her roommate's chair. "Dan."

"Ionet." He eased down as if the seat might be hot. "This is about the board, I guess?"

"Sorry it took so long. Others had to weigh in. But we have a resolution."

He folded his hands in his lap. Waiting for it.

Chugh blew on the Brasso'd buckle to dry it. Only the most dedicated bothered to strip off the clear protective lacquer and polish the naked brass. He could see her nipples through the damp gray USNA T-shirt. Uh-oh . . . great timing, Dan. He grinned uncomfortably and slid his hands down to cover his crotch.

She held the buckle to the light and glanced at him. Could she tell what he was thinking? "The jury was divided. Some wanted to recommend Davis for separation. Official misrepresentation. Concealment of evidence. Others felt you were the one in the wrong. Davis counter-charged you with lying."

"I wasn't called back."

"Well, no. That's not how it shook out. Your little . . . demonstration made us realize further investigation was necessary. We advised the commandant to call in the NIS."

The Naval Investigative Service was the Navy's FBI. Chugh went back to rubbing with a clean rag. Dan said, "So it went to . . . like, a *criminal* investigation? Uh, so, what was the outcome?"

"The *outcome*." She threaded the web belt into the buckle and clicked it closed. Coiled it. Snapped a rubber band over the package. Twisted in her chair to file it in a locker as austerely organized as the one in the midshipman sample room. “One of Mr. Davis's accomplices decided to cooperate. Seems he witnessed the note being typed. Unfortunately, he claimed he wasn't present when the death occurred. It may not have been suicide. But the NIS decided the evidence wasn't sufficient to prosecute for murder either.”

Dan nodded. Waiting for the hammer, yet still fascinated by how her breasts moved under the thin cotton.

“But the supe decided it would be best for the service if Davis wasn't commissioned. He was separated. An ‘other than honorable’ discharge.”

Dan shifted on his chair. “And . . . his buddies?”

“This is in confidence, okay? We boarded them for lying and concealing evidence. The one who came clean got honor remediation. The other's being separated.

“And that, I think, is all you need to know. ” She glanced over her shoulder and raised her voice. “You can come back in now, Veronica.”

* * *

He stood in the passageway, trying to take it in. So, maybe absolute justice hadn't been done. An OTH discharge, the worst you could get without an official court-martial, was a black mark. But it was far from a murder charge.

At least Davis hadn't gotten off scot-free.

Maybe he did tend to imagine the worst. Assume everything would go to shit. But sometimes, fucked up as it seemed, the system worked. Kind of. In a way.

He might have a future in the Navy after all.

* * *

Over the next few days things improved. Classmates nodded to him in the passageway, said “good morning,” or just patted him silently on the back. One woman whispered, “I admire how well you held up.” Dan remembered how Richmond P. Hobson had been treated, back in the day. Maybe not the best role model. But Hobson had endured, and prevailed.

Now he had finals to worry about. And one afternoon, he found an envelope in his mail slot. The linen stationery smelled of lavender.

From Mignon. At last. He took it into the head to read it at the sink.

Pretty much what he'd expected. She had to concentrate on her studies . . . a trip to Ireland that summer . . . he didn't seem to care as much as she did . . . and she'd met someone else.

"Crap," he muttered, staring at his image in the speckled mirror. Should he have tried harder? Seen her more often? And how could he have done that, on restriction all the time?

He started to tear the letter up, then thought better of it.

The battalion Dear John board was full, but he made room for one more. Stole a thumbtack from a last year's posting. Stood looking at it, unsure how to feel. Angry? Disappointed? Relieved?

But like she said, maybe it was for the best.

* * *

A week later grades went up. The word ran through Bancroft like a stomach virus. He jogged down to the first deck. The printouts, taped to the wall like a Beijing newspaper, were surrounded six deep by jostling, anxious-looking mids. He elbowed to the front and traced down to his class, his section, and finally his midshipman ID code.

Thermo, 2.5. Passing. French, 3.5. Tactics and seamanship, 3.5.

He started to sweat, searching for his calculus grade. It wasn't there. He started over, running a finger down the list, ignoring the grumbling behind him.

There it was. In his haste he'd scanned past it. He peered closer, making sure he was reading the smeared dot-matrix numerals correctly. Yeah.

A D.

Barely passing.

But still, *passing.* "Thank you, Mrs. Colson," he whispered.

Now all he had to sweat was the conduct grade. Which wasn't on the academic printout. That wouldn't be great, not with those demerits from obliterating the governor's garden. He'd pay with a low class rank, and losing his pick of the cherry assignments on service selection night.

A voice behind him. "What's the good word, roomie?"

Dan swung around. "Ted. You're talking to me now?"

His roommate shrugged. "Hey, you came to my play. Never said how you liked it, though."

"It was better than getting my wisdom teeth pulled. I'm out of the woods on grades, anyway. You?"

"Checking now." Scherow pushed past as Dan backed away, sensing the world reshaping around him, the possibilities opening up.

* * *

The Plan of the Day scheduled a mixer that Saturday. Students from four Beltway-area colleges had been invited. He was still down for extra duty, but at the last minute, when he reported in, it had been canceled. No one seemed to know why. He jogged back to his room to change out of the marching uniform.

Smoke Hall had couches and a soft-drink bar set around a parqueted floor. The site of dance training and other events that didn't rate the magniloquence of Memorial Hall or the seating capacity of the auditorium in Mahan. One of the mids from WRNV, the Academy station, was disc jockeying Donna Summer. Dan signed in, got a paper cup of Coke at the "bar," and caught Corwin Haley's eye. Drifted over beside the redhaired mid. One of the few classmates who'd continued to speak to him even when he was in exile. "Hey."

Corwin nodded. "Hey."

"You and Kendrick on the outs?"

"No, that's still on. Just alert for targets of opportunity."

Dan nodded and took a swig of Coke. "Me too."

The invitees were filing in from the buses. In high heels, skirts, carefully groomed. Chatting nervously among themselves. The sweet scents of perfumes. Haley slapped his back. "Happy hunting, amigo."

"You too."

He eased into the mix and chatted up a couple of possibilities. They looked even more uneasy than he felt. No wonder. Imagine being herded onto a bus like draftees, then having to stand around to be evaluated like livestock at a county fair. Pretending not to notice while a bunch of horny guys circled you like jackals seeking the weakest prey.

A flash of dark, smooth hair caught his eye. Not tall, but with a dancer's posture. A short plaid skirt showed off great legs. She wore not heels or pumps, like the others, but cordovan riding boots. Her cheekbones were high, her lashes dark. He'd never dated anyone who looked like her.

Actually, they didn't *have* girls like her where he'd grown up. She stood alone by the half-open French doors, nursing a cigarette and inspecting a bust of Admiral Stephen Luce.

He put his rudder over and steered alongside. "Uh, hey. Here from Trinity?"

She turned. "No. Georgetown."

"I hear it's a good school. Dan."

She eyed his hand, and after a moment took it, surveying him coolly. "Shan Chan. But the girls call me Betts."

He'd expected an accent, but she sounded like anyone else here. "Well, welcome aboard."

"'Welcome aboard.' Really, Captain?" She smirked. "Are we on the *Minnow*?"

His face heated. "Not exactly. Uh . . . wanna dance?"

Eric Clapton was rasping "Wonderful Tonight." She looked around. "I guess. Maybe one."

He steered her around the parquet as the Average White Band started "Pick Up the Pieces." He tried to maintain a reasonable distance, so it didn't seem like he was feeling her up. But, shit! A boner was stirring. He leaned farther away. "So, where are you from?"

"Delaware. Dover. Not far from the base there."

That wasn't what he'd meant, and the glint in her eye said she realized it. She added, "My *parents* are from Canton, if that's what you meant."

"Sorry. I—yeah, I guess that *was* what I meant. I'm an idiot! Sorry."

She nodded, seeming to accept the clumsy apology. And didn't walk away, or say she had to powder her nose. So after another dance he took her down to the Steerage and got them shakes. They sat in one of the booths and talked. "I'm studying physical anthropology. I want to get my master's, maybe a doctorate. Work out west with the Pueblo tribes, the Zuni, the Navaho."

Another supersmart woman. He liked that. But then he said something dumb about fossils, and she corrected him. "That's a paleontologist." She started to get up. "I'd better—"

"No, wait. I'm sorry," he said, putting his hand on hers, and after a moment's hesitation, she sat again. "A doctorate. Can you afford that?"

"Oh, my dad's done pretty well."

Yeah, if she was going to Georgetown somebody had money. "That's cool. You've got everything planned out." Poise, brains, *and* a knockout bod. Shining hair the color of oiled walnut, and that smooth, smooth skin. The only drawback was the smoking. She offered him one from a pack of Slims. "No thanks," he said. "You don't actually inhale those things, do you?" And they had what was almost an argument over it, until he apologized again.

She said, "Don't you? Have plans, I mean. What do you want out of life, Dan?"

"Oh, you know . . . see the world, serve my country. The usual stuff."

"Serve the country. Like, by killing people you don't know?"

Maybe they weren't on the same page. He said, a little bitterly, "Only if they need killing."

When they went back up to Smoke Hall, Mrs. Marshall, the Academy's social director, was tinkling her little bell. "The dance is over, everyone. Time for our pretty guests to leave, unfortunately. But I thank y'all *so much* for coming!"

He shook her hand reluctantly. He'd enjoyed being with her. At least, until that last jab. "Uh, walk you to the bus?"

"Oh, we didn't take it. I drove." She waved at someone across the room. Introduced him to her roommate, Moira, also from Georgetown.

Really? A girl with a car . . . think of the possibilities. Since he'd managed to damn near total his own. It was still out in town, at the body shop.

He walked them out to a scarab-green VW Bug. "Looks nice, but it leaks like a sieve," Betts said, patting it. "I think it was in an accident before Dad got it for me, because somebody fixed the back window, but they didn't seal it right. Anyway, I can fill it up for four bucks." She opened the door and slid in. A flash of smooth tan thigh, slender yet muscular. Apparently catching his glance, she tugged her hem down as her roommate snorted derisively. Shit, another faux pas. He'd have to retune his high school reflexes for a girl like this.

He leaned on the door. "Feel free to say no, but—could I get your number?"

She studied his face, as if he were some ancient potsherd found in the wrong layer. "Maybe. What did you have in mind?"

"Well, I'm on restriction right now, but I might be able to get away. If I can march enough of my demerits off."

"Ooh, *demerits*," her roommate said in mock horror.

Shan Chan smirked again, twisting those pretty, full lips. "For what evil deed?"

He considered fibbing. But faced with the dark arch of those questioning eyebrows, decided to level. "Well, I got . . . really drunk, last semester, and drove my car into the governor's garden. Here in town. Wrecked it. The car, I mean. The garden didn't come off too well either, I guess."

She frowned, as if weighing whether he was kidding. Glanced at her roommate. Then, finally, laughed. She grabbed a crumpled toll ticket from the dash and scribbled a number.

He stood clutching it, watching them drive off. Looking after the little car until it vanished around the tennis courts. Sensing, dimly, that something had just happened he'd always remember.

* * *

And the days zipped by, faster and faster as June Week and graduation hove in sight. The Final Swim. Hundred of mids fought one another as much as the overchlorinated water, climbing and elbowing, panting and splashing as they circled the pool for hours. To climb out at last, or be pulled out, exhausted, wheezing, arms shaking . . . As service selection neared, the firsties argued over which communities were the best. The Navy's needs came first, but graduates had a degree of choice for the first assignment. Going in order of class rank, one at a time, to pick from what was still available.

Dan had pondered his options. Aviation? He doubted he had the self-confidence. Sub duty? His math grades nuked that. But he'd enjoyed a third-class cruise. The open sea, watches on the bridge . . . even the storm they'd steamed through had been more exciting than frightening. Maybe a missile cruiser, or one of the new high-tech destroyers.

Unfortunately, when the final class rankings were posted, he was only a hair off the bottom. Not anchorman, but not far above that equivocal honor. The conduct grade had bumped him down. That, and the backlash for turning Davis in.

* * *

When the fateful night arrived, he and Scherow kept the radio on in their room. WRNV was covering the action, like a draft pick night, hour after hour. Teddy went down and came back grinning; a new-construction frigate out of Louisiana. "Just what I wanted. That's where Zusana's family's from." He bounced gleefully around the room, until he noticed Dan wasn't as happy. "Um, gonna crash early," he said. "Break a leg." He flicked his half of the room lights off with a high kick. Within seconds the familiar buzz-saw snoring began.

Yeah, Dan thought sourly, no wonder "wives" was Academy slang for roomies.

* * *

Late that night he stood in Smoke Hall again, one in a long line of over-caffeinated, on-edge mids. They faced five vertical corkboards with printouts thumbtacked to them. A bored-looking lieutenant dozed behind a desk.

"Lenson, DV," an enlisted woman called.

Was he too late to score a decent billet? Dan hustled to the section marked SURFACE LINE.

Then halted. Nearly every billet was lined through. Taken.

He ran his finger down the remaining choices. Transports. Tankers. Ammo ships. Tenders, which hardly ever left the pier. And ships undergoing overhaul. No one wanted to be aground in a shipyard, dodging sparks and dealing with sullen yardbirds. The glamour ports, San Diego and Charleston and even Norfolk, were all taken.

The other printouts, then . . . restricted line . . . naval intelligence, dental, meteorological. He could go to sea as a pork chop, but that siloed you into the Supply Corps. Very few of whom, he'd heard, ever got to drive ships, much less command them.

Behind him in line, other mids fidgeted. One cleared his throat loudly. "Let's go, mister," called the lieutenant. "Get off the dime, okay? I'd like to go home sometime tonight."

Dan sucked air through his teeth. O-*kay* . . . there was one destroyer-type left. USS *Reynolds Ryan.* Home port Newport, Rhode Island. He'd never heard of her, but the hull number meant she was ancient. A rust bucket? Gunnery officer sounded okay. Why had no one grabbed it? Like Scherow, everyone wanted new ships, fast tracks to early promotion. And Newport was reputed to be a chilly backwater.

"Any day now," muttered the mid behind him.

Fine. Dan clicked his Skilcraft and inked the code on his palm. Went to the desk and presented his ID. Yawning, the lieutenant scribbled on a form.

"Is that it? Sir?"

The officer looked startled. "You still here?—Yeah, you're done. Okay, over there, next in line."

Dan turned away, starting back to his room. But changed his mind mid-stride, and pushed through the French doors out onto the balcony.

The wind smelled of seaweed and salt. Not much of a view below, just a roof with aluminum flying-saucer ventilators studded along it.

Beyond that lay only darkness and night. The black expanse of playing fields, then the crazy-canted blocks of the seawall. A hollow tolling clanged from Dewey Basin, halliards bonging against hollow masts. Past that lay the Chesapeake, twinkling like bioluminescence beneath a Caribbean moon. Side lights. Masthead lights. The red and green gleams of channel markers. From out there faintly droned a long-drawn-out moaning; a ship, making its way past the Bay Bridge, out to sea.

Okay, he thought. Got my orders. Got my ship. Now I can leave this fucking place behind. And not one minute too soon.

If you ever really could leave such things behind. He was starting to suspect he might carry it forever. The promises and disillusionments, lofty ideals and petty politics. The everlasting regs. The narrow fucking boxes every mid had to cram spirit and mind and body into, over four long years.

One thing was for sure. Once he walked out that gate, he was never, ever coming back.

Standing alone, in the dark, he could feel his life shifting. Altering. As if he already stood on the heaving deck of a destroyer, leaving home behind for a long cruise.

USS *Reynolds Ryan*. Maybe not the newest and shiniest ship in the Fleet. But still, a Navy man-o'-war.

All he had to do was obey orders. Do his duty. And he'd never have to make a tough decision again.

Standing there, smiling in the blazing dark, he opened his arms to that bright and boundless future.

26

The morning sun was just rising, a blazing-red flame torching the bay horizon as Dan rounded the seawall and started his jog back. He was taking it slower now. A lightning-sharp jab from his knee half a mile ago, when he'd essayed a wind sprint, had reminded him he wasn't twenty anymore.

Today's schedule was full. Event after event, capped by the last formal parade of the year, with the most prestigious guests.

Summer at last, after a harrowing year. This was Commissioning Week, with the Ring Dance, concerts, and receptions. The Herndon climb, when plebes became youngsters. Awards ceremonies and tours of the guest ship . . . which he was jogging past now, the gray hull of a Wartime Improved destroyer looming above the seawall. USS *Cobie Kasson*, a decorated veteran of the Pacific War. Even this early, mids and their families were queuing to go aboard.

May Week would end with graduation, when the first class received commissions as ensigns, US Navy, or second lieutenants, US Marine Corps.

An unforgettable week for everyone, from supe to the youngest mid in the Yard.

The knee administered another jab. "Ow. *Shit!*" he hissed, barely catching himself before he went down. Crap, that had really hurt.

He slowed to a walk as he approached the boat basin. Sighing, he looked after a yawl as it put-putted out into the river, decks crowded with mids and dates. He'd placed an order for a new boat, but it wouldn't be delivered for months.

And Blair had made an offer on the house across the river. It looked out on a sheltered inlet, so he'd have deep water and a pier.

He still couldn't quite believe he'd be retiring. The Navy had been his life. How would he fill the remaining years? Living with Blair twenty-four seven, once she left the Pentagon . . . That would take some getting used to, as well.

He lifted his gaze to a blue sky streaked with only the faintest tint of rose. Seagulls whirled screaming as another yawl cast off. He closed his lids, enjoying the sun on his face, the blood-scarlet brightness.

It looked like the weather would be perfect today.

* * *

Zero eight hundred. In fresh high-collared whites he stood with Leslie Stocker on the Bancroft steps. The companies fell in on the worn golden bricks. Swords flashed. The clear, assertive shouts echoed around T-Court.

As muster proceeded the 'dant brought him up to date, muttering out of the side of her mouth. "Like I figured, once I put the word out so many minority and queer mids joined their little club it changed everything." She squinted into the sun, hands locked behind her. "Might even have changed some minds, once they hashed things out. And the social media bullshit . . . that's dying down too. When we didn't even give them a 'no comment.'"

Dan nodded. Yeah, that was good news. "But don't let your guard down."

"Roger, sir. The battle never ends."

The ranks of men and women, starched whites glowing so brightly in the sun he had to squint too, snapped to parade rest. The brigade commander halted before the steps. Came to attention. The bright steel of her blade flashed in the air, and from the roped-off area where the parents and tourists stood came oohs and aahs as if someone had executed a perfect gymnastic routine. "Ma'am, sir! The Brigade of Midshipmen, present and accounted for."

Solemnly, they returned the salute.

* * *

Back in Dan's office, Mrs. Marsh reminded him there was a signing at the Mid Store that morning. "Mr. Naylor. He wrote the book about—"

"Yeah. I remember." Naylor's latest volume was about the prospects for a postwar peace. "I'm gonna skip it, I think. If I go, it might look like an endorsement. Have you seen Nan yet? She was supposed to be here this morning."

"I called. Your daughter's delayed on the road, but she'll be here for the reception."

Dr. Nan Lenson certainly seemed to be spending a lot of time away from the Yard, considering she was supposed to be living here. Acting as his cohost, when Blair couldn't. "Thanks. What else we got?"

"Zero nine hundred, meeting with a possible donor. Torgild Schrade. He mentioned ten million, to go toward rebuilding."

More glad-handing, and he'd never liked the guy, but he forced a smile. "Look forward to it. Then?"

"Ten hundred, staff conference room. Master Chief Wenck's retiring; thought you might want to say something."

"Absolutely. Anything back on his DSM yet?" Dan had put him in for the Distinguished Service Medal, quite a few notches up from the usual decoration for a retiring senior enlisted. But Donnie had earned it, both in peace and war.

"I'll call again. Make sure they understand we're running out of time . . . then the Brigade change of command. T-Court, noon."

Yeah, no breathing room today. He smiled at her, went to sit down, but his knee jabbed again. "Ow. And could you maybe . . . locate a couple of Aleves?"

* * *

The meeting with Schrade went well. Ten million would help, and there didn't seem to be any strings attached. The conference went smoothly too. He spoke without notes, and Wenck kept shaking his head and looking embarrassed. Another change of uniform, and Dan headed back to T-Court for the change of command.

Not his own; not yet. Once again, he stood beside Stocker between the age-greened cannons of Bancroft Hall. Once again, swords flashed.

He tensed as a howl grew in the distance. Then relaxed as thunder filled the sunlit Yard. The Blue Angels, arriving for the graduation flyover. Welded wingtip to wingtip, they drew a wide circle over the river, the town, the Bay. Then arrowed in for a final pass just above the Chapel. The scream of turbines was past deafening.

"Sir, ma'am, I stand relieved," Midshipman Commander Oshry shouted as the Angels faded in the distance.

"I have the watch," the newly appointed striper reported.

Once again, Dan and the 'dant returned the salute.

* * *

That afternoon he strolled out into the garden behind his house, LeCato trailing him, the aide looking harried. Dan suppressed a wince, trying not to limp. All those years of running had to be paid for, it seemed. But his house staff had the party catered, flowers set out on tables. The buffet tables were crowded solid with hors d'oeuvres and finger foods, Maryland crab cakes, steamed shrimp, penne pasta salad, chicken with pineapple and red peppers, lemonade, iced tea. A uniformed and sunglassed trio from the band were playing light airs. The azaleas were in full bloom.

His daughter, in a long pale-jade green dress, joined him in the receiving line. Her hair was styled differently, long enough now for a pageboy cut. She looked healthier, with even a hint of tan. A new tattoo on one bare shoulder.

With a start, Dan registered a guy beside her in slacks and an open-necked shirt. Glasses. A studious look. Sparse brown hair, already in retreat, and some kind of stubbly almost-beard like detectives wore on television. "Great, you made it," he told her, eyeing the guy sideways. "And I really like that dress."

"Thanks, uh, Dad." She rubbed her mouth. The same way he did when puzzled or nervous.

"Valerie said you hit traffic."

"That was one reason I was late." She took the hand of the man beside her. "This is Owen Brockmeier. He teaches at American U."

They shook hands, Dan glancing toward the receiving line. They should be over there now. He almost said, *This isn't the guy you were dating last year.* But bit his tongue. "Good to meet you, uh, Owen. Are you—would you be why my daughter's spending so much time in DC?"

"Actually," she said quietly, holding out her left hand, "he's striking for a promotion. As you'd say."

It took him a moment to register the ring. Not an immense stone, but a diamond nonetheless.

"The sunlight, um, really makes it sparkle?" she said. Tentatively, as if he was going to disagree.

This was news. "Hm," he said, checking the guy out again. He carried himself well. The handshake was firm enough. But they were engaged, and she hadn't even brought him home for inspection? "Uh, this is a, um, surprise. But . . . hell, if you're happy, I'm happy." He shook the guy's hand again, forcing a smile.

"Actually, Admiral, we have something else to tell you too," Brockmeier said.

"Call me Dan. Yeah? I look forward to talking some more. Right now, you'll have to excuse us. The greeting line. Help yourself, have some lemonade."

He and Nan welcomed the first guests, two women accompanying a female first class. He asked how far they'd come, about their daughter's career plans. Handed them off to Burke-Bowden and turned to the next folks in line.

In a *long* line. Nan stood beside him, chatting brightly with each parent or alum about the weather and the gardens, then inviting them to the buffet as the trio swung into a jazz tune.

"I'd have liked to have met this guy before you were engaged," he asided between guests. "But if he's nice to you—then, fine. This other news—?"

"Oh, that. How would you feel about being a grandfather?" She patted her midriff, smiling.

He stared, forgetting to breathe. Then forced a welcoming smile for the next couple. "Dan Lenson. Great to see y'all. So glad you could make it."

Was she afraid of his reaction, that she was telling him at a public event? He wasn't *that* hard-ass of a dad.

Was he?

A grandfather. He'd thought of it now and then, as a theoretical possibility, but not imminent. Now, apparently, the keel had been laid. When the line dwindled, he got to talk to Brockmeier a bit. He taught economics. Assistant prof. He seemed . . . all right. Not nearly good enough for Nan, of course. But maybe she could have done worse.

This would take some getting used to. He considered cautioning his prospective son-in-law about all the radiation Nan had gotten in the bombed-out Midwest. But . . . that was her story, not his. She'd tell him, if she hadn't already. And have all the risks and percentages at her fingertips.

"Lemonade, Admiral?" His aide held out a beaded glass jangling with ice.

Dan took a long sip of the sweet tartness. Lifted his face to the sun again. And smiled.

* * *

He was sitting it out under the arbor, Nan beside him. Along with everything else, she had an offer from a biotech startup in Baltimore. "The headhunter counteroffered and got me an extra thirty thousand base. Plus options. And my own parking spot. I'd come in as VP of Research."

"That's fantastic," he was saying, when his phone vibrated. He didn't recognize the number.

"Lenson," he said tentatively.

"Admiral? Hold for Senator Peache, please."

The congressman from Maryland. Good news, or bad? He said, still on hold, "So. Got wedding plans yet? Where do the two of you plan to live?"

She looked at her lap. "Well . . . Owen's apartment's too small for two. Much less three. I was wondering, since you and Blair won't be using the house in Arlington . . . at least for a while, to start with? We'd pay rent, of course. And we'd keep a bedroom ready for you."

He nodded. "Absolutely. I'll talk to Blair."

A voice came on the line. The same honeyed-smooth tones as at the committee hearing. *"Admiral? Hollister Peache here."*

Dan turned away, cupping the phone to his ear to mute the music and chatter around them. LeCato stepped between him and the crowd. "Yes, sir, Senator! Good to hear from you."

"Just thought you should hear this first from me. USNA 2100 looks to be a go."

He swallowed, waving away an aggressive bumblebee. Wondering if he'd heard that right. "You're saying . . . ?"

"It's in the budget, and the leadership assures me it'll pass."

"So . . . we're keeping the Academy here?" It felt too good to believe.

"In Maryland, at Annapolis, yes. Though we didn't get the funding we asked for, for your reconstruction—what I call the Lenson Academy." A chuckle; Dan started to object, but Peache was still talking. *"That is, we didn't get it in the defense budget. Which your wife's still determined to cut."*

"We didn't ? Sorry, I don't follow, Senator."

"Not in the defense budget. We shoehorned it into the infrastructure stimulus. We have the votes. Both sides of the aisle. Start planning when to start construction . . . I might suggest some bidders to consider, later in the process."

Dan mumbled something, thanked him for his efforts. He'd been so prepared for failure he wasn't sure how to respond to success.

Peache signed off, and Dan lowered the phone. Blinking up at the Chapel dome as the clatter of conversation around him continued. He'd have to tell Bonar. Finalize a schedule and milestones. Start the process for delisting a few of the oldest buildings from the National Register, though some would probably have to be moved rather than demolished.

It would take years, of course. But he could get things rolling before he left.

The bee came back, hovering near his chest, obviously attracted to the bright colors of his ribbons. The aide moved in to wave it away, but Dan shook his head. Stepped back, slowly, into the arbor, until the scents of the flowers distracted it, redirected its simple senses, and it buzzed up and away, losing interest in him.

Burke-Bowden came over, carrying an iced tea, looking self-important as usual. "Good news, Admiral?"

Jeez, word traveled fast. Or maybe his deputy had his own sources. Dan nodded, letting a smile break. "I think so. Yeah."

A victory. Not for himself, but for the Academy. It would sail on, for the rest of the century.

Which was all anyone could ask for, after all.

He let his gaze return to his daughter. Slim. Radiant. She looked happy. Laughing, smiling up at the young man she'd chosen to share her life with. A new beginning after so much darkness.

He steeled himself against the old feeling creeping back. That he didn't deserve any of this. But like a determined insect, it kept returning.

He'd just have to keep dodging its sting.

* * *

He'd kept the visit close to his chest, not released beyond his personal staff. And his house staff, of course; they had to be told why the Secret Service was casing the place, inspecting the basement, scanning for bugs. He doubled the guard at the gate too.

When the armored limo eased to a halt in front of the Supe's House, he was out front to welcome the vice president. Justin Yangerhans moved in a scrum, an aide beside him, six Secret Service agents boxing them in. Five paces back a lieutenant commander in whites swung a worn-looking black satchel, a backup of the "football" that followed the president herself. Dan remembered when he'd carried that fatal briefcase himself, years before.

Dan's former commander in the Pacific was grayer than during the war. Towering, bent, he still resembled Lincoln. The first thing he said was, "Tell me there's a head here, Dan."

Dan showed him to a small bathroom in a converted closet. "Not very big, Mr. Vice President, but it's historic. Franklin Roosevelt stayed here now and then before he headed to Cairo and Yalta. He wanted a toilet on the ground floor."

Yangerhans nodded, looking exhausted. "Neat," he said, and closed the door. A Secret Service agent stepped in front, facing out.

Blair led Dan a few paces away. "Ready for some good news?"

Apparently this was his lucky day. Could she too be . . . no, unlikely. "You bet."

She told him about the appropriation. He smiled and nodded, making sure to look surprised. He didn't mention Peache's call. Maybe it wasn't in the defense budget, but since Blair was Yangerhans's former campaign manager, Dan was sure she'd had more to do with the appropriation than even the senator from Maryland knew. "That's great," he said. "I've got news too. It's about Nan. She's engaged—"

"And expecting. She told me already."

He shook his head. As usual, behind the curve. "Oh. Well . . . now, if I could just get a little kiss from the SecDef—"

She looked stern, but gave him a peck on the lips. The Secret Service looked on stone-faced. Yeah, they'd probably seen a lot worse. Like he'd witnessed himself in the West Wing.

When the veep came out, Dan introduced him to Nan, and the three of them led him through the house. Yangerhans admired the original oils and the girandole mirrors that had belonged to Commodore James Lawrence. He caressed the glossy varnish of the captain's table from USS *Constitution* and sat for a moment at the Reid desk, where the US flag had been designed.

Seeing how tired the man looked, Dan cut the tour short. A bar was set up in the sunroom. Sunlight glowed off polished wood and antique brass. Overhead fans stirred the warm air. The Secret Service dispersed to the windows, staring out at the Chapel, down at the garden. One raised a hand, murmuring into a mic. A sniper waved back from the roof of Dahlgren Hall.

Yangerhans asked for a tall tonic, lime. "Too friggin' hot for alcohol," he sighed, gradually folding himself down onto a wicker settee. Blair and Nan settled on either side; Dan took a chair facing their guest. The military aide waited at the door, the satchel between his white bucks. "We've got to stand out there for how long?" the veep added, wiping his forehead.

Dan grinned. "Only as long as you want to, Mr. Vice President. You're the boss."

Yangerhans nodded. He looked like he had a lot on his mind. "So, how's it going here?"

Dan spread his hands. "Some challenges. But I think we've got 'em snubbed off. For now, at least."

"You're here how much longer?"

"It's a three-year tour, Mr. Vice President."

"Jeez, Dan. It was 'Jim' during the war. Plans, after that?"

"I'm timing out, sir. Jim. The US Code says I have to retire after this tour."

"You look like there's still a few years left in you." He turned to hand the drained glass to one of Dan's house staff. "Refill, please?—Y'know, retired senior officers sometimes get called back. For special duties."

Dan shot a glance at Blair. No signal came back. "Well . . . we're buying a house here . . . and I was hoping to get some serious sailing in. Maybe even do an around-the-world."

His wife snorted. "Over my dead body," she said, at the same time his daughter murmured, "Oh, Dad."

Yangerhans nodded sagely, not appearing totally invested in the conversation. His lids drifted downward. Then his head began to nod.

Dan said, "You know, Jim, we don't have to be out on the field for two hours yet. If you wanted to grab a few minutes, there's a spare bedroom upstairs. I could send a sandwich up too."

Yangerhans stirred. He glanced at the aide, then at one of the security people. He heaved himself up. "You know, I'm gonna take you up on that. This job . . . anyway. Lead me to it."

Dan showed him up the curving stairs, preceded by two agents, and followed by the aide with the ever-present satchel.

* * *

The Color Parade was the last full-dress march-past before the graduating class walked. The lines of blue and gold and white snaked onto the field. With Blair, Burke-Bowden, and Stocker, Dan took his position on the green. Back straight. Head up. Squinting in the blinding afternoon sun. Sweat trickled under his choker whites. A sailboat floated motionless as a photo in a recruiting brochure. The parents, tourists, alums, invitees fanned themselves under the tents. The awnings offered shade, but no relief from the heat.

The band played four ruffles and flourishes, then "Hail, Columbia" as

Yangerhans made his entrance, striding out to take his place beside Dan. He stood relaxed and gangly, looking peppier after his nap.

The National Anthem. A man and woman took a knee, to scowls from the Old Grads. The Rowdy Twins, seeking the limelight as usual. The alums around them stared and muttered. Finally, surreptitiously, while they were kneeling, they abstracted their chairs, so they'd have to stand for the rest of the afternoon.

Yangerhans made his remarks, complimenting the Brigade, then awarding decorations. Master Chief Wenck's had come through just in time. The color honoree—no longer a "color girl"—in traditional white dress, sun hat, and pearls, presented the award pennant to the winning company. The cannons' flat-sounding reports thudded back from the granite of Alumni Hall and the concrete of the ugly new parking garage and the Edwardian façades of the senior officers' mansions, with muted echoes from Cemetery Hill.

Hands behind him at parade rest, Dan muttered, "Is there some way to shorten this next year? Like, as the heat index rises?"

Burke-Bowden, shocked: "We've been doing it this way since 1867, Admiral."

"Well, maybe it's time for a change."

Shorten them, sure, but he understood now what they accomplished. The way he understood now what a lot of what he'd once considered mindless rote was for.

The loud, clear voice of the brigade commander rang out. *"Pass . . . in . . . review."*

The band struck up, and the blue-and-gold guidons rose.

The slightest zephyr cooled his face, bringing with it the salt-scent of the river, the Bay, the sea. The color company reached the turn point, and he could call from memory *column left, harch*, through the blare of the trumpets, the beat of the drums, as they headed toward him down the field.

Dan came to attention between the vice president and the secretary of defense as the band struck up "Stars and Stripes Forever." Burke-Bowden stepped to the mic. He announced the lead company, then the name, home city, and state of its commander. A sword glittered in the sunlight, then snapped down. "Eyes . . . *right.*"

Dan lifted his arm, aligning his fingers in the bent-wristed Navy salute, as the so-familiar smells of bruised grass and acrid cannon smoke arrived on the wind. They plucked obscure neurons and glia, calling forth the mystery of memory, more durable, more ageless, somehow, than always-fleeting reality.

Suddenly he was twenty again. The glaring heat. The sun slanting through the choking dust. The tightness of the leather-stiffened choker collar. The gleaming blade of the dolphin-decorated saber tight against his shoulder.

Then another column left, into the homestretch, as you matched cadence and dress and cover. A line of white gloves, swinging as one, and suddenly and inevitably the band would hit those slow, deep, brassy notes that made the hair prickle on the back of your neck. And *eyes right* and you snapped your head around to meet the calm, level gaze of the dignified old man who'd stood ramrod straight, so many years before, returning your salute.

Now he held that salute himself, meeting the gazes of young men and women as they in turn marched past. Their shining unlined faces seemed to glow with an inner light. An ideal, preserved against all odds in an age when faiths and beliefs had gone west with the fey.

Of duty. Of country. Of being true to oneself.

That was the final secret the Academy guarded, in its deepest and most sacred heart.

Was it illusion? Fantasy? Even forty years later he couldn't say for sure.

He stifled a sneeze as the wind gusted, as the pollen-laden dust blew over them.

Unbidden, more memories rose. . . .

Boarding his first ship. Pushing through a curtain of steam into a life that would present challenges beyond anything he'd foreseen.

Hauling down the flag, and sailing as a pirate on the high seas.

Cradling a newborn in his arms in a leaking skiff in a hurricane.

Boarding a North Korean submarine, to confront the enemy face-to-face.

Trapped in a wrecked, sinking helicopter.

Staggering through the howling white of an Arctic blizzard.

Screaming as a Mukhabarat torturer turned up the electricity.

Holding an invasion force to the flaming wheel of combat, when every voice urged retreat.

After it all, why was he still uncertain? Still wondering, at the sheer mystery of existence?

But I got what I wanted, he thought. Seen the world. Served my country.

And even learned a few things.

What glory was: a snare, an illusion masking the brutal reality of war.

What duty was: accomplishing the mission, without thought for yourself.

What integrity was: telling the truth, and keeping your word.

What honor was: acting so you could live with what you'd done. No matter what others said.

What the truest compass for a life was: the one you calibrated for yourself, from your own experience.

And who he was, himself: A man, a sailor, a leader who'd tried his best to meet what life had thrown at him. And done not too badly, he hoped, in the end.

"Eyes . . . *front*," came a high, youthful shout, and a saber whipped down.

Yangerhans lowered his hand from his heart, and Dan dropped his own salute. Burke-Bowden droned on, announcing the next company. Nevada. Michigan. California. Puerto Rico. North Carolina. Texas.

They came from all over. The best the country could muster. To be welded into one. United. Indivisible. Just like the pledge.

He thanked whatever gods might be, that he'd been part of it all.

* * *

The drumbeats faded. The last company left the field, trailed by the band. The air shivered empty. The dust blew past, sparkling in the scarlet sunlight. The reviewing party relaxed, mopping foreheads, easing backs, retiring for iced tea in the shade of the VIP tent.

Dan started to follow, then turned back. To stand for a moment yet on a field echoing with ghosts.

His gaze lifted again, to trace the graceful arc of a shaken-out spinnaker. The heart-stopping curve of a hull as it heeled, sending a widening ripple out over the cat's-paws of a freshening breeze.

Departing the bounds of land, and aimed forever outward, to the open sea.

Acknowledgments

Ex nihilo nihil fit. For this volume I owe thanks to many organizations and individuals. First, Eric M. Durie at CHINFO East. For overall help and encouragement, the Surface Navy Association and the Naval Academy Alumni Association, Hampton Roads Chapter; to Charle Ricci and Cara Burton of the Eastern Shore Public Library; Jennifer Bryan of the US Naval Academy Special Collections and Archives Department; and from USNA administration folks present and past: Alana Garas, Colleen Krueger, Sara Sanchez-Maldonado, Luke Kremer, Steve Vahsen, Ted Carter, Jennifer Erickson, C. Herbert Gilliland, Sean Buck, Will McShane, Adam Taylor, for useful background.

Many Academy details are from my time there. They were polished during a residency as Distinguished Visiting Writer and from my articles over the years for *Shipmate*, the USNA alumni magazine. Also, bows to my classmates, especially Richard Enderly, Karl Schwelm, Mike Hichak, and Warren Schultz.

Printed and online sources included: for MIDREGs codes and phrasing, as well as particulars of conduct violation processing, various editions of COMDTMIDNINST 1610.2.

Watchstanding instructions: COMDTMIDNINST 1601.10L, "Bancroft Hall Watch Instruction," April 20, 2015.

Honor procedures: personal observation and USNA Instruction 1610.3H, "Honor Concept of the Brigade of Midshipmen," April 13, 2010.

Discharge procedures: Commandant of Midshipmen, US Naval Academy, COMDTMIDNINST 1920.1 H, "Midshipmen Voluntary Resignation, Involuntary Separation, and Qualified Resignation Procedures," July 24, 2018.

Also, COMDTMIDNINST 1710.14S, "Extracurricular Activities," July 22, 2022, and Naval Audit Service Audit Report, N2018-0041, "Sufficiency of United States Naval Academy Infrastructure," June 7, 2018. Meghann Myers, "Military Sexual Assault Reform Is Slow Going, But That's the Plan," *Military Times*, September 21, 2022. And Doug G. Ware, "'They Want Purpose': Gen Z Is Vital to Solving Military's Recruiting Problems," *Stars and Stripes*, November 18, 2022.

Details of the institutions of The Hague were based on a personal visit and ICC procedural documents. Specifically "Understanding the International Criminal Court," International Criminal Court, Public Information and Documentation Section, accessed March 9, 2021. Also *The Rules of Procedure and Evidence from the Official Records of the Assembly of States Parties to the Rome Statute of the International Criminal Court, First Session*, New York, September 3–10, 2002 (ICC-ASP/1/3 and Corr. 1). And Ben Smith, House of Commons Paper Number CBP 8430, "Russian Intelligence Services and Special Forces," October 30, 2018.

About Chinese submarine operation: Christopher Carlson, "Inside the Design of China's Yuan-Class Submarine," *Naval Institute Proceedings*, August 31, 2015.

Mark Episkopos, "China's AIP Stealthy Submarine Force: A Worry for the U.S. Navy?" *The National Interest*, November 19, 2020.

Ministry of Foreign Affairs of the People's Republic of China, "The Chinese Government Resumed Exercise of Sovereignty over Hong Kong," accessed March 2, 2021. Also, "Statement by the Ministry of Foreign Affairs," May 20, 2020.

For the Æthelstan-Alfred controversy, Matthew Firth and Erin Sebo, "Kingship and Maritime Power in 10th-Century England," *International Journal of Nautical Archaeology*, 2020.

I also thank many others (they know who they are), both retired and still on active duty. If I left anyone out, deepest apologies!

Let me reiterate: these sources were consulted for the purposes of *fiction*, not reportage. Neither characters nor cases were based on actual people. My reflections may not represent the opinions of those I interviewed. Close readers will note I also took some liberties with the time frames of various events and policies, again, for the purposes of fiction.

My deepest gratitude goes to George Witte, editor and friend of nearly four decades, without whom this series would not exist. And Sally Richardson, Young Jin Lim, Ken Silver, Naia Poyer, Kathryn Hough, Kevin Reilly, Ciara Tomlinson, and Brigitte Dale at St. Martin's / Macmillan.

To Lenore Hart, anchor on lee shores, and my North Star when skies are clear.

And finally, to all my faithful readers for lo these many years. Thank you for an unforgettable voyage!